Maze's Center

RUBY DUVALL

Copyright © 2021 by Ruby Duvall

All rights reserved. No part of this publication may be reproduced, distributed, or transmitted in any form or by any means, including photocopying, recording, or other electronic or mechanical methods, without the prior written permission of the publisher, except in the case of brief quotations embodied in critical reviews and certain other noncommercial uses permitted by copyright law.

ISBN: 979-8528436333

Cover Design by Ebooklaunch.com
Editing by Susan Barnes and Laura Helseth

This is a work of fiction. Names, characters, places, and incidents either are the product of the author's imagination or are used fictitiously. Any resemblance to persons (living or deceased), places, buildings, products, actual events, or organizations is entirely coincidental.

Author Note

Dear Reader,

Most of the characters in my Dark Court series have Japanese names, many of which sound the way they're spelled, but romanization has its limits. For example, Jun is pronounced *joon*, like the month. And the r in Mikari (*mee-KAH-ree*) sounds like a mix between r and l—a "tapped r."

For anyone unfamiliar with Japanese pronunciation, or for anyone in need of a refresher on who's who, you may refer to the series' *dramatis personae*, accessible at rubyduvall.com, where you'll also find audio clips of the characters pronouncing their names.

Reader Discretion Advised

Story contains on-page violence (*some occurring between the two main characters, involuntarily*); torture that occurs off-page to a secondary character (*no implied rape*); gory body horror (*secondary character, post-mortem*); past/ongoing trauma for FMC (*succubus curse*); past trauma for MMC (*institutional abuse, combat stress*); and several sex scenes with explicit detail. HEA guaranteed.

GOZU HIGHLANDS

LAKE IWAKO

OMINE RIVER

NANSEN TEMPLE

TETSUTANI

KOICHINO

GENBI TEMPLE

OKUSUSO

SETEI MOUNTAINS

BAKUGI FOREST

YUUGAI

MT. NAGURA

AJIRO TEMPLE

EIROKU

TOUKA PASS

HISANOCHI MOUNTAINS

PART ONE
Bitter Regret

Chapter One

Daylight was fading behind a mantle of snow when Mikari reached the farmstead nestled among fir trees. The plunge into full winter was drawing near, so the couple who lived here had lowered their storm shutters, insulating their home and protecting its summertime veranda. Light shone through a few small cracks in the thick wood panels. No doubt the occupants were in the middle of dinner.

Exhaustion more than gravity pulled Mikari from the back of her reindeer, her booted feet crunching in the thin layer of snow upon the ground. She took the liberty of stabling her mount with the two cows in the nearby barn, though doing so was a risk. She had promised never to return, after all. The young couple could turn her away.

But her cursed hunger was like weighted chains about her waist, so heavy that her feet dragged as she walked from the barn to the farmhouse. If she didn't sate it soon…

She hadn't wanted to come here. Another day's ride away, there lived a widow who was expecting her and would fulfill her particular needs. But she'd been determined to go several days out of her way to deliver the unhappy news that the skeletal remains of a missing young woman had been fished out of the Omine River, still partially wrapped in a half-rotted sheet of rough hemp.

Plenty of bodies ended up traveling down the Omine, so the chance to examine the young woman's skeleton had been pure luck. If Mikari had not been passing through Akawase when the remains had been discovered, the town's residents would have buried them and forgotten them in short order.

Knowing enough information to identify the skeleton had also been extremely lucky. According to the person who'd reported the young woman missing, she had a misshapen arm as a result of a badly healed childhood injury. If not for that exact detail, her remains would have revealed only sex and approximate age.

Even the fact that Mikari had written down the missing woman's description had been luck. Most people in her profession did not take on such work.

She had been hoping that news of the woman's demise would bring closure, if not relief, to the person who had reported her disappearance, but they had since passed away. No one else had cared.

What a waste, she thought, as disappointed in people as she was in the number of days she'd lost.

Upon reaching the farmstead's door, Mikari hitched her bag higher on her shoulder. The neck of her three-string lute, carefully wrapped in thick cloths, protruded from the top of her leather pack.

If she were here in her professional capacity, it would be customary to greet the homeowners while wearing her fox mask. But she wasn't here as a bard, so her mask hung from the waist of her white overcoat, beneath which she wore the traditional red clothing of her profession: a loose, front-closing shirt made of lamb's wool and a woolen split-skirt that allowed for riding.

Most people in Gozu wore at least three layers on all but the warmest days of what passed for summer here, but Mikari wasn't most people and could get away with two layers atop her hemp undergarments.

It was quiet inside. Had they heard her footsteps approaching? She closed her eyes, bracing for the worst. After knocking, she heard Keiko ask something like "who could that be," then the scrape of the inner door sliding upon its track.

A second later, the heavier storm door opened and Keiko's husband, Koba, appeared. His face looked fuller than when she'd last seen him over a year ago, and he'd grown a beard, although not a very good one. Pity.

Still, she was relieved to see he had been eating plenty, which boded well for her. Taking a deep breath, she was also relieved to discover that his desire hadn't faded, the scent of it sweet and cloying.

He loved his wife, but he lusted to see another woman give his wife pleasure—while taking his own, of course.

"Mitsy?" he asked with disbelief. "Why are you here?"

"I wouldn't be if I had any other choice." She did her best to sound apologetic, but mostly she sounded desperate.

Keiko appeared behind her husband, looking surprised. She had also gained a little weight. Her brown hair was much longer, too, and hung loosely about her shoulders. The scent of her desire was mellower than Koba's but still sweet.

If Mikari's particular hunger resided in her stomach, that part of her would be growling.

"Maze take you, Koba, let her inside already," Keiko bade.

"But we agreed," he said, turning to his wife. "No more. Not when we're still trying."

"It's been well over a year. I don't see how she could have been the source of our difficulties," Keiko said, gesturing to Mikari. "Come inside, Mitsy."

Mikari didn't hide her relief. She bowed her head in gratitude, kicked the snow from her boots, and stepped through the storm door. Koba sealed them inside.

"That said"—Keiko sent Mikari a worried look—"this really must be the last time. I heard in town that the new empress has scouts poking around, offering money in exchange for information. They don't say they're from Houfu, but you can tell they're not from Gozu.

"A man came through a few days ago asking about unexplained illnesses or deaths, especially when a stranger was visiting. He asked if anyone remembered such strangers refusing food."

Mikari stiffened. Like any other Gozuan, she hadn't given much thought to the news of a new ruler in the land south of the Setei Mountains. Power in Gozu was held by the priests—and the Keeper in particular, who was the region's highest divine authority.

However, rumors of imperial scouts asking such strange and specific questions put a chill in Mikari's veins, regardless of whether this new empress would wield any political power in Gozu.

Koba grimaced. "*Aj'*, it's only a matter of time before this empress sends more than just scouts." To Mikari, he said, "You know better than most how much unexplained loss there is in Gozu."

Mikari nodded. Indeed, the fact that she'd found the missing woman's body had been far more surprising than the woman's disappearance.

Though tragic, any number of horrible fates could and would befall both the innocent and not-so-innocent in Gozu. Among the dangers were bandits, avalanches, and the demons that came out at night. Although, not a single one of the Damned One's monstrous creations had been seen in months.

People weren't dying right and left, but they did often vanish. Only a small fraction was ever found.

Koba ushered everyone into the home's cozy interior, through the earthen foyer where they kept their ovens and toward the raised, heated wood floor. "If the empress's goons keep asking about odd strangers and suspicious deaths, people'll start pointing fingers at outsiders and whoever they don't like."

"It's probably safer to stick to the cities and towns that know you," Keiko suggested.

Mikari handed over her pack to Keiko and sat on the raised floor to remove her boots. "Do any of your neighbors suspect me?"

Koba and Keiko exchanged a look that lasted longer than Mikari liked. "Anything they might say to a scout would make them sound ridiculous," Koba began, "but that old farmer up the road and his wife... Maze take them, they're observant. They notice how we look after you've gone, and they've seen you without your bard's mask enough to wonder at your youthful look. Eight years you've been visiting. And then there's your hair."

Ah, of course. Even though she carried with her the personal seals of several prominent city leaders certifying her as an active bard in good standing, her profession didn't always protect her from accusations of magical corruption, which only happened to those with black hair. Worse, she had no brand to show anyone that she had been properly cleansed. She had tried to have one fabricated, but her body had healed the singed skin as if it had been no more than a scratch.

"It's beautiful, you know. Your hair," Keiko said. Having stowed Mikari's pack, Keiko drew a black lock from the heavy hood of

Mikari's overcoat and rolled it between her fingers, before pressing her lips to it. "Like the rest of you."

Mikari had grown used to people touching her, at least the ones who knew better than to seek more than a pet or two. It no longer made her heart pound and her stomach clench as it once had. Now all that moved her was the feeding itself. Seeing how receptive Keiko and Koba were, Mikari knew she would eat well tonight.

With a carefully practiced smile, she pushed back her hood and followed Keiko onto the raised floor. Steam rose gently from a covered iron pot pulled to the cool side of the nearby sunken hearth, and a wide mattress with thick blankets had already been laid out on the other side of a standing partition.

Koba followed, silent but for his deepening breaths. Mikari was aware of the aroma of her hosts' dinner floating in the air, but the sweetness of Keiko and Koba's lust quickly overpowered it.

"You don't want to eat your dinner first?" Mikari offered, even as husband and wife both pulled at the leather ties of her overcoat. "I had such an arousing conversation planned."

"Food tastes better afterward," Koba said, sweeping away her outer layer of clothing.

"I wasn't that hungry anyway," his wife concurred.

Relieved that she wouldn't have to bother with seduction, Mikari made a sound that was more of a purr than a laugh. It always excited her donors, and Koba and Keiko were no exception. "And here I was convinced I'd have to persuade the two of you."

She took the lead, tugging at the thick cloth belt of Keiko's front-closing dress. The second the three of them reached the bedding, Mikari tossed the dress away and guided her donor down to the soft mattress. She was so hungry she didn't bother undressing much before starting on Keiko's pleasure, only enough for some skin contact.

Koba was somewhere nearby, watching her push his wife's legs apart. He would join them soon—he never waited long—and he would feed her, too, in the only way that was safe for them, lest he overstimulate her.

She guided Keiko to her first orgasm in minutes. Sexual energy flowed from Keiko to Mikari in soft waves, like mist. The taste was fruity and light but faded quickly.

After eight years of the occasional visit, Mikari had learned where to touch Keiko and how. Unlike some of her other donors, Keiko preferred little to no talking. Anything Mikari said was usually for Koba's arousal, such as a harmless lie about how good Keiko's body tasted though she didn't much care.

Only the prospect of feeding truly stimulated her; she hadn't felt carnal desire in a long time. Hadn't ever desired anyone but one young man. If he still lived, he wasn't young anymore.

Koba, on his knees at Mikari's side, touched her arm. She got to work on Keiko's second orgasm while pleasuring him with her free hand. Whenever Keiko needed a short break, Mikari used her mouth on him. The second time she switched to him, he came down her throat. More energy flowed.

The taste of Koba's lust was sickly sweet. A man of visuals, he focused only on the keenest of his desires. Keiko, on the other hand, had private fantasies for which Mikari provided the stimulation. Fantasies to which Mikari's special senses gave her insight.

Tonight, Keiko imagined that she was the new empress, and the entire court eagerly waited in line to pleasure her. Her lust was more mental than visual, and its quickly disappearing fruitiness was more like what Mikari would taste from someone masturbating.

Mikari gave them a break after Keiko's second orgasm. Warm from all her exertions, she stripped down to her undergarments and cleaned up a bit, hardly taking note of the black lines and circles scarred onto her midriff. And neither Keiko nor Koba noticed them at all.

Only Mikari could see the evidence of her corruption. A small mercy despite being a constant reminder of her weakness. And all the more proof that her transformation into an eater of lust was divine punishment.

She chatted with her hosts while they ate their dinner—quite ravenously, she observed. They knew not to bother offering her a portion.

From their conversation, she learned that Keiko and Koba had brought in an excellent yield from their fields and their sizable herd of sheep. Their bounty had not only allowed them to eat well but also to purchase rarer spices and ingredients, which accounted for their fuller shapes.

Unfortunately, they'd yet to conceive their first child. Mikari did her best to appear sympathetic, but the topic only reminded her of what she couldn't have, and she struggled to express the appropriate condolences rather than blithely change the subject.

At the end of their meal, part of her was curious about the small round dumplings they'd made for dessert, but she was much more interested in whetting her hosts' carnal appetites once more.

Koba was cleaning up when Mikari slid her hands into Keiko's barely shut dress and whispered a few words that played into Keiko's empress fantasy. They worked. Koba managed to finish his task, but his gaze was locked on what Mikari's hands were doing beneath Keiko's clothes. Mikari waited until he glanced at her face before licking her lips and lowering her mouth to Keiko's body.

Keiko was recovering from her third orgasm of the night when Mikari, having shed her undergarments, coaxed a second one from Koba. He barely made it to his proper spot on the bed before passing out.

Mikari leaned over Keiko, who looked blissful but exhausted. Her complexion had paled, but she was still awake. "Can I try for one more?"

"Is he all right?" Keiko asked, even though her husband lay right next to her.

"Mm-hm. He's asleep."

"Will you take care of us, then? After?"

Inwardly triumphant, she gave her generous donor another practiced smile. "Of course, my empress."

Mikari carefully lay over Keiko to maximize skin contact and squeezed her hand between them. The more skin that touched, the more energy she could siphon, although penetration always yielded more. And even though Mikari strictly avoided any act that would stimulate her in return, she did have other options.

Keiko did her best to wrap her soft limbs around Mikari despite her exhaustion, and Mikari paid close attention to the fantasy Keiko was weaving in her head. Complementing it would help her donor reach one last peak. However, Keiko seemed unable to focus. Her mind was searching for something new but still related.

Mikari moved her lips to Keiko's ear. "The imperial studs have arrived, empress. They like what they see."

The scent of Keiko's lust bloomed beautifully. Her mind took over the fantasy, and at the right time, Mikari slid her fingers into Keiko's body. A moment later, her donor gasped, then groaned harshly, energy seeping into Mikari from every inch of Keiko she touched. Even after Keiko lost consciousness, Mikari extended her climax with small motions until she'd wrung every drop she could.

Her skin tingled when she pulled back from Keiko's slack form. Though the lull of her hunger never lasted more than a few moments, the relief was so keen she nearly giggled.

She wanted more—to continue feeding, regardless of the frenzy she took great pains to avoid. With a touch, she could rouse Keiko, coaxing from her another orgasm. Then another. And another. Until her breath ceased. She could easily take the couple's lives, and their deaths would sustain her for at least a year.

A pang of shame always followed such thoughts. More than she feared dying of hunger, she feared the sort of broken creature she'd become if she killed on purpose, although she didn't dare focus on how narrow the margin was. But that the thought even occurred to her, no matter how quickly she dismissed it...

Thankfully, smothering her guilt had become an easy habit. Her donors had nothing to fear from her. And now that she'd eaten, did she not have the freedom to be on her way in the morning? To go where she pleased? To see another day with a body as young as she'd been the day of her corruption?

Life couldn't get much better than that. There was nothing more she could ask for. Nothing more she could have. Ever. This was it. She had to pretend she was comfortable with her life—with her freedom—or she would start screaming and never stop.

Her hunger now managed, Mikari felt nothing when looking at her donor except a bit of gratitude. Oh, Keiko was nice enough. So was her husband. But Mikari had learned not to think of her donors as anything more than that. Not friends, and certainly not lovers.

She would hardly admit it to them, but they were more like the studs Mikari had invoked for Keiko's fantasy. In fact, Mikari had often thought of her network of donors as her "stable," and Koba and Keiko hadn't been the first to be put out to pasture. She made a mental note to find a new patron in the area the next time she visited, *before* risking starvation with a lengthy detour due to bad roads.

With renewed strength, Mikari settled Keiko more comfortably in the bed next to her husband. Neither of them would likely wake until well after dawn. She wiped both of them down, set a pitcher of water and two cups within easy reach, then gave herself a hand bath using soap scented with *oroimebi*, a common but fragrant flower found in most parts of Gozu.

She took care dressing, for her garb was both a symbol of her independence and one of the most important ways of protecting it—and herself—in place of a brand.

As a bard, she made quite a good income. Enough to secure comfortable, if temporary, lodgings, for she was always traveling. She even earned enough to afford Temu, her rather expensive mount.

Reindeer weren't fully domesticated, and breaking one for riding was tricky, but the benefits of owning one outweighed the extra attention she drew in more rural areas.

Unlike reindeer in the south, Gozuan reindeer imprinted on their rider and would defend them if attacked, or attempt escape if stolen. Their antler velvet, once shed, could be used in poultices and drafts. And unlike Gozuan moose velvet, which had more robust healing properties, reindeer velvet did not cause unwanted side effects. Especially unwanted for her.

Considering the times Mikari had met with hostility on the road, including having her horse stolen, Temu was well worth the large sum she'd paid.

She had learned several ways to defend herself, some of them by accident, but as a woman traveling alone, she had thought it prudent to have a mount that wouldn't run the second she encountered bandits, wild animals, or…other crows like her—those with black hair and a hunger that food could not sate. She hadn't come across another corrupted crow in weeks, but every chance encounter had the potential to become violent.

While Koba and Keiko slept, Mikari inspected her white fox mask and her lute for any damage. Both were well made and she devoted a lot of time to maintaining them, but the extreme cold in which she often traveled could warp, dry, and crack the wood.

She noticed a small fleck of black paint missing from the nose of her mask, reapplied it from a kit she kept in her pack, and left her mask to dry a safe distance from the hearth, which she kept burning for the sake of her hosts. Feeding her usually left her donors feeling cold.

She then tuned her three-string and quietly tested its sound, fingers lightly brushing the tightly woven silk threads while she listened with her ear next to her hand. Once satisfied it was in good condition, she loosened the strings and repacked it.

With nothing else to do until dawn, Mikari sat near the fire and silently recited epic tales, both as practice and to avoid forgetting them, starting with *Aya the Vigilant*—an ever-popular request.

Most people knew the gist of the holy warrior's tale—she slew countless demons and was responsible for separating the Damned One's most fearsome general from his book of destructive magic. But the ability to recite her rather lengthy story required a bard's dedication.

Unlike Mikari, most bards only knew an abbreviated version, altered to avoid any mention of the temples' iniquities or any hint that Aya had been a powerful magic user, changing the color of her hair from black to brown.

Mikari spent a couple of hours reciting Aya's tale in her head before moving on to the story of the Blondie Uprising, and the bold assassination of the last black-haired empress three centuries ago. That one was more popular lately after news had reached Gozu of a new black-haired ruler in the south. A young and beautiful one, she'd heard.

According to several people fleeing north into Gozu, a horde of monstrous demons had descended upon the capital of Houfu—the blond king's seat of power—killing not only most of the citizenry but also the king and his family.

A few days later, a young woman and more than two hundred of her black-haired followers had taken over the palace in Houfu, and she had declared herself empress.

The news had shocked and frightened many in Gozu, for reports of other demon invasions on cities and towns throughout the central plains also began trickling north, and many had feared a similar attack. Were the barrier charms that encircled every major settlement no longer repelling the Damned One's demon army?

Gozu's panicked citizens had turned to the Divine One's temples for help, and the priests had demanded offerings in exchange for "the considerable effort" required to inspect and bless the sacred prayers that made up the barrier charms.

Within days, reports of demon attacks in the central plains had stopped, and none had ended up occurring in Gozu. Thus, many had assumed that the temples were to thank, further entrenching their power. Mikari had heard differently, but could not bring herself to believe that the empress had used magic to protect them, not from so far away.

Months had passed before much else happened. Bits of news made it to Mikari's ears, but nothing truly noteworthy or credible.

She then spoke to a merchant, who had seemed perfectly sane, but insisted that this new empress—Shumei was her name—had taken a small group of her best warriors into the Damned One's plane of existence and defeated him there. They'd *literally* crossed into Oblivion, killed a god, and come back again, he'd said.

Mikari had repeated that shocking rumor in more town centers across Gozu than she could recall, although with a strongly worded precaution to all listening that little could be verified at the time. Many people had scoffed in disbelief, but a few had observed that they'd not had any demon sightings in weeks.

And now there were imperial scouts in Gozu, asking questions that made Mikari nervous.

Oh, if only she had the ability to sleep. If only she had something else to do besides sit by the fire with her thoughts—anything to distract herself from her most painful memories.

Things she'd said that she wished she could take back. Moments she wished she could do over. Even moments that had been her happiest. She definitely couldn't think of those, not when she had rejected the young man responsible for them.

Even at the age of sixteen, he had been tall and broad, larger than any of the temple guards. She hadn't known he was her age until weeks had gone by, for he had seemed closer to twenty than her tender fifteen.

By the time she'd dug through her early memories of him to their first tryst beneath the temple maze's *runtida* tree, the flames in the hearth had nearly died, and the cold of an early winter night was pressing in. Throat aching, she revived the fire.

Keiko woke shortly before dawn but fell back asleep after Mikari helped her drink some water. When the sky was light enough for Mikari to depart, both of her hosts were still slumbering soundly. She put on her boots and overcoat, picked up her pack, and left quietly, only to freeze halfway outside.

Her body knew something was wrong a second before her mind did. The hairs on the back of her neck stood up, and she held her breath.

Someone was watching. She looked behind her at the inner door, but it was still shut. No one moved beyond, and no one was peeking at her from the darkened corners of the home's enclosed veranda.

She eased open the storm door in front of her. Outside was cold and silent. The snow had stopped sometime during the night, and the sky was clear and pale. There were no tracks on the ground except for what looked like rabbit. As far as she could tell, she was alone.

And yet her skin prickled with warning. She supposed she should be used to the sensation by now. Every once in a while, she felt as though she were being spied upon—unseen eyes staring at her with an unknown purpose. But it had been happening more lately, and she dared not think upon why that might be.

Determined to ignore the unsettling feeling instead, she quickly made her way to the barn, marring the pristine layer of snow. It was only a couple inches of powder, but in a month, the sky would regularly drop enough to bury her up to her knees and the old snow beneath each new dusting would harden into ice. Thankfully, Temu was quite suited to Gozu's climate. Her thick pelt and saddle blanket would keep her warm, and her hooves had already hardened and tightened for winter travel.

The reindeer doe and its two cow hosts lifted their heads when Mikari entered the barn. She considered how much longer her human hosts would sleep and decided to feed and milk their cows while her doe munched on a generous helping of hay. Partway into milking the first cow, the "watched" feeling faded.

The sun was above the trees by the time she was ready to depart, and the white landscape reflected its light. Leaving the buckets of milk by the home's front door, she covered them with wooden lids and surrounded them with packed snow. Then, without a glance back, she put on her fox mask and rode toward her next destination, keeping her reindeer at a trot.

Her route took her past the neighbors of whom Koba had complained, hearth smoke rising from the farmhouse roof. From the corner of her mask's eye hole, she spied the wife standing at the entrance of her home with her arm raised, no doubt peering at Mikari from across the hundred feet or so of sunlit snow that separated them.

Would the elderly farmers simply shrug at her passing and go about their day? Or would they rush down the lane to call on Koba and Keiko? Would they demand to know why their neighbors looked as though they'd come down with an illness, cheeks red with fever and eyes bloodshot?

Mikari told all her donors to pretend they were having the worst hangover of their lives, but to see one's neighbor with the same "hangover" again and again whenever a mysterious stranger visited?

She could do something about the nosy neighbors now that she'd fed. Infusing a few words with power to convince the old farmers they weren't interested in their neighbors' visitor last night was well within her capability.

But if she did that, she'd have to spend some of the energy she'd harvested only hours ago. She hated doing that. The less she needed to feed, the better.

So, still facing forward, Mikari pulled her mount to a gentle stop. She let a few seconds pass, her warm breath like smoke sliding up her mask. Then she turned her head, slowly, and stared silently at the farmhouse.

The old woman retreated inside with a haste that said she understood Mikari's unspoken warning. The bang of the storm door slamming shut echoed across the snowy terrain.

"Hm," Mikari said, lips hinting at a smile. She knew she shouldn't be amused, especially when the old woman was right to be suspicious, but the idea that someone thought she'd harm them was ludicrous. If only her younger self could see her now, intimidating people into silence with a single look.

What would her younger self say if she saw some of the other things Mikari did now, how often she was alone, and how often she wasn't?

The thought wiped away any humor she felt. Mouth flat with dejection, she jostled the reins and moved on.

Chapter Two

The hush of night filled the halls of the imperial palace. Though it was late, Jun was awake in his quarters and reading. Or trying to, at least.

The glow of a paper lantern on his writing desk offered just enough light to see the book open before him, but he'd been staring at the same page for the past hour, his mind too absorbed in remembering the last few days...and the past in general.

A year ago, he would never have believed he'd see the day when magic was openly accepted rather than practiced in secret, let alone that he'd be an imperial commander training soldiers whose magic would supplement a larger force.

Nor would he have imagined the amount of paperwork involved. Correspondence, research, evaluations...

His combat-weary body preferred the comforts of living at court to the stresses of constant travel, though it meant enduring the formal sitting position during meetings, which required resting his arse upon his heels.

But having access to the court library had become an unexpected pleasure, despite containing only a handful of texts on magic, the rest of which the blondies had burned during the Uprising.

And yet, he would soon walk away from it all, though he doubted his knees would thank him.

He stroked his beard, eyes drawn to the newest items crowding his desk—a handful of reports atop a leather case that held a unique hand mirror.

As a result of the Damned One's defeat two months ago, the army of demons to which he'd given "life" had crumbled to dust, thus ceasing to be a threat. Or so the court had thought, until rumors of "human-born demons" began arriving.

Though tales of humans being turned into demons were commonplace, the particulars of their origins varied greatly. Some stories suggested they were wicked humans who had pledged their souls to the Damned One in exchange for supernatural strength and immortality, feeding and killing to retain the false god's blessing.

Other stories told of humans tricked into giving up their souls and feeding on emotion only with reluctance, to avoid a rather unpleasant afterlife. Still more tales insisted that any crow could potentially become an "eater" if they ever succumbed to temptation and dared to use magic.

He'd heard that last one a lot growing up in Gozu. There, magic was so feared that any family with crow children was expected to give their child to the nearest temple when they reached the age of twelve, where they were confined and monitored until their power manifested.

Families complied with this practice far more often than not, as Jun's had.

Though decades had passed since he'd become a ward of Nansen Temple, it still sometimes hurt to recall how little his parents had resisted. Not at all, in fact. No doubt they'd been relieved to have one less mouth to feed, especially one whose latent magic would supposedly corrupt him if the priests didn't perform a cleansing ritual as soon as it matured.

The empress and her Dark Court—so named for its black-haired members—didn't yet know whether human-born demons were all crows or not. Nor could Jun say for certain whether he'd ever come across one in the twenty years he'd spent as a mercenary, despite having clashed with all manner of criminals, from bandits to politicians.

Like everyone else, he had assumed—hoped—that they had disappeared along with their grotesque cousins. But while some recent claims of encounters with eaters were rather dubious, others could not be so easily dismissed.

So, in response, the Dark Court had established a special group of imperial agents that would investigate the more credible reports, and if a demonic threat existed, eliminate it. Thus far, only one rumor out of the Barrier Forest seemed genuine, but the agent hadn't yet caught up to its source.

Despite his background, Jun had rejected any notion of joining the group. He had no desire to return to what amounted to mercenary work, preferring instead to remain at court, where he could settle down and start a family at long last.

To that end, he had been keeping company with a fellow member of House Rose since midsummer. Kumi was a couple of years younger than him and likewise interested in marriage. She was amiable and attractive. With her, he'd felt certain that his magic would not be averse to what crows called…well, they called it many things.

The "second climax" was the most common term, if laughably inadequate. "Glimpsing the Garden" was another euphemism, implying a euphoric preview of an afterlife in the Divine One's Garden. Too poetic for Jun's tastes. The list went on.

Crows had a physical orgasm like anyone else, but once both lovers reached their peaks, their magics could meld to achieve a second, strength-sucking release that would haunt the magically lacking were they ever to comprehend how intensely the mortal form could feel pleasure.

It certainly haunted Jun, having occurred only once in his life, long ago. Since then, his magic had always closed up tight during sex and refused to participate. Still did, as it turned out, which he'd unfortunately discovered when he and Kumi were first intimate.

The poor woman had been so gracious toward his failure, kindly nodding as he'd clung to the theory that his recent, harrowing mission into Oblivion was to blame for his dysfunction. They'd tried again more recently, only then for his flesh to fail him as well. The memory still made him wince.

He hadn't argued when she'd subsequently declared their relationship finished, for the devastating truth had finally sunk in…

His heart was still in Gozu, with someone who hadn't survived her cleansing and now only existed in his dreams—which his time in Oblivion had twisted into nightmares. And while his bleakest memories of life as a ward had become less painful to recall, the guilt he felt over his escape had only calcified.

If Jun truly wished to move on, from her and from all that had happened there, he had to go back. To do what exactly, he wasn't yet certain. But moments after hearing that rumors of demons had been uncovered in Gozu, he had resolved to figure it out while hunting them down.

Which was how he'd found himself in the imperial council chambers earlier today, sitting before the dais and petitioning to be sent north.

The empress's reaction to his request had been subtle, a twitch of her eyebrows and a blink. Next to her, her consort and high general, Vallen, had remained placid except for a slight downturn of his mouth.

"I know there will be no help or easy escape once the southern pass closes for the winter," Jun had argued. At most, he'd have a scant few weeks before that happened. "And I'm well aware of the hostility I'll encounter if—or rather when—I'm asked to present a cleansing brand."

Each temple had its own mark, simple in design, but a special setting powder known only to the Primaries caused the mark to glow, making the brand nearly impossible to replicate.

The empress's response had been tactfully shrewd. "Commander, I'd like to think I know your character well enough to believe you're *not* asking to be sent into dangerous territory—alone—because of your recent romantic disappointment, but I cannot fathom any other reason."

As a rather private person, Jun didn't appreciate being a subject of court gossip, but while the empress's concern with his incitement was unflattering, it wasn't far off the mark.

Her confusion had been otherwise understandable, considering his enviable rank and the fact that no one at court knew where he'd grown up, only that he'd traveled extensively as part of a mercenary group. He could still speak and write Gozuan as though he'd never left, but his accent had all but disappeared.

"My reason, Your Imperial Grace, is that I am the most qualified for this mission. I know the language and the customs. And I have experience in tracking down dangerous individuals."

"Your group spent time in the Northern Highlands?" she'd asked, referring to Gozu by its name in the Common tongue.

"Only once. Our leader, Masanori, decided he hated the cold. But they were in the right place at the right time to smuggle me out as a lad."

The empress's reaction had been less subtle this time—a jolt of surprise that had jostled her headdress of golden spikes and filigrees arranged in a sunburst. "You grew up there?"

Jun had lowered his head in contrition. "I apologize for never telling Your Imperial Grace. Or the High General."

"You were once a ward, then?" Vallen had asked.

"At Nansen Temple. One of the better ones, I believe."

"You still haven't explained why you seek to return," the empress had noted, her hand splayed protectively over its favorite spot just below the sash around her waist, where a new life was growing. "You being uniquely suitable cannot be the reason."

"I...made certain sacrifices to keep my magic," he'd said, struggling to be as forthright as he could manage. "Left behind everything I knew...and loved. I see this mission as an opportunity not only to serve the court but also to make peace with my past...and cease sabotaging my future."

She had regarded him for a moment and then looked to Vallen. Whatever their eyes had conveyed to each other remained a mystery to Jun.

"How soon can you leave?" had been her response to him.

Relief had briefly softened his posture, before grim determination hardened it once again. "The sooner the better, as far as I'm concerned."

"Tomorrow, then." She'd surprised him by adding, "But you'll not be traveling alone."

The empress had gone on to explain that her objectives in the region went far beyond chasing demons.

Opposed to any sort of large-scale military strategy, she had been sending missives to Gozu's Keeper for months, in a diplomatic effort to bring an end to the ward system and cleansings, offering instead to send members of the Dark Court to train Gozuan crows to use their magic for the benefit of their communities.

All of her missives had gone unanswered, so the empress was sending a pair of brownie emissaries to negotiate in person, having finally recruited a Gozuan-speaking translator just yesterday.

Guarding them would be two of her imperial agents with whom Jun had only a minor acquaintance, their faces not quite clear in his mind. Both were nearly half his age, one an autumn crow, the other summer.

Their presence alongside the delegates would almost certainly invite trouble from the locals, but their access to magic conferred the most protection, not to mention a reliable way to stay in contact with the empress.

Giving up on reading his book, Jun reached for the scouting reports the court had received from Gozu. Once winter set in, they would come only infrequently, if they made it south at all.

The first rumor involved three separate claims of local women disappearing shortly after they'd been seen in the company of a brown-haired man wearing a "nice" or "flashy" brocade overcoat.

Each had left behind their personal possessions, without a word to anyone, but only the informants had suspected treachery *and* been concerned for the apparent victims, whose communities had shunned them for one heartless reason or another.

Of particular concern was one informant's allegation that the man had flirted as though he somehow knew her "most private fantasies," a hallmark ability of lust eaters, and yet the informant could not recall much about the man other than he was young and handsome—not even the color of his eyes.

With only a scant description of the suspect and a general area to search, there was precious little to go on. But Jun had pursued wilier targets, and the timing of each disappearance suggested the lust eater would soon be prowling for another victim.

Jun leafed through the reports for the other of the two claims, regarding a fox bard who, according to an elderly farmer, had been feeding on his married neighbors—regularly, for years.

Even outside of Gozu, the region's traveling bards were known for their musical talent and animal masks. They were a highly respected profession requiring both talent and discipline, not a costume for some human-faced monster, whom the farmer had witnessed feeding on a mist-like energy coming from her foolish prey. Given how rare fox bards were, Jun felt certain he could find her.

"Eliminating these remnants of the Damned One's corruption will be your top priority," the empress had told him while one of her aides fetched the magical speaking mirror he would take with him, to be assured of his continued safety. It was either that or another agent would be going with him. "But once you find your targets, you must do everything in your power to escort them back to Houfu, rather than take their lives."

Confused by her edict, he had furrowed his brow. Eaters were predators, even if some did manage to avoid killing—no doubt because corpses tended to draw a great deal of scrutiny. "May I ask why?"

"You'll no doubt find unrepentant eaters out there, but I believe at least some of the creatures described in the reports we've received can be saved—and made human again."

"What?" he'd blurted. "Is that even possible?"

"We've been to Oblivion and back, Commander," Vallen had answered wryly. "Saw its collapse. And I'm old enough to remember the previous empress. Almost anything is possible."

"Yes, I'm starting to see that."

Whenever Jun looked at the high general, he saw a handsome but hard-featured man of perhaps twenty-five, but Vallen was far older—as was Jun's fellow commander, Rosuke.

Hardly anyone knew the finer details, Jun included, but Vallen and Rosuke had been cursed by someone from the old Dark Court, and they'd lived through the Blondie Uprising as well as three hundred years of blondie reign.

Now they were mortal again, their curse broken, and the knowledge they carried of the old court, which blondies had nearly erased from history, was invaluable.

"A cure is especially possible when you have the counter-ritual for unmaking a lust eater, written by Bane himself," the empress had said.

The Damned One's high general? He's real? Every part of him had tensed with awareness—even his magic.

While he'd never questioned the Damned One's existence, to him Bane had always seemed like more of an imaginary figure, one created to malign magic as a source of corruption, for Bane was not only a ruthless strategist but also a brilliant spellcrafter obsessed with magical experimentation.

Vallen had nodded as if he'd heard him. "We're certain the spell book containing the counter-ritual is genuine, and his name is in it."

News of a powerful spell book in the empress's possession hadn't come as a surprise to Jun, only the name of its author. Months ago, he and several others had accompanied the empress through a portal created by a spell from that book—thankfully, the only thing left of Bane besides scary stories.

None of them had expected to come back from Oblivion alive. The empress and Elder Mai very nearly didn't. And while Captain Kiyoshi had carried out the mission into Oblivion with honor, his mind continued to struggle with the things he'd seen and experienced there.

So did Jun, truth be told. Though the details sometimes changed, he dreamt almost every night of the same horrifying moments that also haunted Kiyoshi.

When the empress's aide had returned with the speaking mirror, they'd handed it directly to Jun. Curious, he had taken it out of its traveling case.

As expected, the mirror hadn't reflected him, instead functioning as a window into another room in the palace, where its twin sat propped up on a table. As the name implied, one could speak through the enchantment linking the two mirrors—across any distance—but doing so required additional magic.

The artifact itself was beautiful, a circular slice of glass set into a scalloped wooden plate painted with red lacquer, the handle embellished with white flowers. And on the back—

Sweet Garden. The design was of a wind bell, tilting in the breeze, forever caught in a single, silent note. A heartsick feeling had gripped him, his magic shrinking in sympathy.

"You can trust me. With our lives and our future. Please, Mikari."

A cool wind skated over the top of the temple's hedgerow maze and elicited soft tinkles from the bronze wind bells dangling in the runtida tree above them. Mikari lifted her hand to brush back an errant lock of her black hair, and moonlight revealed the glimmer of tears.

"I...I'm sorry."

Mikari had fled, vanishing into the maze where they'd so often met in secret—the last he ever saw of her.

"Is something wrong?" the empress had asked, perceptive of his disquiet.

He'd almost asked for a different mirror, but the baffling need to keep it had been stronger. Wind bells were thought to have the power to guide souls through the Maze, and he was in desperate need of guidance.

Though the concept of the Maze was a common tradition across the empire, Gozu had a particular fascination with the cleansing of one's soul that it represented, and every Gozuan temple had a maze on its grounds. Worshippers wishing to make offerings, give prayers, or seek answers from divination first made their way through the maze, which encouraged meditation and patience.

Because the wards' souls were "in need of purification," maintaining Nansen's maze was one of their primary duties. Thus, every ward quickly became an expert at navigating it, even in the dark, which had proven useful the night of his escape.

"I'm humbled to receive such an invaluable object, empress," he'd evaded, putting the mirror back in its case to avoid meeting her eyes.

The sinus-opening scent of camphor pulled his mind back to his quarters. The next bundle of incense on the time-keeping burner out in the hall must have caught, its unique aroma indicating the start of a new brace, with the two hours of camphor marking the start of midnight.

Praise the Divine One, for he hated the scent of the previous brace. Of the Twelve Braces, each with its own particular bouquet, he only disliked the dark and cold odor of patchouli-infused coal wood.

Even if he didn't have an aversion to the scent itself, he would always associate the fragrance with another era, another place. One where he had been confined to his cell from the brace of patchouli until the brace of mint, when the priests would wake them for chores.

In another two hours, the slightly sweet brace of rose would fill the halls of the palace. Jun was usually in bed by the time the bundles of rose-infused agarwood began burning. In bed, but not always asleep. Rather, he slept in fits and starts, like his neighbor across the hall.

He thought he'd be fighting sleep for hours to avoid missing the start of rose, but he was wide awake when the floral scent replaced camphor.

He had never snuck out of his cell before, which he hoped meant that the preceptor on duty wouldn't bother to check on him. Knowing he'd soon be alone with her was more than enough incentive to risk being caught. He had the swollen cock to prove it.

When he reached the maze's center, having made each turn with hardly a thought, he was both surprised and thrilled to see Mikari already waiting beneath the tree. She perked up at the sight of him.

"At last" was his final thought before he had her in his arms.

Maze take him. Mikari had branded herself on so many things in his life. He had strived in vain to shed all associations with his memories of her, but she was as much a part of him as the sexually impotent ball of magic curled up inside him.

With effort, Jun returned his attention to the medical text open before him, which explained the most common pathways of disease and reliable methods for diagnosing illness. The book was as old as he was, but it remained a good resource.

Then a terrified shout shattered the still quiet of the night.

Chapter Three

Jun shot a startled glance at his door, despite knowing instantly who was waking up the residents of the west wing. Frowning, he tossed aside the blanket he'd laid across his lap and stood.

By the time he was sliding his door open, other officers were groaning or shouting.

"That's two nights in a row!"

"Not again."

"We're trying to sleep!"

Jun glanced up and down the hall before emerging from his room. The only light, besides the one behind him, came from a standing lantern at the far end and the incense burner a few steps away.

A nearby door opened just as another yell of terror erupted from the room across from his. A fellow officer, sleepy-eyed and hair mussed, stepped forth as though preparing to take care of the disturbance.

"You can go back to bed, Captain," Jun said to him as he crossed the wide hall and slid the door open.

Kiyoshi's quarters were similar to his. Stuffed bedding on a wooden frame, an armor cabinet and writing desk, and shelves for books or art or whatever a person might collect or keep. Despite the weak light, Jun could see Kiyoshi writhing in his sleep, sobbing in between howls of despair and grunts of desperation.

Jun crossed the room and firmly grasped the sleeping man's shoulder. He knew not to take hold of Kiyoshi's arms or hands—that would only elicit more panic, and sometimes violence. Jun was bigger and more experienced than Kiyoshi, but the younger man could still deliver quite a blow.

He gently shook the captain awake.

"You're safe, Kiyoshi. You're in your quarters," he told him. "Oblivion is destroyed, Kiyoshi. You're safe."

"No!" Eyes flying open, the young captain seized the front of Jun's robe to throw him aside, but Jun was braced for it and hardly budged. He couldn't say the same of his now-rumpled clothing.

The moment Kiyoshi recognized Jun, he fixed his gaze upon him, and the tension in his body slowly seeped away.

"Commander Jun?" He looked around as though confirming his location, then sniffed the air. "Camphor?"

"Just began burning." Jun straightened his robe and turned to sit on the edge of the bed.

Kiyoshi groaned in frustration. "I've only been asleep an hour?"

"Same one again?"

The captain sat up and nodded tiredly. "Always. And you?" Jun gave a firm nod. "I'm sorry to have disturbed everyone. My nights are wretched enough without humiliation on top of it all. I wish I had your fortitude."

"You simply need time. The one I heard in Oblivion...I've been dreaming of her for years." He shrugged. "I know she's dead. Even in my dream, part of me knows. The echoes of the weeping willow cannot truly affect me."

The Damned One's demons had all been distorted versions of the Divine One's creations, flora and fauna alike, and the soul tree—or weeping willow—had been no exception. Encountering one had been the closest the empress's small party in Oblivion had come to failing their mission.

The empress and Elder Mai had been immune to its effects, but the four officers had suffered an intense psychic bombardment, one that had beckoned them to some distant spot deep in the Damned One's dead forest, where a monstrous growth had waited, eager to devour them.

If not for Elder Mai keeping them back, using whatever painful means necessary while the empress dealt with the willow, none of them would have survived.

And even though Jun's recurring nightmare didn't tear screams from his throat, claiming the dream didn't affect him was an outright lie, one he'd told to give Kiyoshi some hope.

The dream did distress him. Greatly. He always woke with a gasp and a pounding heart, his clothes damp with sweat. Once the terror began to fade and reality asserted itself, he'd silently weep.

"But I know that my sister is alive," Kiyoshi insisted. He shut his eyes tight, and in the gloom, Jun spied the shimmer of tears on the captain's cheeks. "I've scried upon her. I've seen for myself that she's safe. Why won't this dream leave me?"

"She's promised a visit, hasn't she? She and her family? Perhaps it's time to arrange her travel."

Kiyoshi nodded and wiped his face. "Yes, that's…that's a good idea." Jun prepared to stand and leave the captain to the rest of his night, but Kiyoshi stopped him with a hand on his arm. "Would you…again, Commander?"

Jun sighed. He disliked relying on magic for something that mundane remedies could heal—things like friendship, affection, support, and time.

But the captain looked weary. Jun would be departing from Houfu in a scant number of hours, making this the last time he'd be helping Kiyoshi for at least a few weeks if not months. And Jun was convinced that a visit from Kiyoshi's sister would go a long way toward unraveling some of the captain's lingering trauma.

"Lie back," he instructed. Kiyoshi sagged with relief, then laid his head upon his pillow and smoothed his rumpled bedclothes. Jun brought his hand up to the captain's face and centered himself.

Suimin. With the spell mentally primed, he touched Kiyoshi's forehead. The captain went slack, head listing a bit to one side. His expression smoothed into one of peace and rest.

"I must say, I'm surprised to see a winter crow wielding such powerful sleep magic," a deep voice said from the doorway.

Jun glanced over his shoulder at the unexpected visitor—one of the agents assigned to the delegation.

Like Jun, Seita wore only a calf-length sleeping robe, but it was tied indecorously loose to reveal a vertical swath of his lean, lightly-haired chest. His high cheeks were the sort of smooth that didn't need a razor very often, and his hair was cropped close to his head. Though the lad leaned casually on the frame of the open doorway, his gaze was sharp, mouth set in a determined line.

"Not something to be used lightly," Seita remarked, in a thankfully mild tone. Jun didn't currently have the patience to deal with any grumbling over him casting magic from a different season's affinities.

Though Jun was a winter crow, with a talent for "hearth and shelter" magic, he had been born on the autumnal equinox, giving him a small advantage in autumn magic. And *affinity* did not mean *to the exclusion of others*. Any crow could conceivably cast the spell he'd used on Kiyoshi.

And yet, quite a few in the empress's court were rather proprietary of their season's innate talents. Seita, as an autumn crow, would have an affinity for "culling and decay," which included sleep, enervation, and wind magics.

Unperturbed, Jun stood and walked to the door. "You're a long way from the barracks."

"I keep wondering about something," Seita said, backing up into the hall and moving rather deferentially out of Jun's way. "And rumor has it, your lamp is usually lit well into the night."

Jun stared at the young crow, noting his slightly jutted chin as he closed Kiyoshi's door. "I'm listening."

"It's about our mission to dissolve the ward system—"

"That's the delegates' mission," Jun corrected him. "Yours is to provide escort and ensure the empress remains informed. And while I have agreed to share whatever I can about the ward system with the delegates, my mission is to eradicate a pair of demons."

"Understood, sir. But protecting the delegates means I need to know what prevents more wards from fighting back—or running away like you did."

"They're children, lad," Jun said, shaking his head. "At the mercy of cruel priests and crueler guards, both with special training, special tools, and convinced of their moral superiority. And what crow knows how to control their power the day it manifests?"

"How were you able to escape?" Seita asked.

"I—" Pain clutched at Jun's chest as he remembered that dismal night.

"Please, Mikari."

"I...I'm sorry."

"I was thrice lucky," Jun said at last. "First, even though wards are to be cleansed as soon as possible once their magic manifests, I was delayed more than a day. Never learned why."

In truth, both his and Mikari's cleansings had been delayed, their magic having manifested within hours of each other. The moment it was discovered, they were locked up at separate ends of the wardhouse.

"Second, Nobuhara was the guard outside my cell that night. Self-righteous bastard most of the time, but out of nowhere, he asks me, 'If I unlock your door and take a walk, can you make it to the service gate on your own?'"

Jun had hesitated to answer, certain that Nobuhara intended to taunt him, but the guard had been clearly nervous.

Jun had responded with one word, *"Mikari?"* To which Nobuhara had said, *"Her too."* And at Jun's firm nod, Nobuhara had fished the key to the door from his sleeve.

Of course, Jun had asked him why he was doing this, but Nobuhara's only response had been a silent glare. And after unlocking Jun's cell, he had just as silently walked away. Jun had barely had enough time to say, *"Tell her she knows where to meet me."*

"Obviously you said you could get there," Seita prompted, bringing Jun back to the hall outside his quarters.

"I did. And almost made myself into a liar. Seconds from the service gate, one of the priests' aides caught sight of me." After Mikari's rejection, immense heartache and the blur of tears had ensured Jun would stumble at the wrong moment. "But I was lucky a third time. Hideaki was a cleansed crow still living at the temple. He'd been there for decades, but when he saw me, all he did was lift his hand and smile."

Jun would never forget that moment, so full of grief and terror. Though Hideaki had been barely in his fifties, stress had left deep lines in his face, and one could hardly tell his thin, white hair had once been black. But his soft smile had transformed him—the only joy that Jun could recall ever seeing on the older crow's face.

At first, part of him had almost been relieved to have been caught, for nothing that would've happened next would've been his choice. But Hideaki had bid him a silent farewell, and Jun had taken it as a sign that escape was his destiny.

"From there, I ran all night to my sister's home, and she hid me for a few days until she'd arranged for Masanori and his mercenaries to take me south."

Masanori had never let him forget who had gotten him out of Gozu, or how much it had cost in bribes. The bastard had brought it up whenever Jun had balked at any of the jobs the group accepted.

"And here I thought my childhood was shit," Seita muttered. "I hope every single one of those so-called priests wanders the Maze for eternity."

"As do I," Jun said darkly, thinking of a few in particular—those senior priests who had achieved the ability to channel ambient magic. Individually, it was only enough for barrier charms and simple divinations, but collectively, they could perform cleansings and sunder a crow from their magic. Or, on rare occasion, their life.

"We have a long trip ahead of us in the morning," Jun rasped, hoping to end the conversation before it upset him any further.

"Yes, of course. Thank you, Commander." Seita executed a prompt bow.

"Get some sleep," Jun bade from the threshold of his room.

Seita nodded as he turned in the direction of the barracks, before stopping short. "Your sleeve is torn, by the way. Were you aware? Left shoulder."

Glancing down, Jun saw a fresh tear where his left sleeve met the body of his sleeping robe. Kiyoshi's doing, he was certain. When he raised his gaze, Seita was already halfway down the hall, walking away.

Jun shut his door and returned to his writing desk, where he loosened his belt enough to open the top of his robe and slip it off his shoulders, giving him the slack to lay the ripped seam on his lap. *An easy repair*, he thought, examining it.

With his hand over the tear, he took a deep breath to center himself. Others of his house had to recite a word or two of Mahou—the language of magic—in order to cast a low-effort spell like this. But Jun had been repairing his things in this manner for years and simply focused in the same way one aimed an arrow. Magic filtered up his arm and into his fingers.

Shuuri. Invoking the Mahou word for *mend* in his mind, he sent fine tendrils of power into the rent seam of his robe. Frayed bits of thread stretched across the hole, grabbed where they'd broken apart, and pulled tight together, sealing the tear.

Similar magic could mend flesh, even egregious injuries, theoretically. Winter crows, like Jun, had an affinity for it. But magical healing required far more stamina and experience, and a thorough understanding of the human form.

He already had the former thanks to years of healing his fellow mercenaries' various injuries, and for the latter, he had been reading the court library's numerous volumes on biology and attempting to finish the medical text on his desk before retiring for the night. He would be leaving first thing in the morning, and couldn't take it with him.

His robe mended, he slipped it on, tightened his belt, then pulled the book closer, only to stare at it with apathy. He would be killing demons in Gozu, not diagnosing disease. According to Rosuke, demons didn't contract mundane illnesses. Nor did they sleep, eat regular food, or beget offspring. They were sterile.

Frustrated, he put the book away then sank onto the edge of his bed, head heavy and heart weary.

Like Kiyoshi and his beloved sister, what Jun—and his magic— needed was proof. Once he'd done his duty for the empress, he would find where Mikari had been laid to rest, then lay his grief to rest beside her. Come spring, he'd return to Houfu for good and, Divine One willing, be renewed enough to make a good husband to someone. Perhaps even a father, albeit much later in life than he'd originally hoped.

With a resigned sigh and a flick of magic, he plucked out the light of the lantern near his desk and let in the darkness. Then he settled himself in his bed and waited for his nightmare to begin.

Chapter Four

Another choice to make. To regret. A literal fork in the road.

From atop her mount, Mikari stared at the roughly chiseled words on a black stone marker. The snow-capped rock hadn't been brought to this junction or otherwise altered apart from the information carved upon it; it had simply been a convenient boulder.

Going left would lead her inland to Tetsutani, her usual destination on this side of Gozu. Tetsutani was a thriving town with an active mine and a thirst for bardic entertainment, and one of her donors lived there. Going right would take her to Koichino, the second-to-last settlement before the road continued into the Setei Mountains, and from there, the southern lands.

Normally, the choice would be clear. Though she might have the energy to reach Koichino and loop back around to Tetsutani, she'd much rather take the left road and head straight there.

However, normally, she wasn't being watched.

The stomach-sinking feeling that she wasn't alone had begun several miles back, and the closer she'd come to the stone marker at which she now found herself, the harder she'd prayed for those malicious, unseen eyes to look away.

But they hadn't. They had followed her here.

Never had the creepy sensation lasted so long. She delayed as long as she could at the marker, dismounting to stretch her legs, repacking her belongings, briefly conversing with another traveler headed the way she had come, and casting surreptitious glances at every possible hiding place in the surrounding landscape. But whatever was watching her was quite patient.

Choice made, she swung up to her saddle, then steered her mount to Tetsutani with an air of purpose. The prickle on the back of her neck indicated her invisible stalker followed and continued to tail her for another half-mile.

Then, at last, the sensation abated. Mikari waited another moment before turning her reindeer around and coaxing it into a gallop. She reached the stone marker in a matter of minutes, all the while worrying that the unseen presence would return its attention to her.

Thankfully, it didn't. And at the stone marker, she followed the rightward path that would take her to Koichino.

Though she didn't like traveling so far from her nearest donor, history told her she'd suffer worse if she did what she preferred. Not one choice she'd ever made to pursue greater freedom had ever turned out right. With her cursed luck, some sort of disaster would be waiting for her on the road to Tetsutani, and she'd end up expending all the energy she'd gathered just to save herself.

Mikari tried to be happy about her decision. After all, Koichino wasn't all that far out of her way. And if she wanted news from the south, especially news of the empress and her agents, Koichino would be the best source. Southern merchants would be making one last trip through the pass before the winter storms filled it with snow, and merchants always had excellent gossip.

Koichino was the right decision, she told herself. And nothing horrible or life-altering would happen. She'd fill her pockets with enough income to put herself up at the Silver Hammer Inn in Tetsutani and depart from Koichino wondering why she'd ever hesitated to visit.

JUN WAS UP BEFORE DAWN, roused by the brace of mint. He packed his saddlebags and dressed almost without thinking, donning several layers of wool in understated colors, including a hooded overcoat. His shirt and undershirt were tucked into a fitted split-skirt, which was loose at his thighs but tight below the knee to allow for physical confrontation, beneath which he wore the pants of his formal military uniform, for extra warmth. His hefty sword sat in its unadorned sheath attached to his waist. Fur-lined leather boots completed his ensemble.

In the hall, a well-rested Captain Kiyoshi bid Jun farewell and wished him good luck. A few other officers leaving their quarters for the day expressed similar sentiments, but with quiet awe, as if astounded by the idea of volunteering to spend the winter stalking demons in the frozen highlands of Gozu.

He was one of the first to arrive at the imperial stables, already bustling with activity. He spotted Seita adjusting the fit of his horse's saddle, and there were several hostlers readying mounts for the rest of the delegation.

Jun would be traveling with them through Futakata Pass to the small market town of Koichino, where Scout Saneo would hopefully be waiting with new information about the suspected lust eaters. The trip would take at least a week, plenty of time for the delegates to learn all they could about the temples from him.

No matter where the scout's intelligence led him, the delegation would be making their way to Ajiro Temple, the Keeper's seat in the region, and doing whatever they could to gain the favor of any local authorities they met along the way, their ultimate goal being an end to cleansings.

A longer-term strategy for reclaiming sovereignty from the Keeper was still being formulated.

"Commander, sir." One of the stable's grooms hastened over. "The high general ordered me to prepare his horse for you."

Jun quirked his chin with surprise. "Is something wrong with my Houfubara?" A sturdy, reliable horse bred in the fertile plains surrounding the capital, the gelding was a little small for a man of his size, but he knew how to pace him. The horse had looked reasonably healthy when Jun had last checked on him.

"No, but my Gozuan stallion is younger and stronger."

Jun turned toward the new voice and found High General Vallen leading a truly remarkable bit of horseflesh toward him. The animal's thick ebony coat gleamed, his chest was broad, and his muscular legs gave him an impressive height. His gait was strong but relaxed, ears pointed forward with interest, eyes alert.

Jun shook his head. "Why would you lend me your horse? I have a perfectly serviceable mount."

"Yes, one that has not seen a Gozuan winter and would need more frequent rests to carry your weight." Vallen held out the stallion's reins. "My duties as both high general and consort will be keeping me here for the foreseeable future, so I'll likely not be needing Nugun for quite some time. And he prefers adventure to sniffing at mares in the stable yard."

Jun accepted the reins, smiling softly at the animal's name. It was Gozuan for "midnight."

"Ah, there she is," Vallen murmured, gazing warmly at someone over Jun's shoulder. Certain it was the empress, Jun turned and bowed.

The crisp morning saw her in layers of pink, and the fur-trimmed hood of her coat was up—no elaborate headdress. Walking beside her were Commander Rosuke and Elder Mai, similarly wrapped up in warm clothing.

Jun hadn't seen the couple since their joining ceremony three days ago, and their mouths still bore the shadow of Mai's dark purple lip stain, which Rosuke had thoroughly smeared during the final Kiss of Power. Unlike other cosmetics, lip stain was exactly that—difficult to remove without time or a great deal of scrubbing.

But despite what looked like a bruise around his mouth, Rosuke was still the most handsome man in the court, Maze take him.

The empress's eleven-year-old brother, Oka, hopped and leaped beside her more than he walked. His blond hair was mussed, as though she'd attempted to get him to put his hood up and failed. The boy's eyes and cheeks were bright with excitement, and he instantly left his sister's side to run about the stable yard.

"May I, Commander?" the groom asked, hands extended toward the saddlebags draped over Jun's shoulder. Jun transferred them with a nod and released the stallion's reins into the groom's possession.

"I'm surprised the commander let you give him your horse," Empress Shumei said to Vallen once she was near enough. The high general offered her his arm, which she took. To Jun she said, "You strike me as stubbornly self-sufficient."

He allowed himself a small smile. "Stubborn, but not stupid. I wouldn't say no to the high general. And..." He glanced at the stallion stamping its hooves with impatience as the groom attached Jun's saddlebags. "Nugun *is* impressive."

"The horse should match its rider," Rosuke said, grinning. Next to him, Mai rolled her eyes good-naturedly.

"You know, Nugun brought Vallen and me together," the empress said, smiling softly. "There was a small creek between my village and my family's field. His horse needed a drink, and as it so happened, so did I."

Vallen gave a pained chuckle. "I appreciate the romantic angle you've chosen. Our first meeting was...fraught."

Mai stepped within arm's reach—still a rare act for her, though she was improving. She had once been well known for avoiding proximity to others, especially men. And especially men like Rosuke.

"I came to wish you good luck, and to give you this." From her clothing, she produced an understated dagger wrapped in a black leather sheath.

Jun knew without looking that its blade was made of a dark metal. Elder Mai had taken the dagger into Oblivion, where she had discovered at a critical moment that it was a living object, so old and so infused with memory that it had manifested a soul of sorts, one of the rarest magical artifacts even in the time of the old court.

The dagger could speak, projecting its simplistic thoughts into the wielder's mind, and it warmed in the presence of powerful magic. But its most remarkable property known to date was its ability to reappear in its sheath regardless of where it was left.

"Vallen, Rosuke, and I have done a few experiments, but we haven't learned much more about the dagger," Mai explained as she laid the weapon in Jun's hand. His palm tingled in response, curiosity drawing his magic there. "We don't know where it was before the merchant who gave it to me had possession of it, or who forged it. The most we've determined is that it's made of aetherite, which hasn't been prospected since the previous Dark Court, meaning it's at least three centuries old."

Jun frowned. "Hmph, first a fine horse and now a rare artifact. I hope no one is expecting me to be fighting for my life in Gozu."

"Don't forget the magical mirror," Rosuke said, holding up his finger.

"I have a feeling," the empress hedged, instantly sending a chill up Jun's spine, "that all will prove to be essential."

Everyone there could understand the empress's phrasing for what it truly meant. She was often pulled into communion with the Divine One in order to hear his guidance, and *"I have a feeling"* was her way of conveying it. To others, she seemed to be asleep, but in truth, her mind was in his Garden. And for a few minutes after waking, she spoke only in Mahou.

Evidently, the Divine One had spoken to her about Jun's mission. Jun would give almost anything to know the entire conversation, but he likely wouldn't learn much more than what the empress had already revealed. The Divine One was consistently light on both detail and context, Jun had heard.

"We're hoping you'll discover more about the dagger that we can't learn in the relative safety of the palace." Mai shrugged her shoulder. "After all, it only spoke to me once, at a moment when the danger to me was greatest."

Jun held his tongue but frowned at the implication that he might soon find himself in a similar situation. The moment Mai referred to, she had been inside the Damned One's throne room. Jun had volunteered to chase down human-born demons, not fight a god—again, he supposed.

"Thank you for entrusting me with it." He dipped his head. In a lower voice, he added, "And congratulations."

Mai looked at him with bemusement. "On what? Oh, my joining?"

He glanced at her midsection before answering. "Of course."

She and Rosuke might believe that no one had noticed, but many in the Dark Court had seen the signs.

Mai no longer attended her combat training, and she sometimes looked at her meal with disgust, picking at it and choking down fewer bites than usual. Rosuke had always been attentive toward his now-wife, but he had never given her so many concerned looks, nor treated her as though she might fall at any moment. One of the captains under Jun's command had even insisted he'd seen Mai sneak in to see one of the court's midwives.

Rosuke's surprised smile told him he'd picked up on Jun's subtlety.

"May your joining marks reflect the strength of your union," Jun said to them.

"Thank you," Rosuke said, rubbing the front of his neck as though anticipating the patterned band of color that would soon appear there. "You feel confident using your mirror?"

Jun nodded as he attached the dagger to his belt. Normally, a crow's innate magic alerted them to an active scrying sensor. The sensation was rather like a prickle on one's skin, similar to gooseflesh. But the speaking mirror was always active and had been enchanted to deaden awareness of it.

Thus, sending out a call was straightforward, but receiving required an additional spell to help him sense an attempt to communicate with him through his mirror. It was an effect that he'd need to cast every day, and it only worked if he kept the mirror within a short distance.

Satisfied the dagger was secure, Jun straightened his overcoat. "The mirror's simple enough to use. I'm more worried about breaking it."

The empress smiled in response, but there were nervous furrows between her brows that made him as tense as a cornered cat.

"Any other advice for me, Your Imperial Grace?" he asked her, pointedly enough that he hoped she understood his true meaning.

Empress Shumei regarded him for a moment, and a sort of calm enveloped her. "I know you'll conduct yourself with bravery and honor," she said at last. "The rest…I have a feeling…is out of my hands."

Jun responded with a stiff bow and silently strung together several curses.

After a few more words of farewell, the empress and her entourage went to greet the three brownie delegates who had just arrived—two women, one of them at least ten years Jun's senior, the other not much younger, and a round-faced man with more gray hair than brown. All seemed healthy, however, and ready for a long trip.

Their other escort, Kie of House Rice, was already engaged in conversation with them. By all accounts, Kie was a tenacious and dedicated soldier—and easy to get along with. Her long hair trailed down her back in a thick plait, and her smile was just a little crooked, jutting to the right as she grinned at something the male delegate was saying.

"He's ready for you," the stable groom said. Jun accepted Nugun's reins and thanked the groom, who scurried off to whatever other task needed doing. He laid his hand upon the stallion's neck, stroking it as he spoke.

"Nice to meet you, Nugun," he murmured in Gozuan. The horse

shifted restlessly but accepted Jun's hand upon it. "Let's take good care of each other, hm?"

The horse didn't answer, of course. Jun swung up into the saddle and settled once his other foot found its stirrup. Nugun shifted forward as though anxious to start moving, but Jun quickly quieted him, marveling at how much higher he sat upon the Gozuan stallion than his gelding.

In moments, the delegation was mounted and ready. The empress spoke a few words, but Jun could hardly pay any attention, too consumed with the realization that in a few short days, he would be back in Gozu. And not long after arriving, he would be on his own.

"Good luck," Empress Shumei said, nodding with finality, her gaze lingering on him for a full breath.

Jun clenched the reins in his hand. What had the Divine One told her?

Nothing that he needed to know, he decided, urging his horse to follow the others toward the yard's exit, where Oka stood to wish them all safe travels.

Jun's mission was to locate the lust eaters active in Gozu and offer them a cure. Simple. He had chased down plenty of cagey criminals as a member of Masanori's mercenaries, and had a feeling of his own that he'd run into one of his targets in no time.

And when they inevitably tried to run or fight back, well…he would just have to slice their heads clean off.

Chapter Five

Three days of excellent weather and dry roads quickly conducted the delegation to the city of Kohan on the shores of Kanamizu, a large freshwater lake. Another four days would see them through Bakugi, the massive forest of pines on the southern side of the Setei Mountains.

Jun was rather used to chatty traveling companions, and his current company was no exception, but the conversation was far different from that of his former mercenary group.

Rather than war stories, tales of sexual conquests, and attempts to insult each other for entertainment, the delegation spoke of their families, their ambitions, and the mission that lay ahead of them.

Kie was an only child, and Seita had been raised by his great-uncle. Neither liked to read, and both enjoyed learning to fight, especially with magic.

Natsu, the older of the two brownie women, had decades of governing experience. Though her town had been destroyed during a demon attack, she had successfully led the two-hundred-odd survivors to Houfu. Iwa, the other brownie woman, had been Natsu's wife and aide for nearly twenty-five years.

Noriaki, the last of the delegates, had grown up in Gozu but had moved to Houfu, where he'd then married. Now a widower with a grown daughter thriving in House Moon, he would be the delegation's translator.

Throughout their journey north, Jun told the delegation about his life as a temple ward, recollecting for them the drudgery, the constant surveillance, and the frequent abuse. No one pressed him whenever he asked to stop for a while.

The only food the wards ate was what they pulled from the temple fields and foraging. The only privacy to be found was in one's cell at night, and even then, the preceptors sometimes did rounds, shining light into their rooms and disrupting their sleep, usually in retaliation for any perceived defiance.

Even in their education, the preceptors in charge of the wards' diurnal schedules were strict and exploitative. The crows with the best handwriting copied books for the temple's profit. Artistically talented crows shaped, painted, and glazed ceramics—again, for the temple's profit.

Musically gifted crows played songs or performed dances as part of the temple's various rites and rituals, many of them done as services procured by the public. The fees paid went directly into the priests' pockets.

To the group, Jun acknowledged that he was lucky to have even received an education. He'd heard that some temples forced their wards to manufacture goods from dawn to dusk, not bothering with reading, writing, music or art lessons.

He then told them a particularly harrowing story of a ward who had been denied food for ten days as punishment for stumbling into several shelves of pottery, resulting in their destruction.

The ward had already suffered from a weak constitution, likely what had caused his disastrous stumble, and his weight had plummeted. Jun and others had tried to sneak him food, but he'd been kept under close watch.

Every crow had feared he would die, but somehow, the ward had survived all ten days of starvation…only to collapse a few days after his punishment had ended. His heart had given out.

"Divine One have mercy," Iwa rasped. She was riding ahead of Jun, so he couldn't see her face, but he knew he'd wrung tears from her when she wiped her eyes, head hanging low.

"I'm sorry," Natsu murmured, riding next to him. "For that poor ward, and for asking questions that dredge up such horrible memories."

Indeed, Jun's wardship had been full of grueling work and random cruelty, but...

"There were bright spots," he admitted. "Friends." *And a lover.*

Iwa looked back at him, eyes still misty, but she was smiling. "I'd love to hear about them."

He grimaced, not at her request but at himself, and a Gozuan interjection slipped past his teeth. *"Aj'*, to my shame, I must admit that I don't recall much that's happy. Only flashes."

He remembered some faces but not many names, and an inside joke but not where it had come from. A ward whose name was on the tip of his tongue had had a bad habit of slapping Jun's arm overly hard whenever he wished to be friendly.

Life back then had not produced many happy moments, and time, as well as the need to forget, had eroded the details. "Anyway, half of them were already cleansed and discharged by the time...Mikari arrived."

He could hardly believe he'd just spoken her name. He hadn't meant to, but she had been a major event in his life, one that oriented his sense of time, having occurred right in the middle of his years at Nansen and thus dividing his wardship into two separate halves.

But it was too late to take back his words, and he refused to insult her memory by lying. So, he confessed. Sort of.

"She became a ward at fifteen and...would come to occupy my full attention." And unlike the friends who had faded from his memory, grief had kept Mikari painfully fresh in his mind.

"Oh," Natsu stammered, quickly comprehending all that he hadn't said.

Kie noticed the inconsistency. "She wasn't taken at the age of twelve?"

"Her parents were older. Before her, they'd been childless," Jun explained. "For fifteen years, they managed to hide her existence, but the isolation drove her to run away, and she was caught."

Natsu murmured something that sounded like "Her poor parents."

"So, what was she like?" Iwa asked.

Jun couldn't help a nostalgic smile. "Shy at first, before I found out how sweet and playful she could be. And so ambitious. She was years older than the newest wards but had to remain with them for classes and work until she caught up in her literacy, which she managed in only a year. The only time we spent in the same room that first year was music class. In that, she already excelled."

"What was her talent?"

"Her father had been a bard in his youth and owned a lute, which she'd taken to playing before she'd even begun to form memories. By the time she'd become a ward, she had already mastered the instrument. She stunned all of us, even the preceptor, with her skill and her singing voice."

He had been attracted to her from the start. At fifteen, she'd already grown quite tall, nearly to his shoulder, which was saying something. And the sweep of freckles across her face, from one ear to the other, had pulled at his gut, tempting him to kiss each one.

But the moment he'd first heard her play the lute and sing was when he'd begun losing his heart to her.

His throat thickened. "She would have been a wonderful bard."

"Did she not follow in her father's footsteps?" Natsu questioned, before realizing her error. "Forgive me. You escaped, of course, so…" She fell silent, leaving the obvious unspoken. *You wouldn't know.*

Oh, but he did know.

Thankfully, the subject was dropped.

Futakata Pass was the easier of the two routes through the Setei Mountains, but the road still zigzagged countless times in its ascent, and minor rockslides had rendered parts of it barely suitable for someone on horseback, let alone the wheels of a merchant's wagon. And yet, judging by the deep tracks in the rocky soil, several travelers had managed it despite at least one cart breaking a wheel, which had been carelessly left on the side of the road.

Still, it could have been worse. He and the delegation could be urging their mounts through a blizzard and several feet of accumulated snow, all while praying that no avalanches occurred. Instead, the sky was calm, if gray, and there was only a dusting of snow upon the ground.

Jun was rather impressed by his stallion's stamina and agility. If it weren't for his traveling companions, he would've reached the other side of the pass well before sunset.

As his group crawled along, careful of their mounts' footing, he wondered whether he'd recognize any part of Futakata Pass, the same route his former mercenary group had taken out of Gozu. However, nothing looked familiar.

What he did remember was the wild panic he'd felt at seeing the spiky horizon of Bakugi for the first time, for another, smaller forest of pines lay on the northern side of the pass—the hysterical thought had occurred to him that perhaps the path taken him back to Gozu like a loop in a maze.

Daylight was fading by the time the delegation reached the other end of the pass. They'd been told that Okususo, the closest village, was another two- or three-hours' ride ahead, so Jun and Kie began scouting for a campsite away from the road.

Luckily, they found an abandoned hunting cabin still structurally sound, and though it was a snug fit, it was dry and kept the wind out. Jun, Kie, and Seita each took turns keeping watch.

By morning, snow had begun to fall. A broken stirrup delayed them a short while in Okususo, but then they rode practically without stopping in the hopes of reaching their intended destination before sunset.

However, night had fallen by the time they spotted the lanterns of Koichino through a curtain of snow. All around Jun, there were sighs of relief.

Winter had barely begun, but Jun could already feel the sharp bite of Gozu's bitterly cold nights. Snow clung to him in clumps. He urged his mount onward, as eager as everyone else for dry shelter, a hot meal, and a cozy bed. With luck, Scout Saneo would be there to meet them.

Koichino's architecture was typical of Gozu—steep, gabled roofs made of dark-brown thatching that extended nearly to the ground and which were shaped to encourage snow to fall off. Every building had lowered its storm shutters.

The village's most prominent feature was a large market square that was currently locked up for the night, but in the morning, Jun's group would be there trading the luxury goods they'd brought from Houfu for currency. The imperial treasury hadn't been able to spare much to finance their mission, so they'd been given the commodities that would fetch the most money: dried fruit, jerked boar meat, rice powder, and fine damasks.

Despite their collective need for rest, the party was wary as they neared the largest of the village's inns, a three-story building with curling, decorative elements straddling its roof line. They had avoided the expense—and trouble—of seeking lodgings the previous evening, which meant that tonight's procurement would be their first close interaction with anyone north of the mountains.

In Gozu, cleansed crows generally had the freedom to travel, unlike their southern counterparts during blondie reign. But anyone at any time could demand to see the brands of the crows in their party, which none of them had. And unless a crow was well known to the local populace, the chance of being "inspected" was high.

With luck, however, simple good behavior would avert most attempts to discover the status of their magic. Bribes and intimidation would be fallback options. Violence would be a last resort.

The group decided to send Noriaki inside to seek accommodations. A few moments later, a pair of young boys wrapped in fur-trimmed clothing appeared. They gave Jun an extended look but said nothing as they led the horses away two at a time.

"Seems they've noted your hue," Seita muttered. "Either that, or they can hardly believe your size." Both Seita and Kie's hair was hidden beneath their hoods, but Jun's beard, even in the lantern light, was that of a crow.

"They wouldn't refuse us rooms, would they?" Kie asked.

Seita scoffed. "I'm certain they'll try."

Jun released a rough sigh and hiked his saddlebags over his shoulder. "Let's get this over with." He strode toward the stone walkway leading to the inn's deep-set entrance.

Annoyed as he was, he dutifully tapped his boots on the snow bar, calmly opened the door, and made sure to remove and store his footwear in an unused slot of the entryway's large shoe cabinet. The rest of his group moved to do likewise.

Half the village seemed to be crammed into the inn's main room, the other half taking up the tables and cushions of the inn's more private back area. Over the din, Jun thought he heard the gentle plucks of a three-string, one possibly still being tuned based on the lack of a melody.

Past the entryway to the left was a wide wooden counter, where he spotted Noriaki speaking to a shrewd-looking older man wearing what Jun supposed passed for a friendly smile. On the counter was an open book and a writing kit. Spread across the rest of the surface were several trays, some bearing cups and pitchers of wine.

A doorway behind the counter led to the inn's kitchen, but a split length of cloth obscured the proceedings beyond. A thin young man who bore some resemblance to the innkeeper retrieved a tray and deftly carried it to one of a dozen tables spread about the open area to the right. Two braziers were spaced for utmost effect and glowed warmly.

A few of the other patrons glanced at him as he approached the counter where Noriaki was counting out kols. The innkeeper was so intent on the money that he didn't notice a new presence until Jun stood at Noriaki's shoulder.

The innkeeper's head jerked up, then up again when he didn't immediately see Jun's face. Jun swept back his hood and stared blankly into the other man's stunned gaze. Noriaki fidgeted beside him, no doubt sensing the imminent conflict.

The innkeeper recovered quickly, eyebrows slamming down, mouth pinching into a frown. "No rooms left," he snapped in Gozuan. "Not that I'd rent to a crow."

Jun glanced down at the man's hands hurriedly sweeping Noriaki's kols toward him. "It seems you just did." He gave his answer in Common, certain that the innkeeper spoke the language of the southern merchants who often stayed in his rooms.

The innkeeper froze and then frowned even harder, lips practically disappearing—which then became his name in Jun's mind. No-Lips glared at Noriaki and continued speaking in Gozuan. "You failed to mention you had a crow in your party."

"What was that?" Natsu asked in terse Common before Noriaki could even summon a reply. Jun glanced behind him at Natsu and Iwa, both glaring with disapproval.

Seita and Kie were taking their time in the entryway, likely expecting they'd be keeping their boots on. The patrons seated within earshot of the counter—not many due to all the chatter—were all silently watching but trying not to be obvious about it.

Jun translated the innkeeper's last retort for Natsu. She approached the counter with such purpose that, despite her soft footsteps and unhurried pace, Noriaki quickly sidled out of her way.

"It's three crows, in fact," she said to the innkeeper, chin raised high in reproach. "Our party of six is here on imperial business."

No-Lips glanced concernedly between the three of them at the counter. Behind him, the head and shoulder of a person's shadow appeared on the white curtain hanging upon the doorway.

"In fact, you have the pleasure of hosting one of Her Imperial Grace's highest officers." Natsu swept her hand toward Jun with a courtly air. "As well as her specially appointed emissaries."

No-Lips made a rude sound. "Even if you were telling the truth, *he's* not staying here. None of them crows are." He jabbed his finger in the direction of the entryway. "I don't care if they've got a brand, they're tainted."

"What in the Maze are you doing?" a brownie woman hissed in Gozuan as she punched through the kitchen's curtain. No-Lips wheeled around. "Are you *asking* for trouble?"

"I don't recall making any threats," Jun said, keeping his voice even.

"Your presence is a threat," No-Lips seethed in a loud whisper.

"Idiot!" The kitchen woman pinched the innkeeper, eliciting a satisfying yelp. Pincher was surely either a wife or a sister, for the young serving boy took after her more than the innkeeper. "You know there's an empress now. You know where half our business comes from. We can't afford to turn up our noses, not with only a few rooms let out and winter almost here."

"I thought you had no rooms left," Jun said to No-Lips, only mildly accusatory.

The other man gestured desperately at the bustling main floor. "We're full, see?" To his angry relative, he spoke through his teeth. "We can turn our noses up plenty."

Pincher drew her head back in astonishment, voice dripping with sarcasm. "You mean they *didn't* all come here to see the bard and *won't* be going back home once she's done?"

Their argument continued, but Jun heard none of it. He whipped his head around and cast his eyes across the main floor.

A bard was here. A female Gozuan bard. But although there were plenty of women among the inn's patrons, none wore the telltale red clothing.

"Where is she?" he asked Pincher, who seemed startled by his sudden question. Or perhaps it was the edge in his voice.

"W-who?"

"The bard," he clarified, switching into Common for Natsu's benefit. "You said everyone was here to see a bard."

AT THE MAZE'S CENTER

"She's getting ready in our back room." Pincher spoke in passable Common, but her Gozuan accent muddled certain consonants in her speech. "It's her last night before she moves on." Jun didn't hesitate to start folding up the wide sleeves of his overcoat and keep them from impeding the movement of his arms.

The motion drew the innkeeper's attention downward, and he pointed sharply at Jun's waist. "That's a sword."

"Your eyesight remains keen, sir," Jun grumbled.

Pincher gave No-Lips a dismissive wave and reverted to Gozuan "There's at least ten other swords in here. You've never cared before. Just like you didn't care when that pack of thugs was scaring our other guests last week and nipping a whole case of rice wine. *I* had to kick them out."

"Where is your back room?" he asked of her as he finished pinning up his sleeves. She pointed out a particular sliding door on the other side of the many tables. Only after giving him directions did she think to ask him, "Why?"

"What's going on?" Natsu whispered at the same time.

"We may have stumbled across someone we're looking for," he said under his breath, casually turning around.

His fellow crows were also preparing for a fight, having read his body language. Kie was pinning up her sleeves, and Seita had simply removed his overcoat. Both had kept their boots on. Jun considered putting his boots back on and stomping their mess across the inn, but perhaps that wouldn't be necessary. Still, he adjusted the position of his sword at his side. The rare dagger Mai had lent him remained quiet on his other hip.

"I need to speak with the bard," he said over his shoulder, hoping the suspect remained civil, but prepared for if she did not.

"But she's due to start any—"

Three crisp, high tings filled the air, the measured shake of a bell stick. The din instantly quieted down, and all heads turned expectantly to the door across the way. The serving boy hurried over to slide it open.

Out of the dim back room and into the brighter main hall, a Gozuan bard in full regalia silently stepped forward, hands perfectly positioned upon the three-string tucked against her body. She wore a long white wig in honor of Tei, the first Gozuan bard, a brightly painted fox mask, and the top-to-bottom red clothing of her profession.

"They're staying, and that's final," he heard Pincher whisper.

"But—"

"Do you want to repair the stables this year or not?"

The bard brushed a beautiful chord with her agile fingers, then another as she slowly entered the main room. Each strum came a little faster until the melody settled into place.

A melody Jun recognized. One he didn't think he'd ever hear again. He told himself the song was likely standard in a bard's repertoire, but Mikari would often sing it while the wards were spread throughout the maze and tending its many hedgerows.

It was the story of the shepherdess Meke and the farmer Kubo, who were cursed the night before their wedding by a jealous hermit. Until the sun rose, they would not be able to speak without revealing their true feelings for each other.

Though the lyrics were simplistic and some rhymes a bit stilted, the entire song could be understood from either lover, showcasing their mutual lack of trust.

The bard moved about the room as she played the introduction. Then she stopped in the midst of her rapt audience and took a breath.

Why can't I speak?
Why can't I spill my heart to you?

The air in his lungs left in a rush. His skin rippled with shock. His magic bucked and flailed, lashing him with heat. The room spun and fell away, and only the bard remained.

My love for you, it runs so deep.
Their darkest depths a mystery.
My fears live there,
And I cannot know if they'll make you go.

He knew that voice almost better than his own, its silkiness and the sweet rasp of its high notes. He'd heard it laugh, whisper, and moan. He'd heard it weep and plead. Every night, that voice called for him. He couldn't have stopped his feet from carrying him forward even if he tried.

Why won't you speak?
Why won't you spill your heart to me?
Can it be true your love is weak?
As shallow as a muddy creek.
I beg of you,
Please hold me close and don't let go.

The bard moved on from the chorus to the first verse, slowly turning in a circle so that all might hear her. Though her voice was achingly familiar, it was also stronger and clearer than he remembered. Each note was perfect, achieved with such ease that no one could doubt her talent.

If any of the patrons were reacting to Jun's obvious intrusion, he didn't notice them. Every part of him was focused on the bard. She was the right height, the right shape. He knew she'd fit perfectly against him, tall enough to tuck her head under his chin.

By the time he was in arm's reach, she faced away from him and was singing the second verse, which introduced the hermit's curse.

He said nothing, throat thick with emotion—too many of them, felt too deeply. His magic was similarly inflamed. Only with his many years of experience at commanding it was he barely able to keep it contained, and even then, only with vague awareness.

She had sensed him. Perhaps the heat of his body, or the subtle radiation of his barely controlled magic. Perhaps she saw the other patrons' confusion. He didn't know. But her fingers upon her lute faltered, the song coming to an uncertain pause. She turned, and he saw only the shadow of her eyes through the holes in her mask.

She gasped, coming fully around. He could see none of her face except the exquisite line of her jaw, one he swore he'd tasted and stroked.

At last, he was able to manage a single word. And even to his ears, his voice sounded twenty years younger.

"Mikari?"

Chapter Six

Mikari's next breath drove pain into her chest, the air having disappeared from the room. Every hair on her body stood up, producing an all-over sting. Her heart thundered in her ears.

And that was before the man in front of her spoke her name. The man whose face she hadn't seen in so long, and yet he was as familiar to her as if she'd seen him yesterday.

The span of twenty long years couldn't tarnish his dark-sable eyes that stared so intently at her mask, or the wonderful breadth of his shoulders that she used to seize while in the grip of pleasure. Twenty years couldn't keep his low, rumbly voice from tugging hard at a place deep inside, as though the string that had once drawn them together was making itself known, having never disappeared in the first place.

Oh, but he had indeed aged. There were fine lines around his eyes, his skin was a little weathered, and there were streaks of gray throughout his short, slicked-back hair and his full, neatly trimmed beard.

She had always known he'd be devastating with a beard…and oh, had she been right…but the temple had required clean-shaven wards. And though he had been a wonderfully large young man, the warrior before her was hulking with muscle.

Yes, a warrior. He had the aura of one—the posture and most

certainly the strength. She didn't need to see that he was armed to know he carried a sword.

Jun. Her first and only love.

Was this the reason she'd felt a cold stare on her nape while tuning her lute only moments ago? Had she been sensing plucks upon their string of fate, each one driving her toward this cruel reunion?

She inhaled to speak, and the air brought with it a scent so heady and satisfying—so complex, combining sweet and savory and spice with perfection—that her body lit up with instant arousal.

A raspy breath shuddered out of her, sounding as much like fear as wolfish hunger, for she was both terrified and captivated by the thought of how utterly and *superbly* he would feed her.

Too late, she realized she shouldn't know him. Couldn't. Much too late, she realized where she was, what she was, and all that she had done. All that had happened in the decades since she'd last seen him.

She did her best to recover, but the catch in her voice seemed to betray her shock, her panic, and her intense desire. "Pa-ardon?"

He stepped even closer, overwhelming her with the singularly mouth-watering aroma of his lust. It was like nothing she'd ever breathed before. Rich and fulfilling. The sort of meal that would send you straight to the Garden. Her undergarments grew damp between her legs.

"Mikari, is that you?"

She briefly shut her eyes as his voice sent a hot wash of incomprehensible emotion over her. "I d-don't know of whom you speak. Please sir, as you can—"

"Mikari. It's Jun. You must—" He lifted his arms toward her, and she backed away, as mindful as she could be of her cramped surroundings. "...remember me." His voice faded to a whisper. His eyes shone.

"A-as you can see, I'm in the middle of a performance." She heard grumbles around her, as if her declaration had woken her frozen audience to reality.

"I know it's you," he said with the barest wobble. "You think I don't know your voice?"

Her heart jumped in her chest, leaving it aching. Sweat covered her in a fine sheen, and her hot breath puffed behind her mask. "You're mistaken."

Desperation flashed across his face. "Impossible. Please, remove your mask. I need to see you." He reached for her again, more quickly this time.

"Please, sir!" She darted back, instinctually drawing her lute to her side. Her audience continued their grumbles, angrier this time.

"Hey, you can't do that," came a woman's voice.

"Stop interrupting the song!"

"You can't go looking under a bard's mask!"

Jun turned his eyebrows up at her, his amazed shock turning into incredulity. "Why are you doing this?"

Choosing which exit to take—definitely the rear—she made a slight right turn without looking, still moving backward and hoping she didn't trip on either a table or a person. On impulse, she dropped her three-string into the nearest person's lap.

"How are you here?" he asked, closing in on her. "I thought you were dead."

"I'm not whoever you think I am," she pleaded, grateful that her obvious anxiety wasn't at all suspicious, especially as he continued to stalk toward her.

The audience tossed supportive shouts, and a few disparaged him, their insults toward him slicing at her heart, but no one moved to stop him. He was, after all, a large and unfamiliar crow.

"I thought you were *dead*!" he bellowed, practically shaking the timber beams of the inn's roof. "Where have you been all this time?"

"You *don't* know me. Please," she begged, nearly at the edge of the dining space.

"Take off your mask. Take it off!" he demanded, stride lengthening. His arm shot toward her face.

She batted his hand away, perhaps harder than necessary. When he moved to reach for her again, she shoved him with one hand on his wide chest. He stumbled back, legs knocking into a group of people seated on the woven-mat flooring. She didn't remain to see whether he fell.

Instead, she ran, summoning every aspect of her inhuman physicality. With one mighty push of her foot, she launched toward the still-open door of the back room, which led to the rear hall and exit.

Amid the chorus of yells, none were as loud as Jun calling her name. Footfalls pounded behind her, but she was already in the back room.

With a flick of her wrist, she slung the door along its track, closing it behind her and swiftly setting it up as a delay. By the time a large body crashed into it, ripping the mulberry paper stretched across its now-cracked wooden frame, she was on the other side of the room and pulling on a tower of boxes full of dry foodstuffs. They smashed to the floor behind her as she entered the rear hall.

Unfortunately for her, the hall was empty of any other obstacles she might lay down, so she grabbed whatever traction her sock-covered feet could manage on the clean, wood floor and plunged toward the back door, swiftly crossing the distance. Then, feet skittering to slow her momentum, she ripped open the portal before flinging herself through.

It was full night. The wind had picked up, and heavy snow fell. Already it was thick upon the ground. She heard another crash behind her, and a deep, mindless shout.

She darted toward the inn's stables, thankfully positioned directly in back. She had no overcoat, no lute, and no footwear, but she'd replace them all if necessary. And yes, she would be terribly cold, but the creature she now was could handle it.

The stable doors were fully open, beckoning her as she raced across the snow-covered gravel and hard-packed dirt of the rear lane. She definitely wouldn't have time to saddle her reindeer, but she had practiced riding her bareback for a reason.

Only at the last second did she notice someone barreling toward her. A woman, Mikari sensed. She gave a hard kick forward and spun in a controlled circle to avoid her new pursuer's outstretched hands. The woman flew past her.

Jun roared her name again. She heard the torment in his voice, felt his pain. Its sharp stab nearly swept her feet out from under her, but she firmed her knees and pressed on.

Another was running at her, a man she didn't recognize. There was little chance she'd have time to drag her mount out of its stall now, but she dove into the stables anyway, for they had a back door.

One that was currently closed. And obviously chained shut.

"*Aj'!*" Then she noticed the two stable boys. Both were stiff with surprise, eyes wide and staring. She ran past one and pushed him into the path behind her. A second later, there was a sick-sounding thud and a pair of pained grunts.

The other stable boy was inside a stall with an enormous black horse, too far out of reach, but the unsecured door of the stall was not. She sprinted past, pulling the door open at a blocking angle, then yanked at a stack of baled hay, spilling several on the ground behind her.

Even with her inhuman strength, there was no way she could rip apart the thick iron chain locking the rear doors of the stable. Instead, she planted her foot and kicked hard at the wood. It absorbed the first blow, then made a splintering sound with the next. A third strike ripped off the iron plate securing one end of the chain to its door.

She chanced a look behind her as the broken door shuddered open. The man was still struggling to his feet after colliding with the stable boy. The woman had caught up and was well past him, dodging around the open stall door. They both had black hair, Mikari realized.

But there was no time to ponder that observation. Only time to run.

She slipped through the broken door onto another gravel lane and turned left—the wrong direction, she was about to learn. She would have to come back for her reindeer. She couldn't replace it so easily. How she would successfully retrieve it, she didn't know, but she'd think of something.

Out of the deep shadows behind the stables, a massive form snatched her and bore her to the ground. She and her captor fell into a fresh snowdrift, but its fluffy texture didn't do much to cushion them. His heavy body knocked the air out of her, and before she knew it, her mask was torn from her head.

Alarmed, she pushed past the discomfort, bucking hard, and threw off her pursuer. Sucking in a breath, she popped up to her feet, but a hand grabbed her leg. She tried to twist out of his hold, but whoever had her was just as strong as she was.

He yanked her off her feet and into the snowdrift, this time on her back, knocking the air out of her yet again. Icy wetness seeped into both the front and back of her clothing. She dragged in another breath as her captor straddled her stunned form and locked her arms in place against her chest.

The man over her froze, and the light from a nearby lantern revealed his face. Jun had caught up to her, even overpowered her. Now he was staring at her, and his expression… He was utterly heartbroken. She mourned how familiar it looked.

A second later, the black-haired woman appeared behind Jun,

followed by her male comrade. Both were panting, but Mikari was too engrossed in the face above her to note much else about them. They began speaking in Common.

"Is it…really her?" the woman gasped.

Jun's face twitched as though words had failed him.

"It has to be," the man said. "No human moves that fast without magic. Didn't think we'd catch one this soon."

Mikari lurched beneath a fresh wave of grief. Jun was one of the empress's agents, and he was here to kill her. Oh, she couldn't bear for him to carry that burden.

"Let someone else end me. Please," she said in Gozuan. Jun jolted above her, eyes glittering with hurt that then deepened into rage.

"I'm not here to kill you," he ground out, his grip on her wrists so tight her fingers tingled. "Not unless you force me to."

Switching back to Common, he spoke over his shoulder to his comrades. "It's her, the bard we're looking for."

"And is she also…?" The woman trailed off.

"Yes." The word was a snarl. "It's been twenty years since I last saw Mikari. And she hasn't aged a single day."

"IF YOU'RE NOT HERE to kill me, then—"

"We'll discuss it somewhere warm and dry," Jun growled, pulling Mikari along.

He knew she might try to escape again, a realization that hurt almost as much as the first time she'd run from him, but she didn't resist his hold on her arm as he led her along her path of destruction back to the inn.

Still, he didn't dare dismiss the magical enhancements to speed and strength that he'd been forced to tap in order to capture her—more evidence that she was no longer human.

She hadn't hesitated to put her mask back on. He briefly considered forbidding her from wearing it, but it was indeed rude for the public to see a bard's face in their professional capacity. In his earlier shock, he had forgotten, and he had no wish to further antagonize the townsfolk deprived of their planned entertainment for the evening.

Later, though, in the privacy of one of their rooms, he would see her. He would carefully observe every twitch of emotion as she answered his many burning questions. He had at least a hundred of them.

They walked through the broken stable door and wended their way through the scattered bales of hay. Those, at least, would be quick to tidy. Kie set about doing so while Seita spoke to a stable worker whose hand was cupped around the back of his head.

Mikari had yanked the poor lad in Seita's way, ensuring a painful collision. When asked whether he'd be all right, the lad glanced at Mikari with angry confusion but nodded. Jun made a mental note to examine him later, grinding his teeth at the recklessness of her action.

He hardly felt the cold as they silently trudged the distance between the stables and the inn. Could hardly feel anything but the agony of betrayal—breath-stealing shocks of pain as though a red-hot knife was buried in his chest.

He fought for a measure of calm, at least enough to answer questions without snapping, knowing he'd have to deal with the havoc he and Mikari had left behind.

The delegates, bless them, made it easy on him. Jun was braced for a loud and chaotic reaction when they returned to the common room, but the crowd had been largely dispersed. Anyone not already gone or bundling up to leave had relocated to the private dining alcove, its doors pulled nearly shut.

At the reception counter, Iwa and Noriaki were engaged in a low, heated discussion with the innkeeper—once again lipless—and his slightly less incensed relative. Nearer to the entrance, Natsu stood in close conversation with a few agitated townsfolk, including an older man whose blond hair as much as his air of privilege identified him as the town's mayor.

If he was like any other blondie with authority in Gozu, he reported almost everything that happened in Koichino to the nearest temple Primary, including any incidents involving an unfamiliar crow shouting at a bard and chasing her from the inn. Recognizing the consequences of his madcap behavior, Jun barely held back a wince.

Natsu caught sight of them emerging cautiously from the rear, one bard in tow. Her keen eyes quickly noted his grip on Mikari's arm, and she subtly tipped her head as if to say, *I'll take care of it. Go.*

Mikari pointed at her three-string, lying safe on an unoccupied table, and they walked close enough for her to retrieve it.

Jun spoke low to her. "I assume you have a room here."

She gestured toward the stairs. "Second floor, to the left."

"Take us there."

Her rented room was perfectly spacious for one or two occupants, but four people made it cramped. Though the air within was cool, he was certain there soon wouldn't be a need to locate and light the room's ceramic brazier.

To the right was a large, open shelf with a row of damask-covered cabinets above and a larger matching cabinet below. Tucked between it and the door was a small, unlit standing lantern.

Mikari's things were few. Her fine-leather pack sat half-empty in the storage alcove past the cabinets. Inside its open top, he could see a couple of books and spare clothing. Her beauty items lay perfectly spaced along their cloth wrap.

The only other items in the room were the inn's: a decorative painting, a cleanly folded mattress ready to be laid out for sleep, and the accompanying bedclothes, including a complimentary robe.

He heard Kie's voice behind him. "*Ka.*" Reddish light gently flared. Jumping, Mikari twisted around as much as his hold on her allowed. He looked over his shoulder at Kie, who had conjured a small, ruby flame on her thumb.

"Divine One's arse," Mikari breathed, watching Kie lift the lantern's paper frame and light the wick set inside the concealed dish of oil. Mikari then looked to Jun, or at least turned her mask toward him. Not being able to see her expression made him clench his teeth. "Can…can you do that?"

"Yes," he said tersely. "Now, take this thing off." His large hand easily spanned the mask's width, and he none too gently lifted it off her head. Instead of the awe he'd heard in her voice just now, her expression was one of insulted surprise.

Divine One's arse, indeed. She looked exactly the same. Lustrous skin. Wide, high cheeks flushed from the hot, close air of her mask. Eyes that somehow always smiled, and a dusting of freckles across her face, from one ear to the other. Damn it, she looked young enough to be his—

Taking her mask off had dislodged her white wig, so he angrily dragged it off as well. Her long, wavy black hair spilled out, along with the fragrant scent of *oroimebi*.

Maze take him, she was the Mikari of twenty years ago. Or rather, she looked like her. There was no way she was the same person. Not after all this time, after what she had become. The knife in his chest twisted.

Even so, it was all he could do to keep his irritated magic from reaching out for her. Not once in the last twenty years had it reacted so fiercely to anything.

"Not a single gray hair on its head," Seita observed from the threshold.

Jun's back teeth met with a click just as Seita grunted sharply. Jun threw a glare at the open door, where Seita was jutting a petulant jaw at Kie and rubbing his side where she'd jabbed him.

"On *her* head," Kie corrected him. "And you should think of the commander before you speak."

Jun refused to acknowledge their exchange and returned his attention to Mikari, who regarded him with affected calm, eyebrows slightly raised.

"I would have removed those myself"—she nodded at the mask and wig in his grasp—"if I had a hand free." She lifted her lute in her unrestricted arm. "May I set this down?"

He frowned at her censure. And damn it, he *felt* censured. Then he leaned across her narrow room to set her wig and mask down next to her pack.

Sensing his unspoken permission, she set the body of her three-string upon a small stand he hadn't previously noticed. The simple wood supports looked as though they folded for travel.

"I'll go tell the others where we are," Seita mumbled. Jun supposed he wasn't the only one feeling censured. Seita then left, sliding the door of Mikari's room shut behind him.

"Now what?" Kie asked with a sigh and a shrug.

Jun looked to Mikari, her shoulders pushed back in a show of courage. "Now it's time for some answers. Have a seat." He steered her toward the back corner, then lowered her to sit upon the woven-mat flooring before reluctantly letting her go. The room had a window, but it was small to minimize heat loss, too small for a grown woman to squeeze through.

Only when she crossed her legs did he notice the heavy swing of her wet clothing. Their tumble into a snow bank had left them both soaked.

He searched the cabinets for the rest of the room's amenities, resentful of his immediate, protective response, and silently berating himself. From one of the upper cabinets, he drew out a pair of towels. One he handed to Mikari, and the other he pressed against his damp clothes.

"Are you cold?" he asked. She shook her head as she squeezed the towel around the soaked hem of her split-skirt. He sat and tried not to grunt like a tired old man while doing it. *Aj'*, why did he feel the need to hide such a thing? "Then let's start at the beginning."

"Oh? And when would that be?" Mikari asked, features perfectly schooled. Gone was the devastation and panic from their earlier confrontation downstairs. In their place, an untroubled look.

He tensed his jaw. "Tell me what happened after we parted."

"I would call that an ending rather than a beginning," she coolly observed. The swiftly delivered blow landed right where she wanted it. "You wanted to keep your magic, and I wanted to be free."

Her manner set him on edge. Who was this creature staring at him with Mikari's eyes? "It's obvious what I mean," he ground out.

"Mm," she said after a pause.

But when she didn't continue… "What happened, Mikari?"

She flinched, not quite hiding it, and drew a swift breath. "I've never told anyone the whole of it before. I'm not sure how to…how to say it."

He made an effort to soften his tone. "When you're ready, then."

She nodded, still blotting her damp clothing. Her gaze slid to the floor and stayed there. "I…I did what I'd intended. I submitted to the cleansing ritual."

"Why?" Kie interjected.

Jun found the interruption aggravating. "Kie, please." She murmured an apology.

Mikari answered her while glancing coyly at him. "Once our magic had manifested, Jun wanted me to run away with him, but I…" Her gaze grew distant. "I was tired of having this…curse hanging over me.

"For fifteen years, my whole world went no farther than my parents' sheep farm. And for another four years, no farther than the temple grounds. Even before my magic manifested, I hated it for all the harm it had done to me. I wanted to be rid of it and go wherever I liked, with no need to hide or worry about it ever again."

Jun held back a grumble. What Mikari didn't say was that she hadn't been as happy with him as he'd been with her. Not enough to justify the struggle.

"And so, you submitted to the cleansing ritual," he prompted.

Mikari nodded. Her shoulders tensed. "But it failed."

His brow furrowed. "What?"

"The inquisitor did his best, but my magic had already found my weakness and used it to corrupt me."

Jun went stiff, digging his fingertips into his knees as tiny revelations hit him one after another, snowballing into an icy ball of dread that sat heavy in his gut.

"What's an inquisitor?" Kie softly asked, as though she didn't wish to intrude.

"A traveling member of the clergy, appointed by the Keeper," Mikari explained. "He's trained to recognize crows whose magic is particularly dangerous, sometimes before their taint even manifests."

Any such determination would be a lie, however, for magic was a neutral force, *not* a source of corruption as the priests had claimed.

He should have realized that his and Mikari's cleansings had been put off to accommodate the inquisitor, whose visits had always been irregular in length, their timing never known in advance. His arrival had always preceded a spate of cleansings.

Jun had never met the inquisitor—only willful wards who were either at or supposedly near their magical maturity did, so he didn't know what the inquisitor looked like. But the inquisitor's aides had been ubiquitous throughout the temple whenever he'd visited, all of them eerily similar in appearance as though they were related by blood. Their most apparent role was to observe and thereby study the wards, often accompanied by a priest.

"Dangerous how?" Kie asked of Mikari, eyes narrowing.

"The danger can be twofold. A uniquely powerful manifestation of magic, or a moral weakness. Either can lead to corruption. A crow with both is sent to the inquisitor. For me, the latter was…licentious behavior." She gave the impression of wry calm, irritating him to no end. "In other words, I am weak to lust."

Flashes of their secret trysts in the maze came to Jun unbidden. Fingers in his hair, open lips pressed to his skin, and the sweet press of her breasts. The soft knelling of wind bells rang in his ears as his body tightened with remembered pleasure.

And wanting. So much crudding wanting. Parting at the end of their trysts, which had been far too few, had been agony. The more he'd learned about her mind and her heart, the more he'd desired to be loved, possessed, to be buried inside her in every way.

But they'd both agreed they couldn't risk a pregnancy. So, in those moments when talking had turned to flirting and then seduction, they'd done other things.

At least until the night they couldn't stand it anymore.

Mikari's cool gaze melted a degree, as though she also remembered.

"This corruption," Jun began, forcing the memories away, "how does it work? You don't age, clearly."

He was highly averse to hearing, in any detail, the method by which Mikari fed. Indeed, the old farmer's story of a bard and a young married couple seemed to be true, and according to Vallen and Rosuke, the mist rising from their bodies would have flowed into her, feeding her their pleasure.

But another part of him ached to know.

She lifted her head a notch, still wearing that same, untroubled expression.

"I can tell who will feed me, and I can read their desires. Fulfilling those desires creates pleasure, which I then consume."

"You have sex with them," he said, barely avoiding a more vulgar alternative.

She held his gaze. "I do."

"And you enjoy it?" *Aj'*, why had he asked? Why, when any possible answer she could give would gut him?

The way her mouth tightened told him she'd not appreciated the question. "About as much as you'd enjoy a meal. What I feel is more like hunger rather than desire. However, some people do offer more satisfaction."

"Satisfaction?" he repeated with clenched teeth.

"Not everyone lusts, and not in the same way. A thin soup may quiet a rumbling stomach, but there's nothing like a gourmet meal."

"But how do you tell?" Kie asked.

"I could demonstrate," Mikari lightly offered, still so crudding untroubled. "Would either of you mind if I shared my insights about you?"

Before Jun could vehemently refuse, Kie spoke up. "No, go ahead. I'm curious."

Mikari turned her focus to Kie and sniffed the air, squinting in concentration. Sweet Garden, was she *scenting* Kie like an animal?

"Hm," Mikari mused. "I have your permission?" At Kie's nod, she continued. "You would not feed me even if you consented to sex. You feel no lust at all, for anyone—regardless of gender. You're indifferent."

Kie raised her eyebrows in surprise, a sardonic smile on her lips. "Does that make me a 'thin soup'?"

"Rather like a summer wind. Pleasant but…not food." She shrugged. "Happens more than you might think."

"Hmph, rather inconvenient for you," Jun groused.

"On occasion," she confirmed, the corners of her mouth tight. "Usually, the reason someone cannot feed me is they're not attracted to me—or they wouldn't consent, which no longer makes it lust." She gave the length of him a warm look, and her cheeks plumped. "But there are rare persons who constitute a five-course dinner."

He clenched the towel in his hands, his wet clothing forgotten. To the Maze with her unrepentant, promiscuous attitude. He hated it. Almost as much as he hated how instantly her words and her gaze had speared his loins with heat.

Had she yearned for him at all, for what they could've had? Had she regretted their parting the way he did, every day? Had she ever thought about tracking him down?

The more they spoke, the clearer it became that she hadn't done any of those things. He had been alone in his grief, which was quickly transforming into loathing.

"You eat by absorbing a mist?" he forced himself to ask, staring into her placid eyes in an attempt to avoid imagining it.

"Sexual pleasure can be a full-body experience, felt everywhere, and it does indeed seep out like mist. But it's concentrated in the genitals, and I can absorb more with penetration of some sort. Penis, fingers, tongue—"

"The cleansing ritual," he hastened to say, glaring at his lap as he fought a fresh wave of jealousy. "How exactly did it fail?"

"The inquisitor prepared me first. Then he—"

"Prepared how?"

"I was undressed and given a blessing."

"A blessing as in a prayer?"

She shook her head. "I don't know. The blessing was rather short and I didn't understand it, but I felt less anxious afterward."

"And then?"

"Then he had me lie upon a table. His aides stood as witnesses, but none of them spoke. I remember staring at them and wondering why the priests weren't there. The inquisitor began praying over me, and I started to feel dizzy. After that, I don't...I don't r-recall much."

He could tell she was holding something back. She refused to look at him, her gaze skipping around.

"How did you learn the ritual's outcome?"

"I had a lucid moment, and that's when the inquisitor told me. He was quite disappointed. He seemed to take some of the blame for the ritual failing, but he said that because I gave in to lust, lust would be all I could eat."

Jun made a soft sound of confusion. "Why would he say that? Gave in how?"

"I...my soul was tested. I was tempted, and I gave in to that temptation. That is..." She took a steadying breath. "It was all a blur. Much of it didn't even seem real." She tossed the towel aside, having done her best to dry herself. "At some point, I passed out. When I woke, I was well outside the temple grounds. I assume I escaped."

"Commander, that doesn't make any sense," Kie said.

"That's twice she's called you that," Mikari interjected. "How high a rank is commander?"

Jun rolled his shoulders in discomfort. "The second highest. I answer to the empress's high general, and he only answers to her."

She looked impressed, but what then came out of her mouth was anything but. "And yet you're here in Gozu, at the start of winter, chasing creatures like me?"

Creatures like her? Then she was aware of others. Other eaters. Had she met them, or simply heard about them?

He was about to ask, but Kie continued as if the tangent hadn't happened. "What she described didn't sound like the ritual we were told. And the way she feeds, it's not quite the same, either."

"What are you talking about?" Mikari asked.

Jun took a deep breath as he gathered the words. "The Damned One didn't only command his army of demons. He also had human servants. One of them wrote down vile magical rituals, including one for creating lust-eating demons from humans."

"We suspect there are other kinds," Kie added. "Other metaphysical ways to feed."

Mikari laughed humorlessly. "You're saying I'm a demon?"

"We're saying you're a predator," Jun bit out.

She betrayed a brief glimmer of pain before her expression turned cold. "And have you, *Commander*, never threatened anyone or caused them harm? Tell me, what experience allowed you to ascend so far in the empress's ranks?"

He recalled the stable boy whom she'd injured with her recklessness, and his gut roiled with anger. "A skilled mercenary is one who prevents violence rather than inflicts it." An argument he'd made to his group's leader many times, especially when Masanori's temper and greed not only lost them reputation but also created enemies.

She gave her lips a sardonic twist. "And you were skilled, is that right?"

"Very. More importantly…" His voice dropped to a snarl. "I can still claim to be human." She had no answer to that and compressed her lips, all amusement gone.

"My orders are to take you to Houfu," he said with more composure. "The empress plans to cure you, or at least start working toward that end."

Mikari loudly scoffed. "But I don't want to be cured."

Chapter Seven

Jun responded with a bumbling mash of words, his shock so great that the noisome assault on her stinging nostrils began to abate at last. She had never cared for the pepperiness of angry lust, and yet his managed to be vibrant, even exciting, promising heat. Never had she met anyone with such pungent desire.

Mikari forged ahead. "I also have my bardic obligations. News to spread, messages to deliver. I can't disappear for what would be at least four months—"

"You can't be serious," he sneered. "What kind of—"

"Oh, I'm quite serious," she insisted, hoping he couldn't hear the low-humming panic in her voice. She couldn't go back to hating what she was and praying for an escape.

"I very much like my life. I'm free to go where I want, and I earn a good income doing something I love. Something I'm quite good at." She gestured at her three-string. "And not only do I remain young and healthy, I also have at my disposal those physical abilities that nearly delivered me out of your grasp."

Mikari tried not to cringe at the naked disgust on Jun's face. She almost didn't manage it and braced for further argument.

But instead of voicing his obvious sentiments, he reached into his clothes and drew out a thin, leather case. What it contained she couldn't guess. She watched with interest as he unwound its ties and flipped it open.

"A mirror?" she asked, frowning with confusion. What bizarre bit of theater was this?

Jun didn't reply, only gazed at his reflection while he traced his fingertip over the glass, as though drawing something.

She noticed that there was a design on the back, but he was holding the mirror at a low angle. She dipped down to look, and her heart stuttered.

"I don't think I'll ever hear wind bells again without thinking of you, Jun."

"Nor I. Their power is now yours."

Wind bells were traditionally hung to beckon and purify a soul on its way to the afterlife. Outside of religious paintings, they were not a common design element.

Why did he have this mirror? And why was he now staring at it?

She directed a questioning glance at the woman whom Jun had called Kie. "Do you also have orders to take me to your empress? You and…the other man?"

"Seita," Kie clarified. "And no, he and I are escorting a trio of delegates. Tracking down eaters is secondary."

"Are you and Seita also commanders?"

Kie shook her head. "We're both working toward captain. We don't have an official rank."

Mikari felt Jun's gaze upon her as she continued chatting with Kie about their organization and their mission. She was astonished to learn that the empress had decided to try diplomacy in Gozu. It wouldn't work, but perhaps the empress would surprise her.

She also wondered whether having a pair of crows escort the brownie delegation would end up being more of a hindrance than anything else. They wouldn't get far without someone demanding to see their brands, and though bribes were often a successful solution, they quickly added up. Even as a bard, Mikari's white wig was far more protection in some places than her profession was.

When Kie began describing something called the Pull of the Empress, Mikari realized that she could finally learn whether Empress Shumei had truly magicked herself and a few others into Oblivion to defeat the Damned One.

But before she could get there, Jun cleared his throat in order to… speak to his reflection? "I need to speak with Commander Rosuke. It's urgent. Tell him we found one."

"At once, sir," the mirror spoke. A woman's voice. Mikari's eyes bulged in instant amazement.

"You're *talking to someone*?" Practically pouncing on him, Mikari shoved her face in between him and the looking glass.

Shockingly, the mirror's reflection wasn't of her. Instead, she saw another room, one that had to be inside a grand building. There were intricately painted standing screens, brightly lit walls of solid-wood sliding doors—a young crow woman hastily opened one on her way out—and what appeared to be a grid of tables that sat low on sparkling-clean, woven-mat flooring. Her view of the room remained fixed as though she were looking out from one of the many other mirrors displayed on the tables.

"Incredible," she said, truly awed. "I had no idea magic could do this."

As she took note of everything in the reflection, the faint pepperiness tickling her nose shifted to something sweeter: pining.

She had smelled it before on grudgingly faithful spouses and from those whom she'd had to rebuff. Anyone who yearned for what they couldn't have. But whereas their pining carried the odor of chewy rice cake so burnt it would crunch, Jun's smelled like roasted sugar. The darkest, smoothest caramel…with a pinch of salt.

Though it was nothing like that first, exhilarating whiff she'd taken of his lust down in the common room, it was much more tempting than the peppery odor he'd blasted her with when she had described him as a five-course meal.

Maze take her, she'd known full well that flirting would anger him at least as much as it aroused him, but she hadn't been able to help herself—he smelled too good. Better than anyone ever had, which was truly alarming. She had to hope that the shock of their reunion was to blame for exaggerating his effect on her…and not a sign that she was a danger to him.

"Is this a room in the capital?" she asked him, speaking softly because he was so close.

He cleared his throat. Twice. And yet his voice still sounded a little hoarse. "I believe it is in the east wing of the residential palace."

"Who is Commander Rosuke?"

"You're about to find out."

"I should go find Seita," Kie cut in. Jun gave a small start as though he had forgotten anyone else was in the room.

"Go," he said to Kie. "I can handle her."

Mikari couldn't suppress a small smile. Jun had hardly been able to handle her when they had been temple wards.

Kie rose to leave the room, and Mikari watched with as much feigned innocence as she could muster. Once the other woman was gone and the door shut behind her, Mikari returned her gaze to the mirror, its reflection unchanged.

Then with her special senses, she peered into Jun's fantasies.

Normally, those capable of feeding her pictured what they wanted to do to her—or at least imagined a certain act or position with a faceless person. Or persons. The ones Mikari avoided at all costs were the ones who thought of violence and degradation. The brackish scent of their lust always gave them away.

But Jun was fully in the moment, soaking up every detail of here and now. He was taking in her scent, admiring her hair, and savoring the press of her body.

She did see a few flashes: lips at her ear, fingers sliding into her hair, a shaky gasp. But if he desired anything more prurient, it wasn't currently his most urgent fantasy. Exerting more pressure would show her his most private fantasies, the ones he hid, but his perfect awareness of her was too entrancing to dig further.

"I like your beard," she murmured. "You wear it well."

"Hmph," he grunted. "Let's not chat as though we're just old friends catching up."

"Are we not?"

"What do you think?" he said in a hard voice.

"I try not to hurt anyone, you know." She felt his gaze on her but avoided meeting it. "I'm careful when...when I feed." The topic seemed to kill his desire, for the scent of his lust began to fade. "Why did you think I was dead?"

He gave a growly sigh. "After I escaped, I made it to my sister's, and I hid there for a few weeks until I had my opportunity to get out of Gozu."

Jun had, of course, told Mikari all about his older sister, Toyome, when they were wards—the only member of his family who had ever treated him as such. He had missed her terribly, and when Jun had made the decision to escape, he had insisted to Mikari that his sister would help them.

Mikari wondered if she should tell Jun that she'd met Toyome, briefly, and knew where she lived as of a few years ago.

"While I was staying with her," Jun said, "I told my sister everything."

"Including me?"

"I told her everything," he said forcefully. "And while she was out one day, she happened to meet someone who had just been released from Nansen."

"Someone we knew?"

He shook his head. "One of the younger wards. His magic manifested early, and he was begging in the town square for scraps. His family had all died of a fever while he was confined to the temple."

She closed her eyes and whispered a curse.

"Toyome gave the boy some food and asked whether a ward named Mikari was sent back home. He told her that you'd died during your cleansing. She broke it to me as gently as she could."

Mikari firmed her jaw. "Someone must have lied, then. Not that it isn't the closest thing to the truth."

"It's not close at all," he said, the harshness of his tone forcing her to meet his gaze. He had such a masculine face: sparse eyelashes, a sharp brow and jaw, an aquiline nose. All of his features put together were truly heart-stopping, even more so when he looked at her with such naked hurt. "The truth is far worse."

Her eyes stung, but she didn't flinch. She couldn't show any sign of weakness. If she did, he might see that she wasn't perfectly content.

They saw it at the same time: movement in the mirror's reflection as several people hastened into the opulent room. First was a beautiful man with long hair tied back. Right on his heels was another equally handsome man and an exceedingly well-dressed young woman, whose hair was held back by several strings of gold beads. Both had a matching tattoo around their necks.

Mikari's gut told her who the woman in majestic attire was, but she had to ask. "Is that who I think it is?"

"Indeed," Jun said. "That is the empress."

GRAPPLING for just a shred of composure, Jun used the mirror's versatile travel case to prop it up amongst Mikari's things in the storage alcove, then adjusted the angle.

Though their bodies no longer touched, his heart still raced from her nearness. In fact, it hadn't beat at a normal speed for a while. Despite the counteracting forces of thirst, hunger, and bone-deep exhaustion, his magic remained nauseatingly agitated, and his cock was so stiff he could feel his heartbeat throbbing between his legs.

But it was the metaphorical knife still stuck in his chest that caused him the most pain. He had no solid ground to stand upon anymore. No rationality left.

His shock at finding her alive and no longer entirely human had left him as disoriented as he was in his nightmares. His grief for her had been based on a lie, and yet the thought of letting it go, letting *her* go, seemed like blasphemy.

Why would he once again hope for her approval, when previously he'd been found wanting? Why even consider the possibility, when their current circumstances were somehow more hopeless than when they'd been wards?

He hardly recognized the selfish person she had become, which meant she had been right in her refusal to run away with him. She had been correct in thinking they wouldn't have been happy together.

No one in the mirror seemed at all concerned that a demon was calmly sitting next to him, instead more surprised to learn that he knew her. His churning disquiet was undoubtedly as obvious as the beard on his face, so Rosuke took the apparent lead in their conversation.

After introductions were made, he started off with easy questions, such as whether Jun's party was all right and where they were. Then he pivoted to interviewing Mikari directly. Jun wished he could say for certain that she was seated in the formal position as a show of respect for the empress, but he didn't trust whether he could know that about her anymore.

Mikari gave her age—her real one—and explained how and when

she had become corrupted. When she revealed who had directed her cleansing, everyone in the mirror shared a look of concern.

"Were you in a great deal of pain during the ritual?" Rosuke asked.

Vallen clarified. "Sharp, as though you were being gutted."

"There was a little discomfort. Mostly I felt listless." Mikari lightly touched her sternum. "Perhaps a bit...pressed."

"Was there anything written on the floor around the altar?" Vallen asked. "Or perhaps a floor covering that seemed out of place?"

"There were always rugs in the offering room."

So that was where they did it, Jun thought. The offering room of Nansen's main building was where the priests accepted the public's gifts to the Divine One—usually food or wine—prior to any scheduled ritual. The room was large but easily secured and therefore private.

"Afterward, did you find yourself with a new sense of sorts?" Rosuke asked.

She nodded. "I could smell desire."

Vallen and Rosuke raised their eyebrows. Both had similar responses.

"Smell it?"

"You can smell someone's lust?"

Jun took a hard swallow. Had she scented him, too?

Vallen and Rosuke looked at each other, then back to Mikari. Rosuke moved on to asking how Mikari feeds, and Jun kept his gaze firmly rooted to the floor. Again, she surprised them.

"You can get energy from skin contact alone?" Rosuke asked, evidently confused.

"A far lesser amount, but yes, I can," she confirmed.

"And how long do you typically go between feedings?"

Her reply this time was a little quieter. "A few weeks at most."

Jun clenched his fists so hard he swore his skin would split. He simply couldn't comprehend how she could've accepted what had to be casual, empty passions. Not that he hadn't settled for the same, Maze take him.

Unless their affair had not been as quite as extraordinary to her as it had been to him. Another twist of the knife.

"Jun," came the empress's coaxing voice.

He lifted his face to find her gazing at him with sympathy, and a realization hit him. The empress knew what Mikari meant to him. She didn't need to see his aura of grief, she knew, perhaps had known the morning he'd left.

What in Oblivion had the Divine One told her?

"Vallen wants you to look for something," the empress said, as though he'd missed hearing it.

"And what is that?" he asked unsteadily.

Vallen replied. "I need you to see if she still has her metaphysical organ. You'll need to reach out with your magic."

"Excuse me, my what?" Mikari asked.

Jun was shaking his head before he knew to stop himself.

"It has to be done, Commander," the empress said.

Sweat poured down Jun's neck, and he was close to vomiting—that was how badly his magic yearned to touch hers, but he refused to let it.

Thankfully, Kie chose that moment to return to the room with Seita and Natsu in tow. Relief flooded him.

After apologizing for the interruption, Natsu gave a brief and undeservedly diplomatic account of the fallout from capturing Mikari. Fortunately, the delegation had still managed to secure rooms, but for a steep price, and had brought up everyone's belongings. She requested to give her full report after their meeting was over, then left.

Vallen repeated his request for an examination of Mikari's magic, rather than rehash everything for Kie and Seita.

"I can do it," Kie volunteered.

Jun closed his eyes in a long blink, and silently thanked her.

"What's going on?" Mikari asked, shifting uneasily as Kie approached.

"It won't hurt," Kie assured. "Nothing about this will alter you." She pressed herself against Mikari's side and took a breath.

Jun's gaze jumped between their faces. Mikari seemed uncertain, then she stiffened almost imperceptibly. Kie stared at nothing in particular, mouth pulling into a bemused frown.

"What do you feel?" Rosuke asked.

Kie made a pensive sound. "I sense something, but it's...cold and limp. Almost as if—"

"As if it were dead," Jun heard himself say.

No one spoke for a moment. But as Kie drew back from Mikari, he knew what everyone was thinking. The cleansing ritual had indeed smothered Mikari's magic.

"That settles it," Vallen said. "Whatever happened to her wasn't done with the ritual we know of."

"Mikari, is there anything else you can tell us?" Rosuke asked. "Anything else you can recall about your cleansing, even if it didn't seem real?"

She hugged her stomach, her expression disturbed. "I remember being tested. Tempted, that is. But it had to be a dream because...I saw Jun in the offering room."

"What?" Jun gasped.

"But he had already escaped the night before," she finished.

"What happened then?" Rosuke asked.

"W-we...began making love. It—"

"I *wasn't* there," Jun insisted.

"I know," she replied, hastily bobbing her head. "I-I know that now."

"But it felt real?" Rosuke pressed. She nodded. "How did you realize it wasn't?"

"B-...because when my mind cleared, just for a moment, I looked a-at the man beneath me and..." A shadow passed over her face. "It wasn't Jun."

Sweet Garden. She must have been horrified. Her intimation sent him reeling, forcing him to throw his hand out and catch himself.

"Did you recognize him?" Rosuke asked.

She shook her head, and the shadow fell away. "That's when the inquisitor told me he'd failed, and that I'd been corrupted. The next thing I remember is waking up outside the temple grounds."

"Divine One's grace," Kie breathed.

"No, I refuse to believe that your magic corrupted you," the empress said to Mikari. "Whoever this inquisitor is, he is to blame. Perhaps he found what he thought was a cleansing ritual, but he wielded it no better than a child playing with a knife. In any case, you'll come to the capital so that we can work on a cure."

Jun shook his head. "She said she doesn't want to be cured."

The empress's eyes flashed. "Mikari, you don't want the only other option there is."

Mikari blanched then nodded in resignation. "I understand."

The empress released a tight sigh, looking pensive. "All things considered, perhaps it would be best for Kie to escort her back here."

"That won't be necessary," Jun quickly asserted.

"I'll decide what's necessary, Commander."

"This is *my* mission. It has to be me." Holding her gaze, he tried to convey how desperate he was to reconcile his most painful regret, even though it meant spending a week in Mikari's company. "I have to be the one to do it."

"Are you sure?" The gentle worry in her voice insinuated he was clinging to false hope —an impossibility after everything he'd learned tonight. Jun nodded.

Seita spoke for the first time in a while. "You'll need to leave as early as possible and ride fast. It's at least two days to reach the other side of the pass and already it's turning into a blizzard outside."

"Can you make it another week or two before feeding again, Mikari?" Vallen asked. "We can arrange something once you're here."

She nodded woodenly. Jun's fingers ached from clenching them.

"Kie, Seita," the empress said. "Escorting the delegation is still your main priority, but the pass is likely to close before the commander can return to Gozu, so I need you to devote some attention to searching for the other lust eater. Did you meet with Scout Saneo?"

Seita shook his head. "He hasn't arrived yet. Not here or anywhere else with rooms to let."

"I suppose a delay of one day to wait for him won't make an enormous difference. If he doesn't arrive by the morning after next, you may need to take a longer route to Ajiro Temple, one that takes you through the area where the disappearances took place. Perhaps a body's been discovered."

"A body?" Mikari asked, coming out of her mental wanderings. "You're looking for one that…one that kills?"

"A male brownie," Jun confirmed. "No one could describe him much, other than average height and build, and generally handsome. He targets socially isolated women. One disappears about every year."

She was silent for a breath, brow delicately knitted with intense thought. "One of the women, was her left lower arm a bit crooked?"

There were various sounds of surprise. "A badly healed break in childhood. You know of her?"

Mikari expelled a sharp breath. "I-I must've spoken to the same person your scout did. I'd lost all hope of finding her, but…her body was discovered in the Omine a couple of weeks ago."

"How did you know it was her?" he asked. Fox bards could, of course, choose to investigate missing persons. But whether they were proficient at it...

"She was mostly skeleton," she conceded, "but I know how to determine age and sex from bones. Both matched. And the old break was as clear as day, bent exactly as described."

An unexpected bubble of warmth burst in his chest. Pride, if a little grudging. And why wouldn't she be brilliant in this? She'd always been clever.

"You're saying a lust eater killed them?" she asked.

"We suspect so. At least three women, but possibly more. We believe he'll find another victim soon."

"I'm sure I could help," she offered. "You and I, we could—"

"We're going to Houfu," he insisted. "Not...roving about just to give you ample opportunity to escape." A convincing enough excuse, considering he'd had to grapple for one.

Her cheeks flushed with irritation. "If you'd at least hear me out first—"

"The less time I have to spend with you, the better," he barked.

There was a flash of pain in her eyes, followed by a wash of cool serenity. The silence that fell filled him with hot shame. Refusing to show it, he firmed his jaw and focused on the glow of the lantern.

He couldn't imagine anything more unendurable than being stuck with her for months. She'd have to feed eventually, at least a few times. And whether she fed from him or from another, each time would drive the knife deeper into his chest.

Then came a breath of sound. "As you desire."

It was a subtle hint, one that flicked the knife's handle. She fulfilled desires, after all. It had become her purpose.

There was little said after that. The empress reminded Kie and Seita to keep their eyes on Koichino's blondie mayor, who now seemed unlikely to become an ally. Then the meeting was over.

Out in the hall, Jun conversed with his fellow imperial agents. Kie suggested a watch rotation on Mikari's room in addition to a simple *lock ward* upon her door, which Jun agreed to. Seita then showed him to his room, where a covered tray of food awaited. Jun removed his outer layer of clothing to let it dry and forced himself to eat his dinner of savory stew and slices of pickled winter vegetables over rice.

He then tracked down the stable worker whom Mikari had used to delay Seita. The lad hesitated to let Jun look at his injury, but he relented when Jun lied and said he was a physician.

The bump on the back of the lad's head was large and tender, but with some subtly applied magic, Jun relieved his pain and reduced the swelling. The gratitude on boy's face helped ease a little of Jun's heartache.

The brace of cherry blossom, which came before patchouli, was still burning when he fell asleep, his physical exhaustion overcoming his mental turmoil. When he woke again, head and heart aching after a particularly intense nightmare, he was inhaling the brace of rose.

He sat up tiredly and scrubbed his hand over his face. A scant moment later, Seita tapped at his door to wake him.

"Just checked on her," Seita said once he'd emerged. "She's staring out the window."

Jun nodded, then took up his post by Mikari's room, putting himself between her door and the way out, his back to the wall. Tears threatened to fall, as they had all evening. Each breath was an effort.

Then a sweet sound floated to his ears. A crooning melody. Jun closed his eyes and put his head back. Mikari was humming in her room. And she had chosen the tragic tale of Meke and Kubo.

Hmph, such a mawkish story. The lovers' weakness was ridiculous compared to the forces that had ripped Jun and Mikari apart.

And yet her voice comforted him. His heart slowed and the tension seeped from his shoulders. His stressed magic quieted.

Eventually, the song came to an end. Did she need no sleep, the same as Vallen and Rosuke when they had been lust eaters? If so, how did she usually pass the night hours?

Perhaps he didn't want to ponder that too much.

Chapter Eight

Komatsu idly rubbed at a bit of blood that remained stubbornly embedded in the creases of his knuckle. Friction and hot water eventually carried it away.

Unlike his master, he did not care for blood. Too messy. He would have killed without shedding it, but if the scout's body were discovered, his death had to look like the result of a robbery. With luck, however, the animals would have him.

Sighing heavily, Komatsu tried to enjoy his time in the soaking tub, having already scrubbed himself off with a separate basin of water. But despite being clean at last after a satisfying kill, he was far from content.

The bard should have arrived by now, and yet there'd been no sign of her: not yesterday when he'd first expected her, nor this evening upon his return to the Silver Hammer Inn, where he'd been idling for more than a week.

If he had the same connection to her that his master did, he'd scry upon her to know what had delayed her. Not that bards had set schedules. They ambled wherever they pleased at whatever pace they wished.

But this particular bard could not dally for long before seeking her next meal, or linger long enough in one place for anyone to start questioning why she never removed her mask.

Her ruse was clever, he'd give her that. She didn't skulk through

Gozu's maze-like terrain the way many of the others did, emerging only to feed.

But she was now a week late, one fewer left for him to help accomplish his master's great work.

They had planned to have more time to gather his entire covey. Nearly two dozen remained on the other side of the Setei Mountains. Winter would be arriving early, but the bard plus a handful more would be enough. They'd have to be.

After so many years of furtive preparation, to have only weeks left—possibly even less—before the great harvest...

The thought stirred his loins, and they hardened further as light, familiar footfalls approached the bathing chamber. His lips curled upward.

There was a gentle knock upon the door, then a soft, hesitant voice. "Master Komatsu? Are you all right? There's b-blood on your overcoat."

Hmm, yes, he supposed he should account for that. He could simply pluck the observation from her mind, but a more compelling option saw him adjusting his magical glamour with half a thought.

"It's just a scratch," he said, affecting a grumble that he knew would only intrigue and concern the young maid beyond the door.

Nene was the sort of downtrodden, yet still innocent, young miss that he and his master both preferred, but she harbored the sort of secret, base longings that he alone enjoyed.

He'd known within a day that she'd be the next one he took. No one would miss her. She wasn't the type of beautiful that was sought after, nor did she have anything tying her to the town but her position as a maid.

He'd overheard the innkeeper scold her for completing her work too soon, calling it suspicious. The miserly churl had reminded her that she'd be out on the street without his generosity. After a bit of surveillance, Komatsu had confirmed that she owned little and had no family, no lover.

Not only could she easily vanish without a peep of concern from anyone, but she'd also come willingly. And he knew his master would soon need another blood meal, although not before Komatsu enjoyed her a bit. Of course, he'd deliver her perfectly healthy, but she'd be far more trusting after a night or two in his bed. At least, until she found herself at his master's mercy.

AT THE MAZE'S CENTER

Softening her toward him had been easy. All she'd needed from him were a few kind words and the impression of restrained interest, as though he were drawn to her but maintaining a respectful distance.

And now he'd give her a chance to witness him injured and stoic.

"All that blood from just a scratch?" she asked, pushing into the room as though her anxiety had forced her. Like all the other female employees, Nene wore a forest-green dress with black edging. Over her heart was a hammer embroidered in silver thread.

Despite her ugly, ill-fitting dress, he could tell she had nothing but lovely curves beneath. Her black hair was messily tied, as usual—her forehead a little too large, her cheeks too round and constantly flushed.

She quickly realized she had invaded his bath, and the scarlet in her cheeks spread to her hairline and down her neck. She stared at him wide-eyed, her fascinated gaze sweeping his reclined form and pausing briefly at the delicate glass bell hanging from a cord around his neck before she noticed the jagged tear down his forearm. The injury wasn't real, but she had no way of knowing that.

"T-that's not a scratch," she breathlessly exclaimed. "How did it happen?"

Another tweak to his glamour reddened his cheeks. "My horse stumbled and I fell. Landed badly. It's already stopped bleeding." Right on cue, a drop of blood seeped from his illusory wound.

"You need a poultice. A-and bandaging. I'll be right back!" Moving swiftly, she closed the door behind her and her footsteps quickly faded.

Certain the task would take her a few moments, he smirked as he reached for a slim case sitting by the tub. He always had it near, never farther away than the edge of a room and almost always closer, for the object inside was both powerful and fragile.

He wiped his damp fingers on a nearby towel before drawing the mirror from its padded, wooden case. The view it offered was of his master's sanctum, an underground chamber formed eons ago by flowing lava.

Ancient, glowing lanterns hung from dusty pilasters on thick, timber supports, the pitted walls of the stone chamber hidden behind enormous tapestries and ample shelving stuffed with books, scrolls, jars of components, and all manner of rare artifacts, including an enormous scrying pool which his master used to monitor his covey.

Nestled within one set of cloth hangings was a raised bed, where this year's blood meal lay, barely breathing as his master's dark head moved subtly over yet another bite to her flesh. Komatsu waited to send his voice, not wishing to interrupt or disturb.

There was no need for his master to hold the woman down. No need for manacles either, which would only interfere with access to her delicate wrists and ankles. After countless feedings, she was too weak to resist and too deeply entranced even to remember her name.

The months she'd spent in that room had left her with a deathly pallor, and her formerly luscious figure had shrunk despite his fellow servants' attempts to feed her, not that proper nutrition would save her. Locating a replacement had been timely. Soon she would be free of the cycle, and Nene would lay in her place for however many weeks remained.

His master raised his head, fangs shining in the yellow light. Showing no surprise when Komatsu finished tracing the symbol upon the glass, his master instead turned toward the mirror's twin with staid grace, rising smoothly from the altar, his strong, lean body unfolding like a blade emerging from a sheath.

Though he looked and moved like a weapon, it was his piercing gaze that awed and terrified. A blue so sharp and pale it was like ice. No glamour could overcome the cold calculation in his eyes, nor the vast intelligence.

Even through the mirror, that gaze sliced into him as his master stalked closer, lips glistening but clean. His long, tapering fingers moved with quick efficiency on the glass.

"The bard is in Koichino."

Komatsu sat up straight. "She doubled back?"

"Spooked, no doubt. She's always been sensitive to my gaze."

"*Dazu*," he swore, reverting for an instant to the old tongue, before the world had been made anew. "The empress has three agents escorting a delegation that's soon to arrive through Futakata." He quickly described what the scout knew about the six total members of the delegation, which hadn't been much. "They know about the bard, master. They're sure to run into her."

"You also learned this from the scout?"

Komatsu nodded, flushing hot at the memory of invading the young brownie's mind and stealing his secrets. He'd learned everything the scout had discovered in Gozu and reported to the empress, as well as his next objective: meeting the delegation in Koichino.

Wielding such sheer control over another had never failed to arouse Komatsu, but he'd yet to seek release, wanting to be clean and inside Nene first.

She would return soon, he reminded himself. She'd imagined herself on her knees before him, and he'd gladly grant her that fantasy.

In theory, any magic user could develop the ability to pry knowledge from another's mind. Komatsu was particularly talented at it, for he had the sort of intellect that quickly absorbed and organized details. He could even manipulate or erase memories to a small degree. Thus, his master often called upon him to make use of his gift.

Alas, invading waking minds was the only power of a dream eater he'd managed to master. The chaos of the dream state lay deeper in a person's psyche, and he'd never been able to make sense of it. Thus, he nourished himself on lust instead.

"They know about me as well, master, though they don't have much." He stood up to leave the tub, reaching out with his free hand for a towel. "I'll ride to Koichino and collect the bard, prevent them from meeting her."

"Arizo." The command hit him like a whip. Komatsu stilled instantly next to the tub, having forgotten that his master hated when he couldn't see someone who was speaking. The disapproval in his gaze was colder than the air on Komatsu's wet skin.

"I've already begun closing the pass," his master said. "Remain where you are until I give you our next step."

Komatsu had several questions but knew better than to ask them. "Yes, Master Bane."

Without further discussion, his master swiped at his looking glass, silencing Komatsu's mirror.

And just in time, for he heard the patter of Nene returning. Barely suppressing a smirk, he put away the speaking mirror and grabbed a towel.

"I brought needle and thread just in—" Nene burst into the room then halted in place, a deep gasp catching her throat.

He paused in the middle of sawing the towel across his back, pretending to be frozen in surprise while letting her take in his full nudity, including the heavy shaft between his legs.

Unlike him, she was genuinely overcome with shock and didn't even seem to notice when she dropped a thin roll of bandaging, her gaze fixed upon his manhood.

Relaxing his expression into one of desire and invitation, he lowered the towel with seductive slowness, displaying himself for her. He wore little glamour, only enough to disguise his general appearance and turn his tied-back hair brown. The rest of him was real, from the lean muscles of his chest to the firmly planted soles of his feet.

"Do you see what you do to me, Nene?" The question was a rough breath of sound. "The ache is a thousand times worse than the scratch on my arm. Tell me you ache as well."

She made a helpless sigh, the creamy sweetness of peaches wafting forth. "I do."

Inwardly triumphant, he stalked closer, scooping up the wad of silk bandaging from the floor before stopping a hand's breadth away, filling her vision with only him. "Then let us give each other relief."

PART TWO
Piquant Desire

Chapter Nine

A heavy snow still fell when the sky began to brighten. Gusts of wind had formed the wet flakes into enormous drifts that made Jun anxious to leave. He wolfed down a simple breakfast, surrendered his share of the trade goods to be sold at Koichino's market, which likely wouldn't open that day, and gave his farewells to the delegation and his fellow crows.

Then he collected a resigned Mikari, who again wore her wig and mask, and escorted her to the stables.

The two stable boys were friendlier this morning than at Jun's initial encounter with them. The one whom he had helped frowned when Mikari gave her apologies for hurting him, and he thanked Jun again for treating him the previous evening.

"I thought I'd have a headache all night," the boy said, "but it didn't even feel tender anymore after you helped me."

"Glad to hear it," Jun replied. Mikari turned her head toward him but said nothing.

He was taken aback when the two boys led their readied mounts toward them, for one of the horses wasn't a horse at all.

"That's yours?" he asked Mikari, even as she accepted the reins of her mount, a Gozuan reindeer fitted with a handsome saddle.

"I was about to ask you the same," she said, a smile in her voice. "Your horse suits you."

He quickly fixed his saddlebags to Nugun's back. "It belongs to the high general. I expect it was almost as expensive as your reindeer and tack, which makes me wonder how a bard was able to afford it."

She drew a steadying breath, having read the barely concealed meaning in his words. Jun had to admit he didn't know how much a northern bard earned from their profession, but he assumed not enough.

"She is a valuable asset," Mikari equivocated.

"We'll get the door when you're ready," a stable boy said.

Jun nodded, then turned to Mikari with the length of rope he'd been carrying inside his overcoat. "Get on your mount," he ordered her.

She became as still as a statue, and the shadow of her eyes was unmoving. She said nothing for several heartbeats.

Then she gave a puff of laughter. "Never thought our first time with rope would be like this." She moved to mount her reindeer, not seeing the tremor of shock that crossed Jun's face. Still, she had to know that he would be taken aback by the instant mental picture.

He forced any expression from his face as he tugged off her mitts to tie her wrists together, hands crossed and palms down so she could grasp her pommel. He tried not to think about the many times her hands had touched him, or where they had touched him. Then he put her mitts back on as best as he could. He had learned not to bind prisoners' wrists while they wore some sort of gloves, for that made wiggling one's hands out much easier.

"I shouldn't be surprised you're so good at this," she said in an intimate tone. "I'm now completely at your mercy."

He exhaled hard, and couldn't help glancing up. With his height, it wasn't far. But of course, he couldn't see Mikari's face. Even the fall of her white wig hid the lines of her jaw, so he couldn't guess whether she was smiling. She had to be, who was he kidding?

Aj', and just a moment ago he had been proud to have resisted hardening at the idea of what she implied.

"Mercenaries are, after all, commonly hired to haul around criminals, isn't that right?" she added, well after he'd had plenty of time to get the wrong idea, or rather the right one. The one she'd wanted to plant in his head.

She deftly tugged her thick hood over her head despite her bound wrists, and he swore he saw a twinkle within the twin shadows of her mask.

Not responding, he yanked on his mitts, gathered the reins of her mount in his hand, and pulled himself into Nugun's saddle.

"Door, if you please," he called to the stable boys. One hastened to comply, and the other performed a bow of farewell. Jun guided their mounts outside as the two boys bid them safe travels.

The icy wind was cutting despite the many thick layers of clothing Jun wore, and he was only a day into Gozu. Though he had never been to the northern coast of the region, he knew that those who lived there never went outside in less than six or seven layers. He tugged his scarf higher.

"We'll not stop much," he said to Mikari, voice raised to be heard over the dull roar of the storm. She acknowledged him with a nod, white wig whipping in the wind from where it peeked out of her hood. He then turned his horse toward the southern road and began their journey back to Houfu.

BUFFETED from behind by the wind, they reached Okususo about an hour before sunset, having taken time only for Jun to eat and relieve himself. The snowstorm had yet to relent, and despite her inhuman endurance, Mikari's body ached from huddling tight to her able mount.

She was looking forward to more than just a place to warm up, though. No doubt they'd have to share a room at the village's tiny inn. Jun might think he could maintain the distance between them, but she knew he still desired her. And despite herself, she craved to know how much, and what made his scent uniquely heady.

Last night during her interview and this morning in the stables, she had gotten whiffs of his lust. She knew he had pictured her tied to a wide, framed bed, where she had been writhing and begging for his touch with whispered gasps.

His mental image had been far more stirring than she'd expected. If she weren't so certain she'd break free of her bonds, she would've made such a scenario her first priority of the evening.

Yes, she had enough energy to avoid feeding until they reached the capital, but that didn't mean she didn't desperately want a taste of Jun's pleasure. More than a taste, if she was lucky. She wondered how she might elicit that first wondrous aroma he'd given off. The one so enticing it had nearly overwhelmed her.

Mikari had never been to Okususo, so she wasn't sure what sort of reception to expect. Some towns cheered upon spotting someone in bardic attire. Others hardly glanced her way. And a few saw bards as musically talented beggars.

Okususo seemed to be the second type, although the reason the villagers largely ignored them was the horrendous weather, which forced anyone outdoors to huddle into their furs and move quickly.

Rising above the tall, swaying pines that surrounded the low roofline of Okususo were two massive peaks of the Setei Mountains. Through the cloak of falling snow, she could see that the pass beyond was already solid white.

They arrived at what looked to be a large home that had been remodeled into an inn, and Jun helped her dismount. The bit of his beard above his scarf was more snow and ice than hair. He untied her wrists, tucked away the entirely unnecessary rope, and held onto her arm as they navigated through the two layers of doors.

Like the previous inn, there was a central dining space directly off the entrance, but this one was much smaller. A pair of male patrons played a card game at one of a handful of empty tables. Both looked up as the inn's glowering, elderly proprietor approached the new arrivals in the entryway, which was so cramped that Mikari was forced to stand almost directly behind Jun, who kept a surreptitious hold on her elbow.

"I suppose you think I'll rent you a room," the proprietor grouched.

"Is this not an inn?" Jun asked drily, having brushed the snow from his face and uncovered his head.

"I'd need to see your brand first." Jun's grip on her elbow tightened. The proprietor then spotted her, for she could hardly be seen beyond Jun's considerable girth, and his scowl and tone both lightened. "You've a bard with you?"

"Well met, sir," she greeted cheerfully. "I hope your village has the appetite for a little news and entertainment."

"Don't you bards usually travel alone?" he asked her.

"Not always," she said. "Some bards travel with their mentors, others with a merchant caravan. In my case, my poor husband couldn't bear to be left at home." The hold on her arm became a band of steel tight enough to make her discreetly pry at his fingers, pretending instead that she was seeking to touch his hand.

Jun put his mouth by her ear. "What are you doing?" The words were low and terse.

Ignoring him, she spoke to the innkeeper with gentle admonishment. "I must say, sir, no one else has shown me the disrespect of asking to see my husband's brand."

Jun straightened with a mild jolt as the innkeeper sputtered. "Yes, well...with us being so close to the pass, it's..." He lowered his voice. "I'll make a quiet exception for your husband, madam bard, if you use my inn for your songs and whatnot. I also serve food, and I need the customers."

"I'd be delighted. What do you say to a free room and stabling in exchange?"

The proprietor frowned. "You'll be making your own tips, won't you? Securing fees for messages and all that?"

"Does that mean you're offering a cut of your extra profits tonight?"

"I'm not implying that at all."

"But didn't you just say my presence would draw customers to your establishment? If I must pay you for your services, surely you can pay for mine."

Jun made a sound in his chest that was either a laugh or a cough—she suspected it was the former. The innkeeper's frown extended nearly past his chin while he attempted to do the math in his head.

"Very well," he snapped. "One free room and stabling. But I keep my profits."

"Oh, and a big meal for my husband," she threw in. "I'll just pick off his tray."

The proprietor didn't answer, only glowered, and turned to dress himself in additional layers. He would be their stable groom as well, it seemed. She and Jun quickly removed their wet boots and overcoats.

"I see your game, you know," Jun rumbled the moment the innkeeper left. "It won't work."

"Oh? Did I not secure us shelter with little effort or expense?" she lightly whispered. "I highly doubt we would've gotten the same were it known that you're unbranded and I'm your prisoner. Besides, renting two rooms would be a waste. I don't sleep."

"But I do. And I'll only do so with a locked door between us."

She swiftly blocked whatever scurrilous scenario he'd concocted in his head. "Well, you can't sleep in the hall. The innkeeper will wonder whether we're really married."

He shot her a glare, a smoky-sweet scent floating forth. "And whose fault is that?"

A breathy laugh shook free. "I know you're tempted. You can't hide it."

He leaned in close, eyes snapping with ire. "Unlike you, I can control myself."

She prayed he didn't hear her quick, indrawn breath.

He was right, in a way. And yet rigid control was also the only thing keeping her from killing anyone. Again.

"I suppose we'll see, won't we," she softly challenged.

That evening, as promised, she performed to a full dining room. She sang requested songs, recited an epic about Masayo, the second of the blondie rulers—it was almost entirely fictional—and announced the latest news from as far as Yuugai and Houfu, though she was careful not to mention anything that might draw attention to Jun.

When the brace of patchouli began, she guided everyone through a series of drinking songs, complete with bawdy lyrics. The innkeeper, delighted by his sales, swayed to the music as he replenished drinks. Jun sat in the corner the entire evening, aggravatingly impassive. If anything, he seemed all the more withdrawn.

She finished her entertainments at midnight. As the dining room began clearing out, an older brownie woman approached Mikari to request that she deliver a letter to the woman's sister in Tetsutani, which had been Mikari's previously intended destination before a creepy prickle had sent her directly into Jun's path.

"I'm afraid I can't, madam," Mikari told her. "My husband and I plan to traverse the pass in the morning."

"Surely it's too dangerous now," the woman said. "Every hour of this storm that goes by, the greater the risk of avalanches."

Jun, in the middle of a quiet conversation with the innkeeper, glanced at them with a troubled look, then nodded at something the innkeeper said.

"I'm afraid we have to try," Mikari answered.

At last, they were shown to a room at the far end of the rear hall— the smallest the inn had to offer, she could tell. But it was far from a problem. Mikari reminded the proprietor of his promise to send dinner to "her husband," accepted his offer of a basin of hot water for her evening ablutions, and then gratefully removed her wig and mask.

Jun remained at the threshold, arms crossed, his attention sharply centered on her as though he'd been waiting all day to see her face.

Maze take her, he was large. She hadn't forgotten, but he was even broader than he'd been in his youth, his body filling the open doorway. She couldn't wait to spread him out on the bedding, all that warm, hard flesh straining and flexing beneath her.

Just imagining it had her private flesh thrumming with tingling tension. She ignored the fact that she hadn't yet scented him, telling herself that merely recalling his more enticing aromas was enough to provoke her hunger.

"You can't put it off forever," she teased. "You might as well come in."

"I'm fine here."

A coy, practiced smile lifted her lips as she looked him up and down. The affectation had become rote. "Yes, you're certainly fine. I'd like to make you more so."

He curled his lip with disdain. "Is this how you choose to act with your lovers?"

For the third time that day, his words sent pain shooting through her. This time, however, she couldn't hide the hurt behind a mask, so she turned her back to him before her smile faltered and pretended to dig through her things.

"My interest in you is not an act." Softer, she added, "Neither is it a choice."

Her corruption demanded her interest. She simply couldn't help it. She managed her hunger well, but it was always there, a heaviness she couldn't put down. And with Jun—well, what did it matter whether her heart or her corruption wanted him? The latter was what she had to listen to regardless of what the former wanted.

Jun was silent and unmoving. The tempting redolence of dark, buttery caramel embraced her, only now there was a hint of sour citrus. She curled her fingers tight around her beauty kit, hunger gnawing at her.

"Sir and madam bard, your hot water," the innkeeper announced, far jollier now than when they'd first talked.

She heard Jun move aside so the proprietor could deliver his burden. Mikari turned her head a degree but kept her face hidden, mostly out of habit than for any deference toward etiquette. She was not currently serving in a professional capacity.

"Will you need anything else this evening?" the innkeeper asked.

She shook her head. "Just his dinner."

"You'll find it waiting in your room, sir," he said to Jun on his way out.

She straightened with surprise and turned. "What?"

Jun looked at her from the hallway, his hand on the door. He pointed at the wall to her left, beyond which was another room. "Knock if you need anything." Then he pointed at her. "And don't cause any trouble."

"You're not staying in here?" She stood, too despondent to recognize that she'd asked a stupid question. "Don't...don't you need to keep an eye on me?"

Rather than answer, he slid the door shut, then muttered something on the other side. She moved to open it again, not sure what coaxing thing to say when she did, but when she tugged on the door frame, it didn't budge.

How had...? There was no chain or bar, on either side.

She tugged harder, to no avail. "Jun?" she called.

"We leave early. Get whatever rest it is that you need." Then he walked away, footsteps light despite his size. She wanted to call his name again, but something in her held it back. Possibly the lump in her throat.

She heard him speak briefly to the innkeeper, thanking the other man for the food and accommodations. He had evidently made up some lie about his snoring waking up his "wife." The proprietor told him it was no burden thanks to the business she had brought in. Jun then entered his room, but she heard little after that.

After one last futile yank on the door, which didn't shift even a hair, she sat in a huff in the center of her room. Alone.

Chapter Ten

The morning was blustery but clear. Fallen snow choked the small village, hip-deep in some places where the wind had gathered it. Jun had slept as well as he had the previous night, meaning not for long and not peacefully. His nightmare had disturbed him twice, the second time nearly drawing out a cry of alarm.

He had stared into the dark the rest of the time, pondering what Mikari had murmured earlier, and the flash of pain she'd tried to hide. *"My interest in you is not an act. Neither is it a choice."*

Did she suffer, after all? She had told him she didn't want to be cured, that she enjoyed her freedom, her youth, and her strength. If that wasn't true, for what reason would she reject a potential cure?

Perhaps she'd meant that her compulsion to feed simply was what it was, that she thought nothing of indulging it. Perhaps that wobble in her smile had been yet another practiced reaction, one meant to soften his heart and his resolve. And which nearly had.

When he removed the *lock ward* from her door, Mikari was fully dressed and sitting next to her packed things in the center of the room. She already wore her mask, so he couldn't see whether she was sulking. He asked if she was ready, and she merely nodded.

He was also ready to depart, having eaten a sad-looking breakfast. Lukewarm tea, under-seasoned soup, and two ill-formed rice balls, neither with enough filling to even know for certain which type of fish roe they'd contained. His dinner hadn't been much better, but it had at least been sufficient in quantity.

Within moments, the proprietor retrieved their mounts. Jun bade that he retreat to the warmth of the inn rather than send them off, preferring to bind Mikari's wrists without a witness. She made no comments this time, and they set off without delay.

The sun had just risen over the shoulder of the eastern mountain peak when they reached the tree line and the start of the pass. Jun stopped their mounts and studied the surrounding terrain.

It didn't look good. A lip of snow overhung the western peak to their right, so the slope beneath was wind-loaded.

Though the path ahead wasn't completely buried in fresh snowfall, there were signs of a smaller, previous avalanche. Worse, the rising sun would be hitting the snow-packed slope just as they were traveling through the pass.

"That's quite a cornice," Mikari said, pointing with her bound hands at the massive brow of snow on the eastern peak. It was the first thing she'd said that day. "It won't take long for the sun to put cracks into it."

He let out a growly sigh. "And if the slab slips while we're in the pass, our bodies will be buried so deep they won't be discovered for months." About how long he was now stuck with Mikari unless the weather decided to skip winter that year.

The only other way south was by sea, via the strait that cut between the western edge of the Setei Mountains and the rocky, barren island off the coast. Two powerful winds met at the south end of the strait in winter and could sink ships of all sizes.

Even if they left for the nearest port town in the next moment, the journey would take three or four weeks, and it would be even more dangerous than traversing a mountain pass the day after a blizzard.

He spat a blistering curse.

"I'm willing to try it," Mikari said airily, as though she'd merely been presented a dish she'd never tasted.

Stunned, he looked back at her. "Are you mad?"

"The longer we wait, the higher the sun will rise."

"Absolutely not," he snapped.

She spoke with laughter in her voice. "Well, the only other way to be rid of me is for us to part ways for now and meet back in Okususo in four months time."

A strange sort of pain slid through him like a slow-moving knife. "You think I'll let you out of my sight again?"

She sighed, shoulders sagging. "What else can we do?"

"You can hand over all your valuables," a gravelly voice answered.

Jun pulled his horse's reins to turn about just as a pair of arms as hard as iron banded around his middle and roughly hauled him from his horse. He landed hard, pain shooting through his shoulder as his mount whinnied in alarm. He didn't feel a pop, so it wasn't dislocated, thank the Divine One.

Mikari let out a yelp, her reindeer bleating. Before his magic could numb his injury, Jun was grabbing for his sword and rolling to his feet. He had it halfway out of its sheath when a slovenly man with bloodshot eyes pointed a blade at him.

Bandits surrounded them from wherever they'd been hiding among the trees. He counted six, all of them bearing weapons...of a sort. Mikari had also been dragged from her saddle. A burly man with a second chin and wearing a filthy straw coat had one meaty paw on her arm and a filthy dagger at her neck. Jun didn't need to see beneath her mask to know she had to be frightened.

"Watch it!" one of them yelled.

Mikari's reindeer also did not appreciate the bandits' hostility. The doe still had her antlers, and she dropped her head to charge at the smallest bandit, a dirty man in a tattered overcoat, who barely dodged the animal.

"Steady, Temu. Steady," Mikari commanded, a tremor in her voice.

The reindeer shifted restlessly but obeyed her rider. Jun commended Mikari's instinct. Her mount was likely good against one or two attackers, but six? One of the bandits grabbed her mount's bridle. Another already held Nugun's.

If they were lucky, the bandits simply wanted money. Jun knew his way around a sword and he'd learned a lot of combat magic in the last few months, but he didn't know any method—mundane or magical—of keeping that dagger at Mikari's throat from slashing her jugular the second he tried to resist.

"That's right," the slovenly one holding Jun at sword point said, his cheeks red from the cold and a night of drinking. "Don't get any ideas."

They had to be the same pack of thugs that had terrorized the inn in Koichino some number of days ago, stealing a case of rice wine before

Pincher had driven them off. They appeared to be still drunk from the previous evening, and Slovenly had probably been the one to lead his five companions out early for a little robbery. Perhaps they had run out of alcohol.

Aj', if only a swaying drunkard weren't holding a blade two inches from Mikari's neck. Jun could take on six inebriated men who obviously weren't terribly lethal with a sword.

"What'd I say, boys?" Slovenly slurred. "The perfect spot for catching prey. A rich pair of travelers with fine mounts. We'll be drinking for at least a month." He grinned, revealing a horrendous set of teeth. The other five chuckled their approval. "And we'll have some entertainment. Let's see her."

Every muscle in Jun's body went tight. "What?"

Another of the thugs swept back Mikari's hood, then clumsily removed her mask, yanking it from her face rather than lifting it up.

The bandits slowly gasped in awe. Jun had yet to see Mikari's face in the full light of day since their reunion, and she was all the more radiant, glowing with health. Her full, smooth lips were the palest pink, and they were the first thing to draw his attention before he moved on to the delicate flush of her cheeks just beneath her band of freckles.

He had expected to find trepidation on her face, but surprisingly, she seemed to be nothing more than mildly annoyed.

"Good morning, Miss Bard," Slovenly crowed.

"You know it's rude to see me without my mask," she gently scolded, as though they were unruly children.

"Oh ho, we'll be seeing a lot more than that."

"You'll be lucky to see another day," Jun growled. He had been willing to hand over his coins and leave without a fight. Now, he would gladly leave with the bandit's head.

Slovenly guffawed. "And how'll you manage that? You're certainly big, but there's six of us, and you look a bit long in the tooth."

He was only forty! Was it his beard that made him look older? "This old man will demonstrate what a sword can really do," he snarled.

Mikari giggled, eyes twinkling with delight. Jun's jaw dropped.

"Oh, don't listen to him," she said to Slovenly, gesturing dismissively at Jun. "He was trying to force me through the pass. Do you see?" She lifted her bound wrists as proof, and more than one bandit pointed in surprise. Divine One's arse, they hadn't noticed?

"I would love to entertain my rescuers. In every way." She pursed her lips prettily. "There will be plenty of drink for me as well, right?"

The bandits lustily cheered, drowning out Jun's objection.

"Mikari, what are you saying?" he rasped, his stomach in his feet. She couldn't be serious. Even if she were willing, these brutes would—

A wondrous smile lit up her face, her eyes practically sparkling. Jun's heart leaped, and for an instant, he was ready to trust and agree with anything she said. She was on his side after all, and would never betray him.

No, that couldn't be right. She had tried to run from him, and when that didn't work, she'd tried to seduce him repeatedly. She didn't want to be human again, but he simply couldn't allow her to go on as she was. And not just because he'd been ordered...

His magic pulsed inside him, throwing off the compulsion Mikari had just cast. Taken aback, he glanced around.

All six bandits were gazing at her as if hanging on her every word.

"All I ask," she said, a hum in her throat, "is that you let my former captor leave with his horse and weapon."

"We still get his money pouch, right?" Slovenly asked, blinking hard as though aware of the compulsion, at least on some level. Indeed, he was likely the least drunk.

"Of course," she crooned. "We'll need it for tonight's celebration, won't we? And a celebration requires alcohol."

"S'fine with me," Burly said, licking his lips.

"All...all right," Slovenly agreed. He turned to Jun with a sneer. "Hand it over."

Jun slowly reached for the strings of his money pouch while staring pointedly at Mikari. "I hope you know what you're doing."

"I'm leaving with my rescuers, of course." She gazed up dreamily at Burly. "Would you mind untying me?"

Without hesitation, Burly lowered his dagger toward her bonds. "Fine with m—"

"N-no," Slovenly said, shaking his head as though dizzy. "Not yet." He snatched the money pouch from Jun's hand. Unfortunately, Burly obeyed Slovenly. The dagger went back to her throat.

"No matter," she said, quite agreeably. "Ooh, tied up sounds fun." Drawn by the implied carnality, Slovenly looked at her. His shoulders slumped the instant she snared him again with the sight of her inviting grin. "Off you go, Jun." She swatted at Jun with her bound hands. "The faster, the better."

Get out of range was what she had to mean.

Jun bucked at the idea of riding away and leaving her behind with six armed, drunk thugs. But that dagger was still there, right at her neck. And even though he hated the idea that Mikari had ever been in similar situations, he acknowledged that she had to be experienced at handling the dangers of travel.

He mounted his horse and grabbed Nugun's reins from a bandit so engrossed in Mikari that he wasn't even aware of him.

Jun scowled at her, hating everything about the situation. Her response was to tilt her head and arch one brow, as if to say *what are you still doing here.*

Pointed in the direction of Okususo, he urged Nugun into a canter and rode with his head cranked around. Mikari and the pack of bandits circling her began to recede.

Five horse lengths. Fifteen. Thirty. Burly stepped away from her as though he'd been ordered. Slovenly shoved his hand into her overcoat and down her split-skirt. Mikari gasped sharply, nearly shrieking, then tried to cover it with an excited laugh.

"Damn me to Oblivion," Jun swore, wheeling Nugun around. He kept the reins in one hand and put his other hand on his sword hilt.

It happened fast.

Mikari tapped Slovenly on his forehead, sending the bandit leader stumbling. Before Slovenly even landed on his arse, Mikari reached out, snatched Jun's money pouch, and ripped her wrists apart as though bound by nothing stronger than a thin, fraying thread. Well, so much for that.

The other bandits were too focused on Slovenly's lurching descent to stop her from scooping a handful of snow from the ground, which she then flung about her head in a powdery spray, yelling something that he couldn't quite parse over the distance.

All of this occurred in the time it took for Jun to draw his sword. He was astonished, mouth hanging open.

The bandits' reaction to her spray of snow was instant. A few wheeled around as if drunker than ever. One bandit swiped his sword at his own arm, sending a spurt of blood flying. The last raised his weapon as though intending to swing it at the nearest person. All were yelling incoherently.

A *confusion* spell?

Mikari snagged her mask from one of the off-balance bandits, jumped past Slovenly lolling about on the ground, and leaped onto the back of her reindeer as effortlessly as a bird.

There was another shout of pain, but Jun didn't see from whom. Mikari demanded all his attention. Even though she had a money pouch in one hand and her mask in the other, she managed to seize her mount's reins and prod it into a run, the white hair of her wig flying behind her.

The sight made his heart soar.

He hastily sheathed his sword. Mikari reached him by the time he had Nugun turned back around, and together they raced away.

Mikari took one last look over her shoulder before the pines whipping past swallowed up the site of her near kidnapping. Two bandits were on the ground, the rest flailing about in confusion.

She was damned lucky none of them had resisted her abilities. While immensely relieved, she now had another urgent problem.

She glanced over at Jun, who had remarkable control over his horse's gait, matching its speed to her reindeer's. He was looking at her as if she'd grown horns. As though he hadn't also repeatedly taken her by surprise these last two days.

Not only was he a veteran mercenary—an honorable one, she had no doubt—and now a commander in the empress's forces, he was also an experienced wielder of magic, working to rid the world of monsters. He had chased her down despite her inhuman strength and speed, locked her room at the inn with a mere mutter, and spoken to someone a week's travel away through a mirror.

He had also treated the stable boy she'd injured. She couldn't forget that. The man was so insufferably heroic, he'd fit right into any of the epic tales she recited. And *he* was shocked?

At best, all she had done was cause a distraction long enough for the two of them to get a head start. The bandits' confusion would fade at any second, and if she and Jun wanted to survive the morning, they couldn't stop or even hardly slow until they reached Okususo. She could only hope that the bandits elected to retreat.

"Now I understand how you managed to afford your mount," Jun said with a glance at the money pouch clutched in her hand.

She couldn't help laughing at his appalling remark. "Does this mean I've been promoted in your mind from paid bed companion to roadside robber? Or is that a demotion?"

He gnashed his teeth at the road ahead. "You're saying you've done neither?"

"I'm saying I'm a dedicated bard, and I work hard," she avowed, too insulted by his aspersions to let them simply roll off her back. "You failed to notice that the only thing I took from those bandits was what they stole from you." She tossed the pouch at him, not caring if he caught it and rather hoping he wouldn't. But he did, the boor. "You're welcome, by the way."

He frowned, tucking the pouch into his clothing. "Not that they had anything worth stealing," he said under his breath. "I certainly noticed the power of that charming smile of yours. I'm sure it helps when you're working a crowd."

Mikari gasped. "I would never!" How dare he accuse her of such a thing? Especially when he'd been sitting there all last night while she'd entertained an inn full of people.

She couldn't have avoided subjecting him to her particular ability any more than she could've blinded him to her smile. And unsurprisingly, he had shaken off her coercion, for he'd always had a strong will. Even as a ward, he had been decisive, dedicated, and constant. No wonder he held a high rank in the Dark Court.

Such admirable attributes were what had first drawn her to him, even more than his breathtaking physique. She had seen him protect the other wards on countless occasions, never failing to take what action he could, even though his efforts sometimes failed.

Once, he had offered to remake every single ceramic another ward had accidentally shattered, in addition to his usual quota. Doing so had taken him ten grueling days, but in the end, the preceptors had deigned to let the censured ward eat again.

Unfortunately, the ward's health hadn't recovered, and his death a few days later had been a blow to all of them, especially Jun.

And yet, despite a hundred past instances of his valor, remembering his good qualities was quite difficult at the moment. Had he always been this judgmental? Or was she special?

"Were you ever going to tell me you can use magic to bias others?" he asked.

Not if she could've helped it, no. "Does it count if it sometimes doesn't work? We were lucky they were drunk and stupid because my coercions usually aren't that reliable." She blew out a breath. "Anyway, I avoid using it whenever possible. It's too draining."

He snapped his head toward her. "Wait. Does that mean…?"

"It does," she said, nodding. "I need to feed again."

"How soon?"

"Tonight. Or I won't see the morning."

He turned to face the road, looking as though he was going to be sick. The longer he was silent, the tighter her chest felt. Did he have nothing to say?

"Please, will you help me, Jun?" she begged, not bothering with her usual seduction tactics. "I promise to be careful."

"Not even as a last resort," he barked, refusing to look at her. Which was just as well. She wasn't wearing her mask and couldn't use it to hide the pain that his tone as much as his words had inflicted.

But she wouldn't cry, not even as she and Jun raced away from the quickest route to Houfu, unexpectedly struck with dismay at being cut off from a possible cure. She was furious with herself for even entertaining the notion, despite knowing better.

Now, she'd have to find and seduce someone in Okususo before morning, and she doubted she'd have many palatable options, if any.

She glanced at her mask clutched in her hand, its strap broken from when a bandit had wrenched it off her head. Fortunately, it would be simple to fix.

All things considered, she was lucky to be no worse off after their brush with bandits than a broken strap and the unpleasant prospect of a hastily arranged "meal." Though she had feared for Jun's safety more than hers—possibly unnecessarily—terror still churned in her gut at the thought of what those thugs would've done to her.

Their collective lust had reeked, but the one threatening to cut her throat had been the closest, his desire fetid, not unlike the half-eaten animal carcasses she'd come across over the years.

Today hadn't been the first time she'd been threatened with physical harm, but such encounters were never easy. Each one chipped away at her.

It was nearly midday when she and Jun made it back to Okususo—without further incident, for which Mikari was grateful. This time, their arrival was met with interested looks rather than hurried glances.

Though her hunger was already weighing her down, she dismounted and held her mask before her face as she and Jun walked their well-exercised mounts toward the inn.

On their way there, the old brownie woman from the previous night emerged from her home, wrapped up as though she meant to go somewhere on an errand. Spotting them, she paused at the threshold.

"Was it as I feared?" she asked when they neared.

"Worse," Mikari answered. "We were met with bandits."

"Oh, Divine One have mercy. Are you both all right?"

Mikari awkwardly nodded. "We're unscathed."

"Did something happen to your mask?"

"Just a broken strap."

Jun abruptly paused and turned. After refusing to feed her, he had kept his gaze firmly fixed to the road. "From when they tore it off?"

She shrugged. "There's no need to concern yourself. It's my problem."

He turned back around with a scowl.

"I'm sure I can fix it," the old woman called, now behind them. "I'll come by the inn once you're settled." Touched, Mikari turned to bow her head.

The innkeeper happened to be outside when they arrived. He frowned upon seeing them, but not out of rancor. Rather, he seemed resigned. "Pass too dangerous, then?"

"The pass as well as the road in general," Jun confirmed. "Has anyone in the village had trouble with a pack of bandits?"

"Bandits?" the innkeeper echoed, eyebrows shooting up. "There's always at least a couple roaming around, sometimes in a group, but they usually go farther north once the snows start and the pass closes."

"They were likely holed up somewhere before they found us," Mikari observed as she switched which hand held her mask. Her arms were tiring quickly. "Might we negotiate another night of lodgings with you?"

"I'd also like a brief word with your village leader," Jun tacked on. "Assuming they'll agree to speak to me."

The proprietor nodded. "I'll make sure he does." He turned to Mikari. "Same arrangement as last night?"

"Agreed, but we'll not be requesting a second room this time."

Jun went rigid. "No, I—I might snore again."

The innkeeper waved his hand as though shooing a fly. "Madam Bard's room was in perfect order this morning like she'd never even slept—hardly had to do much. So, if I end up with one to spare—"

"I would be grateful," Jun said quickly.

"Husband, dear." Mikari beckoned him to lean down, which he did with reluctance. "I don't need my own room tonight," she whispered, "because I'll be elsewhere."

He drew in a slow breath as though reining in his patience. "You're not leaving the village." Spoken like a command.

"Jun," she softly chided. "I can't leave the only plentiful hunting ground within a day's ride. But I am going to leave your sight at some point." She shifted her mask just enough to touch her lips to his earlobe. "I don't allow an audience when I feed."

He swiftly straightened, the wind at his back buffeting her with a sharply sour odor, one so bitter it made her eyes water and her throat dry up instantly. She imagined it was like *ushoji* tea being left to boil until all that remained were the burning dregs.

How dare he be hurt and jealous? *He* had spurned *her*. And not just an hour ago on the road. Twenty years ago, he had chosen power over love.

Only after their magic had manifested had he spoken to her of running away from the temple, only after they'd come together on more than a physical level, for the first and last time, a wondrous night that had haunted her nearly every night since.

The pleasure of that moment had terrified her. It had been too sharp, too overwhelming in the truest sense of the word, taking over her mind and connecting her to Jun for one intensely spiritual second. Though that one second had been pure joy, it had also been a loss—of self, of control, and of reason. It had felt bottomless.

And it had driven a wedge between them. Mikari had realized that the priests were right, that her magic would corrupt her. It would addict her to that unequaled high and compel her to do reckless things in the pursuit of as many of those transportive seconds as she could elicit. It would destroy her.

She hadn't wanted that to happen to either of them. She had been deliriously happy with Jun before her magic had developed.

All of her other concerns with escaping the temple had been secondary, although none had been trivial. She hadn't wanted to risk the consequences if they were apprehended before they could flee Gozu. And even if they made it out, the southern lands still had plenty of challenges for a pair of crows, especially ones without a community.

But Jun had insisted that losing his magic would be like losing his hands and eyes, as though he had known any different before. He had chosen the high of its power over a safer existence together as cleansed crows.

Unfortunate, then, that she had become the one chained to an addiction while Jun had full control of his magic.

"Hm. Look at us." She lowered her mask, not caring that the innkeeper could see. Her arms were tired anyway. "Neither of us is getting what we want."

His face turned an angry red, looking as though one more sardonic reply from her would have him yelling.

"W-...this young beauty is your wife?" the proprietor softly exclaimed, looking from her to Jun, whose foul mood made him seem even older than his forty years. "At first, I was surprised that you managed to marry up, before I discovered you're both crows, but now..." His bushy brows wiggled over a slight smile. "Now I know why you weren't content to stay at home."

Mikari managed not to wrinkle her nose with distaste, but Jun didn't. Though the stinging bitterness of his jealousy wasn't pleasant, it did overpower whatever scent the innkeeper was putting out, for which she was grateful.

She supposed the old man hadn't mentioned her black hair when seeing it last night because she'd helped him make a healthy profit, but who knew if she'd make him quite as happy tonight. Bardic performances required concentration and energy, of which she had far less than yesterday.

"I'm older than I look, sir," she said before Jun could muster a rebuke. "And thank you for your discretion." She bowed her head.

"It's...it's not about your hair," the innkeeper muttered. "I don't care, but the village leader does. He has little tolerance. Next to none, in fact."

"We shan't cause any trouble," she promised, hoping she hadn't just lied.

He nodded then pointed at the nearby entrance to indicate they should head inside. "Same room as last night. I'll take your animals to the barn."

Jun quickly removed his saddlebags and slung them over his shoulder with a slight wince. Determined not to care about his pain, she handed over her reins. The proprietor walked their mounts away, and she and Jun entered the inn. The tiny entryway only allowed one of them to remove their boots at a time, so Mikari did so first.

Gone were the two men who had been playing cards yesterday afternoon in the central dining space, which was unfortunate, for both had been attracted to her.

Instead, there were two blonde women, likely a mother and a daughter, both picking at the remains of a meal and casting curious glances her way. She couldn't begin to guess why they traveled, but it stood to reason that they were also planning to traverse the pass before it closed. Like Mikari and Jun, they were too late.

She glanced at Jun, who had seen the direction of her interest and was now glaring at her. She would need to get some space between them if she wanted to scent anything of the two women besides burnt *ushoji* tea.

Leaving him to remove his boots in the entryway, she held her mask before her and approached her potential donors.

"Well met, ladies." She bowed her head, and the women graciously reciprocated. She focused on one, then the other as she spoke. "Forgive me for intruding on your meal, but if you're staying here tonight, I'll be entertaining from the hours of cherry blossom through camphor."

She took a deep, subtle sniff. Both women felt lust, the older woman especially, but both preferred men. Exclusively, Maze take them.

"We look forward to it," the older one replied, smiling blandly, distracted by something over Mikari's shoulder. Cloying sweetness tinged the air.

Mikari turned to find Jun still scowling at her. She scowled back even though he wouldn't see it, annoyance digging at her like an itchy navel. Should she tell him that the older blonde woman wanted to sleep with him? No, there would be no guaranteed way to avoid sounding jealous, whether she was or wasn't. And she certainly wasn't.

"I'm going to freshen up," she told him, then made her way to the rear hall without waiting for a response.

Inside the room, she knelt before the storage alcove, set down her mask, and shrugged off her satchel. Jun entered but kept his distance as he set his things in the opposite corner. She determinedly turned her back to him and drew her lute from her pack.

The head of her instrument jiggled unexpectedly, sending a jolt of alarm through her. Breath held, she carefully unwound the lengths of linen, but her fervent, silent pleas were in vain.

Her lute was broken at the neck, the body connected to the head only by the strings, which still had enough tension to pull the now-broken section out of place. She drew a soft gasp of pain, her heart breaking.

Her mentor had given her this instrument. It was almost as old as her corruption.

How much worse could her situation get? First, she had been involuntarily reunited with the only man she'd ever loved, and he despised her. She had been forced to travel with him, causing all sorts of confusing and unwanted feelings, only to find the pass primed to bury them in a literal mountain of snow, dashing any hope of a cure for at least several months.

Then they'd been accosted by bandits who had broken her three-string. Worst of all, she had to feed, and Jun wouldn't submit himself, so she would have to hunt for a new donor while he watched, or rather, glared.

"What's wrong?" Jun asked in a grudging tone, instantly turning her despair into resentment. He didn't actually care, so why ask?

She gave a mirthless chuckle. "Nothing, it's not your concern."

"Stop saying your concerns are not mine, dammit."

"Aren't they?"

"Tell me what's wrong."

She forced out an exasperated groan, throat tightening dangerously. "Leave me alone, Jun." *Leave before you see me cry.*

He stomped over, which only took a single step in that tiny room, then loomed above her, bringing with him a blend of pepper, citrus, and ginger. And for a moment, he didn't move or speak, having seen the problem for himself.

"Let me fix it," he said at last, the air sweetening. "I'm certain I can."

She twisted to look at him crouched next to her. He appeared earnest and...truly concerned.

"Let me fix it," he repeated.

"There's no point," she whispered, barely holding back tears. "I must suffer, I cannot avoid it. If not this, then something much worse."

He absorbed that with a scowl, then silently knelt. Reverently, he picked up the two pieces of her lute and carefully removed the strings.

She watched anxiously, too weak to resist a spark of hope, as he studied the break and fit the two pieces together. Then he pulled in a breath as though centering himself.

Her lute made a strange squeal where the break had occurred, and the fracture across the fingerboard began to fade. She pressed her fingers to her lips to stifle a gasp. Divine One's grace, he was really doing it. He was mending her instrument with magic, the power she had asked him to give up.

Less than a minute later, he took his hand from the top half of her lute, and the neck held as if it had never broken.

He cleared his throat and held it toward her. "Solid objects are easier."

Mouth hanging open, she accepted her instrument. The neck was smooth where it had been broken. No sign of damage at all. "Easier than what?"

"Flesh," he said. "It has a soft, complicated structure."

She gaped at him. "You can heal flesh? I-is that what you did for the stable worker?" She had thought he'd given the boy a medicinal tea or a cold compress for the bump on his head.

He nodded. "Check the sound."

Fumbling with astonishment, she managed to restring her lute and tune it. Her relief as she played several pitch-perfect chords was keen. It sounded beautiful. Beautiful and unbroken.

"T-thank you." She paused to swallow the wobble in her throat. "I don't know that I could've... Thank you, Jun."

The second she met his gaze, she understood what he must've felt when she'd charmed the bandits: ensnared. His intense and bittersweet expression was a poignant contrast to his honeyed scent—the gently sweet and creamy variety, not at all cloying.

The air between them thickened, and she swore she heard the metallic ting of a wind bell rather than the soft, accidental strum of a lute string. Heat surged in her veins as his dark-sable gaze focused on her mouth. His lips parted on a soft breath out.

She tried to ignore her roaring hunger. Jun had made his preferences clear, even if his body didn't agree. But when he closed the distance between them, her insides leaped with joy, and she couldn't move away.

Her eyes slid shut with the first, lingering brush of his lips and velvety beard. She tasted honey drizzled over dense sponge cake, and a hint of salty remorse.

His mouth was warm and soft, his kiss light, but she knew it could be hot and hard, commanding a response. The shaky breath he took as his fingers slid behind her neck filled her heart with agony.

A spill of warm, moist air preceded a heavier, more indulgent kiss. She felt the tip of his tongue, which she let in with a quiet, carnal moan, and it was all she could do just to cling to the front of his overcoat.

The meeting of their lips was both new and familiar. Her flesh remembered well the sure slide of his tongue and the possessive grasp of his hand around her nape, but she had never kissed him as the creature she was now, had never seen where his mind went.

Like her, he was marveling at the softness of their mouths moving together, nothing but wet, silken heat. His hand behind her neck pulled her closer, and the word *mine* swam through her head, making her heart trip. In his mind, he pictured bearing her down to the floor and parting her legs with his wide body.

Wetness bloomed there in response, and she was struck by how much she'd missed his touch, even more than she missed food and sleep. She missed the connection, the mutual possession, the flood of joy that came with knowing he wanted only her. The mere thought of their bodies becoming one, at first with trembling passion and then with desperate lunges...

She abruptly pulled away, panting and shuddering, the wave of want rising inside her slowing to an uncomfortable stop. She had let it grow far too strong, for she knew exactly what would happen if he made love to her ever again.

She'd plunge into orgasm within minutes if not seconds, and then her corruption would be in control. And he would be too weak from pleasure even to be aware she was killing him.

"Mikari," he uttered, still clenching her nape, so close she could feel the brush of his beard on her cheek. "Tell me, did you ever actually—"

"Pardon me," someone blurted, startling them both.

The old brownie woman stood wide-eyed in the open doorway. She held up a sewing kit as well as a carefully sealed letter, likely the one meant for her sister.

"I didn't mean to peep. But I'd rather not have to come back later." Her brows tweaked with confusion. "Aren't you awful young, Miss Bard, to be with a man of his age?"

Before she could think of a reply, Jun sucked in a breath as though woken suddenly, snatching his palm from her nape. He regarded her with quickly dawning horror, disgust flashing across his face, turning his scent sharp and sour.

Did he think she'd employed her wiles upon him? She hadn't, and yet shame over her lack of control stung her cheeks, stifling her. Shame and disappointment.

Jun lurched to his feet then staggered back, eyes darting about. "What am I doing?" he rasped before retreating from the room. The brownie woman quickly made way for him.

As ever, the pain of his rejection hurt far worse than even the powerful cramping of her denied hunger. Turning away to blink back tears, she slammed the lid on her heart, resolved to let it bleed in the dark. Stupid, weak heart.

His refusal to feed her was for the best, she determined, as was his departure just now.

She knew he wouldn't let her die if she didn't find another donor, but the safest way to feed from him would require that he keep his hands to himself out of pride. She didn't know whether she could resist if he decided to reciprocate.

Of the two of them, her control would always be weaker.

Chapter Eleven

Jun stalked to the front of the inn, past the two blondies at whom Mikari had been staring, and shoved his feet into his boots. He was boiling hot and needed a blast of cold air, which he got when he burst outside, sucking the chill into his lungs. He got halfway to the inn's barn before stopping to contemplate a snowdrift.

If it weren't guaranteed to turn the heads of any villagers going about their business, he would shove snow down his pants until his ardor cooled. Even then, he wasn't entirely sure the icy mush would have any effect on his stiff, aching loins.

He had kissed her, tasted her. Maze take him, he had been seconds away from a lot more. Part of him did desperately want to feed her, to unleash his magic that still urgently grasped for her, and to let her suck every drop of strength from him.

That part of him exulted in the thought of nourishing her with his body, of sustaining her with his desire for her. It relished the idea of her begging for him as though it would save her life—because it would.

But his heart knew that twenty years hadn't bridged the gap between them, only widened it. He had grown older, as so many had deigned to point out that morning, much to his aggravation.

Even if Mikari were cured in the next few minutes, she would not become his age, nor he hers. He wanted to think a difference of twenty years wouldn't matter, but it did.

And while Jun had come to appreciate the glib, reckless woman she had become, one who he'd learned was as much of a mask as her fox guise, their lives had also gone separate ways, no doubt as they would have even if he and Mikari had left the temple together.

She was fully committed to her bardic profession—her anguished reaction to her broken three-string had more than proven it. And his eventual future lay far to the south, likely with someone else.

He would, of course, find some way to keep her alive if she found no one else. Telling her he wouldn't even be a last resort had been a lie. But he couldn't be just a convenient source of energy to her. He couldn't let his body or his heart be used and later discarded, not when she'd already made it clear once before that he wasn't enough as he was.

But until and unless she had no one else from whom to feed, he would keep his distance from her.

What he would do when she disappeared with another, he could not know, even as his hands drew into tight, shaking fists, but he supposed he would soon find out.

Once his arousal had faded to a simmer, he returned to the inn to find that the proprietor had summoned the village leader, a man whom Jun had seen observing Mikari's performance last night.

The tall, thin blondie stiffened with dislike at the sight of Jun, then shot an angry look at the innkeeper.

The blondie's voice was curt. "You did not say the bard and her crow brute had returned." To Jun, he said, "Be glad you have your life and your master. I do not care if you've lost a money-string."

"Money-string" implied a small number of lighter, low-value currency carried on a linen string, usually what parents gave their children as an allowance or as errand money. It also suggested poverty or an unskilled laborer. In Jun's case, it implied that he was a leech.

Anger surged, burning away any lingering lust. For that, Jun was grateful to the village leader, the latest in the long line of self-important curs he'd met over the years. He deserved a reward for the perfectly composed response he gave.

"Luckily, my wife and I escaped with my money pouch, though we feared losing more than that. I felt the need to warn the village and offer my skills as a former mercenary in capturing these bandits. I believe I know where they are."

No doubt they had also found the abandoned hunting cabin where he and the delegation had stayed three nights ago. If they had any sense, they'd have tried their luck with the pass rather than go back there.

The blondie snorted, barely concealing a flinch when Jun revealed that he'd been a mercenary. Jun had no wish to return to such work, but he'd make an exception for Slovenly and the rest.

"And I suppose you'll need a big reward for slaying six imaginary bandits, hm?"

Jun froze, his gut turning to ice—metaphorically and metaphysically—the air around him growing chilled. "Never said there were six," he growled.

Fear flashed across the blondie's face with the realization that he'd made a mistake, confirming that he'd had something to do with those drunk thugs.

"What'd I say, boys? The perfect spot for catching prey. 'A pair of travelers with fine mounts.'"

The village leader certainly wouldn't be the first arse to expose Jun to danger. As a mercenary, he'd lost count. But the mere suspicion that the blondie's prejudice had almost gotten Mikari kidnapped, or worse, made Jun want to break the man's knees.

"That's a rather high number for this area at the start of winter, and all in a group, *hm?*" Jun pressed. The proprietor turned to the village leader with stunned anger.

"A lucky guess," the blondie said, shifting uneasily. The man was a terrible liar.

"I'll pay," a woman called out. Jun had forgotten that the two blondie women were in the common area, perfectly within earshot. "We need to get south, which will be difficult enough without the threat of bandits."

"You'd still be risking death by snowslide," Jun warned her.

"As I said, difficult enough," she said, pushing her back straight.

He named a fair price, to which she agreed. The village leader drew himself up as though he wished to argue, but his common sense triumphed and he walked out with his nose up.

Jun was contemplating what to tell Mikari when she and the brownie woman emerged from the rear hall. She carried her good-as-new lute, to which she'd attached a shoulder strap, and also wore her newly repaired mask.

Sweet Garden, he could still taste her on his tongue, a hint of the sweet winter nut *rundona* from whatever powder she used to clean her teeth.

At the same time, a group of brownies arrived with a bit of a ruckus from outside—tradesmen by the look of their clothing.

Mikari stopped within arm's reach of Jun and said her goodbyes to the brownie woman, thanking her and inviting her to return for another performance that evening. The woman promised to do so, then walked past him with a concerned glance.

Behind him, the merchants were speaking to the proprietor in Common, upset to learn they would be stuck in Gozu for the winter unless they risked their lives in the pass.

"I'm heading out for a while," Mikari told him discreetly, her manner as cool as snowmelt. "Feel free to have dinner without me."

He couldn't resist a flippant response. "Hmph, likewise."

"Oh?" she said, chin lifting. "And where will you be?"

"Look, a bard," a tradesman said, snaring their attention.

"She's performing here tonight," the innkeeper hastened to say, no doubt hoping her presence would mollify the merchants' frustration with the weather.

"Starting at cherry blossom," she clarified, brushing past Jun, her question forgotten and her manner warming considerably. When he realized why that likely was, his stomach went tight.

She explained her typical evening of entertainments, and one of the merchants, a handsome young man with a small mole on his chin, gave Mikari an assessing look, as though he were contemplating what she looked like out of her bardic attire. When she mentioned that she took requests, he smugly asked whether she was "open to a private performance."

Jun took a step in Mikari's direction before he could stop himself, hands clenched.

"I am, in your case," she said with coy emphasis.

Her response practically gutted him, turning his knees soft. The innkeeper looked at Jun with confusion, for her meaning was hardly ambiguous.

And he'd be damned if he stood there watching another second.

Shaking with frustration, he stomped past everyone just as Mikari bid the merchants farewell, and he ended up reaching the entryway before she did, forcing her to wait while he put on his boots.

The tradesmen quickly returned their attention to haggling over the innkeeper's rates, with Chin Mole demanding a steep discount for a week's stay, claiming the innkeeper had given them a false idea of how long they had to return south and entertaining the foolish hope that the pass might become traversable in the next few days.

Mikari spoke to him in a murmur, one for his ears only. "You can't be jealous while also refusing me." He swiftly straightened from tying on his boots.

"I'm not jealous," he hissed. "I'm disappointed at your lack of discretion."

She stepped closer, crowding him in the small entryway, her voice mocking. "I can smell the difference. I know you still want me, in either case."

"What I want no longer exists," he said in a grating whisper, "if indeed it ever did."

With that, he turned and left, eager for a fight.

Chapter Twelve

Mikari plucked merry chords as she walked along the village streets, beckoning anyone who was about with musical sways. Never was she more grateful for her shoulder strap, which made it possible to carry her lute without succumbing to fatigue.

Jun was nowhere in sight, nor had she seen him when she'd emerged from the inn, heart bruised. Shame had hit her anew when she'd tucked her mended lute against her body—Jun may have fixed it, but there was no fixing the conflict between them.

However, her work offered the usual balm to her self-loathing, starting with the first smile she elicited.

Fingers never stopping, she took every opportunity to promote her services and to invite the villagers to an evening of songs, gossip, and games back at the inn.

She secured another message to deliver, this time to a recipient in Koichino. Easy enough. Another person paid for her interpretation of an augury he'd sought a few weeks ago, one that he suspected had been botched.

After hearing his description of the ritual, she was forced to agree, telling him the divination had failed to achieve an answer to his dilemma, whether good or bad. And yet the temple had claimed he'd see a bad outcome.

Eventually, she had a handful of children following her, whom she led to the small, central square where she played several whimsical songs. One was about a group of birds bickering in mid-air over a stolen sweetcake, which shrunk as they fought over it until there was none left to eat. The children were delighted to learn silly gestures for every verse.

Another song about wind through the pines was familiar to them, and they all sang along. A few adults even joined in.

The sun was near the horizon when she sent the little ones off to their dinner, their parents giving her surprisingly generous tips. Though she tried not to, she couldn't help slouching with exhaustion, bare hands aching from the cold despite her supernatural resistance.

A few hours remained between now and cherry blossom, during which she'd rest and warm up. Hopefully, she'd have the energy to perform without anyone noticing a difference.

She began the walk back to the inn, breaths labored.

"What in the Maze is that?" someone behind her exclaimed.

Mikari turned just as more cries of surprise rang out. Several people were jogging to get a look, a few leaning out of their open storm doors.

Over their heads, she saw a horse and its rider ambling up the lane. She instantly recognized Jun, who was a bit flushed and disheveled but otherwise unchanged.

Before him walked a line of men tied one to the next, six in all, and each one bloodied. Several limped. Almost as instantly, she recognized the bandit who had brandished an ill-maintained sword at Jun, if only by his hair and clothes, for his face was misshapen with bruised swelling.

Now she knew where Jun had been. He had gone out alone and captured six criminals, though he could've remained in the village rather than take on such a dangerous task.

She stared, awed and stuck in place as though ice had encased her boots. Keen awareness of him washed through her, speeding up her heart and heating her from the inside, thawing her icy fingers and then some.

He was a towering man on a towering stallion, as broad across his shoulders as his mount was. Though his expression was stern, he rode with ease, gripping his horse's flanks with thick, powerful thighs.

Maze take her, he was potent. Brave and true.

How had she ever thought she could have him, keep him?

AT THE MAZE'S CENTER

"Hey, that one stole my sister's chickens a month ago," one villager shouted, pointing at one of the thugs.

"I know you," another yelled at the large one who'd held a knife to Mikari's throat. "You hit me and took my money pouch and my boots. H-he's wearing 'em right now!"

Villagers surrounded the procession of bandits. No one was yet throwing anything, but a few spat at them.

Then someone realized that one of the criminals was the village leader's uncle, and the shouting grew much louder. Behind her mask, Mikari's mouth was wide open.

Okususo's blondie leader quickly strode toward the scene, followed by a younger man wearing a sword—likely some muscle, though she doubted whether the swordsman was there to protect anyone but the blondie.

Mikari remained where she was, watching as the irate villagers and their deceitfully indignant leader worked out what to do with the six criminals, cataloging the event in her mind out of well-ingrained habit, for one of her duties was reporting interesting news and this counted without question.

She itched to write it all down, along with a dozen other tidbits gleaned over the afternoon, so that she could boast every detail of Jun's heroism far and wide.

However, the self-assured look he aimed directly at her as the bandits were led away would be hers alone to treasure and bemoan. *Bear witness*, it said, arrowing her with desire.

Only when he was forced to look away did she find herself able to move. Overwhelmed, she retreated, returning to the inn as quickly as her trembling limbs would let her.

***

THE SUN HAD DISAPPEARED beneath the horizon when Jun stepped into the inn, seeking food and warmth, free at last of the villagers and their awed gratitude.

Not that he didn't appreciate it. He was glad that his unwise but unregretted decision to take on six bandits had brought them some justice. He was even more glad that he'd only sustained a few minor cuts and one nasty bruise, though his wrenched shoulder from earlier that day still pained him.

But he hadn't gone after those thugs for the village, or for the blonde woman who'd tried to trap him into a conversation after paying him, or even for himself.

Aj', that last one was partly a lie.

At first, once the bandits made their intentions clear, he had been determined to take a pound of flesh from each of them on Mikari's behalf, to make up for his helplessness at the time. It was the least they deserved on top of the rout she'd delivered them, as impressive as it'd been.

But after that profound moment in their room, glimpsing the hidden hurt in her fawn-colored eyes, kissing her and discovering the same joy and blistering need he'd felt twenty years ago, and then realizing that her heart would never be within reach, her hurt never his to mend...

He couldn't stop Mikari from slowly unraveling him, but he'd stitch himself back together in other ways, seizing control whenever possible to avoid coming completely undone. He wasn't proud of it, but nothing short of menacing those thugs until they'd cowered and begged would have eased him.

Mikari occupied a table in the common area and was concentrating on the open book in front of her, a writing kit laid neatly beside it. Her wig was in place, but her mask sat next to her lute on the floor by her cushion, indicating she was not accepting any requests.

The innkeeper greeted him like an old friend and offered him a meal. Jun thought about taking it in his room, as most other guests seemed to be doing. There, he could update Houfu through the speaking mirror about the state of Futakata Pass, and then hide for the rest of the night.

Instead, he found himself sitting at the farthest table from Mikari, neither composed enough to go closer nor strong enough to take himself elsewhere.

Not once did she look up to meet his gaze while he awaited dinner, and yet he couldn't help staring, noticing the dark circles beneath her eyes. She had grown paler.

Hopefully, the innkeeper would assume that Jun was giving her space to work, or at worst that there was marital strife, rather than suspect they weren't married.

Mikari had begun to write on a blank page when his meal arrived. Jun hardly noticed the taste, only that it was unpleasant, too focused on her movements—controlled and precise, just as they'd both been taught. He desperately wished to know what she was writing, his curiosity burning even brighter when she put away one journal and brought out another.

When the innkeeper returned to collect his tray, he gave Jun a sort of pitying look, which answered the question of what the man thought of their physical distance. He shuffled over to Mikari and asked if she wanted dinner.

Her gaze nearly touched Jun. "No, thank you."

"I've not seen you eat today. Could I tempt you with some soup?"

She gave the innkeeper a tight smile. "Perhaps later, if I must."

Her true meaning was not lost on Jun, but the proprietor gave a confused nod before returning to the kitchen. *"A thin soup may quiet a rumbling stomach."*

A few moments later, she packed up her journals and writing kit, gathered her mask and three-string, and retreated to their room where the rest of her things were, likely to prepare for her performance as she'd also done last night, tuning her lute and warming up her voice.

He itched to stand up and follow. There was still a bit of time before her audience would start to arrive. If he could just wall off his heart and swallow his pride, he'd be able to feed her without driving the knife deeper into his chest.

Only he wanted her too damned much to do either. He wanted the masked bard as well as the woman beneath, whether she was stoic, reckless, fearless, or vulnerable. And in turn, he wanted her to desire him for everything that he was and not merely because she was hungry.

So rather than offer himself up to her, he sat and waited and methodically stitched together the newest threads she'd loosened inside him.

Feeding from others was rote for her. Meaningless. He wouldn't let anyone treat him that way again, as if he meant nothing. Not if he could avoid it.

Night fell not long after she'd left, and villagers began to arrive for the performance Mikari had promised. For the first hour, she played her three-string without singing, providing musical accompaniment while the villagers picked at their abysmal fare and otherwise filled their bellies with rice wine and side dishes that even the innkeeper couldn't foul up, such as pickled vegetables and steamed bean pods.

Jun vacated his table to allow others to eat, taking up a hopefully inconspicuous position against the wall by the vestibule, leaning back with his arms crossed. And yet he still had to endure a few well-wishing slaps to his arm.

Judging by the din of laughter and shouts, practically the entire room was tipsy by the start of cherry blossom, when even more villagers arrived and ordered wine. Why bother with magic, he realized, with an audience happily in their cups?

Of course, he'd already known that Mikari hadn't used her coercions the previous evening. He would've felt the magical compulsion. But he supposed that, in his mind, he wanted her to have done so, for guarding his heart from her would've been far easier if she had.

Her performance that evening was just as entertaining as the previous night. And like then, Jun struggled to remember that the vivacious bard bringing music to this room full of strangers was a lust eater. He tried not to get sucked into her spell—the one she wove without magic.

And yet he found himself watching her so closely that he noticed every little sign of her growing fatigue. In between songs, she dropped her arms as if carrying boulders and shook out her hands. Singing was more of an effort, her high notes less powerful, and she never seemed to catch her breath, not even while bantering with the crowd.

The only thing she repeated from the previous evening was a request by the younger of the two blonde women who wished to hear a romantic tale, written during blondie reign, of a princess falling in love with a brown-haired warrior, forbidden to someone of her caste unless he proved himself in a battle against demons. Afterward, Mikari graciously accepted a tip from the young woman.

"With demons gone, princess, you'll have to settle for the old crow looming back there," Chin Mole quipped in a boisterous voice.

Jun stiffened as everyone turned to gauge his reaction while a handful of people chuckled, some of them awkwardly. He kept his expression resolutely neutral.

If he weren't convinced that he'd be disbelieved, he could reveal that he had played a major role in eradicating demons, not that Chin Mole would have the integrity to be ashamed of himself.

The young blondie stared determinedly at her lap, and the older woman sent what Jun assumed was a disapproving glare at the brownie merchant, for he wasn't at a convenient angle to see it.

"Ah, but with age comes experience," Mikari announced with bardic flare, strumming a chord. "The kind that led to the capture of six brutish bandits earlier this evening."

Cheers filled the inn, and Chin Mole's self-satisfied grin soured.

She strummed a brief melody, one familiar to Jun, from a children's song about Aya the Vigilant. The matching lyrics were, *"A hero with no equal, ten warriors in one."*

Duly prompted, the villagers sang the next line. "In darkness, as bright as the midnight sun!"

Jun squeezed his fists tight beneath the fold of his arms, his chest swelling, shoulders inching back as visceral satisfaction curled warmly inside him. He wished her praise didn't affect him so deeply, but it did.

With deft timing, Mikari turned the room's attention to something new, affecting a sultry, striking tone.

"Speaking of demons." She stepped prettily toward Chin Mole. "Perhaps the handsome merchant can confirm for us one of the most incredible tales I've heard about the empress."

Chin Mole's grin returned. "And what's that, Miss Bard? There's quite a few."

"Is it true that she went to Oblivion and slew the Damned One?"

A bolt of surprise went through Jun to hear Mikari mention something so directly involving him, when he knew she wasn't aware of his part.

"Yes, I believe that's the rumor. Not just her, though. A few other crows went with her. People claim that demons are gone because she defeated him."

"You sound skeptical," Mikari observed. "Is there no proof?"

"The demon attacks stopped, but someone up here told me the priests prayed for divine intervention."

"Well, I can't imagine anyone with sense would be willing to take a midnight stroll outside the barrier charms to find out," Mikari quipped, earning a titter of laughter.

Having restored a relaxed mood, she moved on to any news she hadn't yet related to the village the previous night, touching only briefly on old topics.

She was in the middle of describing a fashion trend in Yuugai, where they layered clothes to achieve a color progression from light to dark, when Chin Mole spoke up again.

"It's too bad the Northern Highlands are so cold. In the far south, there are places where women walk around in dresses so sheer you can see their tits," he said, staring and pointing at Mikari's chest with unnecessary emphasis.

There were several gasps. Some people laughed as though happily scandalized, while others squirmed with agitation. Jun limited himself to a sneer.

True, in *some* parts of the far south, women wore such clothing inside their homes, and pleasure workers of all genders wore sheer clothing inside the pleasure houses, but Chin Mole's crude innuendo all but shouted that he wanted to see Mikari's breasts.

Sweet Garden, he just might, Jun realized, stomach turning.

"I'd say it's time for a drinking game," Mikari announced, a slight strain in her voice, one he almost missed. "Who needs another pitcher?"

She turned away to sneak sips of water while the innkeeper replenished her audience with carafes of rice wine and plum wine.

Once alcohol had been distributed, she told everyone to drink whenever they laughed, and began a thoroughly indecent song about a man sneaking into his lover's room to have sex with her but failing miserably at finding the right hole to plug.

Though the audience was cackling and rapidly growing drunker, Jun silently stewed as he watched Mikari blatantly flirt with the brownie merchant. Every time the young man in her song realized he still hadn't found his lover in the dark room, she turned to Chin Mole and rolled her hips suggestively, practically moaning the bawdy lyrics.

Then she sang about a woman going from town to town, looking for the perfect lover, and she challenged the crowd to guess the strange ways in which each person had sex with her. Whoever didn't guess right, which was everyone, had to drink.

Every suggestion Chin Mole made was the lewdest one in the room, and Mikari laughed with delight every time, fanning herself in feigned shock.

The night ended less than an hour later when the innkeeper ran out of wine. After one last song about improvised drinking vessels—*a lover's mouth is best* was its conclusion—the evening's entertainments were over.

Mikari thanked her audience and collected her tips. The villagers began stumbling out, smiling and still singing, several more whapping Jun's arm as they passed him.

Almost everyone had gone when Mikari removed her mask, signaling that she was done for the night, looking wan despite the spots of red beneath her freckles.

With a coy smile, she approached Chin Mole at his table. The bastard grinned at the sight of her, obviously pleased with her beauty.

Even though Jun had seen this moment coming and done nothing to avoid it, a sick feeling punched him hard in his gut. His magic swelled in warning, urging him to move, to seize and possess.

No choice of lover Mikari could make would ever be agreeable—except himself, Maze take him—but *Chin Mole? Really?*

The merchant was, of course, the most handsome one in the room, not to mention half Jun's age. And hers, technically. Was youth and vitality especially alluring to a lust eater? Was Jun stale in comparison?

Mikari and Chin Mole spoke at a volume that Jun couldn't hear from across the common area, not that he'd be able to stomach their conversation. The conceited smile on the brownie's face said it all, anyway.

Part of him begged for Mikari to look at him, but another feared she would.

She and Chin Mole then stood. Jun nearly shot forward but managed to plant his feet and press his shoulders to the wall behind him. As they wandered toward the rooms in back, his magic scraped at his insides, drawing out a grunt of pain.

He told himself that the only thing worse than this moment would be the day Mikari left his life again. That if he wanted to survive it, he had to guard his heart from her.

The common area was now empty except for Jun, the innkeeper, and two other brownie merchants who seemed to be passed out at their table. The innkeeper frowned at Jun as he moved about the room, cleaning up.

It was all Jun could do not to vomit. Or cry. Or yell. He tried not to think about what exactly was happening in Chin Mole's room, or how long it would take.

Then he faintly heard her voice—a giggle, then a drawn-out sound of wonder.

He jerked away from the wall, bile rising in his throat. Though his feet wanted to take him directly to her, he forced them toward the vestibule.

Knowing Mikari was with someone else was difficult enough. He didn't have to hear it, too.

He had one foot shoved into a boot when a man's shout echoed from the other side of the inn. "It's your crudding fault, you crow whore!" Then a distinct, unmistakable slap.

"What the—?" the innkeeper squawked, the tray of used tableware he held rattling with his jump of surprise.

Jun ripped off his boot and raced toward the inn's rooms. There was a heavy thump just as he entered the rear hall, and his magic tugged him toward a specific door which he flung open without question.

His gaze went to Mikari first, standing in the center of the room. Her cheek was red, her wig absent, and she was hurriedly knotting the last tie on her half-tucked shirt.

Her abused cheek and dishevelment were equally enraging, but it was the shimmer of tears in her angry eyes that put ice into his veins.

Chin Mole lay dazed on the floor, pants open to reveal a pitifully soft member, hands cradling his head as though he'd hit it upon something. Had she stunned him in the same manner as the bandit leader? When her energy was already exhausted?

Avoiding his gaze, Mikari straightened with a visible effort to appear calm. "I'm all right."

"You're clearly not," Jun growled, stalking closer.

How often had something like this happened to her? Was this what she went through just to survive? *I'm a damned fool*, he realized. The perils of travel were bad enough for a lone, female bard with black hair. But for someone like Mikari, with a particular need?

Chin Mole groaned as he heaved himself into a slumped sitting position, looking as though he were about to be sick. More footsteps approached at a bumbling pace. The innkeeper, no doubt.

Priming a *sleep* spell in his mind, Jun snatched the merchant's collar.

Though he didn't need to deliver the magic with his fist, he punched the man directly on his stupid mole, laying him out cold. One yank flung the merchant onto his stomach, concealing his exposed genitals from view.

A second later, the innkeeper appeared. "What's going on?"

"This drunken lout," Mikari said with unfeigned acrimony, "does not know the difference between a bard and a pleasure worker. He requested private entertainment and mistakenly believed that I'd tup him."

"*Mistakenly* believed?" the innkeeper repeated, incredulous. "Why, you were flirting with him all evening. What sort of marriage—"

"I'm a bard, sir. My profession demands that I be witty and inviting," she maintained with the perfect air of someone rudely accused. "A few bawdy drinking songs do not mean that I'm open to another's advances."

If Jun weren't in a stormy mood, he'd be fighting not to smile at her remarkable acting.

The innkeeper grumbled, lips curving into a deep frown. "My gut says you're lying, but I've made good money the last two nights, so I'll not turn you out. I do, however, expect you both to remain in your room the rest of the night and to leave first thing in the morning."

"As if I could eat another of your meals," Jun muttered.

"W-what did you—?"

"Very well, sir. Come first light, our mounts should be readied and waiting outside."

The proprietor made an ugly frown. "They'll be ready." He backed up, stiff with agitation, and waved them out. "Come along, then."

Mikari quickly gathered her wig, mask, and three-string. No one bothered to move Chin Mole onto his bedding. The innkeeper saw them to their room, as if they were children to be punished.

"No more trouble," he sharply reminded them before shutting them inside.

The innkeeper's steps faded, leaving them in tense silence. Jun turned to Mikari with a soft step and contemplated her, wondering what to say.

She had put away her things and stood staring at the plain plaster wall at the back of the storage alcove, chin up and arms wrapped around her middle, her normally straight posture bent with fatigue.

Even seeing her in profile, he could tell her mouth was tight with uneasiness.

And why wouldn't she be uneasy? He'd witnessed what had undoubtedly been a rather low moment for her, one that he'd driven her to, Maze take him. No doubt she was bracing herself for more censure, when he was the one who truly deserved it.

He had treated her callously, simply for surviving whatever vile magic had altered her. He had disrupted her life, failed to keep her safe, and then refused to address the ramifications. He'd proven that he wasn't worthy of her and that she'd been better off without him.

His magic rolled and surged inside him, an ocean battering at the walls of his body. Containing it and the urge to draw her into his arms took nearly all his willpower, for he sensed that she wouldn't want comfort from him right now.

"I'll just wait a few moments before sneaking out," she said in an abject whisper.

He shook his head. "What?"

"I believe one of the other guests will—"

"I'll feed you."

She turned, pulling herself in tight and looking at him with wonder. "But you said—"

"Forget what I said." He stepped closer. "Let me be the one to feed you."

Chapter Thirteen

Out of shock, Mikari didn't immediately respond, tense hope flaring in her chest.

"I vowed to bring you to Houfu alive," Jun said, with an aloofness that sounded forced. "That includes keeping you fed when there's no other option, which there isn't. The innkeeper will eject us if he catches you prowling about."

Prowling about? No other option? As though his intoxicating aroma weren't giving him away.

She knew he hadn't imbibed any alcohol that evening, but he gave off a heady scent that both comforted and roused, like warmed rice wine or a slow, deep kiss followed by the nibble of teeth.

He wanted her and yet hid his desire behind duty. Because he didn't *want* to want her.

The knowledge hit her with quiet devastation, shaming her more effectively than if he'd blamed her for her earlier assault. That he hadn't assigned any sort of blame didn't help much, as he was surely thinking it. Nor was she proud of the sick satisfaction she'd felt when Jun had punched the merchant.

Her heart squeezed painfully, and the air grew hot on her skin, spots appearing in her vision. She teetered, her face tingling.

Jun blurted her name as he darted forward to steady her. "Divine One's grace, you're as white as snow."

"I can't wait any longer," she slurred, lips numb.

"Very well," he said. "You can absorb energy through skin contact, right?" She gave what she hoped was a nod. "So, if I turn away and undress, and then take care of myself, would that work?"

Meaning they wouldn't look at each other, and she wouldn't be the one pleasuring him, merely clinging to his back. It was about as impersonal as a lust eater could get.

"Yes, that'll work." She wouldn't get much energy from the act, but she'd be walking out of the inn when the sun rose.

The imminent opportunity to feed granted her a second wind, but Jun made sure she would remain standing before turning around to remove his clothes, keeping his back to her. Her hunger instantly made itself known as a bloom of heat between her thighs and a galloping heartbeat.

As she started to undress, she was keenly aware of her fingers on her clothes, the rote act feeling unfamiliar. Even the wash of cool air on her legs as she stepped out of her split-skirt had her feeling strangely vulnerable.

Mere nerves, she told herself. She had to be careful, after all. And she was never more grateful that no one but her could see the mark of corruption on her stomach. Especially not Jun. She couldn't stand the thought of him staring at such glaring proof of her weakness.

Jun made a neat pile of his clothing, starting with his finely made pitch-black overshirt that subtly shimmered with a faint pattern. As he revealed greater detail of his impressive bulk, she concluded that she'd certainly have plenty of broad back to hold onto.

Hissing suddenly, he froze in the middle of shrugging off his wool undershirt, tensed as though he'd felt a twinge of pain.

From when he captured the bandits, she realized. The thought of him taking on six bandits quickly went from heroic to terrifying.

"You were hurt?" she asked, fighting off panic. "Why didn't you say anything?"

Still half-dressed, she clutched the dangling hem of her shirt and searched him with her gaze. But all she could see was an old, thin scar on the swath of chiseled skin he'd revealed, one that was new to her.

He resumed undressing and unveiled a mountain of well-defined muscle, including more old but new-to-her scars. There was nothing more recent than a fist-sized bruise on his left side, already yellowing.

"The bandit who unseated me this morning kindly threw me onto my bad shoulder," he said as he folded his undershirt. "It wasn't dislocated, so I'll be fine by morning. My magic will see to that."

Mikari remembered when he'd first hurt his shoulder, nearly a year before their magic had manifested—a fall from a ladder while he was replacing some broken tiles on the wardhouse roof. The joint became dislocated, and the priests did even more damage in their attempts to put it back. Recovery had taken weeks, and his shoulder hadn't been as strong since.

Only somewhat mollified, she picked at her shirt ties to loosen them. "Your magic heals you?"

His hands went to the cords of his split-skirt. "It passively enhances the body's natural healing process, but I haven't attempted to mend the damage with any sort of deliberate effort."

His split-skirt slipped down his legs, leaving him in a pair of form-fitting pants the likes of which she'd never seen before. The sturdy, thick material was high-quality black wool, and it hugged his muscular thighs and his wonderfully rounded arse. Court attire, perhaps?

"Why not?" she asked, nearly breathless with want as her shirt dropped to the floor. In her hand, she'd retained the small square of cloth that she habitually kept in her sleeve. "You did so well at mending my three-string."

"As I said, flesh isn't as easy." He moved to untie the waist-cord of his pants but paused. "I suppose I'm waiting until I feel more comfortable." Then he sat, legs crossed, gripping his knees.

She knew he was speaking of using magic to heal his shoulder, but she couldn't help noticing that he still wore the last of his clothing. Divine One's grace, was he feeling shy?

"That will come soon," she said, stepping away from her discarded undergarments. "It never took you long to become good at anything."

He tensed, sensing her, and drew in a deep breath as she knelt behind him, her fingers lighting upon his shoulders. She couldn't stimulate herself in any way, yet couldn't help risking a glimpse at his sexual desires.

He was picturing her loosely clothed in a gauzy, black dress and sensually writhing upon mussed bedding, one breast nearly visible. The man could turn his head if he wanted to see her chest, but he seemed determined not to.

The expression that her fantasy-self wore...she'd never seen such detail in the heads of any of her donors. Often, the person they imagined was someone else entirely, or they cared more about arranging her body into inviting positions.

But the Mikari in Jun's head had the right eyes, both in shape and color, and they were fever-bright with desire. Her mouth was open in a soundless moan, and she had all her freckles, which lay atop a lovely flush in both cheeks.

He'd thought of her so often—*her* and not some improved version of her—that she could look into his fantasies and marvel that she wasn't looking at a mirror.

"May I rub your shoulder?" she asked, fighting to keep her voice low and calm as she shifted closer, still only touching him with her fingers. "It might help you relax."

"I'm perfectly relaxed," he grumbled, even as the muscles beneath her fingers grew tighter. She couldn't help smiling in amusement. "Anyway, there's no need. In fact, perhaps we should stop talking and…"

"Get it over with?" she supplied. Jun grunted his assent. "You know that the point of this is to feel good, don't you?"

"The point is to keep you alive," he contended.

"There's no pleasure I can offer you?"

"I want nothing from you."

If that weren't such a blatant lie, she would've been offended. "Oh, but I can smell that you do."

She slid into place behind him and pressed her nakedness against his back. He let out a shuddering breath, fingers digging into his legs like claws.

His mind abandoned the image of her partially clothed and instead latched onto one where he turned to kiss her, snaking one arm around her waist to pull her into his lap.

Thankfully, he refrained from turning that fantasy into reality, tension pouring off him as he tugged at the knot of his drawcords.

She peered down the front of him at his lap, noting as she did so how muscular he was, and how much thicker his chest hair had become. His arousal strained the front of his pants, even after he'd loosened them. How she ached to run her hands down his sculpted flesh and rub him through the stretched black wool.

Feeling the direction of her stare, he covered himself with his hands. "What are you doing?" he asked, breaths quickening.

"I can't even watch?"

"You've seen it before," he said through clenched teeth.

Yes, and she had never lasted long enough for him to stroke himself for more than a minute. She had always lowered her mouth to him, or taken him in hand.

"But it's been so long." She touched her lips to his ear. "And even if it hadn't, I'd never grow tired of the sight."

The tension in him broke, and he sagged with a tight whimper. For a split-second, she wondered if he had come already, but then an odd sensation slid through her middle—distant pressure, as if someone were grasping a limb of hers that had grown numb. She pulled in a sharp breath and held it.

His magic was touching her, which she wouldn't have immediately known had she not felt something similar a day ago when Kie had examined her. Only instead of gentle prodding, Jun's magic explored with hard, rapacious strokes. The sensation was...disorienting.

"Oh, Mikari," he softly lamented, tilting his head back.

His eyes were closed, and his throat jumped as he swallowed. Movement drew her gaze downward in time for her to watch him open the front of his pants. His loincloth was straining to contain him, the linen pulled so thin it could not conceal his skin tone beneath, including the flushed head of his cock. Her mouth began to water.

"You remember that night, don't you?" he rasped. "Our last night together."

The images coming from him blurred together, but they were of a frenzied coupling that she'd recalled thousands of times—Jun, snatching her into his arms and bearing her down to lie upon his spread coat. A blissfully cool breeze and the knelling of wind bells. Hot breaths and open mouths. Hands grasping at flesh, shoving clothing away. Their magics, newly manifested, melding with matching desire, drawing gasps and moans. Then connection. Heat. Euphoria. Mikari swore their souls had touched. Her memory of that night still made her squirm with desire.

But it had been an illusion. A false high. A prelude to addiction and destruction. The inquisitor had told her so.

"Of course," she murmured. "Although I try not to."

"It hurts to remember," he said, spoken like a foregone conclusion. Spoken as though he felt the same. She wondered, not for the first time, whether he'd shared such bliss with other crow women in the years since. No doubt he had.

"Yes," she gulped, pain squeezing her heart. She drew a slow breath, but with his warm body against hers and his magic clutching at the numb place inside her, she wasn't able to reclaim much composure.

He turned his head slightly. "Do you regret it?"

Pressing her body closer, she tucked her face into the bend of his neck. "I could never regret it," she confessed in a bare whisper, certain that if she licked the pulse rapidly ticking in his throat that he would even taste like rice wine. "I could never regret any of our time together."

He groaned her name, shifting subtly as he stroked himself. She brushed her lips against his throat and inhaled his fragrance. Her tongue snuck out, stealing a taste of his skin, and he began making low sounds in his throat that were achingly familiar. They weren't full moans, but rather more like tight breaths that brushed his vocal cords.

As wards, each attempt to see each other had been a risk, so Mikari had usually been alone at night, and she had pleasured herself most often to the thought of Jun's soft, restrained groans. She had wondered countless times what he would sound like if they hadn't both had to be very quiet, lest their cries carry out of the maze.

Pulling away from the warm bend of his neck, she opened her eyes and craned her neck forward. Oh, sweet Garden. To think that so much hard flesh had ever been fully sheathed inside her, or that she'd ever wrapped her lips around his thick stalk. Yes, his cock appeared to be an average size compared to his hand, but only an idiot would fail to notice how enormous his hands were.

He was imagining her tucked into the well of his lap, legs wrapped around him. As wards, they had tried the position more than once, but with clothing in the way.

Divine One's grace, she was much too aroused. Jun was too tempting, his fantasies too affecting, her hunger too great. She was in danger of slowly sliding into an orgasm without even brushing the small peak throbbing between her legs. She had to feed now and then get away from him.

"Please, Jun," she softly begged. "Let me touch you."

"Yes, lamb," he whispered, his term of endearment for her emerging so unexpectedly and so poignantly it stalled her breath a moment.

She shifted toward his right side so she could reach around him, heart pounding with as much desire as distress. She expected him to let her take over, but instead he covered her hand with his to make her stroke him exactly the way he wanted.

Maze take her, his flesh was as hard as silk-wrapped steel and wet with arousal. It slipped easily through the tight grip he kept on her hand.

The urgent motion of his fist made her head spin. That and the semblance of control he had over her, even though she wanted to be touching him. His magic, meanwhile, grabbed at the numbness inside her as if through many layers of bedding. There was no satisfaction or pleasure, only frustrating pressure.

His fantasy shifted, and the Mikari in his mind put her hands back, displaying her breasts as she took him deep.

In response, she adjusted the angle and roll of their stroking hands, a needy moan slipping out of her.

The air in his lungs left in a rush, and his free hand reached back to grip her bare thigh, holding her leg tight to his flank. His groans grew louder and rougher. Vaguely, she worried he was making too much noise, but the consequences seemed so trivial compared to her delight at hearing his pleasure.

His hand on hers made three hard pulls, his body drawing as taut as a lute string. She groped for the square of cloth next to her knee.

"M-maze take me, I—I'm—" he gasped. She put the cloth into his hand, and he took it without hesitation.

He came the second he had it in place, grunting in harsh, heavy sighs as pleasure rolled over him, voice hitting a higher register than his usual rumble. She clutched him close, so affected by the sound she nearly fell headlong into a lust eater's frenzy.

"Oh!"

An unexpected pulse of energy hit her like a cushioned blow, making the numbness in her core twitch. She had never fed from a mature, uncleansed crow; apparently, their energy came all at once.

His hold on her hand went slack, and she hastily pulled away, scooting out of his reach, or rather putting him out of *her* reach, lest she crawl into his lap and make his fantasy a reality.

She had never eaten so well on so little. She had been hoping for a day's worth of energy, but a mere nibble of his orgasm had given her several days' worth. Was it because of his magic?

She watched, still shaking with desire, as he cleaned himself up and righted his clothing. Loath to do the same when her skin felt so hot and itchy, she was slow to reach for her undergarments.

"I assume you got what..." He twisted to look at her. "What in Oblivion is that?" he asked in a harsh whisper, eyes flashing.

Mikari froze. He was pointing at her, brows pinched at an incredulous angle. But he couldn't possibly be seeing what no one else had ever been able to see—the first person in twenty years to learn that she bore an indelible mark from her corruption.

But Jun did see it. Indeed, he was glaring at the black scarring as though he might start shouting.

IF THERE HAD BEEN anything left of Jun's composure after feeding Mikari his best crudding orgasm in decades, even without a metaphysical climax, then deceit such as this destroyed it.

Not that his magic hadn't participated, regardless of what he wanted. Overpowering his will at last, it had reached out to a lover for the first time since his youth, since her. And he had sensed precisely what Kie had described—an inert, unresponsive mass where Mikari's magic should be.

He'd heard enough talk at court to know that many crows' metaphysical organs could also show signs of sexual frustration, resulting in breathtaking pain, like being cut open.

But instead of clawing dissatisfaction, his magic had freely given up a pulse of energy and then quietly settled, leaving him so confused he couldn't even begin to understand why he was shaking. Anger? Afterglow?

Or was it self-loathing, after spending his pleasure into a towel while wishing mournfully to be pressed deep within Mikari's cove?

"I said, what in Oblivion is that?" he repeated, turning fully. He pointed again at the most complex magical array he'd ever seen, which stretched from the underside of her breasts to the edge of her pubic hair.

She sought to cover herself rather than explain, cringing with shock as though she hadn't been keeping this secret from him, and he lunged to grab her ankle before she could retreat. Deaf to her yelp of surprise, he dragged her toward him and bore her down with his hands on her arms while angling her to take full advantage of the lantern light.

Divine One's crudding arse! Here was undeniable proof that her magic hadn't corrupted her. He couldn't read much of the Mahou that inscribed the three main rings, but the array's staggering complexity alone was confirmation that her transformation had been neither an accident nor a reckless experiment. The possibility was beyond belief.

He'd barely begun to study the array's three activation nodes when she released half a sob, the heartrending sound penetrating the fog of anger in his mind. He looked up to find her pressing her lush lips together, something like despair glistening in her eyes, and his anger dissipated.

"Y-you can see it? But how?" she croaked. He wiped away a tear sliding down her temple and cupped her cheek. "How, when no one else has?"

"No one has ever seen this? Never commented on it?" She shook her head. "Do you know what this is?"

Grimacing, she nodded. "The inquisitor—h-he warned me that my sexual appetite was unnatural, that my magic was using it against me." Her voice was choked with shame. "He tried to help me purge it, but I was too weak to its temptations. Now it owns me, so I am marked by my corruption."

"Oh, my lamb," he breathed, stroking her wet cheek.

All this time, some part of her must not have been able to dismiss the lie told throughout Gozu that having magic led to moral decay and an eternity in the Maze. That one must shun the temptations of its power, and purge it.

No wonder she'd wanted to be cleansed. She had actually believed her magic would corrupt her, even after—and maybe even because of—the bliss they'd shared. And the inquisitor had only given her "proof" that the priests had been right.

"Magic can sometimes create marks," he said, splaying his other hand over her middle. "But this? Someone put this here."

He returned his attention to the array and its three major keywords, one for each node. Although he could write a couple hundred words of Mahou and understand another hundred more, even if he couldn't pronounce them, only a small fraction of its thousands of symbols had been recovered and translated. Thus, he couldn't begin to comprehend the array's purpose.

He brushed his fingers over the outermost node, which sat just below her sternum. "This keyword means *press*, I'm sure of it." Could it also mean *suppress*? "And this one..." He framed the second node between his thumb and forefinger. "The first character here means *move*, but I don't fully recognize the second one."

"The inquisitor put this mark on me?" she asked in a shaky whisper. "He made me what I am, knowingly?"

Jun nodded gravely. "If we want to start understanding why, we'll have to show this to Empress Shumei."

If anyone could decipher the array's function, it would be the empress. The whole court knew that she deliberately obscured what she was capable of, but that the Divine One had granted her the most magical knowledge by far. Not even Vallen and Rosuke's abilities came close, despite being members of the original Dark Court, for they had lost much of their vocabulary over the centuries of their curse.

Jun couldn't read the keyword in the array's third node, but he did recognize something in the line of Mahou written along the innermost ring—a word that referred directly to a crow's magic.

He stroked his thumb across the mysterious third keyword, scanning its parts for meaning. Mikari softly gasped, flexing beneath his touch.

His awareness opened up, reminding him that she was naked beneath him. He had ended up straddling one of her legs, while her other knee rested lightly against his thigh.

Mikari stared silently at him, one knuckle pressed to her mouth in exquisite coyness, her arm held close to her body, pushing one of her full breasts a little higher.

Sweet Garden, she was still perfect. Every curve, every slope, every freckle seemed designed to be kissed and stroked. She wasn't overly lean, but rather soft at every point where he might like to touch and rearrange her for their mutual pleasure. Her hips were especially generous, molded for his grip.

Loath to remove his hand from her flushed cheek, he let his other hand on her stomach wander to the bend of her waist, drawing from her another audible breath.

"I s-should get dressed," she said, voice growing stronger. "And you should get some sleep."

Indeed, he should sleep. He should take his hands off her and let her sit up to clothe herself. But after the climax he'd had, not reciprocating seemed like heresy. Leaving her un-worshipped was irreverent. He knew how deeply she felt pleasure. Mikari was, from skin to soul, made for ecstasy.

But that had been before her curse. Before the inquisitor had turned all pleasure against her while also enslaving her to it. And Jun couldn't ignore the way she'd retreated from him after he'd fed her, as though eager to put space between them.

And though he now knew that she had been far more scared of her magical maturity than any oppression they might've faced together in the outside world, that realization did nothing to close the gap between them. Their circumstances hadn't changed.

"I don't think a conversation with the capital can wait," he said as he drew back, studiously avoiding any other glimpses of her nudity. His loins were already burning for her again. "You should be prepared to show them the markings on your stomach."

He turned away to dress himself, more careful this time of the soreness in his shoulder as he put his arm through the sleeve of his undershirt. "I promise they'll be respectful."

Mikari made an amused sound, clothes rustling as she dressed. "You assume I have any modesty left."

"Of course, you do," he insisted. "It's only marginally less arousing than your brazenness, which is why my cock isn't hard at absolutely all times." What point was there in denying it anymore?

She let out a soft burst of laughter. "Speaking of brazen," she said in an aside. "Believe me, I took your concern as a compliment."

The room was entirely too warm, but Jun clothed himself in two of his layers. He confirmed Mikari was decent and then took out his speaking mirror to activate it.

Luckily, the mirror attendant was still awake and appeared to be writing. She responded to the tingle of his mirror's twin and left immediately to fetch at least Commander Rosuke if not the empress and her consort as well. Jun arranged the mirror upon a shelf to allow Mikari, sitting at arm's length from him, to see as well.

All three of those summoned arrived within a moment of each other. The empress was wrapped in a deep-red dressing robe, hair loosely pulled back and unadorned. Vallen and Rosuke were likewise dressed for bed, although Rosuke looked rather flushed.

Jun didn't have to guess why. The man's joining mark had appeared, a band of red in a honeycomb pattern, and Jun had heard that the location of one's joining mark became an intensely erogenous zone. Rosuke and Mai had undoubtedly been discovering how intense.

Jun quickly relayed his news about Futakata Pass, the bandits who had accosted them, the means of their escape, and the mysterious markings that had resulted from Mikari's so-called cleansing, which no one before him had ever seen besides her.

Thankfully, no one asked how he had found the markings, although they probably didn't need to. He didn't need a working mirror to know that he looked as though he'd run a race.

"The pass closing is damned inconvenient," Vallen muttered.

"An inconvenience we foresaw, at least," the empress pointed out. "Mikari and the commander may not be able to come to us, but we can still examine the markings through the mirror, assuming they're visible to us and Mikari agrees—"

"Very well," Mikari said, tugging at the ties of her shirt. The empress murmured a small oh, and Jun readied himself not to look.

But he did anyway, glancing at her askance. A bleached strip of hemp was wrapped snugly around her breasts, supporting them and preserving her modesty...which she did have. He tried to remember that as she pushed down the waist of her split-skirt nearly to her pubic bone and then put her hands back to fully display her markings.

"Indeed, I see it," Vallen said. All three of Mikari's examiners leaned closer to their mirror, their eyes narrowing in concentration. Rosuke blew out a slow breath as though awestruck, and the empress quietly asked someone for paper and a writing brush.

The empress spoke as the mirror attendant set out writing supplies for her. "Mikari, has any magic user before Jun had a chance to see these markings on you?"

"No, I've never fed from an uncleansed crow."

Until now. Jun shouldn't feel pleased, but he did.

AT THE MAZE'S CENTER

"Jun, could you...will you bring 'us' closer? Your mirror, that is?" the empress requested. Jun moved to obey, picking up the mirror by its small handle. He put himself before Mikari in as stable and comfortable a position as possible to keep it steady in his hand.

"One thing is for certain," the empress announced after a moment of silence. "This pattern was not handed down by the Divine One."

"Do you know what it does?" Mikari asked, brow tense.

"Yes. But I want to stress that I may not yet understand all its nuances, and I can only speculate as to what the inquisitor had in mind when he placed it on you."

Vallen's voice emerged from the mirror. "All I can tell is that this did not turn you into a lust eater. That circle was likely drawn on the floor around the altar during your cleansing, hidden beneath the rugs."

"Divine One have mercy, this is complex," Rosuke muttered. "Who could have crafted this? Do you see that secondary pattern there?"

"Please just tell us what it does," Jun said tersely.

"Firstly, it suppresses her magic," the empress answered. "Not smother, not cut out, but suppress. As in 'put to sleep.'"

Mikari and Jun's gazes crashed together.

"Firstly?" Jun echoed.

"My magic isn't dead?" Mikari asked.

"No, it's not," the empress confirmed, "and that's because the rest of the array deals with harvesting your magic—transplanting it—either upon your death or upon reciting an invocation."

Mikari held his gaze, the shock on her face sinking into dread as her mouth silently formed the word *harvest*.

"And if the invocation is used," the empress continued, voice heavy with regret, "it will kill her."

Jun's stomach dropped to the floor. Mikari closed her eyes, lips held tight.

"But you can cure her, right?" he urgently asked, turning the mirror to see the empress. "You can remove this curse?"

"In the spring, when she can travel here, it's quite possible. But I have a feeling spring won't be soon enough."

The empress had a feeling. He hated it when she said that. "Is there a way to teach me whatever magics are necessary to cure her myself?"

"We'll certainly investigate that, but Jun, you may not be strong enough to employ them."

Jun gnashed his teeth, realizing she could very well be right. Crow women were nearly always stronger with magic. Vallen and Rosuke were lucky to have been cured by the empress personally, for she was the strongest magic user alive.

"Kie," Jun blurted. "And Seita. We could try to catch up with them. Kie might have the strength for a cure."

"She might," the empress hedged. "But she might not wish to. The ritual we know of is…quite intimate." Even through the mirror, Jun could see the empress's flush of color. Vallen and Rosuke exchanged an enigmatic glance.

"Can we not combine our efforts? I've heard of many spells that can be powered by multiple crows."

"I certainly hope that will be the case," the empress said. "In the meantime…"

Jun's mind raced ahead. If time was running out, it meant that Mikari was still in danger, even in his care. They had to find the means of curing her as soon as possible. And they had just one path forward.

"In the meantime, we need to find this inquisitor," Jun said.

Rosuke made a pensive sound. "Assuming he's still alive."

"I'm certain he is," the empress said. Jun put the mirror back on the shelf and noted that Mikari was dressed again. "No doubt he meant to mark Mikari for later harvest, and cursed her to eat lust so that he had all the time he needed before invoking the array."

"Time for what, I wonder," Vallen mused.

"He can't have done this only to Mikari," Jun inferred. "Even before he marked her, he had been around for years. He must have been cursing crows and then setting them loose. Perhaps he wants to harvest all of them at the same time."

"Oh, Divine One's grace," the empress said, paling, breathless with shock.

"Wait, what would that accomplish?" Rosuke asked.

The empress swallowed, looking nauseated. "He would need a lot of magic all at once in order to seize godhood."

Chapter Fourteen

Mikari heard none of the ensuing discussion, as energetic as it sounded, all of it coming from the three in the mirror. The air in the room felt too close, too heavy. She stared at her lap, hands shaking with the need to claw at the markings on her abdomen. Divine One have mercy, she had been branded like livestock for slaughter.

Never had she hated magic as much as she did at that moment. It had only ever given her one beautiful night in her first nineteen years, and since then, she had been surviving on a half-life. Now it seemed she would soon lose that as well.

"Mikari." Jun's hands engulfed hers, his gentle touch softening her tightly held fingers.

The rich fragrance that floated from him evoked the memory of that fateful night when she had snuck away from her parents' farm to see the village's flower festival. The aroma of sweet dumplings and wood smoke had filled the cool, wet late-spring air. To her, it had been the scent of welcome, of freedom.

Even if she'd known that she'd be caught and questioned by the villagers, she still wouldn't have been able to resist going.

"I wish I had turned left," she whispered.

Jun stroked his thumb across the back of her wrist. "Left? When?"

"Days ago. I was deciding whether to go to Tetsutani or Koichino. I intended to turn left, but instead I went right." She lifted her eyes and met his concerned gaze. "If I had gone left, we likely wouldn't have run into each other, and I wouldn't know any of this. I wish I didn't. Before, I was at least content."

"That's a lie, Mikari. I didn't see it at first, but you were never content." He cupped her face in his warm hands, and she realized how cold she was. "And even if you did truly accept your life, I'm glad you turned right. Because now, together, we're going to find the bastard who did this, free you of his curse, and then kill him."

Together. We. "But I...I'll need to feed again, and soon," she reminded him.

"I'll feed you." He pulled her face closer, no hesitation in his voice. Thrilled at the immediacy of his response, she reached out to curl her fingers into the rich material of his shirt and drew a full breath for the first time in many minutes. *Oh, if only!*

"Feeding me is tiring, especially over time."

"I feel fine."

"You won't after a while."

He shrugged. "A problem for the future." Again, no hesitation. She had already shed a few tears and didn't plan on losing any more, but it was damned hard to hold them back. It was even harder not to kiss him, especially when the direction of Jun's hot stare told her he wanted the same.

Oh, how would she resist him? Hoping that she would be free of her curse before it killed him was tempting fate yet again. And even if she managed not to drain him before he cured her, fate could still punish her. Jun might leave her again, which he almost certainly would if he ever learned what she'd done to that poor, nameless man the day she'd been cursed.

She wanted this chance to save herself, despite knowing better, but there was no way Jun would let her go off on her own. They would be traveling together for an indefinite period of time, and he'd insist on feeding her every time she needed him.

Could she harden herself to the heat in his eyes? Could she push him away once he grew too weak, though the freedom she felt with him was all she'd ever wanted?

Could she see this through and come out mostly whole on the other side, even if she ended up alone? She dreaded the answer, even while hoping that this time, fate would be kind.

Please, let fate be kind.

"She's right to worry," came another voice. The high general. Vallen, she believed his name was. "But not for the reason you might think."

Jun, having seemingly forgotten they had an audience, seized up with obvious discomfort. His warm hands left her cheeks, but they didn't go far, landing instead on her shoulders.

He turned to the mirror, keeping one hand on her. "And what's that?"

Rosuke was the one who responded. "Your magical stamina will start to suffer before your body does. By the time you face the inquisitor, you might not be able to channel much."

"Wouldn't that take months?" the empress asked.

"I'd like to think so, but Mikari is a different kind of lust eater—more powerful, I suspect," Rosuke said. "Anyway, if Jun wants the chance to cure her, he'll need all of his stamina."

"He'll at least have a few weeks, won't he? Vallen fed from me for a while before you were both cured, and I only felt a little fatigued at the end."

Vallen what?

Her consort snorted. "Your stamina was enormous by then, and yet you still slept nearly eighteen hours after a…vigorous session."

"H-he fed from the empress?" Mikari asked.

Jun seemed just as thunderstruck as she was. "That was your curse? How you lived so long?" There was anger in his voice—and shock. "You were lust eaters?"

Mikari gasped, seeing them anew.

"We were," Rosuke soberly replied. "However, the ritual used on us wasn't the one that made Mikari. She's different. We don't believe the same cure will work for her."

No wonder the empress was willing to rehabilitate creatures like her. Or even knew it was possible. She had fallen in love with one of them.

"Why didn't you tell me?" Jun asked, still upset.

"Can you not imagine the reason?" the empress asked in return. "Were it widely known that two former demons hold high ranks in the Dark Court—regardless of whether they've proven their loyalty and their honor—people will think they're right to beware all crows. And whatever chance we may have of pressuring the Keeper to abolish the ward system will vanish."

Jun's voice became thin. "Did you kill?" Mikari froze at his question, even though it was directed at the mirror.

Vallen shook his head.

"Once," Rosuke admitted, rigid with discomfort. "The night I was cursed. The hunger was so powerful, I couldn't even think to resist it. I couldn't think at all."

But I could, Mikari thought, guilt crushing her. She couldn't bear to watch Jun's reaction, convinced he was horrified.

"Once you locate this inquisitor," the empress then said, "you should look for a book or a scroll, perhaps several. With luck, you'll find your exact cure."

Mikari had a flash of memory. "I-I might've seen it. In the offering room. There was a prayer book by the altar, but not one of the temple's. It had butterfly-type binding, and the cover looked like obsidian." Mikari had only seen the hand-sized book for a couple of seconds and had assumed it contained the prayers the inquisitor would use to cleanse her.

"That has to be it," the empress said. "Reach out to us as soon as you find it, the moment you're safe."

"We will, Your Imperial Grace," Jun promised, calmer now as he gently squeezed Mikari's nape in silent reassurance.

The warm weight of his hand was a guilty pleasure as it drifted down her spine, its heat penetrating the thick wool of her shirt, tricking her into thinking his palm spanned her entire back. She fought the urge to arch like a cat and wondered if he even realized he was stroking her.

"The array itself is too complicated to copy accurately through the mirror, but I've written down the Mahou it contains. We'll send word if we discover anything."

"Understood," he said. Then he turned his head to Mikari, a gentle smile on his lips. "Still wish you had turned left?"

Mikari gave a small laugh in spite of herself. Jun couldn't know what he was getting into by letting her feed exclusively from him. Truth be told, Mikari wasn't entirely sure, either. She'd never fed from a fully mature magic user before. Would he last longer than a handful of feedings?

Her hunger ached to know, and she was already showing a concerning lack of restraint by not shunning his touch.

"What made you change your mind about going to Koichino?" he asked. At last, he took his hand from the small of her back.

Mikari recalled the creepy sensation that had put her off her intended destination, and her nape began to itch. She rubbed her hand there.

"It was simply a bad feeling." Mostly the truth, albeit a version that did not make her sound quite so paranoid.

She certainly had cause for concern. Powerful magics had been worked upon her, and the empress worried the inquisitor would soon put some sort of plan into devastating action. But what could any of them do about a tickle on her neck?

"There's something else you should know," Rosuke said. "We received a report from Seita and Kie's group earlier this evening. Someone discovered a body on the road to Tetsutani and brought it to Koichino. Kie is fairly certain it's the scout who was supposed to meet you."

"Sweet Garden," Jun muttered. "Was it bandits? Temple loyalists?"

"Could be either. Anyway, the delegation can't be much more than a day ahead of you."

Vallen spoke next. "We will, of course, inform them to be wary of the inquisitor and his servants. With luck, and Natsu's silver tongue, they'll be allowed to meet several Primaries while on their way to the Keeper's temple, and they might be able to extract some information. But they told us they've already had difficulties."

"Gozuan hospitality?" Jun asked without inflection.

"A temple loyalist learned of the delegation and sought them out at the market in Koichino. The man made several harsh comments, then a fight broke out."

"Everyone is all right," the empress quickly added. "Seita employed sleep magic, which quickly ended things. Luckily, it can also soothe strong emotions. Natsu managed a calmer conversation with the man after he woke."

Mikari wasn't surprised to hear that they'd encountered hostility. "Am I right in assuming you already know of some potential local allies who can persuade the temples? Or at least pressure the more practical of the priests?"

"Only a couple," Rosuke admitted with a shake of his head. "Our scouts were told to avoid unwanted attention, and if they had started asking questions about loyalties..."

"Then perhaps I can help," she offered. "I know a lot of people. A few are quite powerful, and a couple of them even like me."

The trio in the mirror looked at each other thoughtfully.

"Mikari and I should rejoin the delegation, at least for now," Jun said, returning his hand to her lower back. She held her breath. "If we want to track down the inquisitor, we must learn which temples he visits to find victims, meaning we should head to the nearest temple first. I assume that's also where the delegation is heading, and if Mikari is with them, she can help smooth their way. I, for one, don't think I could've secured lodgings these last two nights without her winning over the innkeeper. And she can introduce Natsu to more of the right people."

Mikari fought a grin and settled for a small smile. Though she was ecstatic to hear him recognize her strengths, hearing him describe their fake marriage as *winning someone over* nearly had her giggling. Despite his gold heart, life as a temple ward had made Jun into a rather good liar, and a good lie always contained a kernel of truth.

The empress hummed pensively. "It's a good plan for now. Another couple of days might change things again, especially with that other lust eater still at liberty, but you'll have to travel north anyway." Rosuke and Vallen nodded in agreement.

Not much was said after that. Jun and the empress had a brief exchange that Mikari didn't understand, about maintaining a "detection" spell. Then the meeting ended, and he packed away the mirror.

All that was left was for Jun to get whatever sleep he could. Come the dawn, they would start catching up to the delegation, which would be waiting for them in Tetsutani.

Mikari was glad, for once, that the creature she had become didn't sleep. After the revelations of the past hour, she wasn't sure she'd have been able to get any rest even if she still had the capability.

Jun snuck out of the room, saying only that he'd return quickly. She assumed he was relieving himself. While he was gone, she readied the room's bedding for him, unfolding the thick mattress and neatly laying the fresh-smelling comforter upon it.

At least the innkeeper was capable of providing comfortable amenities, if not palatable food. Mikari hadn't needed to taste the man's consistently ruined meals to know they were hardly fit for human consumption.

Perhaps before she and Jun left in the morning, she should track down the kind brownie woman whose letter she had promised to deliver and obtain for Jun a better-cooked breakfast than what he'd been given the previous morning.

Jun returned, his beard glistening in the lantern light, indicating he'd found a way to wash up. Mikari, sitting cross-legged, had taken up her usual position by the long, thin window common to most buildings in Gozu. Even a small village like Okususo kept a couple of shielded lanterns burning overnight, and their light would let her watch the wind play with the snowdrifts.

Jun glanced at the readied bedding and began removing the outer layer of his clothes. "What will you do while I sleep? Or rather, what do you usually do?"

"In my head, I review the catalog of songs and poems any bard should know. Sometimes I practice my lute—softly. Sometimes my things need mending."

"I can't imagine that always fills the hours."

"Not really, no."

Now in his undershirt and closely tailored pants, he was looking at her as though waiting for her to elaborate, but she certainly wasn't about to tell him of the countless hours she'd spent remembering him, yearning for him, and knowing that every day that passed pushed him further away from her.

She changed the subject. "I noticed that Commander Rosuke now has a tattoo on his neck like the others, although his doesn't match theirs. Does it have something to do with the court?"

Jun paused in the middle of untying the two halves of his undershirt and stared at her with the most inscrutable expression. "It's a joining mark. Magic users who wish to be metaphysically linked complete a joining ceremony. The link lasts until death, and not long after the ceremony, identical marks will manifest, often around the neck, which indicates couples in a love match."

"Then it's a symbol of their union? Their love?" she asked, both fascinated and intensely jealous.

"It's like a wedding ring, only you can't remove it. Magical joinings are deeper than that. Unbreakable. There's no such thing as divorce when it comes to joined crows."

"I see," she said, half-wishing she hadn't asked. She'd obsess over it all night. "Well, feel free to douse the lantern. I'll not need any light. There's a sleeping robe in that cabinet." She pointed at the correct one.

His gaze followed the direction of her finger, but his feet didn't move and he shifted nervously.

"Are you worried I'll pounce if I see you naked?" she asked with a sly smile. "Should I promise not to look? Or would you rather I wait in the hall?"

There it was again, a heady whiff of the flower festival. As smoky-sweet as the dark-caramel fragrance he often exuded, but more complex, with faint notes of budding fruit trees and the dizzying singe of alcohol.

His voice emerged, soft but deep. "You could do more than look." He lifted his gaze, pinning her with a molten stare.

Maze take me. The invitation, paired with his scent, was overwhelmingly stirring. In the space of a single breath, heat and wetness rushed to the crux of her legs, the rest of her tingling. Her nipples pebbled so quickly they smarted.

Alarmed, she pressed her shoulder tight to the wall by the window, the smile fading from her lips as she broke eye contact.

"No need. Good night, Jun." Amazed that she'd kept her voice even, she stared out the window and tried to appear disinterested as though she weren't more tempted by his offer than he could ever comprehend.

The room became chilly, the air thin. Gone was the flower festival. In its place, the odor of lingering smoke. A few tense breaths passed before she heard sharp motions behind her as he changed into his sleeping robe. She'd never focused so hard on her reflection.

The lantern was still glowing when he slid into bed, and she gasped when the light went out despite Jun being well out of reach.

He had to have done it with magic, she realized. She almost made a comment but held her tongue, for if Jun meant to feed her over the next few days and weeks, he would need all the sleep he could get.

AT THE MAZE'S CENTER

"HELP! HELP ME! JUN!"

Mikari was calling for him, weeping, begging, scared for her life. He strained to hear the direction of her voice, but her pleas echoed. Should he turn the corner, or go back the way he'd come?

Not that it would make a difference. He never found her any faster, despite how desperately he searched night after night. When it came to her, he wasn't capable of anything less.

"Help me! Please help me!"

He turned the corner, snow falling so thick and blowing about with such force that he could hardly see ten feet ahead. He'd fallen more than once, battered by the shearing wind until he was stumbling on half-frozen legs through knee-deep snow.

"Jun!"

Only when it was too late—when her pleading became tortured shrieks—would the snowstorm finally end, the sky clearing to reveal a full moon the color of blood.

But not yet.

I hear you, Mikari. I'm coming!

His extremities were stiff with cold, and his lungs burned in the frigid air. Howling gusts of wind blasted him with specks of ice and snow.

"Jun? Wake up, you're dreaming," whispered a familiar voice. He felt an unexpected spot of warmth on his chest. Another on his cheek. They slowly moved in a gentle caress.

The snowy maze quickly faded, but his panic did not. Panting, he opened his eyes to darkness, barely able to discern the vague outline of someone leaning over him.

He became aware of a hand rubbing soothing circles upon his bare chest, of heat and sweat coating the back of his neck, and the fistfuls of bedding clenched in his fingers.

The whisper returned. "There you are. You're safe."

"Mikari?" he croaked, his throat on fire.

She hummed an affirmative, her cool fingers stroking the side of his face. "You were having a bad dream."

Jun might have expected humiliation to wash over him, but he was too relieved. Unlike all the other nights when he'd woken from his nightmare, he wasn't alone. This time, she was here.

Reaching out, he slid his arms around her waist. She came willingly into his embrace, half-lying upon him, her chest and heartbeat pressed to his head. He listened to that steady sound and the air moving through her lungs.

"Do you want to talk about it?" she asked, combing her fingers through his hair. The sensation sent goosebumps down his body.

"It was a nightmare, that's all."

"I thought I heard my name."

He winced. "I didn't know I'd spoken."

"You don't have to tell me about it if you don't want to. I just hope I wasn't the villain of your dream."

He held her tighter. "No, no. I'm always trying to save you."

Her hand stilled. "Always?"

A foul curse crossed his mind. His tongue was unable to form any further response.

She pushed up, putting space between them while still in his hold. "How long have you been having nightmares?"

He wanted to lie. He wanted to appear stronger to her. But he couldn't hide this from her, not even in the darkness. Not when she was the person whom he'd wanted the most whenever he woke with terror.

"A very long time." Decades, in fact. "But they're worse lately."

"Since finding me?" she asked, hesitant.

"No." He took a constricted breath. "Ever since Oblivion."

"S— Oh, Jun." She pressed herself against him, gripping his shoulders. He felt the warm spill of her breath on his chin and banded her closer.

"I was honored to be chosen for her mission. I still am."

"You really went there? *How?*"

"A portal, opened with magic. No...not a portal," he added, voice hollow. "A maw."

"A-and the Damned One? Did you...?"

"I was not there. Only the empress and another crow woman. Rosuke's wife, now."

"What was it like?" she asked, awed.

"My first impression was of how thin and dry the air was. And it was so still. There was no wind. The moon overhead shone red, and it never moved." He swallowed, thinking of what the moonlight had first illuminated. He would not talk about that, nor the everlasting horror of what he'd seen in the sky the moment the Damned One had died.

"Is that what you dream of? That place?"

"It's where I end up. And there's a tree," he said. "Something we encountered, a plant-like demon. Most of us didn't see it, but it...it put a vision in my head. To lure me to it."

"Lure you?" She paused. "You mean kill you."

"Yes. That vision is what haunts me. Every night, it's you I hear, calling for my help. I search for you, and I do find you. But I can never stop the tree from killing you."

Somehow, it was the same *runtida* tree that lived at the center of Nansen's maze—a lofty specimen with a wide crown of pendulous stalks of leaves, hence its name, which in Gozuan meant "crown."

Even though the tree of his nightmare was bare of leaves, "fruit" hung from its branches—round flesh-colored objects with human faces that whimpered and screamed, the souls of previous victims whom the tree had smothered, crushed, and eaten like fertilizer.

Jun had not seen the weeping willow of Oblivion with his own eyes, but in its mental projection to him, it had known to take the form of the *runtida* tree.

And every night, it ate Mikari.

Whenever he reached the maze's center, he'd find her buried up to her chest in the tree's roots, clawing desperately at the ground. He always rushed forward—no weapons and no plan of attack, his only goal to grab however much of her he could and pull her free.

But the tree would never let him have her. A second before he could touch her, she would give one final scream as it snatched her into its root system. Then she would fall silent forever.

"Oh, Jun." Mikari molded herself to him, her cheek against his, her lips by his ear. "I'm here. I'm safe." She pressed a pair of kisses to his temple, her softness laying so comfortably over him. "I'm safe, and I'm not going anywhere." A puff of air passed over his ear, and he could hear the smile in her voice when she said, "Even though I should."

"Do that again," he said in a bare whisper.

Her grip on his shoulders loosened, then firmed again. He felt her head turn slightly.

"This?" She kissed his cheek at the top edge of his beard, lips clinging to his skin. It sent a tingle down his neck, one that got more than just his magic's attention.

He clenched his teeth. "Yes, that. Keep going."

Her weight upon him shifted, becoming heavier where her forearms were braced against his chest, giving him an unexpected thrill. She pressed more kisses to his face, a slow, sweet trail from one cheek to the other and across his forehead.

Unthinking, he allowed his magic to touch hers, and it did so with hard strokes, as if striving to penetrate her magic's torpor. She stiffened against him, a small sound of distress escaping, and her weight began shifting away.

"Don't stop," he said in a rush, clutching her closer. "I know you're still hungry."

Another puff of air, but this time her voice was sad. "I'm always hungry."

He sent one hand down her back and palmed her thigh, noting the way she arched and the soft sound of pleasure she made. And yet she shifted her legs out of reach.

His throat tightened, but he managed a plea. "Mikari."

"First, let me ask…are you sure?"

"Yes, I'm sure," he growled, lifting his head. He found her mouth with his lips, but she turned her face to avoid a kiss. The rejection was like a sharp jab to his chest.

"Mikari, why—?"

"It can't be like before. You need to give me full control."

Full control? But he'd already kissed her. Maze take it, he'd already fed her once.

"I don't understand," he said.

"I'll take no pleasure. Only give it."

"Kissing you gives me pleasure." He bent one leg, planted his foot, and pulled her over him, bringing the soft press of her abdomen against his eager arousal. "I want to taste you and touch you. I want to hear you moan, lamb."

She gave a choked sigh as she rolled her lower body off him. "I-imagine that, if you wish. But I don't want such attentions. I only want to feed."

"You wish me to lie here unmoving?" he asked, voice hardening. He still didn't understand. Why wouldn't she want to feel any pleasure? Unless… "Are you saying you wouldn't want this, with me, if it weren't for your hunger?"

"I…" Her hesitation made his throat close up and his lungs shrink.

He wished he could see her face and nearly cast a spell to allow it. But then her open mouth was on his neck, and she pushed open his sleeping robe.

"I'm saying"—she kissed his collarbone—"it works better this way." Another kiss landed on his chest, and the way she yanked the blanket aside sent a tremor through him. She slid down his body, parting his too-small sleeping robe with hurried motions.

"At least let me touch your arms, your s-shoulders. Anything," he begged, yet again clutching the bedding beneath him, voice catching when she boldly stroked her hand down his naked thigh and pushed it wide.

"I'll let you hold my hair out of the way." She crawled over him, between his legs, and began kissing her way down his torso.

He spread his other thigh without prompting and hastily gathered her silky hair into a messy ball at the back of her head. Divine One's arse, his cock was so hard it would be standing straight up were it not for his loincloth.

The room would be lit next time, he promised himself. So many of their stolen nights together in the maze had passed in near darkness, some of them proceeding just like tonight was, with Mikari preparing to take him into her mouth. And every time, he had wished he could see her better.

"Mm, should I light the lantern?" she murmured, kissing well below his waistline, both of her hands putting gentle pressure on the insides of his thighs to hold them open.

"D-did you see that in my head?" She couldn't have come to the same thought separately.

"I did." As she spoke, she dragged her tongue and lips ever downward. Moaning softly, he lifted his hips toward the electric sensation. "I only peek at the surface desires. I've not delved any deeper with you."

Damn it, he didn't like that. He didn't like her knowing his inner wants while she held back hers. "No more peeking."

She made a pensive purr as she nestled into the cradle of his open, bent legs. Her inert magic was no longer comfortably within reach of his own, but his magic remained content, holding still as though in readiness. He felt the smile on her lips as she touched them to the inner crease of his hip.

"I'll peek all I want." Wet heat then swept the sensitive, thin skin where his leg met his groin.

He breathed out a sharp moan. "Y-you already know all my desires. And how to—" His voice faltered as she gently slid her fingers beneath the edge of his loincloth. "H-how to…fulfill them."

"Do you want the lantern lit or not?" she asked, deftly freeing his loins.

"*Aj'*, to the Maze with it," he said, straining to speak. "I can't wait anymore. I need your sweet mouth on me."

"Me too," she whispered.

Her soft words silenced every thought in his head. He felt her warm breath on the tip of his shaft, and his hand in her hair tightened into a brutal fist, the pain of it making her gasp. In that second when her lips were parted, he splayed his fingers over the crown of her head and pushed her onto his cock.

A harsh groan sounded from low in his throat as he plunged his shaft deep, arse clenching with an upward thrust. He met zero resistance, even when his tip brushed well past the very back of her mouth. Only on accident had he ever gone this far when they were young, and she had always gagged.

Floored, he held her there and had the ridiculous yet no less erotic thought, *she's taking all of me*. A breath later, he let her pull up and was floored again when she pushed him even deeper, then sucked while moaning.

Stars sprayed across the backs of his eyelids, flashing with indescribable colors as he and Mikari worked her mouth over him. Searing heat swamped him, sending his heart into his throat. They were both moaning, her hands clamped onto his rocking hips, his hands sending her head back down every time she lifted it.

He hissed a vicious curse as a climax flew toward him as swiftly as an avalanche. He wouldn't last even a minute, not when she was working him so hard. Maze take him, they were both working him too hard.

Her palm slipped down, cupping beneath his cock. He clamped his teeth hard, every muscle in his body snapping tight, a growl scraping his throat.

Pleasure slammed through him. He bucked, holding her head in place as he came down her throat. Unlike the grasping ripples of an orgasm, the motion of her swallows felt deliberate. Hungry.

Tonight wasn't the first time she'd ever sucked him dry, but *fuck*, had she become good at it.

He was still in the midst of climax, panting in moans, when his magic flicked at Mikari with a tendril of power, catching against her inert magic like a curtain drawn through a window by a strong wind. She jerked as she received his energy, her gently bobbing head pausing for a breath. A few seconds later, she slowly drew away.

All of him went limp. Well…almost all of him.

What he wouldn't give to strip away her clothes and sit her upon his face. To ravage her flesh until she came, then keep going until she either came again or his cock ached too much to continue. Then he'd roll her beneath him, sink into her, and swive her so thoroughly that she'd wake the entire inn.

"Oh," Mikari moaned, resting her cheek against his lax thigh. She was shivering, fingers digging into his hip and leg.

"You all right?" he asked her, languorous. He didn't know whether his lethargy was from pleasure or from feeding her, but the lightness in his limbs suggested the former.

"Q-quite all right." And yet he heard pain in her voice. "You?"

"Crudding fantastic." Not an exaggeration despite how much he still craved her. "Was it enough?"

"Yes, I'll last a while now," she said more steadily. He wanted to ask how long that was, but before he could… "Let me fetch a cloth." She pulled away, and he felt her absence like a missing limb. The door opened then slid shut, and her footsteps faded. He wondered how the room could be spinning even when he couldn't see it.

While she was gone, he righted his clothing and the bedding. Sleep weighed upon him the more his ardor quieted. He was only half-conscious when her footsteps returned, but he dragged himself upright. She handed him a washcloth with the warning that it was cold, and for a moment, its chill woke him up. He cleaned himself quickly.

She left again to dispose of the washcloth, but he remained sitting up, loath to lie back and sleep. Only when Mikari returned did he realize why.

"Come lie in bed with me," he implored of her before he could stop himself.

She made a startled sound, shutting the door with a louder tap than she'd likely intended. "I…I'm surprised you're still awake."

"I want you next to me." He prayed she didn't ask why. He wouldn't know what to tell her. Certainly not the truth.

"But I don't sleep," she said, tarrying at the door. "I'd only toss and turn."

"I don't care."

"T-the mattress is only meant for one pers—"

"Come here," he bade sharply, hating that he was so close to begging. "At least until I'm asleep. Please." And there it was.

There was a breath of silence. "Very well." Then she shuffled toward him.

Ashamed but also pleased, he shifted to make room and opened his arm to her. A sweet whiff of flowers and tooth powder preceded her, telling him she'd taken time to freshen up.

She paused, only partway settled, when discovering he meant to have her in a close embrace rather than next to him. Even held her breath.

Despite feeling like an arse, he nevertheless waited silently in the strained stillness. Was she thinking that the position made slipping away difficult? That he had to know the same?

Rather than balk, however, she let out a slow, soft breath and arranged herself to touch as little of him as possible.

Unacceptable.

Anchoring her against him, he reached down with his other hand, gripped the back of her thigh, and pulled her flush to his side.

"I-I don't wish to make you uncomfortable," she said, stiff as a pole.

"I am comfortable. You fit perfectly." Just the right height to drape her soft leg across his groin.

"We'll be too warm."

"Nonsense. We both know you were constantly under my coat, and not just to seduce. Now let me sleep."

She stopped arguing but didn't exactly surrender, carrying tension everywhere he touched her. Still, he enjoyed the weight of her against him, the reassurance of her nearness. Hopefully, it would keep another nightmare away.

The need to stroke her was nigh overwhelming, but he had already pushed for more than what she'd offered. Instead, he concentrated on his breathing and tried to sleep.

And yet he couldn't help noticing every little movement she made, the places where she relaxed one muscle at a time until she was all softness against him, head tucked beneath his chin. What he wouldn't have given to know this sense of peace every night—wouldn't *still* give.

"Sleep well," she whispered, sneaking her arm across his chest.

He stroked his chin across the crown of her head. "You know, I think I shall."

Chapter Fifteen

Never had the darkest hours passed so quickly for Mikari, even though she spent them tipping between agony and ecstasy.

She hadn't been lying when she'd said she was always hungry. And Jun was far and away the most fulfilling meal she'd ever had. The amount of energy she'd received from him so far would last her a couple of weeks, which delighted and terrified her in equal measure.

She wanted more. Wanted a full taste. Being so close to him was torture. She didn't know how she would resist feeding from him again for two whole weeks, especially if he continued to insist upon such physical closeness.

Worse, the scent of his lust continued to evolve, becoming more irresistible. Now it reminded her of *esorege*—a hot, sweet Gozuan drink, traditionally imbibed in the days between the Snow Festival and Divine Day. Its frothy creaminess carried a soothing blend of toasted spices and a blood-warming kick of alcohol. And it was the preferred beverage for lovers spending the deep-winter holidays together.

Oh, but how sublime it was to lie tucked against him, his strong, steady heartbeat thumping beneath her ear. How compelling it was that he'd wanted her next to him and had said so outright.

As time slipped by, she reveled in fantasies of sleeping like this every night. Only they would both be naked, and she wouldn't be awake and starving for him.

If she could manage not to lose control until she was cured, and if she could avoid making Jun hate her, then being with him *was* a possibility. She wouldn't even dream of such a future in the light of day, but in these hidden, quiet hours of basking in his nearness, she allowed herself a little hope. Real, desperate, foolish, wonderful hope, which he had given her.

Never in the last twenty years had a cure even seemed possible, but now they had a good idea of where to look for one. She had also learned the truth about her corruption, that her hunger for lust wasn't her fault, allowing her to see that night of metaphysical pleasure twenty years ago with new, eager eyes.

Yes, fate hadn't been kind to her, but if given the chance to stay hidden on her parents' farm rather than end up a ward of Nansen Temple, even if it meant never becoming a lust eater, she would still sneak out for a glimpse of the village festival.

After all, following her heart had led her to Jun. If only she'd listened to it when he'd asked her to run away with him.

How could she not see their reunion as the opportunity it was—to follow her heart and trust that she'd be strong enough for whatever followed?

But did that mean telling Jun what she'd done the day she'd been cursed and what she might do again if she ever allowed him to touch her as he wanted? He might despise her for killing that man.

Worse, he might forgive her. And if he were cocky enough to think he could be her only donor for an indeterminate amount of time, he'd likely insist he could handle the consequences of putting her into a feeding frenzy.

Mikari didn't know if she'd have the strength to resist if he offered to pleasure her despite knowing the danger.

Or perhaps following her heart meant continuing to rebuff Jun's advances while trying to avoid smothering any affection he still felt for her. Perhaps it meant never revealing that she'd murdered an innocent person.

Dawn came before she could decide. She was so deep in thought that the rustle of someone elsewhere in the inn alerted her to morning's imminent arrival rather than the light itself.

She wanted so badly to wake Jun with a kiss and a whispered

endearment, but staying with him the rest of the night had been bad enough. If he didn't wake up alone, he'd get ideas.

Not that he didn't already have some dangerous ideas. She'd seen them. And the visual he'd conjured a moment after his climax had nearly done her in. He'd had the right idea when he'd told her to stop reading his inner desires. If only she had the willpower not to look.

She managed to draw her arm and leg back without disturbing him. But when she touched his hand on her waist, his slack embrace tightened, and he turned toward her with a sleepy moan. *Dammit*, she silently cursed, even as her heart twirled with happiness.

He clasped her close, splaying his other hand across her arse, and buried his nose in her hair. Then he took a deep breath, his chest expanding beneath her hands.

"Mm, morning already?" he rumbled, nuzzling the top of her head. "And you're still here."

"How are you feeling?" she asked, ignoring his observation.

"Good, all things considered. Probably because I'm holding you."

"I'm serious," she said, lifting her head. Dawn's light was still too weak to gauge how fatigued he was after feeding her in the middle of the night. All she could tell was that his hair needed combing.

"So am I. Even my shoulder is feeling better. I'll be ready to head out after I eat something and splash some cold water on myself." The tempting aroma of *esorege* wafted up, and he grunted in self-derision. "Hmph. More than just a splash, I suppose."

Divine One have mercy, he was getting hard...again. She could feel him growing against her stomach.

"I-I'll get you some breakfast," she said, pulling out of his embrace. "I shouldn't be gone more than half an hour."

"Do you plan to take over the inn's kitchen?" He spoke with amusement as he rolled to his back and stretched, his broad body exposed by the part in his sleeping robe.

Wrenching her gaze away, she shoved her arm into the sleeve of her overcoat. "I plan to charm a villager into sharing their food—not that I'd use my coercions," she hastily amended. "That's not what I meant."

"I know." A soft rustling signaled that he'd tossed aside the blanket, and she couldn't help imagining how delectable—and accessible—he looked in his rumpled robe. "I appreciate your offer, thank you."

"Of course," she murmured, shoving her head and hair into the cap of her white wig. She wouldn't don her mask, but she preferred that no one else in the village learned that she was a crow. "I'll return soon."

She left without looking back. The rear hallway of the inn was silent, none of the other guests yet stirring. But there was light coming from the front dining space. She continued to bundle up as she walked toward the entrance, tying her belt properly and tugging her hood up, careful not to displace her wig.

Warmth radiated from a pair of braziers in the dining area, and the sounds of cooking echoed from the kitchen beyond. She was tempted to poke her head through the curtain for a glimpse of the innkeeper ruining yet another meal, but he was already upset at her over the commotion last night. She doubted he'd be in a friendly mood.

So, after putting on her boots and gloves, she headed out. The sky looked to be overcast, and the breeze was slight, thus, the chill of dawn wasn't as penetrating as it could be. She made her way toward the home of the old brownie woman, nodding to a man enjoying a pipe outside his door. He lifted his chin in return.

The old woman's home wasn't far, and Mikari was glad to see light coming from the window slits beneath the lower roof in the rear where the earthen-floored cooking area was likely located. She approached the home's storm door and knocked loudly to be heard in the back.

"Who's there?" the woman called.

"It's the bard, madam. You kindly mended my mask for me yesterday?"

The woman made an intrigued grunt. "You're awake rather early." The door slid open, and she beckoned Mikari inside. "You were up late entertaining, weren't you? Yesterday was busy for me, and I only lasted until patchouli."

Mikari bobbed her head in thanks as she entered. "I grew up on a sheep farm, so I've always been an early riser." Even before the curse had taken away her need for sleep, it had been the truth.

She had no need to explain why she wanted to barter for a well-cooked breakfast rather than eat at the inn. After some negotiation, Mikari agreed to waive the woman's message-delivery fee in exchange for half a dozen rice balls and several slices of fried *ruborada* curd made from a kind of bean that grew well in the valleys of the hills to the north. Mikari had eaten a lot of it growing up.

The woman doddered toward the back of her home to fetch the

food, and Mikari, rather than remove her boots to come in, sat upon the edge of the raised flooring. An old ceramic brazier sat a few feet away, warming the main room.

"I doubt this'll be enough for both you and your husband," the old woman called across her home, a pan clattering. "You found yourself a right large man."

The thought of Jun truly belonging to her sent twin pangs of hope and anxiety zinging through her. Despite all the dreaming she'd done last night of escaping the maze of her current existence, she was afraid to hope for too much. While there was a real chance of a cure, who knew where she and Jun would end up?

She opened her mouth to reply, but the words died in her throat. The back of her neck was prickling in warning of a familiar malevolence turning its gaze upon her. She barely resisted the instinct to look behind her.

Her shoulders rose to her ears, and only through sheer force of will did she push them back down. She scooted a little closer to the brazier and rubbed her gloved hands over her arms, the fear making her cold and tense.

"I-it will be more than enough, madam. Thank you," she said at last.

Something in the kitchen began sizzling. "My husband always praised my cooking," the woman shouted back. She went on to say something about the bean curd she was frying, but Mikari's mind raced with indecision.

If the uncomfortable sensation of being watched didn't abate before she left the old woman's home, should she go back to the inn? Would she be risking something happening to Jun? What, she couldn't say.

But if she didn't return in the next half-hour, Jun would come looking for her. They were to set out as soon as possible. Was it too much to hope that she could evade him until the feeling went away?

Her heart told her to go straight to the inn and tell Jun what was happening, but her mind was screaming warnings. Because whatever watched her...it was not on her side, and it would make Jun its enemy, too.

She could practically feel the pressure of the gaze like an icy hand tightening on her shoulder. If she still ate food and had anything in her stomach, she would be in danger of throwing up.

"...to carry it all, Miss Bard?" The brownie woman was walking toward her.

Blinking, she met the kind woman's questioning eyes and did her best not to let her anxiety show. "My deepest apologies, madam. I was lost in thought."

"Oh, I was wondering if you needed a way to carry the food." She held up a drawstring sack made up of smaller, stitched-together scraps of linen, something that would serve as an offering bag for festival time.

"Maze take me, I hadn't even thought to— Yes, I'd appreciate that. Might I give you a kol in return?"

The woman waved away her offer to pay for the bag. "I have a dozen of these. I like to make them from the scraps of the clothing I sew."

The cold hand on Mikari's shoulder pressed harder, its chill spreading across her neck and down her back. "I-it's beautiful, madam. Thank you."

"I'll just need a moment to put it all together." The woman returned to her cooking hearth.

Mikari calmly stood, despite her rising panic. When the woman shuffled toward her holding the bag of food, it took all of Mikari's concentration to keep a placid smile pasted on her face instead of snatching the food and running back to the inn.

"Thank you again for taking my letter up to my sister," the woman said, gently handing over the food. "I know Tetsutani isn't far for a young, well-traveled bard like you, but for all my old bones care, my sister might as well live in Yuugai."

The woman kept talking, saying something about moving to live with her sister, but at the woman's mention of Tetsutani, the cold weight of the invisible presence began crawling up the back of Mikari's skull. Pain followed like a pounding headache.

"M-my apologies, madam," Mikari interrupted, "but I'm a-afraid I must be on my way. Thank you again, and m-may you have a safe winter."

"Of course, Miss Bard. Don't let me keep you."

She let herself out, hands shaking. The day had grown a little brighter, but the overcast sky promised more snow. She walked quickly, practically jogging, but the cold grip on her didn't slow in its advance. More villagers were up and about, but she kept her eyes down and her feet moving.

Jun will know what to do. And if not him, then someone in Houfu will.

She looked up when she neared the inn, and spied the proprietor disappearing into the nearby barn, likely to ready her and Jun's mounts. She hoped he didn't grumble too much if she and Jun didn't end up leaving right away.

Inside the inn, she shucked her boots at the entryway, not bothering to stow them in her haste to reach their room. Other guests were taking tea at a couple of the tables, and she swept past without paying them any heed.

She turned down the rear hallway. The cold sensation had spread so far and sunk so deep into her skin that goosebumps covered her. She kept her hood up and gloves on.

The door to their room was open. Jun stood inside, fully dressed, his back to her. He turned, looking confused, and she realized he was holding the speaking mirror. Upon seeing her face, his tense eyebrows drew even tighter.

"Is something wrong?"

But it wasn't Jun who spoke. That had been her voice.

She tried to correct herself and tell him she had a problem, but her mouth refused to move. The cold pressure had encompassed her head, and it was squeezing hard.

Jun glanced at the mirror in his hand. "I maintain a spell every day that sharpens my awareness of magical spying. In other words, it tells me when someone is attempting to use the other mirror to talk to me. It's like a…prickle on the back of my neck."

Her heart dropped to her stomach. She tried again to say something, to warn him, but her lips stayed silent.

"I felt it just before you arrived." He closed the mirror's case, then shrugged as he tucked it into his clothing. "But no one's there."

All he had left to collect was his sword, standing in its sheath in the corner, and his packed saddlebags, on top of which sat a black dagger. He reached for the dagger first.

The cold pressure squeezed down hard, bringing tears to her eyes. Any yelp of pain she would've made was suppressed by the force that was controlling her. She couldn't even flinch.

This must be one of her agents, hm? He didn't kill you, though. And he has a speaking mirror.

Mikari knew that voice.

"Are you all right?" Jun asked. "And is that my breakfast?" There was a teasing tilt to his lips as he slid the sheathed dagger into his coat.

"It is. And I'm all right," she heard herself say. "We should go."

"Hmph, is the innkeeper pushing us out the door?" He picked up his sword to tie it to his belt. "And here I was hoping for enough time to eat."

Can't kill him now. I suppose tonight will be soon enough.

No! Oh, sweet Garden, how was this happening?

Despite her inner panic, her voice was even and controlled. "How long does it take to eat a few bites?" Her arm held out the sack of food. "I'll meet you outside."

Jun gave her a look as he took the sack from her. A close, narrow regard. "I'll not be long."

Her body turned to her things in the corner, and her feet took her closer.

Now, now. None of that. I think it's time to put that mask on.

A hot tear slipped down her cheek as she donned her mask, all without her willing it. She could only watch as she closed the top of her pack, and she was too upset to notice that her two journals were on top rather than at the bottom of the bag. Once she had her pack on, her body took her back the way she'd come without another word to Jun.

Soon, I'll be shifting my attention to other things, but don't mistake my absence. I own you now. I can turn my gaze upon you at any moment. Now, here's what you'll be doing...

He issued her a series of orders as he directed her body outside, his control over her now absolute, the only exception being the tears falling unseen behind her mask. She was so divorced from her actions, despite seeing and feeling every motion, that she had no idea what her limbs would do next, let alone whether she'd ever be able to stop herself.

In her nearly forty years of life, no other instance of imprisonment could compare.

...and you won't speak of any of this—of me or what I've commanded of you—to anyone or anything. There's no escape from my control, Mikari.

Chapter Sixteen

Jun watched Mikari leave, not liking her behavior. She had been standoffish from the moment he'd woken, but something had changed while she had been out getting him food. It was almost as if a stranger had been speaking to him.

He continued mulling it over as he pulled apart the knot securing the sack of food shut. The sight of his meal had him softly groaning with want. All of it was still warm, but the three thick slices of fried *ruborada* were the most tempting. He shoved an entire slice of it into his mouth—Divine One have mercy, it was delicious—and stared at the empty doorway as he chewed.

After he'd given himself a quick but thorough scrub-down with a hand towel and washed his hair and beard over a basin of soapy water, he had returned to the room to find it empty still. He'd begun to dress and had stared at her open pack sitting in the storage alcove, his curiosity about her journals tugging at him.

Had she written of her previous lovers? How often she visited each one or which of them she preferred? Was there someone in particular she missed?

But the truly nagging question was whether her journals would confirm the suspicion that her affection for him went no deeper than what she felt for anyone else from whom she'd fed.

His insecurity, and a profound sense of guilt, had fed into his still-simmering jealousy, bringing it to an uncomfortable boil. Convincing himself that it was only fair, he'd dug the two books out of her pack. She had been using her abilities to trespass on his inner desires, after all. Why should he not feel free to trespass on hers?

However, the first journal was professional in nature, the numbered pages worn with age and frequent handling. She'd recorded the trickier bits of songs and poems that a bard would need to have memorized, as well as general notes about numerous towns and people of importance.

About halfway through, the content shifted toward bits of news and rumors, with several entries containing page references to earlier notes.

One entry in particular had caught his eye due to how many references it contained. As he'd read, his stomach had begun to sink—then plummet—with the realization that she'd been tracking the other lust eater.

And so far, she'd linked him with *eight* potential victims over the last fourteen years.

He'd flipped back several pages and noted quite a few other threads she'd been following, all of them indicating at least a dozen human-born demons hunting and feeding, which implied an even higher incidence of undetected eaters prowling throughout Gozu than just her and the other lust eater.

Sick with remorse, he'd recalled her offer that first night to help track the other lust eater, an offer he'd not even allowed her to make and which he'd roundly rejected.

The detailed information in his hands put to shame what the imperial scouts had learned over the last few months, and though he'd have to admit to snooping, he made a mental note to ask for the journal properly.

Her most recent entry had been about him, as he'd anticipated, or rather his capture of the bandits menacing the area. But its narrative elided any explanation of why she and an imperial commander were traveling together, and made no mention of their previous history.

Except for the word "triumphant" used to describe his return with six bandits in tow, the precisely written paragraphs had been disappointingly impersonal, the only other conspicuous detail being a small drawing of a wind bell to one side.

No, Mikari's second journal was what he'd truly sought, something personal in nature.

But rather than a series of dated entries with accounts of the past, it was simply a list of foods she wished to eat, places she wished to visit, and things she wished to do, but couldn't. More wind bells filled the margins of every single page.

> *Someday, I'll eat as many sweet rice dumplings as I can stomach. The ones with strawberry bits inside.*
>
> *I wish to see the Black Sands from a safe distance. Is it true you can stand close enough to bake a fish on a skewer?*
>
> *What an adventure it would be to bring bardic tradition to the southern lands. To learn their songs and stories, and preserve them.*
>
> *Do women in the south really wear dresses so sheer you can see their breasts? I bet the weather's so warm that you'd rather be naked. What I wouldn't give to be that warm.*

That last one had been her latest entry, quickly scribbled during some stolen moment last night, likely when he'd first been asleep.

Rather than imagine Mikari dressed in a similar fashion, her lithe form draped in a silk robe so thin it merely fogged the lines of her naked curves, Jun quickly skimmed her list of dreams for his name.

But he hadn't found it, nor any mention of wanting a family.

As wards, her affection for him had been significant. He couldn't bear to doubt that. But if she had ever truly longed for a life with him, that longing had since died.

He knew he should do the same. He should keep her at arm's length, at least emotionally, if he was even capable of that anymore. And after she was cured of the inquisitor's curse, he should set her free to pursue the long list of wants she'd been denied.

Divine One's grace, he wouldn't have a choice. The divergence of their lives and the gap of twenty years was unbridgeable. After a lifetime of restrictions, why would she consent to a commitment to anyone, let alone a man twice her physical age who wishes to be done with adventuring?

But in the darkest hours of the previous night, when he had been confessing his fears and she had been comforting him, there had been no distance then. At least, not until he'd wanted more than comfort. Even then, she had seemed...conflicted.

Did he dare ask for the truth? Could he handle it if she told him, outright, that she no longer saw a future with him in it? The impossibly tangible pain in his chest when he breathed told him he couldn't, and yet the thought of letting her go hurt even worse, the metaphorical knife twisting torturously.

But if that were what she truly wanted, no matter what he offered her—everything short of murder, negotiable in a few cases—then how in the Maze would he endure with enough fortitude to be of use to anyone?

Only one solution—he wouldn't ask after her heart, and he'd retain the small remaining fragment of his own with a stone grip.

A prickle on the back of his neck had woken him from his morose reflections. He had hastily stowed her journals in her pack and gone to check the speaking mirror, only to find no one waiting to talk to him. Seconds later, Mikari had appeared.

Jun shoved the last of the fried *ruborada* into his mouth, carefully packed the sack of food into his saddlebags, and then draped everything over his shoulder. A moment later, he had his boots on and was exiting the inn.

Mikari appeared to be conversing with the proprietor just outside the stables. The old man held the reins of Jun's readied horse, and Mikari had a hand on her reindeer's bridle. The closer Jun came to them, the clearer the innkeeper's consternation became.

"...won't be necessary. Your food is appallingly inedible, so I was forced to procure his breakfast elsewhere," Mikari said once Jun was in earshot. "Here he is. We'll be on our way, then."

A frown pulled at Jun's mouth. The innkeeper hadn't been the most hospitable man, not that they had been ideal guests, and yes, Mikari had grown even bolder since their youth, but her rude remark and imperious dismissal didn't wash with what he knew of her.

She would have thanked the proprietor, or at least bid him a safe winter out of professional considerations. He could think of no reason that would compel her to be unnecessarily cruel.

Jun expressed their thanks instead, and the innkeeper gave Jun a perturbed look as he handed over Nugun's reins. The horse nudged Jun's shoulder, and he absently stroked its velvety muzzle.

"Well, safe travels to you, then," the proprietor grumbled before trudging back to the inn and his other guests. Mikari seated herself upon her mount.

"Eager to be off?" Jun asked before doing the same.

"I must reach Tetsutani as quickly as possible," she said, adjusting her reins. The texture of her voice was decidedly brusque. "Be sure to keep up."

Jun snorted. "It's *we*, you know. And of our two mounts, yours is slower."

She pulled her reindeer's head toward the road leading north, turning away from him without comment.

If they pushed hard, they could ride an hour or two past Koichino and find shelter for the night at one of the family farms along the route to Tetsutani. Another day's ride would catch them up to the brownie delegation and his fellow crows.

Nudging his horse to follow, Jun frowned even harder at Mikari's silence. Something was wrong, he could feel it.

Had she noticed his snooping and was angry about it? There was no way she wouldn't say so. If he'd learned anything about the person she'd become, it was that she didn't hesitate to speak her mind. Unless she'd also realized that taking exception would be a mite hypocritical.

They urged their mounts into a fast trot, but Jun's stallion had an easier gait with its longer, more powerful legs. Nugun, being well trained, knew to keep pace with its companion and held back on its speed.

"How often do you come across other bards?" he called over their mounts' pounding hoofbeats, in an attempt to draw Mikari into some conversation.

She turned her masked face toward him but didn't immediately answer. "It depends," she said eventually, before returning her gaze to the snow-packed road ahead. He waited for her to elaborate, but she didn't.

"Depends on what?" he asked.

"On where I am." No further explanation.

After a beat of silence, he tried again. "Have you ever checked on your parents?"

Rather than answer, Mikari pushed her reindeer into a gallop, widening the distance between them. Nugun quickly caught up. Jun supposed their mounts had warmed up enough for such exercise, but he was certain that Mikari was avoiding conversation with him.

After running for about a league or so, his horse began showing signs of its extended exertion. Nugun could go on for a little while longer if Jun needed him to, but it was still early morning and they had many leagues to go over the next two days. Mikari's reindeer was also tiring. He waited for her to slow its speed, but their mounts took them another five minutes without change.

He whistled to get her attention. "Let's walk them a while," he shouted.

She shook her head before facing forward.

"Your mount needs a break," he insisted. "Mikari, it could stumble."

"She can go on."

Another five minutes passed. Mikari's reindeer was breathing hard, its speed naturally slowing as fatigue set in.

Clenching his jaw in frustration, Jun pulled ahead of her and eased back in his saddle as he pulled gently but firmly on Nugun's bit, forcing her reindeer to slow down to avoid colliding with the much larger stallion.

Keeping Nugun at a walk, Jun looked back at Mikari, and even though he couldn't see her face, he could tell she was bristling at his interference. "It'll take much longer to reach Tetsutani if your mount injures itself," he chided.

"I know her limits," she snapped, directing her reindeer to walk alongside his horse. The smaller animal was blasting out great lungfuls of white air like a roaring outdoor oven.

"What's the matter? You're agitated about something."

"I must reach Tetsutani as quickly as possible," she said with urgency. "That's all."

"*We*," he clarified...again. "And no, that's not all. Ever since you returned from your errand, you've been different. Did something happen while you were out?"

She tightened a degree, but was it anger or discomfort? "Leave me alone, Jun."

"Were you forced to use your coercions?" he pressed. "Are you drained and needing to feed again?"

"No. Now leave me *alone*," she said forcefully.

Scowling, he took a deep, irritated breath. "Very well."

They hardly spoke for the rest of the morning. Mikari continued to push her reindeer, and Jun was repeatedly forced to check her speed. He ate whenever they walked their mounts and was able to put two more rice balls in his stomach. By midday, he had drained his waterskin and was in need of a brief rest to relieve himself, refill his waterskin with melted snow, and eat again.

But Mikari refused to stop.

"I'm sure you can catch up," she said, already urging her mount into a jog.

He lunged forward, legs gripping his horse's flanks, and caught hold of her reins. "I need only ten minutes."

Mikari attempted to shake his hand off, but he held firm. "Let go, Jun. Your horse is fast enough to overtake me down the road, isn't it?"

"It's a ten-minute delay, Mikari. And I've had about enough of this," he growled. "Do I need to bind your hands again, with magic this time, and lead your mount as I did before?"

She stared at him from behind her mask, not moving a muscle. "Ten minutes. Then we move on." She tugged at his grip on her reins, but he didn't let go.

"You first. Get off your mount." If she decided to race ahead while he was emptying his bladder, she certainly wouldn't get far before he closed the distance, but he wanted to avoid such an incident.

She stiffly descended to the ground. He led her reindeer off the road, not trusting her. Then he dismounted and hastily tied their mounts to a pair of branches. Mikari moved away from the road but stood stock-still, hands at her side. She didn't even take off her pack.

He kept an eye on her as he went about his business. She didn't budge, or even look around. He thought about contacting someone in Houfu, but he wasn't sure what to tell them besides the fact that Mikari had become ornery.

He supposed he could tell them about the prickle he'd felt despite no one...

"Wait," he said aloud, darting his glance to her motionless form.

The spell he cast every day augmented his awareness of *all* nearby scrying sensors. His mirror was a sensor, but that didn't mean it would ever be the only one. If someone wanted to attempt to spy upon him from a distance, all they needed was a reflective surface through which to scry.

The chance of successfully doing so depended on a variety of factors, such as how well they knew him and whether they had an additional focus, such as an object he'd once owned or a piece of his physical form, typically a hair or part of a fingernail.

But once the *scry* spell worked, it would tether to him an invisible, floating sensor, and through it, they would see and even hear him. The least taxing version of the spell didn't allow the scryer to speak, but a conversation wasn't usually the point. Spying was the point.

According to Vallen and Rosuke, the abuse of scrying magic had been a constant hassle in the old Dark Court, the giving or exchanging of jewelry with tiny compartments for hair, blood, or tears a gesture of trust.

Most crows could sense the magical intrusion of scrying without a specific detection spell in place, but there were ways to further disguise a sensor or deaden awareness of it. And anyone who wasn't a crow had little to no chance of realizing they were being watched.

This morning, however, Jun had felt a magical presence. And it had raised the hairs on his neck only seconds before Mikari had returned, her personality altered. If indeed there had been another scrying sensor, it must have been following her.

Growing more and more certain he was right, he wondered who was scrying upon Mikari and whether she was aware of it. Her magic was arrested, so perhaps she was one of the rare few without any magic who could sense an invisible gaze.

Or maybe her power, despite being inert, still connected her to that extended metaphysical awareness that crows possessed. She was able to cast a limited type of magic after all. She merely cast spells using a different source of power.

If Mikari did know someone was scrying on her, she might have been trying to mislead her watcher.

Or maybe he was wrong, and she was simply angry. At him, at their quest, or at some other recent offense of which he had no knowledge.

Jun scowled as he repacked his saddlebags, having eaten the last of the delicious food Mikari had fetched for him. She remained motionless, still standing in the same spot and watching him from behind her mask. She was undoubtedly anxious to resume their journey, but he could not ignore his reservations.

First, he'd need to find out whether a scrying sensor was still stalking her. If so, he knew of a couple ways to combat it, although neither was easily done. If not, then he could at least speak to her of his suspicions.

The detection spell that warned him of magical scrying had a limited range, about five or six horse lengths. Mikari was considerably farther.

Leaving the mounts tethered, he slowly approached her, giving himself plenty of time to sense any sort of prickle. He didn't. Just in case, he paused a couple strides away and allowed more time to pass.

Mikari shifted restlessly. "What are you doing? Let's go already." She gestured impatiently at their mounts behind him.

"No one is watching us right now," he said gently. "You can speak freely. I didn't realize it until a moment ago, but someone must have been scrying on you this morning."

She straightened with a jolt, then shook her head in an obvious attempt to pretend she hadn't. "Scrying? I don't know what that is." How he wished he could see her face, but asking her to remove her mask might rile her temper.

"The prickle I felt this morning wasn't warning me of an attempt to speak through the mirror. It was warning me of the invisible sensor following *you*." He took a careful step closer. "You also felt its presence. That's why you've been acting strangely. But there's no sensor at the moment. You can tell me what happened." She shook her head again, harder this time. "Mikari, I can help."

"You're wrong. I'm fine. I must reach Tetsutani as quickly as possible."

He tilted his head. "That's the third time you've said that. *Exactly* that."

"And yet you remain gallingly dismissive," she said sharply, arms stiff and straight at her sides.

He took another step closer. "I understand your urgency, but not the reckless pace."

She gave a frustrated sigh. "What's your point?"

"Tell me why you're pushing so hard, why you've been so agitated. Did the scryer manage to speak to you?" Jun didn't personally know how to wield such high-level magic, but he knew it was possible to talk to a scrying target without a speaking mirror. Had the caster threatened Mikari?

"Ugh," she scoffed, stomping her foot. "I don't know what you're talking about. Now let's *go*. We're wasting time."

He seized her arm when she tried to move past him. "Speak to me without your mask, and I'll consider it."

"Let go of me," she ground out, yanking at his grip.

"I know something's wrong," he insisted. "I'm on your side, you know that, right?"

"You have a strange way of showing it." She pushed at him with her other hand. "Are you certain the problem here isn't you?"

"Where has this hostility come from, then?" he challenged. "You've been different ever since your errand. Is it because I looked at your journals?"

"Why does it matter whether I'm kind to you?" she shot back. "I— Y-you read them?" The horror in her voice sent guilt stabbing through him.

Guilt he resented. "You've seen my secret desires. Why can I not know yours? Or that you never included me in them?"

A sharp tingle washed down his neck as Mikari fervently shook her head. "No, that's not— You see, I had planned to—"

She fell silent, and he saw a change in her posture. It became rigid. Aggressive. His magic responded instantly, sending out a pang of warning. But like an utter fool, he did nothing to prepare himself in the two or three seconds before she unleashed.

Chapter Seventeen

"Temu, attack!" Mikari yelled, seizing Jun's forearm in an iron grip.

He stood there, stunned, as she planted her feet and swung him violently forward with supernatural strength. Only his years of training saved him from being thrown like a sack of rice. Stumbling in the direction in which she'd sent him, Jun barely managed to keep his footing and retain his grasp on her arm.

Her reindeer bleated loudly, but he didn't have the spare focus to pay the animal any attention. A mistake, but one he couldn't avoid, for he had barely recovered from her throw when she tapped him on his forehead.

The small touch hadn't hurt, but the magical force behind it nearly dazed him as assuredly as a thrown fist, and only through sheer willpower did he push it aside. The glancing blow cost him a second or two of focus, leaving him unprepared for the decidedly physical force that rammed into his body.

He threw a hand out at the last second, grasping an antler, and turned the reindeer's head aside before it gored him. The rest of its body crashed into him full-on, including the broken branch hanging from its wildly swinging reins. The collision knocked the air out of him and sent him rolling across the snowy ground until he landed on his side.

Pain radiated from where he'd been hit, from his back where it had collided with the ground, and from his left hip, into which his sheathed sword had smashed.

He didn't wait to get his feet beneath him before calling upon powerful defensive magic that would harden his skin against a lethal blow. Thankfully, he was able to cast *skin like armor* silently, for he was still struggling for air.

The added protection proved to be vital, for in the next instant, Mikari appeared above him, tensed for another attack. His training urged him to roll out of reach and draw his sword, but he would never —*could* never—wield a weapon against her. Instead, he swung his leg, knocking her feet out from under her.

He was on his knees and ready to lunge on top of her before she even landed. What he would do once he had her pinned, he didn't yet know, but he couldn't get the answers he needed when she was trying to stun him. Or worse.

She hit the ground sitting up, legs raised to keep from falling backward. He was mid-lunge when she clapped her palms together. "*Hakushu!*"

Brilliant energy burst forth, hitting him hard and slamming him backward, pain exploding throughout his body as though he'd been rolled beneath his horse. His ears rang as he lolled about on the ground, staring dazedly up at the gray sky, every part of him aching from the force of the magical blow.

If not for his quick casting of *skin like armor*, that blast of energy would have done serious damage and might have even knocked him out, not that he didn't already have a few wicked injuries. But thanks to his magical protection absorbing most of the blow, he was able to push through the pain.

Jun struggled to his feet, gasping and wincing, and stood in time to see Mikari leaping into her saddle. He charged forward. She was kicking her mount into a run when he reached her, and he barely got his arms around her waist before the animal could carry her away. The reindeer's momentum as well as Jun's wrenching pulled her from its back.

He bore her to the ground, intending to cast *sleep* on her so he could think. Everything was happening so fast.

Needing access to her bare forehead, he did his best to hold her with one arm while prying her mask off with his other, which her bulky pack made difficult.

Just as he was tossing it aside, sharp pain exploded in his head. His vision darkened and swayed.

He lost his hold on her and heard the angry grunting of her reindeer. He'd been kicked—hard.

The cold, wet ground met his shoulder and back. He felt a weight upon his stomach and a hand searching inside his clothing.

His magic quickly numbed his newest wound on the side of his head. Divine One's grace, that blow might've killed him if not for his magically hardened skin.

Blinking hard, he cleared his vision.

Mikari had his dagger. She was on top of him and ripping off its sheath. Her face... A lake of tears swam in her horrified eyes. Her cheeks were wet and dripping. Her nose and lip were curled in a snarl that didn't belong on her.

She held the dagger in one hand, its blade pointed down, and lifted it high. Despite his magical protection, he jerked his arms up to protect himself.

Not that he would have been fast enough had she instantly plunged the blade into him—which she didn't. She was frozen over him, arm shaking violently.

"*No*," she uttered low in her throat, teeth gnashing.

Maze take him, she was fighting against something. Something that was controlling her.

Jun didn't know how to counter that sort of magic. Not in the heat of the moment. He knew of an array that could grant powerful protection for a day, but—

All of this whizzed through his head in the space of the single, strained breath Mikari took. Then she brought the dagger toward her throat, chin lifted, hand still shaking with effort, and all thought vanished entirely.

"I'm sorry," she sobbed.

He grabbed her wrist with a horrified howl, both hands pulling hard to keep the lethal blade from her neck. Her strength was immense. Terror so cold it stung washed over him.

He flooded his muscles with magic and was able to drag her hand away from her throat, holding on so hard he was practically crushing her wrist. If he let up for a second, she would slice that beautiful column of flesh wide open.

They struggled for what felt like an eternity, but what was probably only a few seconds.

Heat poured from her hand, or rather the dagger clenched in it, the blade growing so warm that the air around it condensed.

Mikari cried out, and in the same instant, he felt it—a powerful pulse that raced up his arms and over the rest of his body, electric and searing, drawing out a pained gasp. It hit him like a slap in the face, and he wasn't even directly touching the dagger the way she was.

All the fight went out of her at once. She sagged, eyes fluttering, her grip on the dagger going slack. He tossed it aside, and the damned thing steamed in the snow.

Sitting up, he caught her before she slumped to the side, then made quick work of removing her pack and tugging down the hood of her overcoat. Brushing aside the fall of her white wig, he pressed his cheek to hers and wrapped her up tight in his arms.

Her mount had run off a short way, seemingly startled as though it had also been hit with magic. Paying it no further heed, Jun whispered to Mikari in between kisses to her chilled flesh. Endearments, words of comfort, and bits of nonsense as his heart spilled directly from his mouth.

"It's over, lamb. I have you. Just breathe. In and out. Only that."

Strength slowly returned to her limbs. She straightened, taking on some of her weight, but she didn't pull away. He felt her hands against his back, grasping fistfuls of his coat. She began convulsing with silent sobs. One broke free when she gulped in air, the sound shredding his heart.

"Jun," she croaked. "I'm s-so sorry."

She was shivering hard, and even though he knew she wasn't cold, he responded by rubbing warmth into her body.

"Oh!" she gasped. "Are you all right?" She attempted to pull back, but he tightened his hold on her.

"Don't worry about that right now."

"But you must be hurt!"

"Just let me hold you, lamb."

"After what I did?" She clung to him even while shaking her head against his shoulder. "I hurt you. I c-could have killed you!"

"But you didn't. You fought it. And I know the rest wasn't you. You weren't in control," he reasoned. "Your reindeer, on the other hand…I'll not be giving it a hug any time soon."

She gave a surprised, breathy laugh. A smile kicked up the corner of his mouth, but it wilted the second her levity reverted to whimpers.

"It lasted all morning," she said, haunted. "The i-inquisitor wasn't always watching, but I was under his control the whole time. Everything I did and said…if it w-wasn't him doing it, then it was his orders twisting my mind." Her words grew more frantic. "I thought my cleansing would always be the worst day of my life, but this… I've never felt so…so *violated*."

Jun couldn't imagine the helplessness. The fear. And after everything she'd been through—her isolated childhood, her wardship, her fake cleansing, and years of feeding off lust…

Aj', it was no wonder she carried a list of dreams with her. All Mikari had ever wanted was freedom, especially from magic. But this morning, even her bodily autonomy had been taken from her.

And now that his terror was beginning to fade, he shook with white-hot rage. Holding back a primal roar took every ounce of willpower he possessed. He had none left to keep himself from kissing her cheek and gently rocking her.

"I'm so sorry, lamb," he rasped, clutching her tight. "Maze take me, I wish I'd figured it out sooner."

"Thank you for breaking his grasp. For saving me."

"As much as I'd like to take credit, it was the dagger that broke the compulsion."

"The…dagger?" She lifted her head to look for it. "Where did it go?"

"It's magical. Returns to its sheath." He looked for the dark leather cover and found it on his other side. Indeed, the dagger was there. He pointed it out to her.

"Divine One's arse," she said, staring at it. She had pulled back enough for him to see her face. Her cheeks still looked damp, and her puffy eyes were rimmed in red.

"It's a living object," he explained. "Such artifacts are so old and infused with magic that they're practically alive. Elder Mai took it with her into Oblivion." He gave a short laugh. "She'll be fascinated to learn that it can interrupt magic."

"She didn't know?" she asked with a glance his way.

"She lent it to me hoping to learn more about it."

"That was lucky." She blinked in realization. "I should get up. You must be getting cold."

She pulled out of his arms and crawled off him. Indeed, his arse was freezing, but he regretted having to let her go.

They both stood and brushed themselves off. Rather than wear her mask, Mikari hung it from her belt. Jun tucked the dagger away and did his best to hide his new aches, suppressing a wince and a groan. Now that the fight was over, his magic had withdrawn and his head ached terribly. He pushed his hood back, took off his glove, and carefully checked his wound.

"Oh, Jun," Mikari fretted when she saw the blood on his fingers. She stood close and gently turned his head to see his injury. "Temu didn't know any better, but damn that animal anyway."

"It could've been worse," he told her, the center of his chest glowing with warmth as she carefully dabbed at his wound with a clean cloth she'd pulled from inside her coat. "I managed to cast magic to protect myself just before that powerful clap of yours."

She frowned hard. "I didn't even know I could do that."

"Really?" A daunting thought then occurred to him. "Did it drain you?"

He knew the answer was yes when she shut her eyes and pressed her lips together. "I'm sorry."

"Don't apologize for something that wasn't your fault," he said as she dampened the cloth with fresh snow and returned to his wound. "Will you make it until tonight?"

She nodded in reply.

"I won't let him do that to you again," he swore. "We'll not move on until we're both protected."

She furrowed her forehead in worry. "More magic?"

"I know you don't trust it, but I hope you at least trust me."

"Of course, I do."

Her earnest admission nearly lifted him off the ground. If they weren't still vulnerable to attack, he'd kiss her then and there. But the longer he waited to cloak their minds from scrying magic, the greater the risk the inquisitor would try again.

"He was..." She closed her eyes, voice losing strength. "He was going to make me kill you."

"And the push for Tetsutani? Was that also him?"

She moistened her lips. He tried to ignore the way they glistened. "I was supposed to surrender myself to someone there."

"Do you know their name? What they look like?" She shook her head, and he had to bite back a curse. "You're certain the inquisitor was controlling you?"

"I'd never forget his voice," she rasped, the distant look of unease on her face making him want to stab something—preferably the inquisitor.

Instead, he quickly cleared a large patch of snow while Mikari retrieved her still-skittish mount. Then he pulled a small volume from his saddlebags to review the magical array he'd have to draw. Any writing implement, ink, and canvas would work, so he used the dagger to cut the relevant pattern into the half-frozen soil. When it was finished, he and Mikari stood facing each other in its center.

"Prepare to be impressed," he told her with a wry grin.

A small, delighted smile eased her tense expression. "I already am."

"I'll expect effusive praise."

This time, she laughed. "Oh, of course. I'm sure I'll be gushing."

He cleared his throat before centering himself, grin fading. His magic quieted in readiness.

Hands at his sides, he drew from his magic at a carefully controlled speed until the perfect amount of power had built up inside the circle, illuminating its pattern. The air around them stilled, growing quiet.

Mikari stared at the circle and then at him, her beautiful face open with wonder. Maze take him, he wanted to kiss her.

I can right now, he realized. Base instinct told him to apply the spell's magic with a touch to his subject's forehead, but anywhere on the body worked, even through clothing. He didn't even have to grant *mind cloak* with his hand. Any part of him would do. His toe, the tip of his nose... his lips.

He made an instant decision that stirred his blood. And with the array already primed, there was no time to warn her.

One pounding step closed the distance between them. Reaching out, he grasped her nape and slid his other arm around her waist, hauling her against him. She made a gasp of surprise but remained pliable in his embrace. Power flooded his mouth, drawn there by his will.

"*Kokoro no kakushi*," he said on a hard breath out.

His lips surged against hers, and their softness parted sweetly for his tongue. The sizzle of magic between them was as audible as their shared breaths. Its power permeated his brain, warming him like a guzzled cup of *esorege*, shielding his mind from attempts to affect his will while the array enveloped them in a metaphysical cloak that would repel divination magic.

The spell took only seconds to cast, but Jun continued plundering her mouth as if his heart would stop the instant their lips parted.

His magic, humming with passion, groped hungrily at hers. She stiffened with its every stroke but didn't resist his hold. Instead, she serenaded him with transported moans while clinging to him as if in danger of being swept away, her sweet, silky taste only fanning his desire for her.

What he wouldn't give to be somewhere warm and private, in more ways than one.

But he had an empress to update and another half-day of riding ahead of him. He could only hope his erection abated by the time he was back in the saddle, otherwise the next few hours would be torturous.

He pulled his magic back and lifted his head, surprised by how much force he had to use as her hand tightened on his nape. His magic also fought him, its thorny response mirroring Mikari's deeply erotic growl.

"More," she begged in an aching voice, rising to her toes. Her eyelids were low, her lips puffy and wet. He couldn't stop staring at how inviting they looked...

Not until she gasped and shoved herself away from him, staring at him in horror and what looked like pain, her shoulders hunched.

Taken aback, he worried his magic had done something unexpected to her or that the inquisitor—

"Maze take me," she choked out, shaky on her feet. "You have no idea how dangerous that kiss was."

What? Hadn't he made it clear that he would be the one feeding her?

"I'm well aware of the risks, Mikari. I'm not afraid."

"You should be!" she exclaimed, close to tears. His stomach was tight with the need to hold and reassure her, but her cringe of shame stayed him. "I...I've been avoiding it, but I need to tell you why I can't accept pleasure from you."

Dread sank to the pit of his stomach. "All right."

"Something happened during my cleansing," she began, hesitant. "I thought that I was making love with you. And when the pleasure peaked, I...*needed* more. As if it were the only thing holding back an avalanche of pain."

She was staring at some spot on the ground next to him, eyes glassy with memory. "The frenzy made everything hazy, but I...I remember holding that man down, believing he was you, and..." Her shoulders tensed. "And yet I still killed him."

Shock rippled through him.

He'd suspected upon first meeting her again that she'd killed, but only because her attitude had been so unrepentant, even indifferent. The Mikari he'd first met had seemed like a ruthless stranger capable of murder, although he hadn't wanted to believe it even then.

But he had since seen otherwise. Living with a curse for twenty years had hardened her, but it hadn't destroyed the woman he'd fallen in love with. In fact, the Mikari before him was even more amazing than the one he'd known as a young man.

She had pursued a well-respected profession and was damned good at it. She was a seasoned traveler who could handle everything from grumpy innkeepers to bandits.

Just now, she had managed to stop herself from driving a dagger into his heart, had been prepared to slit her throat instead. The willpower that must've taken, especially for someone without magic...

At his stunned silence, Mikari forged ahead. "That's why I shun any stimulation. I can safely feed if I forbid myself pleasure." She looked up at him, full of trepidation. "I've never killed anyone since. I swear."

Jun thought of how he'd spent the last twenty years, and he remembered Mikari asking him during her interview how he'd ascended so quickly to his rank in the empress's army.

Then he thought back to the moment he'd learned that Vallen and Rosuke had once been lust eaters, and the tormented look on Rosuke's face. *"The hunger was so powerful I couldn't even think to resist it,"* he'd said. *"I couldn't think at all."*

At the time, Jun had wondered what he'd done—or not done—to make the others think they couldn't trust him with the full truth. Then he'd wondered, deeply ashamed, whether they'd have been right two weeks ago. He certainly hadn't given Mikari much empathy the night he'd found her.

And he'd failed again last night to give her any, he realized—too busy questioning himself, Maze take him.

He dragged Mikari back into his embrace. "I believe you," he said, resting his cheek on the crown of her head, his voice gruffer than he'd expected. "If I feel any horror, it's because I can't help imagining what you felt when you saw what had happened—not just to the man, but to you. I can see that his death haunts you, but you're not to blame." She released a weepy sigh of relief and slid her arms around him.

He'd at least had a choice when it came to killing during his time as a mercenary. He preferred to think the four deaths and countless injuries he'd caused were justified, but blood was blood, and no curse had compelled him to shed it.

"I just wanted you to know why I rebuffed you last night," she said, leaning back. "And why it'll happen again tonight."

"'It's not you, it's me.' That sort of thing?" he asked.

"Yes, but it's more than just the risk of frenzying. Like I've said, I'm always hungry. The need to feed…well, it complicates how I feel."

His heart shrank. He understood what she was saying, that her attraction to him was, at best, muddled by the curse. At worst, it was the only thing drawing her to him.

But he still didn't like hearing it and couldn't help his chilly tone. "All the more reason to cure you," he said in concession, letting her go and stepping back.

"No, Jun. Do not mistake me." She entered the space between them as though drawn forward, and stared at him with naked yearning, her hands clasped against her chest. "I do want you. I want you so much."

His heart tripped, and he was momentarily struck silent.

"The things I put in that journal were mere yearnings that I knew wouldn't make me happy. I wrote them all down thinking I'd burn the volume once it was full, hoping maybe it would satisfy the Divine One. But I could never have consigned all my hopes I'd ever had for us to the fire. Whenever I missed you, I drew a wind bell instead."

The breath he'd been holding left him in a rush. He wanted to argue that her "mere yearnings" were still important and not to be discarded like spoiled rice wine. She was allowed to want more than a basic existence, to dream and have ambitions. However, hearing how deeply she still treasured their connection had tied his tongue. He'd seen hundreds of wind bells in her personal journal.

"But you…you have no idea how incredibly delicious you smell." She inhaled slowly, eyes sliding shut with an expression of pure want.

Molten desire washed over him. He gave a broken moan, his sex as hard as stone oak.

"R-right now, it's…oh, it's sugar and spice, salt and smoke, creamy and biting." She inhaled again. "It's orgasmic. I'm so liquid inside that I swear it'll start dripping down my thighs."

"*Fuck*, Mikari," he said with choked incredulity, grasping her arms on instinct, his body blasting out heat.

"Oh, I'd fuck you," she promised in a low, sultry voice, nailing him with a gaze to match. His cock kicked, and his simmering magic began to boil within him. "Only…I've no doubt what would happen if I ever sought gratification. I'd cease to care about anything else, not until the moment you've been wracked with more pleasure than your heart can bear, and you take your final breath."

He couldn't help imagining such a demise—a sheen of sweat on her flushed skin, the brutal pressure of her hands holding him down, the vigorous rhythm of her silky nest and breathy grunts—and it made him gasp with need.

Mikari snatched him against her with a keening cry, rising on tiptoe to fit them closer together. She shook with strain, as taut as a drawn bow.

"Y-yes, that's how I'd do it, what I've pictured," she groaned, rubbing her stomach against his aching cock, making him groan in return. "More times than you can dream."

He would also come the second he got inside her—an orgasm was already racked in his balls. He thanked the Divine One when she stopped moving, although doing so appeared to be painful for her.

"I so badly want it to be real, this bone-deep ache for you," she begged. "I don't want either of us to have any reason to doubt it. But my hunger—it's a continual weight upon me, always pulling me toward that fearful frenzy. And I cannot help but think, what if the longing I feel…is to take your life again?" she asked in a bare whisper. "H-how can I know the difference?"

Sympathetic pain seized his chest. He cupped his hands about her neck, thumbs resting behind her jaw.

"There's what you crave, and then there's what you do—and your actions speak to your incredible fortitude," he said, holding her gaze. "But if you cannot trust your heart, then take comfort in knowing that mine is certain."

She blinked in astonishment. Then a puff of stunned laughter transformed her look of anguish into a misty-eyed smile. "I actually believe you. Must be the beard."

He let out a relieved chuckle, his gaze drawn once more to her pink, pillowy lips. To say he looked forward to feeding her tonight was an understatement. He then realized they might not have the necessary privacy at whatever lodgings they secured. Feeding her now was possibly the safer bet.

Or perhaps he just couldn't wait to sheathe his cock in her throat, wishing he could push her to her knees then and there. She'd surely be uncomfortable with the idea. They were out in the open. Anyone could come down the road at any time.

"I'd do it," she whispered, waking him to the realization that he was stroking his thumb across her soft mouth. "I want to. Please let me."

He let out a strangled groan, for once not angry at her trespass into his private desires. Instead, he shoved his hand between them and tore at the front of his split-skirt.

She helped by untying his overcoat, only far enough to push it out of the way, their hands snatching and fumbling at his clothing. When she sank to her haunches, Jun could only spare two seconds to make sure they were still alone before locking his gaze onto her face.

His erection went straight from the warmth of his clothing into the wet heat of her mouth, and the air exploded from his lungs. He squeezed her name out through his teeth, and when her lips touched the base of his shaft, the air came rushing back.

He watched, mesmerized, panting in primal groans, as she swallowed him over and over. The sight was a thousand times more heart-stopping than he'd ever imagined. She kept one hand on his shaft, stroking. The other gripped the front of his thigh to keep her steady.

A tiny part of him still capable of thought wanted to prolong this interlude, but here and now was neither the time nor the place for something more involved, nor did either of them seem capable of slowing down.

He nevertheless forced himself to focus, just long enough to sear every detail of this moment into his brain. He was already thoroughly familiar with the feel of her mouth, the lush, slippery heat sucking him in.

But the way she moved her head, the furrow of effort between her eyes, and the shape her lips took as they moved down his—

Jun rolled to the balls of his feet, every part of him seizing, and clamped his hands onto her head. It was a good thing they were alone, because he released a string of *fucks* that grew in volume and violence. He watched his shaft disappear into her mouth, then everything blurred.

He was aware that he was still upright, his heart pounding, his skin so blistering hot he wished he was naked. The pressure on his sides was from her hands holding on tight.

His magic offered up a tendril of power which her hunger yanked downward like a wild animal offered a fresh kill. This time, he felt the jolt of fatigue as it took more of his energy than he could spare.

Then he became aware of the rhythm of delighted groans, eager swallows, and gentle strokes. His breath burst from his throat as pleasure pounded through him, sharp and deep, scooping him out and siphoning the strength from him one pulse at a time, until his heels were back on the ground and his body was shaking.

Gulping for air, he blinked hard to regain his focus just in time to see her pulling off him. Her pink lips were swollen and wet, flushed around the edges, and she licked them with satisfaction. Trembling, he managed to tuck himself away.

He had no idea what to say. His orgasm just now had almost surpassed the last one they'd ever shared as wards, only he still had the strength to remain standing. Barely.

Mikari slowly rose to her full height, mouth soft with pleasure but eyes dark with pain. Indeed, her pupils were enlarged, and the white of her wig made the twin pools of amaranth on her freckled cheeks pop. She was aroused to a fever's pitch.

Again, he raged at the thought of not reciprocating. Of shunning her blessed taste and wetness upon his lips, tongue, fingers, and cock. He *needed* to witness her in the throes of pleasure, even more than his next breath.

At last, words came to him, deep and scratchy with exhaustion. "The day you're cured, I'll not have another orgasm until I've given you fifty."

She grinned while biting her puffy lower lip. "That assumes I'll survive the first one."

"The second one will revive you," he joked, smiling.

Despite feeling bone-tired and a little weak-kneed, he was light and loose with afterglow. He'd need a few more minutes before attempting to ride. Eyes still grinning, Mikari tugged her gloves back on.

"Why fifty? Is that...how many you've had?" Her smile grew a little tense. "With others?"

He thought about redirecting Mikari, if not reassuring her, but he didn't want all the times they'd spent in another's arms to remain a wedge between them. He hated his jealousy, and if she felt even half as jealous as he did, she surely hated it as well.

"Fifty simply sounded like a good start, but...yes, give or take. I haven't, uh...indulged much."

"I—" Blinking, she paused to swallow. "I avoided it as much as I could," she said, voice dropping in and out. "Having a network of donors helped."

"Donors?" *Not lovers?*

"That's how I think of them, the people I've fed from. I sought them out, after all, rather than the other way around. With you, however, I must admit to having moments when I become..."—she furrowed her brow, as though searching for the right word—"possessive in a way I'm not used to feeling. But, to my shame, I can't know for certain whether my heart or my curse is to blame. You're not like anyone else I've ever fed from."

Could she be describing jealousy? He tried not to cling to her admission, but that she even attempted to assure him that he was special to her gave him hope.

"Would you like to hear something that might help?" he asked, gently brushing her cheek with his knuckles.

"Help with my shame? Or my confusion?" Vulnerability was etched into her face.

"You've done nothing to be ashamed of," he insisted. "I'm in awe of your strength. Yes, I'm jealous. Deeply," he bit out, tracing the edge of her distracting lower lip. "But that's my problem, not yours."

A release of some sort showed on her face. Her shoulders relaxed.

"That last night we were together, that sensation when our magics joined, crows in the empress's court call it the 'second climax.'" Her expression turned fretful. "I...I haven't had a connection like that since you. The only times it was even possible, my magic balled up tight."

There it was again. Vulnerability, furrowing her brow. And yearning. "But I've felt something. It's faint, but—"

"Indeed, my magic's been reacting to you since the moment I recognized your voice at that inn in Koichino. That first night, it was like...a storm inside me," he professed.

She looked practically entranced, cheeks even pinker than before, lips slowly parting. He couldn't stop himself from stroking her blushing flesh. "I've never gotten over you, lamb."

Mikari closed her eyes with a shudder, nuzzling into his touch. "You were right," she said with a bittersweet smile. "That did help."

Maze take him, how he loved this woman, so much he could hardly breathe.

But love couldn't remove the gap in their apparent ages, nor align the disparate paths their lives had taken. He had to acknowledge what would likely happen once she was cured, even if her feelings for him remained genuine.

She would have her freedom, at last. He didn't dare hope that she'd invite or even allow him to travel the southern lands with her, an aging reminder of her difficult past.

If he was lucky, he'd survive losing her, consoled by the knowledge that she was free and happy.

"You're well fed, then?" he asked, forcing himself to step back. The magical pattern he'd cut into the soil had disappeared, leaving only a circle cleared of snow.

Her eyes twinkled. "In more ways than one."

Groaning as desire swept through him anew, he forced his legs to take him toward his mount. "Have mercy on me, lamb. I need to be able to sit in a saddle."

"My apologies," she said, walking beside him, voice threaded with sincerity. "I'm afraid I can't help it."

"Even when we were wards, you enjoyed making me squirm." Her favorite tactic had been to slip him a note, usually only big enough for a single sentence.

"True," she acknowledged. "I loved knowing I was in your thoughts."

"*Aj'*, you were in them almost constantly." *You still are.*

To his dismay, he'd had to burn every note she'd slipped him, lest the preceptors discover them, but he still remembered several of them, including one she'd tucked next to his pottery wheel after Jun's effort to remake over a hundred broken ceramics had failed to save the frail ward's life.

You're the greatest person I've ever known. Always will be.

He'd kept the heartwarming words as long as he dared, their worth to him as large as the temple's grandest mural.

However, most of her little messages had warmed another part of him. One in particular had kept him hard and edgy nearly the entire day, and then at random for weeks after. *I want to kiss you everywhere*, she'd written.

He let her do just that the next time they met, then eagerly returned the favor.

"I need to send word to Houfu before we push on," he said once they had reached their mounts. Nugun had been waiting patiently this whole time, and Mikari's temperamental reindeer looked deceptively calm. "Hopefully, they'll be able to warn the delegation about a potential enemy in Tetsutani."

Mikari nodded and bent down to search through her pack, while Jun reached into his coat and withdrew the speaking mirror in its traveling case.

It made a sound he did not like.

He quickly pulled apart the case's leather ties. *Please don't be broken.*

"Divine One's crudding arse," he swore as he stared at the shattered mirror. The glass had cracked in several places, and shards of it had come loose from the top right of the mirror's face. Rather than the imperial palace's mirror room, each piece of glass now reflected his horrified expression.

"Can...can you fix it?" she whispered, hesitant.

"The magic in it is gone," he ground out. "And I don't know how to put it back—can't, without its twin. All I can do is turn it into something pretty to sell."

Without the speaking mirror, he had no way to warn the delegation that one of the inquisitor's minions was lying in wait at their next destination. He supposed he could wait for the people in Houfu to notice a problem, and scry upon him to learn what it was—he'd feel a tingle and could simply start speaking out loud.

But the effects of *mind cloak* would block their scrying sensor. And even if he dismissed the benefits of his magical protection—which he wouldn't because the inquisitor could then attempt to mentally dominate Mikari again—he'd have no reliable way to know whether a particular tingle of awareness was the inquisitor or the capital.

Perhaps the empress had the strength to overcome *mind cloak*, or could access other, more powerful kinds of divination magic, but he assumed she didn't, based on her distress over communications with her scouts in Gozu.

No, circumstance rather than magical compulsion was what now demanded that he and Mikari reach Tetsutani as quickly as possible.

They could push their mounts as far as they dared and then arrange to borrow well-rested ones at one of the small farms or pocket-villages dotting the road. He knew Mikari would ride all night if he asked it of her, but the clouds overhead promised snow, which would make travel even more difficult, exhausting, and dangerous. And now that a cloud of anger had replaced the afterglow of feeding Mikari, his head was clanging where her reindeer had kicked it.

Still, he had to try.

Scowling and still cursing, he bundled the broken mirror up tight and stowed it in his saddlebags, for he didn't have the spare time, magical stamina, or inclination to fix it. As he tied the bag shut, he noticed Mikari looking at him with a mortified grimace.

Oh, dammit. She had to think he was incensed at her.

He forced his face into something more neutral. "It's not your fault."

"I held back that I'd been feeling someone watching me."

True. But she couldn't have known she was sensing a magical intrusion. Still, he wished that she had trusted him with her worries.

He shook his head and moved to untether his horse. "It's all moot at this point. I can't attempt to communicate a warning to the delegation without dispelling our magical protection, which I won't do while the inquisitor can try again to attack or interfere. So, we'll stick to our original plan."

"To Tetsutani, then," she said, withdrawing something from her pack. She smeared a small amount of powder on a cloth, intending to cleanse her mouth. "I assume we'll travel overnight? Grab fresh horses somewhere? I know of an orchard that might lend us a pair. They'll be fair on price. I'll help negotiate and make sure someone follows us with our mounts once they've rested."

"I'd appreciate it," he rumbled before mounting his horse. He shouldn't have been surprised to hear her suggest the same plan as he'd been considering, but he was.

Mikari turned her back to make quick use of the powder and cloth and then grabbed a handful of snow from a nearby branch to rinse.

Already, Jun's pounding head and aching body demanded that he rest, but it would be hours before they reached the orchard. Hours of cold and wind and keeping his seat upon Nugun.

Then they'd be riding even farther in the dark, on unfamiliar mounts, possibly through driving snow, and they'd arrive in Tetsutani at a frigid, still-dark hour without any knowledge of whether Kie, Seita, and the brownie delegation had met any hostility.

Holding back a pained grimace, he adjusted the length of the reins in his hand and tried to remember just a few moments ago when the only sensation swimming through his veins had been pleasure. Maze take him, the memory would warm his blood for the rest of his life.

"I'm ready," Mikari announced, reins firmly in hand.

"Then let's go." He urged his horse into a trot, one that her reindeer could match.

And he hoped they didn't arrive too late.

PART THREE
Delectable Passion

Chapter Eighteen

"I'm told you can speak Common?"

Pausing in her scrubbing of the hallway floor, Nene looked up at her employer, Master Hayashi, whose mouth was tight with irritation to match his snappish tone.

"Well enough, sir," she said, on guard.

"And what does 'well enough' mean?"

She held back a defiant glare. "Enough for regular conversation." Which he'd learned at her placement interview but had forgotten. All he cared about was money and—when he was drunk—propositioning her.

"Come with me. You can finish that later," he bade. "And fix yourself up. You're as unkempt as a field hand."

Stung, she followed the innkeeper toward the reception area, wiping her hands on her apron and tucking a stray lock of her black hair into her head scarf. She could do little about her red cheeks when Hayashi worked her to the bone, but she blotted the sweat from her forehead with her handkerchief.

"An odd group has just arrived," Hayashi told her, speaking low and fast. "They say they're delegates from Houfu, and only one of them speaks Gozuan. Name's Noriaki. Two of the five are crows. *Uncleansed*," he whispered forcefully.

"I want you to show them to their suite and attend to them during their stay," he said. "But don't let them know you speak Common. Tell me everything you overhear. Understand?"

She had little choice but to nod, although the thought of lying made the corners of her mouth tighten. She was neither good at it nor comfortable with it. They would see right through her.

At least it wasn't some new onerous chore, she supposed. The innkeeper rarely used her for guest relations, but she was certain she'd remember her early training. *When bowing, bend low enough to see your feet. Smile with your eyes. Open and close doors for guests. Move quietly.*

Unfortunately, she forgot half of it the second she laid eyes on the newly arrived guests, who were still checking in. Or rather, when she spotted one guest in particular—an unimprovably handsome young man with black hair cut close to his scalp. Easily a head taller than her, he had thick brows over beautiful dark-brown eyes, and high cheekbones softened by full, petulant lips.

He and the rest of his party were better dressed than she could ever comfortably afford, all of them wearing fine, thick linens and wools. His hooded overcoat and fitted split-skirt had been dyed in beautiful but subtle dark-brown patterns that complemented his warm, sandy complexion. And he seemed quite accustomed to the sword at his waist.

The "neutral" expression he wore for the reception clerk made him look rather unapproachable, but it softened a degree when he noticed her arrival, his posture turning unsure, as though something about her was unexpected. Her beet-red face, no doubt.

His gaze landed on her forearm, where she was branded, and his expression hardened once more, the lines of his cut jaw firming and flexing. The crow woman next to him, whose hand rested casually on the sword at her waist, also noticed it and subtly scowled.

Nene thought she'd become well used to displaying proof of her cleansing, but she found herself untying the linen cord that held her sleeves back and then covering her brand as she performed a belated bow of greeting, not quite managing a smile.

The crows didn't particularly strike her as the diplomatic sort, but the two older brownie women reminded her of Hayashi's aging mother, who still contributed to the running of the inn that was once her and her husband's. She was shrewd but kind, though she more often leaned toward the former.

Nene suspected that her employer restricted his sexual advances toward her because his mother would disapprove. Whether that disapproval stemmed from Nene being black-haired or an employee, she wasn't certain. Thankfully, the woman was still in rather good health.

Speaking directly to the translator in their party, Hayashi confirmed the details of their stay—a minimum of two nights while they awaited others—and said he'd given them one of the inn's best rooms.

If she weren't so used to Hayashi's needless exaggerations, she might've let her incredulity show on her face, but to him, *every* room was "one of his best."

Oh, the inn's accommodations were all nice enough. She and the other maids worked hard to keep every surface dusted, every mattress fresh-smelling, and every lantern well supplied with wick and oil. But the inn's largest and most beautiful rooms were on the opposite side of the building from where the delegation would be staying.

"One of our maids will show you to your suite on the third floor," Hayashi said, prompting her to bow again. She managed a welcoming expression this time. He offered to have a porter carry their things, but the delegation declined. "Very well. Should you need anything, Nene shall provide it. Please enjoy your stay."

"This way, please." Doing her best to appear graceful, she gestured toward the main stairs, then turned to lead.

Behind her, a low voice discreetly murmured in Common. "Hey, Noriaki." The party's translator responded with a curious *hm*. "That pretty maid, what's her name?"

She nearly missed the first rise on the stairs, heart racing with bashfulness and yet twisting with guilt as Noriaki whispered the answer to the male crow's question, for she also wished to learn his name.

How could a mere glance stir her heart to this degree? Had she only imagined herself to be half in love with Master Komatsu?

If so, then she'd been right to deny him the other day. No doubt she was simply aching for some relief and couldn't help reacting to every pretty face she saw.

Of course, she'd been sorely tempted to find that relief with Komatsu. Declining had been both heart- and gut-wrenching, a seed of regret that had sprouted into frustrated arousal later that night while she'd lain wide-awake in bed and recalled the pained yearning on his face.

However, she knew from bitter experience what usually happened when taking a lover. And here at the Silver Hammer, she'd seen other employees become romantically involved with guests over the last two years, and in not a single instance had both sides come away happy.

The worst so far had been a wealthy tradesman staying in one of their largest suites while working out a supply deal with the town's mine. He had pursued one of the other maids for nearly a month and ended up proposing marriage.

But the morning after he'd concluded his business, he snuck out of the bed he'd just tricked his "bride-to-be" into, and left.

Risking such betrayal would be bad enough, but even if Nene knowingly agreed to a mere dalliance, the more common arrangement she'd seen, she had zero doubt that she'd lose her position were the innkeeper to learn she had crossed the line with a guest.

Because if he couldn't have her, no one would.

And so, painfully conscious of the tail of black hair sweeping the back of her shoulders, she smoothly preceded the delegation through the third-floor hallway toward their suite and put any sort of romantic thoughts about the handsome southern crow firmly out of her head.

She started by keeping her gaze politely averted from him as she gave them a tour of the suite and explained the inn's amenities. Noriaki translated for the rest of the group while they settled into the room, his voice scratchy.

"You should order yourself some tea," the male crow said with a sweet note of concern as he removed his sword. "You sound even worse than yesterday."

One of the brownie women sighed. "It's from all the talking he's had to do. First, that hours-long conversation with the mayor of Koichino, then all that time we spent trading in the market, followed by another long conversation with the temple loyalist."

Nene had to stop herself from offering to bring them a refreshment service—she wasn't supposed to understand their conversation, the details of which would no doubt interest her employer.

"Would everyone care for some tea?" Noriaki asked the others. Several heads nodded. He turned to her and made the request in Gozuan.

"Of course." She dipped her head. "I'll have a tray delivered to you shortly. Is there anything else I can do for your party at this time?"

AT THE MAZE'S CENTER

After hearing a quick translation, the same brownie woman spoke. "Word for word, please," she said to Noriaki, who nodded. Then she spoke to Nene directly.

"I'll be blunt, dear. As your employer may have told you, we represent Empress Shumei. And she is...concerned by the Gozuan practice of confining and cleansing crows. Judging by your age and the brand on your arm, you were recently cleansed at Genbi Temple. If this is correct, then I'd like to speak to you at some point about your time there. What the Primary is like, and how they treat their wards."

A subject that Nene didn't care for, nor did she know whether Hayashi would even permit such a conversation, given his subterfuge. She was loath to ask him, wary of being further involved in his machinations.

And if the Primary at Genbi learned that a group of imperial delegates sought to oppose cleansings, and that she'd spoken to them about life inside the temple...

She strove to keep her expression placid and oblivious—at least until Noriaki translated—but her stomach sank as her cheeks turned conspicuously warmer, betraying her racing heart. Only after she'd done it did she realize she'd slipped her branded arm behind her.

No one seemed to notice, however, except for the male crow. She saw it the second he knew she could understand them, his face slackening in surprise.

For once, the blood left her cheeks. She quickly looked away.

"...how the temple treats its wards," Noriaki said in Gozuan, having translated the brownie woman's request—Natsu was her name? She'd barely listened.

"I-I'm afraid I can't," she replied.

"May I ask why?" Natsu asked after a translation delay.

She found herself glancing at the male crow, which made her heart flutter anew, for his expression was...dangerously arresting. Full of righteous anger and compassion.

"It'd only lead to trouble," she murmured, speaking to Natsu but looking obliquely at him. "Excuse me, please."

Though she hadn't yet determined whether they needed anything else from her, she bowed once more in parting, then moved toward the door to take her leave, fighting the instinct to scurry away.

Unsettled and distracted, she failed to close the portal behind her and was halfway down the hall before realizing her error.

Turning abruptly, she crashed right into a warm wall of flesh and reared back in surprise, not apprehending that a low voice had spoken her name until strong hands reached out to steady her, clasping her shoulders firmly before quickly gentling.

She looked up at the male crow and nervously swallowed. His lean, handsome visage was even more devastating when viewed up close, especially when he seemed so uncertain yet determined.

And he smelled wonderful, Maze take her. Clean, hot skin with a whiff of pine sap.

Should she somehow try to feign ignorance, or would lying only make things worse? Her heart wanted her to confess, but...

"You don't have to say anything," he said, barely above a whisper. "We're not—*I'm* not here to make trouble for you, though I realize you may not see it that way."

He had slowly stepped back, giving her a small amount of space, and yet she couldn't breathe any better, not when he was trailing his hand down her branded arm. Warmth gently encircled her wrist.

Her lungs constricted further when something brushed the edge of her burning cheek. His hand, she realized. It tightened into a fist and disappeared, the corners of his eyes tensing in a brief wince, as though he felt sorry for taking the liberty.

"You have my vow that speaking to us will not have any consequences for you. But if there are any assurances that I can give you or conditions I can satisfy, you only need to ask."

He coaxingly drew her arm away from her body, her loose-fitting sleeve slipping down to her elbow with his other hand helping it along, the one that had touched her face so gently. Lifting her extended arm, he held the back of her hand against his chest, right over his heart.

He broke their intense eye contact to look closer at her brand—three intersecting lines capped with small circles. A simplistic snowflake. Sometimes, she could still feel the instant the temple guards had pressed the red-hot iron onto her skin.

His jaw slowly jutted out, brow furrowing with sympathy. He drew his thumb along the edge of the dark-colored scarring, treating the brand as if it were still fresh.

How could she derive so much joy merely from the feel of his gentle grip on her forearm, his rapid heartbeat against the back of her hand, and his thumb stroking her skin?

"This should never have happened," he rasped, tearing her heart out. "Nor the years that led up to it."

Unbearably touched, she wanted so badly to speak to him in Common, to ask him his name and tell him *thank you* and *I want to trust you* and *sweet Garden, but you're handsome.*

But a small delegation was no match against the temples. He could promise her nothing—offer her nothing but his sympathy, as heartfelt and appreciated as it was.

And so, well aware that his companions were bunched up at the door of the suite silently watching, she averted her eyes and replied to him in Gozuan. "I'm sorry, but I can't be involved."

Then she tugged at her arm, which he instantly released, and backed away with another bow before turning to leave. There was only silence behind her.

Even more distracted than before, she made repeated attempts to swallow the lump in her throat and walked on unsteady feet toward a discreet and narrow staircase meant for employees, well-hidden to one side of a shallow alcove.

One of the kitchen staff would be delivering their tea service, she reminded herself. She wouldn't have to see him again very soon, possibly not for the rest of the evening. And in less than two days, he would be gone. She'd certainly never see him again after that.

"Nene," came a distant whisper.

Startled, she spun with a backward hop. There was no one else in the hall, but the door to an unoccupied guest room stood ajar.

Assuming she'd find the innkeeper in there, wriggling his fingers in anticipation of hearing what she'd gleaned, she entered the room wearing a tight frown, which surprise quickly erased.

"Oh! Master Komatsu."

Maze take it, how many more shocks would the day subject her to?

His posture was straight but relaxed, his expectant expression free of any resentment. He dipped his head in politeness, which few people did for her. "Good afternoon. May we speak for a moment?"

How odd. She had not felt this...reluctance toward him before, only secret happiness. Too much excitement, perhaps? That didn't sound like her.

And why did she suddenly find him less handsome, his manner shallow? Why had she not noticed before that he seemed to resemble the aides who'd always accompanied the inquisitor whenever he'd visited?

She did her best to look contrite. "Unfortunately, sir, I—"

He smiled, wide and bright and achingly alluring. Her reservations fell away in an instant, her shoulders drooping with relief. Here was a friend, she thought. An ally. Someone whom she could bring into her confidence, although her heart didn't beat any faster at the thought. Not like it had with the southern crow.

"The briefest moment," Komatsu cajoled, though she'd already changed her mind. He stepped closer, smile turning a little sharper. "In fact, this will take no time at all."

Then he reached for her.

MIKARI AND JUN set out once more, and less than an hour later, snow began to fall, small flakes at first, then large ones, growing heavier until they were constantly brushing it off their clothing. Still, they managed to maintain a brisk pace.

As the hours and leagues passed, Mikari couldn't help picturing every way in which the delegation might come to harm and what sort of look she'd see on Jun's face if they did. She didn't have to imagine his resentment, anger, or disappointment when she'd already seen all three. But his hatred? She'd not seen that yet and prayed she never did.

When she wasn't agonizing over the consequences of the broken speaking mirror, she was bombarded with every horrific detail of her morning and of the violence she'd been forced to unleash.

She tried not to relive it. Instead, she tried to recall her awe when Jun had cast his magical protection on her, suffusing and encasing her in warmth as comforting as a lovingly wrapped wool blanket. Just thinking of the kiss that had delivered his spell still stole her breath.

She also tried to remember the scent of his lust, its complexity and potency, and how much she had enjoyed pleasuring him in broad daylight. Yes, she had fed from him and been well satisfied, but his groans and curses and clutching hands had been far more memorable than the hefty dose of energy she'd received.

If he had touched her in that moment, when she'd been nearly mindless with arousal, she would not have had the strength to deny him.

But despite the other, more pleasant moments she'd had that day, she couldn't help remembering the final moment of their fight—the grief that had ripped her open the second she'd decided what to do, and his terror when she'd brought the dagger to her throat.

She was glad she didn't sleep, for those few minutes of violence would surely haunt her dreams for...who knew how long.

"Are you all right?"

Jun's voice interrupted her baleful ruminations. She tipped her head up and met his frowning concern, which was obvious despite the scarf concealing the lower half of his face. "Yes, I'm still me. I've not sensed anything new."

They had been walking their mounts for a short while to let them catch their breath, but with their next sprint, she and Jun would reach Koichino, where they'd be stopping only long enough for her to deliver a letter and for Jun and the animals to warm up and eat, before pushing on.

Mikari had considered looking for fresh mounts in Koichino, but she didn't think she could trust anyone residing there to bring Jun's prime stallion and her equally expensive reindeer to Tetsutani, not unless they paid an exorbitant sum that neither of them could afford.

The only people along the road to Tetsutani whom she could think to trust were the family that ran one of the largest orchards in Gozu. She would need to hide her face, having visited and performed for them nearly ten years ago, but that shouldn't be a problem.

"That's not what I mean," Jun said to her. "Every time I turn my head, you look like you have a preference in your throat."

"P...preference?" she echoed bemusedly. He had used the Gozuan word *tindu*, which also meant "intention" or "purpose," but he had to have meant *tinto*, which translated to— "Do you mean 'a bug?'"

To have a bug in one's throat was a Gozuan idiom for *nauseated*.

"I—" He barked with laughter. "Yes, I meant 'bug.' And here I thought I still spoke Gozuan perfectly."

"You do," she said, smiling with relief to hear him laugh. "I still wince whenever I think about the time I was reciting *Aya the Vigilant* and said she wore a collar instead of a sword."

He laughed again, the sound lifting the last of the weight that had been sitting on her heart all day. The weight would be back, she had no doubt, but for now she would savor the respite.

"*Kindi, kindu*...my tongue tripped! I was so embarrassed. But hardly anyone even reacted."

Jun's eyes were crinkled with amusement, and she wished she could see the smile hidden beneath his scarf. It made her realize how he must feel whenever he couldn't see her face.

"Your Common is amazing," she continued, having only a passable fluency herself. "You speak it so confidently. Do you know any other languages?"

After only a beat of silence, he proceeded to rattle off an impressive stream of words that hit her ear somewhat like Gozuan but with tighter lips and more y sounds. She looked at him round-eyed, snowflakes flying into her open mouth. "What language is that?"

"Chouja. It's spoken in the far south," he said, turning his gaze back to the road. "But most people there also speak Common just fine. I can carry on a simple conversation in Chouja, but I wouldn't want to be the translator in a trade deal."

"And what did you say in Chouja?"

"I asked if you're all right."

She narrowed her eyes. "That was a lot of words for 'are you all right.'"

"It was," he agreed in an arch tone that sent a warm frisson of bashfulness through her. *Bashfulness.* He went on before she could recover. "But tell me, Mikari, are *you* all right?"

Was she? After all that had happened since dawn? The weight on her heart returned. "I will be, eventually," she said, dissembling a cynical confidence. "You?"

He heaved a sigh. "Physically, I could be better. My head's still pounding. I ache everywhere. And I'm so hungry I could out-eat Nugun here." He patted his stallion's neck. "And before the thought even crosses your mind—no, I don't regret feeding you. Not one part of me," he muttered.

The thought *had* begun to form. "And mentally? I can't imagine how worried you must be about your court companions."

Jun blew out a breath. "Of course, I'm worried. And not just about the delegation. Us, too. But know this,"—he clapped his gaze upon her—"Kie and Seita are well trained, and their mission is to protect the delegates. I'm certain Houfu will warn them that our mirror no longer works, so they'll be extra cautious."

She nodded, but his assurances couldn't banish her frown. Despite knowing next to nothing about magic, even she knew the inquisitor was far more experienced with it than any of them. And far deadlier.

He didn't even need to be physically present in order to be a danger to them, and it stood to reason he was using magic to alter his appearance, the only question being how much. Would she know him if she saw him?

"*Ijaa.*" Jun's demand for attention pulled her out of her spiraling panic, his concerned gaze yet again capturing hers. "Tell me more about bards. This morning, I asked how often you meet one."

Ah yes, this morning, when her mind hadn't been her own and her only other major objective had been to avoid conversation, regardless of tact. She tried not to think of how rude she'd been to the proprietor in Okususo.

"Only rarely, when I'm this far from the Lake Route—there's usually enough work, and it's safer than more rural travel."

The Lake Route was the circuit of roads circumscribing Lake Iwakouri, a large body of freshwater from which the Omine River flowed. Despite Gozu's harsh winters, Iwakouri hardly ever froze, but when it did, it formed a wide shelf of hilly ice that broke into countless enormous shards in the spring.

"But not you," Jun observed. "Do you avoid the Lake Route, then? Less competition?"

"Less attention," she corrected. "But I do have to travel it a few times a year. Parts of it, at least."

He nodded, his bulky upper body expanding with a deep breath that then escaped as mist. She waited for him to ask about his family, some of whom still lived in Akawase, a major stop along the Lake Route. He had to realize that she'd likely know their condition.

"Do you wish to hear?" she gently asked when he remained silent. "About your family?"

He stiffened, not responding at first. "I don't know," he said eventually. "Haven't thought about most of them for years."

"Your sister, then?"

A bit of the tension left his rigid posture. "Is she well?"

"I've not seen her for a few years, but I have no reason to doubt it. She lives in Yuugai with her husband, who's a bookseller, and they have two sons. One is now seventeen, the other fifteen."

He let out an unhappy sigh. "I should have written to her more, knowing how impossible it was for her letters to find me. She's not heard from me in nearly five years."

"She'd be ecstatic to receive a visit, I'm certain."

"Perhaps." He then gave her a careful look. "And your parents?"

She glanced away. "I did send them a message a few months after I was cursed, saying I was alive, but I avoided my old village for years. Once I felt I was ready, I visited for a day. A washerwoman told me they'd died of a fever."

"I'm sorry to hear that, lamb. When did it happen?"

"The winter after my curse began. I…I'm not sure if they were alive to read my message." She swallowed. "I don't wish to talk about this anymore."

He made a soft grunt. "Ask me a question, then."

Well, there was quite the offer. "Any question?" she asked, sliding him a sly grin. "And you'll answer it?"

He groaned a curse. "Please don't take it as an opportunity to give me an erection."

"Oh, but now I'm so tempted. And it'll get your blood flowing."

"Forget it," he grumbled. "Let's run them the rest of the way. Put your mask on, if it suits you."

She did so, smiling.

They weren't in Koichino long. Barely half an hour, but it was long enough for night to fall. Delivering the letter from Okususo took but a few minutes. The same pair of stable boys cared for their winded mounts, and Jun scarfed down a well-made meal that one of the boys ran inside to fetch. All for a reasonable fee.

Mikari risked taking off her wig in sight of the stable workers, having worn the thing all day. She longed for an all-over bath and then a long, hot soak, but settled for brushing her hair. Jun sipped water and watched her movements from his seat at the other end of the bench they shared. A lit brazier sat between his feet to warm them.

"When I offered to answer a question, what came to mind?" he asked, voice low to avoid eavesdropping. Twenty feet away, a stable boy was checking Nugun's hooves.

She began rinsing her brush, dribbling water from the carafe onto the bristles. "I was going to ask why the empress sent one of her highest-ranked officers to Gozu. I would assume she'd rather not risk you, and that you'd have more important duties than chasing demons."

He considered her for a moment before he gave his reply, sounding almost...resigned. "She didn't choose to send me. I volunteered to come, much to the empress's worry. She presumed I was acting rashly from having my heart rejected."

Mikari's insides went cold. "Oh. Is there...someone you love back in Houfu?" She barely got the words out, every inch of her stinging. Like a hopeless fool, she'd assumed that no other woman had captured his interest. The possibility hadn't even occurred to her.

Jun watched her closely, as still as the frozen lump her heart had become. She waited for him to shake his head or to say no, but he paused and her anguish spread upward from her chest.

"While I'd like to say I volunteered out of a sense of duty to the court," he said, "the truth is that I've wanted to return for a long time, even when I was certain I didn't. Even when I was working toward settling down and starting a family with a particular woman whom I hoped to love one day."

Hoped to...one day. She breathed out, her heart knocking against her chest. The burn at the back of her throat told her she was close to weeping.

"Something was calling me," he rasped, "telling me to free myself."

From what? From her? So that he could move on? What else would compel him to come back after so long?

She didn't want him to find some other woman to marry—or, Maze take her, to unite with in a joining ceremony. But what compromise was there to allow them both happiness, assuming she survived the winter and would eventually be cured?

She imagined she'd love Houfu, and she might convince Jun to travel with her once or twice a year to some destination in the southern lands, but remaining with him in the capital would mean giving up her profession as she knew it.

And if Jun still wanted children, he would surely want to have them right away. An itch she still shared, but starting a family was an additional layer of complications, not to mention difficult to fathom after years of hopelessness.

Jun made a pained hiss that drew her attention. Face pinched, he lifted his hand to the side of his head that had taken a hard kick earlier. His hair there remained crusted with dried blood.

"It still hurts?" she asked, turning to him with worry. "I could check the wound. Perhaps a poultice will help? I know of a—"

He shook his head. "The pain will fade sometime tonight. My magic simply needs more time to aid in the healing. And I don't want a ball of wet mush freezing to my head."

She didn't bother to hide her frown but did hold her tongue. He'd fed her three separate times in the last day, but she supposed he knew better than she did whether his magic was struggling.

His eyes crinkled with amusement. "I can tell you want to say something."

She looked away to stow her brush. "I don't have the right."

"And what right is that?"

"The right to worry. To tell you that you're pushing yourself too hard." Her voice fell to a whisper. "The state you're in and the danger the delegation is walking into…it's all my fault."

"Hmph, I wasn't aware that you were the one who cursed yourself and forced yourself to attack me," he said lightly. "I'm also surprised to learn that the times I've fed you were not my decision."

"But if I had only—" Blinking back tears, she stared at the floor without seeing it. She had suppressed her regrets for so long, hoping the pain of them would fade, but it hadn't. "I should have run away with you. I knew I'd made an enormous mistake the second I'd returned to the wardhouse. And I've thought the same countless times since."

"You couldn't have known what the inquisitor would do."

She shook her head. "Part of me knew that the man at my cleansing couldn't have been you." She tied her bag shut with frustrated tugs. "But I was so relieved to see you. I wanted it to be you."

"He must've learned about us. And he used it against you."

"Yes, he violated my love for you. But I violated it first when I doubted it. I submitted to fear instead."

"Mikari, no—"

"Your mounts are ready," a stable boy called.

"Just another moment," Jun responded, then spoke in a soft rumble only she could hear. "Look at me. Lamb, look at me. Please."

Oh, Maze take him, she could never resist his pet name for her. Meeting his gaze, she noted the dark smudges beneath his eyes. He needed rest, preferably with a poultice of herbs, tree pitch, and reindeer velvet extract upon the gash in his scalp.

Regarding her tenderly, Jun reached across the space between them to comb his fingers through her hair, and his wonderfully warm hand found its usual spot just behind her ear.

"Either we both share the blame for our parting," he said, "or neither of us does. All these years, I've hated myself for leaving you there. I should've fought for you, one way or another—whatever would've kept us together."

If she weren't keenly aware of the pounding in her chest, she would've thought that the painful lump in her throat was her heart. A dangerously familiar aroma wafted around her, the spiced air becoming close, and she thanked the Divine One for the pervading odor of animals that spoiled it. Otherwise, she might lose all sense.

"Y-you would've had to kidnap me, and I know you wouldn't—"

"I should have," he said in a dark tone, the tenderness in his gaze turning into something greedy and harsh. "I know I considered it. Pictured it."

"Oh" was all she could say, filled with a sudden fever that burned away higher thought.

Stupidly, she looked at his surface desires, or rather, had never shut herself off from them. Glimpses of his fantasies, always of her, were torturous, but she'd take whatever shred of his desire she could get.

But just now, what she saw in his mind...

She shot up as though the bench were on fire, pulse fluttering. Jun calmly took his hand back, his stare so entrancing that she almost didn't notice the small smile on his lips.

"I told you 'no more peeking,'" he teased, rising to his feet with a wicked gleam in his eyes. "Perhaps I should've added 'or else.'"

He approached the waiting stable workers and spoke to them in a quiet but authoritative tone, gesturing here and there as he managed the final details of their departure. One of the boys had obtained a bronze handheld lantern to light their way through the snowy dark, and Jun confirmed its oil reserve was full, its wick properly set.

She drew her hood up and strapped on her pack without conscious thought, observing Jun with the stable boys with scant attention paid to their conversation.

Jun's fantasy still occupied her mind. In it, she saw herself as if she were Jun. There had been euphoria on her flushed face as her head rocked backward upon a red brocade pillow, which matched the bedding beneath her.

A band of red had encircled her neck, a joining mark, and the familiar shape of a wind bell's copper bulb formed its repeating pattern. Thick gold ropes had wrapped her upper body, restraining her arms behind her, leaving her breasts vulnerable to any and every kind of stimulation.

She'd seen his large hands gripping her hips, pulling her into his deep, gentle strokes, his wet cock glistening every time it made an appearance.

And in Jun's fantasy, her stomach had been rounded with child.

"Maze take me," she whispered.

Mikari had concocted quite a few wild fantasies about Jun, the sort she now knew were not so uncommonly shared by others and that her many glimpses into others' creativity had inspired.

She had pictured animalistic ardor. Slow, poignant lovemaking. Spontaneous midday trysts and...and showing affection anytime and anywhere she wanted, the way a normal couple might. Holding hands as they strolled through a festival. Embracing for a kiss whenever the mood struck and not just the times they could meet in secret. Sharing a bed and sleeping in each other's arms every night.

She had fantasized a life together, growing their love into a family. And it had been more stirring than any of the salacious mental images she'd conjured up.

But Jun had found a way to combine the two. And his fantasy hadn't been a surface desire. Those were always quick flashes in vague rooms, more sketches than paintings.

No, that vision had been his deepest, most privately held fantasy. One he'd come back to so many times it could now manifest in vivid clarity. One that evinced how ardently he wanted to claim her—in multiple, permanent ways.

"He still loves me," she whispered, reeling from the discovery.

And she still loved him too. More than ever. His magic was not the reason for his uniquely heady aroma, and the inexorable pull she felt toward him was not her curse's doing.

For there was no mistaking, no doubting, the painful yearning that had pierced her the second she'd recognized the scent of love. That same yearning had pricked her every time she'd fed from another, had stopped her from recording her most desperate longings in her journal, and had nearly stopped her heart when he'd told her he'd nearly taken a wife.

The curse could make her feel lust, but it couldn't make her feel love. What she was feeling was real, not fantasy. And, Maze take her, it was *deeply* mutual.

Never was she more determined to seek out a cure and seize the life with Jun that she'd been dreaming of for decades. What fate had in store for them didn't matter. Fate could go straight to Oblivion. Their happiness had been left unfulfilled for far too long, so she was going to find a way to make Jun's fantasy, and hers, a reality.

Chapter Nineteen

Mikari and Jun made short work of settling on their mounts. She chose to wrap a scarf around the lower half of her face rather than wear her mask.

Once they were outside, the two boys bid them safe travels from the shelter of the stable, their expressions full of concern. Though demons no longer seemed to threaten travelers at night, the fear was still there.

And then there was the danger of the elements. Snow still fell, the wind was picking up, and the cold had deepened dramatically. Jun and Mikari were experienced riders with well-trained mounts, but one false step could lead to injury or worse.

Jun had already lit the hefty lantern, which held enough oil to feed the wick inside for five or six hours. Hopefully, it would be enough fuel for them to reach the orchard.

She'd wanted to ask whether Jun could light their way with magic, but she didn't dare suggest something that might further drain his magical stamina or draw unwanted attention. Although she doubted anyone else would be desperate enough to travel through a strengthening blizzard.

They spoke little as Jun led them onward, one arm raised to light their way. The falling, blowing snow quickly erased any tracks others had made, and the northeastern road had few markers, which were difficult to spot in the weak lantern light. They could adjust the flame, but the oil would burn quicker.

Still, Mikari had a vague sense of where to go, having been in the area a few times over the years, and she was able to point the way whenever the path forward seemed unclear. Fortunately, the road eventually narrowed into a trail choked on both sides by dancing evergreens, which made it easy to follow.

Several hours passed in slowly intensifying misery. The buffeting wind scraped every inch of skin it could reach, and the temperature continued to plummet, causing even a creature like her discomfort, her body aching from too much time spent hunched over her reindeer. How poorly, then, did Jun fare?

She kept a close eye on him, swamped with worry, and scrutinized every dip of his head, every suspect sway of his body, and every adjustment he made. His normally upright posture became bent with fatigue. Any questions she posed received one- or two-word answers, each given in a gruff, distracted manner.

When it was her turn to pull ahead and lead, he said nothing when she took the lantern from him, its flame low but still steady.

Every chance she got, she glanced back at Jun to check on him. Only once was his head raised to meet her gaze, but his stallion knew to follow her reindeer.

Another hour went by. She didn't ask Jun to take his turn carrying the lantern, and he didn't offer, which meant he wasn't aware of the time. She looked back at him practically every other minute, not liking how low his head hung. And she couldn't help fretting over whether she had misremembered where along the road they'd find Pochi Orchard, or whether the family that ran it would extend them any hospitality, especially in the middle of the night.

Where's their damned sign already?

Perhaps if she'd resisted the opportunity to feed from him, or if her reindeer hadn't landed that kick, or if the mirror hadn't broken, thus necessitating that they be out in this horrendous weather when anyone else would be somewhere warm and resting...

A heavy groan twisted her head around to find Jun slumped forward and slowly tilting to one side. She gasped, stomach diving.

"Jun!" she shouted, startling him into catching himself, before stopping both of their mounts.

"I-I'm fine," he gruffly announced. "Just tired."

"You're lying," she snapped, grasping his forearm in case he lost his balance again. "I'm not human anymore, yet I feel wretched. How's your head?"

"I..." She held the lantern up to see him better. He was bleary-eyed and obviously in pain. "I can endure it."

"Can you try your magic on it?" she dared to ask. "The way you helped that stable boy?"

"I don't think I can...m-muster the concentration. I d-don't understand why—" The last came out in a heavy slur as he slumped forward again.

"Oh, Jun," she gasped, keeping him as stable as she could with her free hand.

Divine One have mercy, how were they to make it to the orchard? His stallion was strong and fit, but it had been traveling for nearly sixteen hours with a heavy man on its back. Could Nugun hold her as well for just a little longer?

She'd have to take the chance.

"Steady yourself for just one minute, Jun. I'll ride with you," she decided, shaking his arm. He nodded, holding his saddle tight.

Moving quickly, she dismounted, set down the lantern, and tied her pack to her reindeer. Then she had Jun scoot back in his saddle and forced the lantern ring into his hand. Once she was seated in front of him, she took the lantern back and he instantly wrapped his body around her.

"Just a little farther." She urged Nugun forward, then produced a pair of clicks her reindeer would recognize. "Temu, come." Her mount obediently followed.

Jun lay heavily against her back, his head on her shoulder and his face tucked into her neck. She was grateful to be both tall enough and unnaturally strong enough to support him. But his hold on her was loose, as though he'd fallen unconscious, so each breath she felt against her back was a relief.

The weather somehow worsened over the next hour, the wind so powerful it made Nugun stumble. Each time sent her heart into her throat and jolted Jun awake, albeit briefly.

Then, at last, a wall appeared to their right, shoulder high and sturdy. The trees beyond grew in orderly lines, their branches currently bare. During Gozu's growing season, they would produce apples, pears, plums, and persimmons.

"We're here," she said, nudging Jun once the orchard's gate and sign appeared at the edge of the snowy darkness. Her announcement was met with a groan.

The sign featured an artistically carved sun beneath which were the Gozuan characters for "happy orchard." Mikari hoped that the family who had been growing fruit there for five generations was still as receptive as their sign suggested.

The gate had no door, only an archway upon which the sign was firmly affixed. The snow wasn't as deep on the orchard's private road, and after a moment, they arrived at the large main house, where a well-shielded lantern glowed beneath the eaves above the entrance.

Mikari extinguished their lantern, dismounted, and helped Jun down. Then she drew his arm across her shoulders and let him lean on her as they approached the house's storm doors.

"Master Yotarou? Madam Kitsume? We beg for shelter, please!" she called, knocking loudly enough to be heard. "Please help!"

She pressed her ear to the storm door while bracing Jun's weight, which seemed to grow heavier by the second. Almost instantly, there were voices and hurried thumps. Just before the storm door would have opened, Mikari moved back.

It was someone she didn't recognize—a young brown-haired man of about twenty-five. He was fit, handsome, and scowling. "What in Oblivion is this?" His scornful gaze quickly took her measure, then Jun's. His scowl hardened.

Mikari dragged her scarf down. "I'm a bard, sir. My name is Mikari, and I've visited previously. My husband and I desperately needed to reach Tetsutani, but he sustained an injury that has worsened, and the weather is too treacherous. We cannot go on."

Partway through her plea, Yotarou appeared, the head of the family as far as she could recall. His hair was much grayer and thinner than when she'd last seen him, his complexion more spotted. But the sixty-something man still glowed with health, and he looked at her with such warmhearted concern that Mikari nearly started crying.

Ignoring the younger man's grumbling, Yotarou ushered them inside, and in seconds, several more of his family appeared, including his stout, sweet-faced wife, Kitsume. Everyone was in various states of dress, and Mikari only recognized half of them. Yotarou's clan had certainly grown since she'd last visited.

Without needing to hear anything more than "let's get them warm," his family began stripping Mikari and Jun of their ice-encrusted outer layers. Mikari's hands and feet ached as her limbs thawed in the wonderfully warm interior, heated with below-floor wooden pipes that carried hot-spring water.

Yotarou didn't bother with any questions that weren't relevant to their immediate safety, and he assured them that they and their mounts would be taken care of. Mikari thanked him repeatedly.

Stripped of their outer garments, Mikari took Jun's arm across her shoulder again, and one of the family's oldest sons mirrored her on Jun's other side. They followed Kitsume down a side hall, past an incense burner still emitting the earthy scent of patchouli. Midnight hadn't yet arrived, but it couldn't be far off.

In the family's enormous kitchen, Mikari declined an offer of food, but Jun was given a small meal that one of Kitsume's daughters prepped in an instant. He stood unsteadily before a tall counter and carefully spooned plain, hot porridge into his mouth while Mikari peeled off his pants and helped him step out of them. The instant his legs were bare, Kitsume wrapped a thick blanket around his waist, then did the same for his upper body once they'd removed his undershirt.

"He's your husband, I heard?" Kitsume asked as Mikari tucked the second blanket around him.

"Yes," Mikari said, more comfortable with the lie than was probably right.

"I wondered why someone with as fresh a face as yours would marry a man with this much gray in his hair," the matron said in a gossipy aside that Jun could absolutely hear. Her eyes twinkled. "Having seen a bit more of him, I now understand."

Mikari didn't have to fake a startled demurral, for in her haste to get Jun warm, dry, and his injury tended, she hadn't put a single thought toward donning her mask. She could only hope that she looked as windblown as Jun did, which would make her appear older than someone at the far edge of nineteen.

They sat Jun down on a stool to finish his meal while another of Kitsume's daughters cleaned his head wound. A bucket was placed next to him without comment, for it was assumed he might throw up his porridge.

Then came Mikari's turn to strip. Although she was anxious to see to Jun's needs first, she obeyed when Kitsume brought forth a set of sleeping robes and told her to remove the last of her clothing.

"We don't have anything big enough for him, but we have plenty that would fit you," Kitsume explained, shielding Mikari's nudity with the inner robe. She then helped Mikari into it as well as a matching outer one. Both were soft and dry, eliciting from her a sigh of relief.

She returned to Jun just as Kitsume's daughter finished combing his hair away from his wound. Surprisingly, the laceration itself seemed to be well on the way to healing. Mikari had also expected to find a knot but could see only a small one.

"Oh, that's not too bad," Kitsume cooed next to her. "No sign of infection at all."

And yet Jun's face was a mask of pain. "I believe blood has collected b-beneath my skull…and is putting pressure on my brain," he said, voice weak. "The bleeding may have already s-stopped, but if it hasn't…"

Mikari sucked in a breath and held it, every muscle tightening with fear as her voice faded to a shaky whisper. "Then what? If it hasn't stopped, then what?"

Jun raised his lovely, dark eyes. "I m-may lose consciousness. But I shall wake in time," he said with aggravating surety. "My…body simply needs a b-bit longer." And by "body," he undoubtedly meant "magic."

"You need more than just *time*," she insisted.

"This calls for a healing draft," Kitsume said decisively before calling out to her daughter by the stoves. "Forget the poultice. Skim the top of that into some goat's milk instead. And mix in a spoonful of the herbs from my green bottle." She pointed to another part of the kitchen.

"You believe a draft will work?" Mikari asked, grasping for reassurance.

"Essence of moose velvet works wonders for injuries."

"Moose velvet?" Her eyes became round, and she looked at Jun, who wore only exhausted confusion. Did he not know? "S-surely you'd rather save such a rare component for your own use," she said to Kitsume. "I have a bit of reindeer velvet in my—"

"Moose is far better for this, and I decide when to use it. Besides, it's already been prepared. Too late now," Kitsume said, waving off her concerns.

Oh, Divine One's grace.

She felt a tap on her arm and met Jun's gaze. He mouthed a question while Kitsume dabbed an ointment on his wound. *Is something wrong?*

Mikari subtly shook her head and did her best to look unconcerned. She hated lying to him, but if Jun learned of moose velvet's most infamous effect upon the body, one completely unrelated to treating injuries, he might refuse to drink it, and he needed its healing properties.

"It's ready," the woman at the stove announced as she brought over a cup.

Jun stared at Mikari as though he sensed her omission. But he said nothing when Kitsume put the cup to his mouth, and drank every drop.

Mikari knew it would take up to half an hour for the velvet's effects to kick in. She had to get him tucked into bed before that happened. He seemed tired enough to sleep through the stimulation caused by ingesting the velvet extract, although his dreams would undoubtedly be affected.

Once Jun had pushed away his bowl, Kitsume escorted them in a familiar direction, her son bringing along a basin containing a hot compress that Mikari would put on Jun's chest to warm him while he slept. They passed a few more family members, including Yotarou, who informed them that their animals had been settled in the barn. Then they entered a narrow corridor, the walls of which rattled as wind buffeted the layer of storm doors on either side.

The guesthouse that lay ahead was where Mikari had stayed for both of her previous visits. Although it was currently one large room, partitions could be added to create three separate areas: one for sleeping, one for taking food and drink, and one for enjoying the natural hot spring around which the guesthouse had been built.

There was no need for a brazier when the spring water offered plenty of heat, but two lanterns emitted soft light. Bedding was already laid out, and their bags had been patted mostly dry and placed in separate alcoves. Nearby was a low table surrounded by half a dozen floor cushions, and in the rear, a tall stack of towels sat within arm's reach of the hot spring's carved stone steps. Only some of the spring's rim had been smoothed, while the rest was made up of the original rocks and boulders.

"Anything else we can get you?" Kitsume offered. Her son, having already placed the hot compress next to the bedding that had been laid out, stood silently behind her.

Mikari glanced at Jun. He was standing on his own power and his eyes were open, but he was hunched and looking dazed. Still, he seemed steady enough. She'd need only a couple of minutes to put him to bed.

"I believe I can manage," she said to Kitsume. "Thank you. You've saved our lives. You and Master Yotarou and your family. I shall, of course, compensate you for—"

"Bah!" Kitsume waved her hands in irritation. "A bowl of porridge and a bit of extra laundry. What's two more people when you live with over two dozen?" Indeed, Kitsume had already told Mikari all about their expanding family, which had gone from sixteen members to twenty-eight. The scowling man who had answered the door was evidently their newest son-in-law.

"Well, there's also the velvet and the stabling—"

"No, I refuse to hear anything about money. Now get some rest, if you can. I'll come check on you two sometime after the start of mint." Assuming midnight had recently passed, that was three braces from now, plenty of time for Jun to sleep off the effects of the draft and regain some strength. Kitsume and her son then left, shutting the door behind them.

Mikari straightened from a bow of gratitude and turned to Jun. "Now let's get you to bed."

"First, tell me...what it was I drank," he said, drained of energy and yet refusing to budge when she tried to coax him toward the sleeping area.

She couldn't look him in the eye when she answered. "Moose velvet is extremely difficult to collect and therefore expensive. But while its healing properties are powerful, most people acquire it for another purpose."

"Which is?"

"A...potent sexual stimulant," she confessed, peeking sideways at him. His eyebrows pinched with incredulity, so she rushed to add, "It's the best choice when it comes to treating injuries. Unless you have access to magical healing, I suppose."

He let out a long sigh. "So, I'll just sleep it off?" More softly, he muttered, "Assuming I'm able."

"That's my hope," she said, nodding. "I imagine you'll have strange dreams, but…" This time when she grabbed his hand, he let her tug him toward the bed. "I expect you'll be dead asleep."

"Can't I enjoy the spring for a bit?" he grumbled as she drew back the blanket.

"You know better than that," she scolded. "Warming your organs comes ahead of your limbs. You'll be plenty comfortable here."

Relenting at last, he slid his big body into the bed. She wrapped the hot compress in a towel, set it on his chest, and then covered him with the blanket.

"You're not joining me?" he asked in a grumpy mumble, eyes already shut.

"I will soon. Now get some rest." She leaned down to kiss his forehead, and by the time she sat up, he was asleep.

At last, she was able to draw a full breath, a heavy weight lifting from her. She was tempted to put off her usual nighttime routine in favor of snuggling up to him and listening to his heartbeat, but she knew she'd be more comfortable if she got through it.

She started by checking their belongings and ensuring that everything was accounted for. Then she made use of the bath, which was in full view of the rest of the guesthouse and thus allowed her to keep an eye on him.

Certain he would remain asleep, she washed in a separate stream of water that flowed down a wooden chute. Then she piled her damp hair on top of her head and sank chin-deep into the hot spring to soak up its heat. It was glorious.

Twenty minutes later, she emerged flushed and relaxed, a towel wrapped around her, and confirmed that Jun was still resting comfortably before she began drying off. Though the temperature in the guesthouse was toasty, the air felt chilly next to her heated skin. Goosebumps covered her limbs, and her nipples pebbled.

Wondering yet again what it would be like to visit the far south and never be cold, she leaned down to dry her legs, only for her hair to slip from its pins and fall in front of her face. One pin landed by her foot. The other bounced and disappeared somewhere behind her.

Whispering a tired curse, she quickly scrubbed her legs dry. Then she tossed the towel aside, picked up the pin by her foot, and turned to search for the other one, which she spotted a step away. She retrieved it, straightening with a toss of her head—

Then froze, for Jun was not only awake but sitting up.

And he was looking at her. At *all* of her.

His hair was sorely mussed, the blankets crumpled as though he'd shoved them off. The hot compress lay forgotten beside him, likely sapped of its heat. His wide chest rose and fell with each deep breath he took. The dark bruises she'd noticed on his torso when she'd been stripping him in the kitchen had all but faded.

She refused to look any lower than that, especially not at the enormous bulge stretching the front of his loincloth.

But Jun perused her without any such restraint. And the *way* he was looking...as if he needed the sight of her in order to breathe. As if he'd kill to have her.

Slippery warmth pooled inside her. Mikari fought to ignore her body's response, but the naked longing on his face called to more than just her flesh.

"G-go back to sleep," she softly bade, a desperate edge in her voice. Thirty feet separated them, and the building's ventilation allowed a slow, steady breeze that put him downwind, but the humid air would all too quickly carry his scent to her.

Still caressing her with his hungry gaze, Jun slowly shook his head. His normal voice was already deep, but desire made it abyssal. "No chance of that now, lamb. Not until this draft wears off." Their eyes met. "Not until I've had my fill of you."

He tossed the blanket aside and rolled to his knees, sending a surge of panic through her. Something fell from her hand and hit the smoothed stone flooring with tiny tings. "W-we can't. I'll end up hurting you."

"Then hurt me," he rasped, sitting on his heels in supplication. "Whatever gets me inside you."

Heat swamped her, making her sway. "D-don't say that. I'll lose control if you touch me. I think I should l-leave." She knelt to grab her clothing.

"I could restrain you. I know a spell," he offered, rising to his feet.

"No, no more spells." She paced sideways toward the door, clutching her robe against her front and shaking her head. "You've already fed me and protected my mind. You and your magic need rest."

Jun stalked toward her, his hulking form filling her vision despite the distance she maintained between them. "My magic and I disagree with you. Although, come to think of it…I believe the right spell is already in place."

What? Had he cast something while she wasn't looking?

"There's simply no way I can trust myself," she insisted. "Please, just try to sleep it off. I-I can…"

Her words faded into a soft sigh as an enthralling scent embraced her, labyrinthian in its complexity, so thick in the air she could almost drink it. The same one had assailed her when they'd first reunited, and it now made her heart and body ache with acute need.

It was as tempting as a dare, as comforting as an embrace, as sweet as a compliment, and as heady as deep kisses. It surrounded her in aromas both familiar and new, evoking a flood of memories and fantasies and hopes. No other scent, real or otherwise, could rival this one.

For it was the scent of Jun's love. And its power over her was total.

Chapter Twenty

Jun's nightmare began as it usually did—a desperate search with countless turns and dead-ends. Wet snow clung to his hair and clothes. Powerful gusts disoriented him with blasts of sleet. Mikari called out for him to save her.

Then he discovered warmth. He knew that he was getting closer, so he traveled deeper into that part of the maze, away from the blizzard. The wind faded. His clothes dried.

He started sweating. And not just because he was running and the air was humid. His skin was burning hot. He shoved off his clothes, but the heat seemed to come from within, a fever covering him in pinpricks. Mikari's pleas for help turned...playful. Seductive. His cock rose, and he altered his gait rather than slow down.

"Come and claim me, Jun."

He did, and there was no carnivorous tree this time. No red moon and no dusty, lifeless earth.

The sky overhead was a brilliant spatter of stars on a black expanse. The ground was a lush, dewy field. Mikari sat on her hip upon a lawn of red brocade, an inviting smile on her lips as she toyed with a length of gold rope. She wore her black hair up so he could see her joining mark, and her sheer black dress hid nothing.

But just as he marched forward to claim her, he opened his eyes to a sight even more affecting, for the woman rubbing a towel over her flushed skin was real. The bed he lay in was real. The private space they occupied was real.

She turned as though to look for something, granting him a full view of her delicious buttocks, and bent over...

He sat straight up, a curse blaring inside his mind.

Maze take him, he'd do anything to have her. *Anything.*

Oh, he knew what it was to desire Mikari, to need her so much it physically hurt. But his overtly drugged state made her pull upon him as irresistible as gravity. Divine One's grace, no wonder moose velvet was such a rare, expensive component.

"You and your magic need rest," she said a moment later as she backed away, her borrowed robe clasped against her.

But his magic was alert and eager, not tired in the least, same as him. And he told her so. However, something else she'd said—*"and protected my mind"*—gave him a surge of hope.

"Although come to think of it...I believe the right spell is already in place," he told her, closing the distance between them.

"There's simply no way I can trust myself. Please," she begged, "just try to sleep it off. I-I can..."

A small sound slipped from her lips before they pressed shut. Her eyelids sagged, and her head tilted back. She was taking in a scent.

His scent. She held the air in her lungs as though savoring its aroma, the robe slipping from her hands. Good riddance.

Sweet Garden, she was lovely. From her lean legs to her gently indented waist to her long neck. He ached to fill his hands with her breasts. Didn't care a whit about the markings on her abdomen. Nothing about them would stop his worship of her, not tonight.

She released a carnal sigh that made his shaft buck beneath his loincloth, then pinned him with a nakedly erotic gaze, skimming her hands down her stomach and between her legs to grip the silky soft insides of her thighs, as though she wished she were already on her back and holding herself open. For him.

He knew he shouldn't exult in the knowledge that she found his fragrance irresistible, not when she couldn't help it, but seeing his effect on her made his cods draw up tight.

The temptation to stroke himself was nearly overwhelming, but he'd be damned to the Maze if he found his pleasure before she did, thrown in headfirst if his cock weren't the first thing to make her climax in years.

Though he ardently wished otherwise, he couldn't be touching her in any way when he came, not without feeding her unnecessarily. But before he spilled himself anywhere else, her sweet pot was going to sanctify his loins.

"You can rely on my magic to protect your free will," he told her.

Her breath rushed out of her. "You're certain?" She shook her head. "N-no, you'd still have to avoid feeding me."

"I'll pull back before it's too late."

She blinked at him. "Wh— You think you can?"

"I'll have no choice." He decisively yanked off his last strip of clothing. "Trust me, lamb."

Her gaze shot downward, and she only dug her hands in harder, mouth open in a silent gasp. "I do. I trust you."

"Then *come here*."

Yielding at last, she ran to him with open arms. He caught her up against him, lifting her, then captured her first needy moan with his lips.

Her soft mouth tasted of *rundona*, her tongue a silken spear that burst his every thought. Indeed, all of her was silky, from her lithe arms clinging to his shoulders, to the stiff tips of her breasts and her long legs that wrapped him up tight. But where she was silkiest was her hot center currently pressed up to his stomach.

He strode toward the bed, his magic guiding him. Once his feet found the mattress, he bore Mikari onto her back then insinuated his hand between them. After a second's adjustment, he set his knees wide, brought his hips back, and pressed deep into her warmth.

Mikari pulled her lips away with a sharp gasp at the same time that Jun barked out a groan. Everything in him pulled tight, from his cods out. His knees and toes dug into the mattress. One of his hands crushed the bedding, and the other cranked down on her hair to hold her mouth in place beneath his.

He hadn't hurt her, he knew that. He'd slid in so perfectly that he wasn't sure how he was managing to hold still. He wanted to move, to coat himself in her slick heat and service her passion, his back trembling with strain.

But something in her voice had stopped him, and he lifted his head just enough to see her expression.

Her face was screwed up tight, cheeks red. Her teeth were sunk so deep in her lower lip that he expected to see blood any second. She was hanging from the edge by her fingernails.

"Let go, lamb. I'll catch you."

She gave her head a tight shake, a grunt escaping her. "Y-you—" Her lip popped free of her teeth, red and swollen. "You should tie me, just in case."

"Not this time." He brushed his mouth over her abused lip and tightened his hold on her, a smile somehow breaking through. "That fantasy can wait."

She groped at his back, whimpering as though too desperate to think anymore.

"I'm going to move now," he warned her, eliciting another litany of incoherent pleas.

But the second he lifted his hips, she fell silent, mouth open and wet lashes fluttering. She slipped, almost unknowingly, into a position of surrender—knees back, arms hooked around his neck, hands molded to the slope of his shoulders.

To his great relief and even greater satisfaction, it meant only one thing.

Take me.

MIKARI HAD SOMEHOW FORGOTTEN the sensation of his body holding her legs wide. She had forgotten the soft brush of his chest hair and the way she disappeared beneath him.

Maybe that was because Jun was now bigger, his chest hair as thick as fur, and his range of carnal experience broader than when the two of them had only ever known each other's bodies. His touch was that of a fully matured man, and he was resolutely poised above her, his next thrust guaranteed to set off an avalanche.

He slid in hard and rolled his hips, stealing her breath. Another thrust had her crying out. Another roll had her grunting. Then he set a fast rhythm that firmly shoved her over the edge.

She slid down, down…even as her orgasm surged. The first jolt of release drew out a whimper. With the next, she began to contort, as if her body sought to achieve some sacred form.

A wave of tension then flooded her with heat. Her thighs shook uncontrollably, and still the final crest loomed, unyielding and consummate. She exhaled on a shuddering sob, only to gasp in air and hold it as bliss washed over her, leaving her twisting in its wake.

"That's it, my lamb," Jun ardently rumbled against her parted lips, his praise pushing her to even greater heights. "I'm there with you. I'm right behind you."

Wetness rushed from her, and the air in her lungs burst forth as sharp moans. Parts of her trembled, and other parts arched and writhed as he drew more cream from her with relentless thrusts and deep-chested groans of approval.

And his scent...Divine One's grace, it was so enrapturing she felt called to confess every secret filthy want she'd ever had.

She was still sobbing with pleasure when he pulled back, breaking her hold on him. He slipped his cock out and fisted it, pumping hard, his expression harsh and wild.

"Hold your legs open for me," he growled. "Give me a pretty picture."

Dizzy and trembling, she tiredly dragged her knees back. Jun no longer touched her, and even the pressure of his magic disappeared, its attentions ceasing.

"Yes, that's exquisite. Now where shall I paint you, lamb?" His fist moved faster. His voice dropped to a rasp. "Tell me where you want it."

She keened, toes curling, as images of pearly fluid upon her thighs, stomach, and breasts flashed through her head, courtesy of Jun. But she had something even better in mind.

"Here," she said, sweeping her hands down to spread her slippery folds. "I want to push it in."

He made a low yelp of shock, jerking forward as he positioned his hips. The hoarse, grating whimpers he made while jetting all over her sex hit her brain like a potent drug, much like the one swimming in his veins. With tight-lipped moans, she helped his seed slip inside her.

Not once did she feel a transfer of energy. He had, in effect, avoided feeding her.

And yet, even despite her denied hunger, she sensed no impending loss of control. She had flung through an incredible climax, but her ardor was no more powerful than it had been moments before.

Yes, she wanted more. As much as he could give her. But the frenzy that had once led her to kill did not manifest.

"All this time, I thought..." *That I chose to kill that man.* She gulped, still catching her breath. Her legs shook as she set them down.

Jun sank to his heels with a tired sigh, spent for now. "I realized that your feeding frenzy must be a form of bias magic, a compulsion to which you are now practically immune. As long as *mind cloak* protects you, you can have all the pleasure you desire."

Overwhelmed, she crossed her arms over her face. She thought she might cry she was that relieved. Relieved and grateful and shocked. "What if you'd been wrong?" she asked, voice muffled.

"I wasn't. Nor was I worried. The only thing that concerned me was whether I'd have the strength to pull out. I'd love to spend inside you, but..." He gestured at his still-healing head wound.

"Oh!" She flung her arms down and rose upon her elbows. "Does it hurt?"

"Only one thing hurts, lamb," he said, dark-sable gaze sizzling. She looked down at his hand stroking between his legs. "Tell me, is it safe to touch you again?"

Thrilling warmth washed over her. Nodding, she managed to speak in a steady voice. "As it's ever been."

He was on her in a heartbeat, shoving her legs wide, his hands beneath her tilting her hips up and pulling her into every thrust. In under a minute, he had her coming again, the bedding damp beneath her bottom.

While she recovered, he retrieved the stack of towels. Then he flipped her onto her stomach, packed enough blankets under her to lift her hips, put a towel in place, and took her again from behind, the wall of his chest laying heavily over her as he held her thighs tight to his and rocked deep. Seconds after she came, gasping and writhing, he broke contact and covered her with his seed.

Variations of the same routine continued for some time. She never left the bed, for her tireless lover fetched everything they needed. He cleaned her, offered her water to replace the moisture sweating and creaming out of her, and even brought over the small, wooden jar she asked him to get from her things.

When he asked what it was, she showed him instead of telling him, twisting off the lid and scooping out a generous amount onto her finger.

Jun smiled wryly as he raked back his sweat-dampened hair. "I think we've established that we don't need additional lubrication. Or does this do something special?"

She gave him a secretive smile as she put her hand behind her to apply the thick oil. "I mean for us to use it elsewhere." A flicker of shocked arousal supplanted his amusement. "Somewhere no one has ever been, but where I've long wanted you to visit." And with that, she sank to her hip, rolled onto her stomach, and put her knees beneath her.

If Jun's energy was starting to fade, her invitation brought it roaring back. He mounted her with a throaty, eager sound, one hand braced on her lower back to hold her still while he worked his hastily oiled finger into her. She trembled, heart ready to burst, as he teased and relaxed the ring of muscle that would soon swallow something much thicker.

"Oh, lamb. Your body wants me here," he moaned as he inserted a second finger, along with more oil.

Her empty sex was practically liquid with heat, aching for more pleasure. He drove his fingers deep, twisting and spreading them. She held out as long as she could before swirling her taut little peak.

"Ah!" she cried out, another climax shivering through her, dripping down her fingers.

"*Aj'*, greedy girl," he growled, sending his free hand between her legs to gather her fresh cream.

She watched, upside down, as he spread her moisture over his swarthy, oil-coated cock, a sight so erotic that, for a brief instant, she was incapable of complex thought, her most tender flesh burgeoning with hot honey.

His fingers left her as he rose and walked his knees closer, the fever-warm and furred flesh of his inner thighs straddling her narrowly spaced legs. More oil. Then the wide head of his cock nudged into place.

Oh, sweet Garden.

"We'll be there soon," he rasped, and she realized she'd spoken aloud just now, the slurred words coming from somewhere in her chest.

He pressed forward until the thick crown made it past her outer ring. Heat radiated from her flushed face, beads of sweat shivering along her damp hairline.

Want compelled her to utter a stream of wicked encouragements. "Feels so good, Jun. M-maze take me, I— Deeper, *please*. I want all of you."

"Mercy, lamb," he uttered in a low, shaking voice. "Have mercy on me."

He was making those breathy moans she loved, slowly readying her with deepening thrusts, each one a sweet invasion followed by a gentle ebbing. Every inch he gained further drained her ability to speak until she was reduced to moaning *Jun* and *please*.

But words failed her when his entire stalk entered her, filling her impossibly well. Leaning his fiery warmth over her, he firmly gripped her shoulder, then slipped his other hand between her legs to nestle two fingers between her sensitive folds.

Rubbing her with exquisite, massaging pressure, he gave her a series of short, deep strokes, as though relishing the novel intimacy—exultant little pushes that evinced the profoundness of his pleasure, which matched her own at having such a long-held fantasy fulfilled.

A deep moan rumbled in his chest. "Your arse is as sweet as your pot, lamb. I'll be visiting often."

His strokes lengthened, remaining gentle, each one promising to be the first hard thrust that would signal his total possession of her. She savored the heat and friction of their connection, mewling mindlessly, astounded by the shivery tension building beneath his fingers and in her thighs.

At last, he surged fully into her, wrenching from her a rapturous cry. No longer cognizant, she surrendered to whatever pace he wanted, knowing it would lead to more pleasure than she'd ever imagined.

He rewarded her trust with stroke after wonderful stroke, holding her in place with his hand on her shoulder, and grunting in soft growls that made her think he'd also surrendered to instinct.

A searing climax raked through her, sending her to a place of shimmering colors upon a warm, shadowy flow, the poignant pleasure somehow devouring, for she felt the hard pulses at an unfamiliar depth, and the quaking sense of emptiness beneath his still-moving fingers left her strangely bereft.

"Sweet Garden, lamb," he said in a broken moan. "You love it."

A scant moment of thrusting later, he carefully pulled out and painted her cheeks again, his beautifully agonized shouts echoing in the guesthouse.

Mikari had vast amounts of stamina, but even she needed a couple of minutes after that encounter. She lay there in a satisfied daze and wondered if she'd be able to walk by the time the draft wore off.

"Maze take me," Jun panted. "I've wanted us to do that…since the second I knew…it was possible."

"And how long ago was that?" she asked, cheek mashed into the bed.

"Heard it from another ward. He read it in a book that he was copying for one of the temple's clients."

"Mm, I would love to get my hands on that book."

He gave a short laugh. "So would I."

They cleaned up again, this time at the washing area she'd used earlier, where there were wooden stools to sit upon while scrubbing and rinsing. Mikari convinced Jun to let her bathe him and wash his hair, a task that took twice as long once Jun pulled her onto his lap.

Afterward, he enjoyed the hot spring for a short while. She sat behind him on the rim, legs split around his sides, feet submerged in the steamy water. The position allowed her to massage his shoulders, and she paid careful attention to the one with an old injury.

He lasted ten minutes before turning to her with revived need. She was on her back in no time, thighs splayed apart, feet braced on his shoulders. She was incapable of speech when the suction of his lips finished her off, incapable of thought when he did it a second time. Then he replaced his tongue with his stalk.

"I'm going to be deep in your pot the next time I feed you," he growled just before lashing his seed upon her sex. She could only nod in acceptance.

The effects of the draft had begun to fade by the time they found themselves cleaned up and back in bed, one lantern snuffed and a mound of laundry piled in a basket near the water closet.

They lay in each other's arms, kissing gently amid tender whispers. The scent of his love filled the humid air, and his magic idly touched hers, although she felt it only distantly.

Drawing her fingertips through the coarse hairs on his chest, she delighted in the shiver that went through him, his thick arm flexing behind her shoulders as he brushed his kiss-reddened lips against hers.

"Mikari, my lamb," he softly uttered, bringing his hand up to her cheek. "Look at me."

She gazed at him with hazy focus, a blissful smile on her lips. When his masculine features sharpened in clarity, she noticed a small furrow between his eyebrows and a tightness to his mouth.

"What is it?" she asked, worry creeping in. "Does your head still pain you? O-or did I—?"

"No, lamb." He gently pressed his thumb to her lips, then stroked it to the corner of her mouth. "I...I wish to ask you something, although I believe I already know what your answer will be."

Sensing it would be a difficult topic, she tried to prepare herself. "Ask me."

Jun stared at her warily, bracing himself as well. "Why didn't you come find me? Did you even want to?"

A tight band of guilt squeezed her chest, building pressure. She couldn't draw breath for a short pause, and a burning began in the back of her throat, spreading up to her eyes. Her next breath came only with deliberate effort.

"I did want to, so very much. But I couldn't, not after what happened," she said, voice trembling. "I'd have only been a danger to you, and...I was so ashamed I sometimes thought I'd suffocate. I had become exactly what I'd feared, and not even the priests could help me."

"Where did you go instead?" Jun murmured, soothing her with gentle touches to her cheek.

She'd known, of course, where Jun would flee after his escape. Even without a mount or funds, she could've found her way to his hometown and his sister.

Instead, she'd gone in the opposite direction, to a small town where one of her former fellow wards had said she'd be returning, a friend with whom Mikari had often performed musical accompaniment during the temple's rituals.

"I went to Uta. She gave me some proper boots and a few kols. The next place I went, a bard was performing in the market. I'd already had trouble with people asking to see a brand, and I realized I'd need the protection of his profession. I asked him to mentor me, and he agreed once I proved I had some talent.

"From there... The man I killed—the energy from his death had given me a reprieve of nearly a year. And I spent as much of it praying as I spent learning from Master Atsuyori. I thought that if I prayed, promising anything I could think of, then the Divine One would cure me of my weakness.

"But the hunger was always there. It never ceases for more than a few moments. And I was forced to question whether I truly knew my heart. Maze take me, how I've h-hated myself.

"And when I eventually had to feed again, or else, I…" But no more words would come as the insoluble turmoil of that day hit her anew. She shook her head, a sob escaping that reduced her to a croak, "I cannot speak of it. I *cannot*, Jun."

"Please try to let it out, lamb," he rasped, his heart knocking against her hand upon his chest. "Let me carry this pain with you."

His anxious countenance blurred as she wept, but he was patient, allowing her a moment to gain control of her voice, though she only managed a stammer.

"I knew I should starve, but I was too weak. I seduced a serving woman and…and it was such a relief to eat, and so much easier than I could stand to admit. And for a moment, I…I thought about killing her," she confessed, choking out the last.

"But you didn't," he said, wiping away her tears.

"No, but I…I fell into despair. I convinced myself that I must deserve this life with a heart as cruel as mine." Her voice turned bitter. "My despair lessened the more I accepted my fate until at last I resigned myself to it."

A dark emotion seemed to pass through him, his warm hand upon her cheek tightening with urgency. "Tell me you don't believe that anymore. Any of it. You deserve whatever life you want." He shook her gently, his arm around her unyielding. "Say it."

But she was too moved to speak, too stunned by his intensity, and too raw from sharing painful secrets. Any response she would've made remained lodged in her chest.

Misinterpreting her silence, he kissed her with demanding pressure, willing her to agree with him, for he repeated his command against her tingling lips. "Say it, lamb. You deserve a happy life."

If she could swoon, she would have. Instead, she forced herself to answer him, the breathless words carrying away her mantle of disgrace. "I deserve a happy life."

I deserve your love.

"That you do, lamb," he rumbled, grasping her hip to draw her against his ready loins. He began a trail of searing kisses down her neck, his beard like soft wool against her skin. "If only I'd been worthy enough to give it to you."

She exhaled hard, the meaning behind his words shocking her, for he had given her more happiness in the few years she'd known him than she'd ever scraped together in the time they were apart. Her bardic duties had given her purpose and fulfillment, but they hadn't made her feel whole or nearly so alive.

And yet, the fearful fool she'd been twenty years ago had denied him. Even now, she was *still* denying him out of uncertainty. And after what his parents had done, giving him up without a fight... It was no wonder he believed he wasn't worthy.

"You were more than worthy, Jun. You s-still are," she softly declared, shivering as his lips found the sensitive skin behind her ear.

Her cursed hunger had been a fever in her flesh for hours now, but as he insinuated his thigh between her legs, an inferno of true desire rose up once again, burning high and bright, turning her supple and yet taut.

Reeling with acute want and incapable of thought let alone speech, she found herself on her back once more, her spread thighs cradling his hips as he covered her with his warm bulk.

She clutched at him with her knees, hands fluttering with indecisiveness as she explored the hard, flexing planes of his upper body. As he gently nudged his way inside her, her arms seemed to remember where to go, wrapping around him to grip his shoulders.

They made love in slow, full lunges, both tensing and reluctantly receding. She kept her face pressed against his hot throat, every muscle tingling with warmth as she tightened her lower half in upward pulls.

Their combined movements dragged her through a long series of climaxes, one after the other in a tumult of ecstasy.

Each one pulled carnal sounds from her throat, but as she jerked and shuddered through yet another tide of pleasure, her voice struck a high, raspy note that made him moan in response. He moved over her with greater and greater need, rocking her beneath him and coming dangerously close to giving her his energy.

She pushed feebly at his sweat-slick shoulders, weak and shaking from a surfeit of sensation, legs falling open. But he was relentless, his hands beneath her bottom tilting her just right and allowing him to reach deep into her liquid heat.

"J-Jun," she forced from her throat.

"Once more," he grated as though gnashing his teeth.

She tried again to separate them. "Too—dangerous."

He curled tightly over her, pounding between her thighs, the pulse in his neck tapping fast and hard against her cheek. Maze take her, he was so near to climax that she was tasting tiny sips of it. Glorious little samples of a divine feast no mortal was meant to have.

She let out a broken cry as trenchant pleasure spilled through her yet again, then gave a sharp gasp as Jun tore himself away from her, twisting and slamming onto the bed with a furious curse. She heard his harsh, hissing groans as he spent himself, and shakily lifted her head to find him clutching a towel against his loins, his prone body frozen in a low, twitching arch.

Moments later, Jun wobbled his way across the guesthouse to put the towel into the laundry basket, then stumbled back over. The poor man looked as worn out as he no doubt felt, and he was asleep the instant he collapsed onto the bed.

She arranged him to be more comfortable, pulled a blanket over him, and then tucked herself against his side. There was no incense in the guesthouse to mark the passage of time, but she estimated that they'd spent three hours burning off his drug-enhanced libido.

They had been three of the most magnificent hours of her life.

Chapter Twenty-One

Jun woke alone, and yet Mikari was everywhere. Her delicious feminine musk was all over the mattress beneath his face, and his body ached from all that he'd done to her in the middle of the night.

She had even been in his dreams, which had picked up right where he'd left off, resulting in the unspent erection he'd been grinding into the bed just before opening his eyes.

Still, he'd have liked to wake up with her next to him as he had done the day before. Maze take him, had that been only yesterday?

He felt a vague sense of guilt wondering how much of Mikari's response to him had been her own desire rather than her cursed sensitivity to lust, and whether the difference remained unclear to her. She had ceased to shun his attentions once he'd proven that she was protected from any sort of frenzy and that he could pleasure her without feeding her, although getting to that point had required a great deal of her trust.

Had he taken unfair advantage of her? Made her feel used?

Someone must have placed lit incense outside the guesthouse door because a crisp, familiar fragrance hung in the air. As a temple ward, he'd become used to waking at the start of mint, and its scent could still rouse him even when he would otherwise sleep.

The snowstorm had ceased, and the guesthouse was quiet but for the soft woosh of outside air that ventilated the building. Low light seeped through the narrow gaps in the storm shutters beyond the small windows of the outer wall. Dawn was just arriving, which at this time of year meant the brace of mint was half-burned.

He sat up, groggy but headache-free, aroused but content. And mildly sore all over, anywhere that had worked to give Mikari climax after climax while taking a few of his own. So, a good sort of sore, even if it did remind him just how many years he'd lived.

After some careful stretching, he washed up, wrapped a blanket around his lower half, and then made his way to the table at the front of the guesthouse, where he'd spotted a piece of paper upon the neat pile of his freshly laundered clothing.

He recognized the paper as having come from one of Mikari's journals, and the writing upon it was in her beautiful hand.

I hated to leave you, but I've gone ahead to ensure a quick departure.
Once you're packed and ready, find your way to the kitchens.
Love, your lamb

He stood there a moment, then two. One would think he'd forgotten how to read, but he hadn't. He understood each word. And they made his heart race.

The note in his hand trembled, and his lips silently formed the single, precious word upon which his gaze remained fixed, although the two words that came directly after were also of devastating importance—*love, your lamb.*

Love.

Filled with both euphoria and impatience, he quickly dressed. He carefully folded the note, even sat at the table to do it properly, and tucked it into an inside pocket of his shirt, right over his heart.

And even though he would have preferred to return later for his things, he packed his bags and strapped on his sword before emerging into the hall, where a small censor was emitting a whorl of white smoke. From there, the smell of food was easy to follow.

The kitchens had been quiet and spacious when he'd previously been here, but now they were noisy and cramped as eight people bustled about with all sorts of pots and bowls. At least a dozen plates of food filled a sideboard, and yet more were being prepared. Jun set down his saddlebags where he hoped they would not be a hindrance.

Anyone not intent on a stove or cutting board glanced up at his arrival, including the woman who had prepared his healing draft last night. She gave him an assessing look before pointing out Mikari, who was tucked in the corner by one of the ovens and conversing with a man whose back was turned to Jun.

Both of them sat upon low stools. The man seemed to be tending to something baking in one of the ovens. Mikari wore her bardic attire but not her wig, and the sympathy on her face opened up into a smile the second she noticed him over the man's shoulder. She swiftly stood.

Dying to touch her, Jun marched over, breaking his stride only once to avoid colliding with someone.

"Excellent timing," she said with a pleased sigh. "The morning meal is nearly ready, but I think there's eno—"

He dipped his head and took her mouth in a hard kiss, embracing her with such insistence that she was forced back a step. Despite a few titters from those present, Mikari responded instantly, softening for him as she twined her arms around his shoulders.

With her in his grasp, some of his urgency faded and he slowed their kiss, if only to savor her better. But he refused to pull back until he'd thoroughly reacquainted himself with the taste and feel of her.

"Well, now," a familiar, matronly voice said once their lips parted. Madam Kitsume stood at the nearby counter, arms akimbo. She appeared to have been shelling an enormous number of *rundona*, which dropped at the start of winter. "I already said last night that I'd come to understand the attraction, but now I *really* understand."

"All of us do," a male voice groused. More laughter followed.

"They're *married*?" a higher voice asked in a loud aside. "But he's so much—ah!" Thankfully, someone cut her off with a smack and a reprimand before she could say *older than her*.

Ignoring their commentary, Jun looked down at Mikari's blissful expression. Her gently smiling lips were wet and puffy, her freckled cheeks much pinker than before.

Indeed, he felt a twisting stab of guilt whenever he noticed her enduring youth, which was often, even though he knew she was only a year younger than him. The gulf between their assumed ages wasn't unheard of, but it was rare enough for their relationship to appear… well, obscene.

He told himself he could tolerate the remarks. He was done holding himself back whenever he wanted to touch her.

"Be careful, Jun," she said in a close voice. "I'm rather weak to you."

"I feel the same, especially after reading your note."

Her fingers played upon his nape. "You seem rather robust to me."

"Last night with you restored me."

"*Ijaa!*" Kitsume laughingly scolded, slapping the counter. "To the Maze with both of you. You're not in private anymore."

Mikari ducked her head in contrition as she withdrew from his arms, but her eyes sparkled. "Is there still time before the first meal, madam?" she asked of their hostess.

Kitsume took a quick look around. "Five or ten minutes. If you still wish to speak to my grandson, you can do it now."

"Grandson?" Jun echoed.

Mikari stepped back to indicate the man with whom she'd been speaking, and who was now rising to his feet. Jun turned to acknowledge him.

The man's brand was the first thing Jun saw, and it stunned him into silence, which Mikari thankfully filled, no doubt to buy him a couple of seconds.

He had seen the brand before, on plenty of people. Too many. But never like this.

"Eiji is actually her second grandchild out of seven," Mikari said by way of introduction. "He'll be eighteen soon."

The tall, muscular crow before him had therefore been cleansed somewhat recently, his status confirmed by the unique brand of the temple where he'd been a ward.

But while most wards were branded on the forearm, Eiji's brand had been seared onto his handsome face. The scar covered his right cheek, barely missing his eye. Even for Gozu, it was cruel.

Even more surprising was how familiar Jun was with that particular mark, its design consisting of opposing arrows.

Composing himself, he bowed his head. "Well met, Master Eiji. I apologize for imposing on your family's hospitality, for which I also thank you."

Eiji accepted the sentiments with a small nod but remained unsmiling. "I'm glad you're all right, Commander Jun."

At the use of his rank, Jun sent Mikari a questioning look.

"We've been speaking a while," she admitted with a small grimace. "I told him your mission, and who we're looking for."

"This happened a year ago," Eiji said, pointing briefly at his face. If he felt grief over the scarring on his face, he masked it well. "About a month before that was the last time the inquisitor visited."

Jun went rigid. "Do you know his name?"

"No, but I overheard one of his aides speaking to the Primary's secretary, asking him to send word once certain wards reached their maturity. The aide had a list of names."

"Did he say where to send word?"

"He did," Eiji confirmed, mouth set in a firm line. "Ajiro Temple."

Jun blinked in surprise, for he had been certain that the inquisitor could not be a real priest, and that any clues they discovered would lead to some secret lair.

But no, the inquisitor could apparently be found at the Keeper's official temple of residence, which meant the region's highest divine authority had to know that the inquisitor was turning crows into demons with his ritual. Perhaps he was aware of even more.

One look at Mikari's face told him she shared his dismay.

"Ajiro Temple is several days past Tetsutani, isn't it?" he asked her.

"It's four if you push hard," she confirmed, "but I've never taken the mountain path up from Eiroku that leads to it."

Jun let his gaze linger on Eiji's brand. "Was that a punishment for eavesdropping? Or is that how Nansen does it now?"

The young crow's stoic mask hardened, voice turning stony. "My cleansing did not go well."

Hardly an answer, yet it explained plenty.

"What about you two?" Eiji asked, gaze bouncing between them. "How did you avoid becoming wards?"

"What makes you think we weren't?" Mikari replied.

"No one here has seen a brand on you."

Her eyes became shadowed. "The inquisitor has a different ritual."

Eiji blinked, his indifferent mask slipping momentarily. "How did you survive?"

"Luck, I imagine. Jun, however, managed to escape Nansen."

Eiji looked at Jun in surprise. "You were the ward who escaped?"

"I—have I been the only one to do it?" he asked, stunned.

He'd always assumed that Nobuhara, the guard who'd freed him, had made a habit of accepting bribes in exchange for helping wards escape, although certainly not from his sister Toyome, who had denied even making the attempt. The only other reason Jun had ever come up with was pure whim.

Now, he wondered if Nobuhara had suspected the inquisitor of wrongdoing—of lying, at the very least—and for once in his life been compelled to protect his charges.

"I'm surprised the Primary didn't suppress it, then," Jun said. "He could've dismissed the guard who helped me and told the rest of the staff to keep silent about it."

"I don't know how he could have. I heard that a guard made a big fuss, right when everyone was rising, about some huge ward attacking him and escaping," Eiji said, leaning on the word *huge* while eyeing Jun. "Still, I always thought the older wards were lying when they'd talked about it. None of them had been around at the time. Figured they were holding onto false hopes."

"Why do you believe that wards sent to the inquisitor don't survive?"

"At least one didn't while I was there," Eiji revealed. "Happened in the first year. Some older wards were repairing the railing outside the Primary's office and saw the inquisitor's aides carrying another ward out of the offering room. Claimed he was dead."

"But you didn't see the ward yourself?" Jun asked in a careful tone.

"No, but no one doubted it." He shrugged. "Anytime the priests wanted to scare or scold us, they invoked the inquisitor. And anyone sent to him disappeared, with no word of them ever again."

Jun glanced at Mikari and saw in her eyes the same conclusion. There could be no doubt that the inquisitor who had targeted her had continued to curse others.

Kitsume then declared the start of the morning meal, precipitating a flurry of activity. Eiji drew a tray full of small ceramic cups from the oven, each one containing a single serving of fragrant morning cake that had risen in softly cracked pieces.

Jun and Mikari kept out of the way as the dishes on the sideboard began to disappear, all on their way to the family's dining space. Once Eiji added a final touch to each cake— a glistening ribbon of candied persimmon—the entire tray was whisked away by another family member.

"You'll eat before you go," Kitsume said to them once the kitchen had emptied of people and food. "One of my brood ate already and is preparing your mounts, but I never send anyone off without a full stomach."

She directed her attention to Eiji, gaze softening even as her lips tightened. "We didn't want to hand him over, but we didn't want to hide him away, either. That's no way to live. My daughter and her husband were planning to take him south rather than give him up until his magic presented."

Her eyes turned liquid. "But I knew I'd never see the three of them again if they left Gozu. I convinced his parents to surrender him to Nansen along with a generous donation, thinking he'd be treated well." She curled her lip in a sneer. "Just look at what my selfishness caused."

"I've told you it was my fault," Eiji said in a steely voice. He stared at the floor without seeing it. "I always thought I could go through with the cleansing, but the second they started…it felt wrong. If I hadn't tried to resist, if I hadn't pissed them off…"

"Allow me to help," Jun proposed, having heard more than enough. All eyes turned to him. "I can't give you your magic back, but if you wish, I can take that thing off your face."

Here was an opportunity to do some good with his healing magic. Jun couldn't erase the trauma of Eiji's mutilation and forced cleansing, but he could give the man a reflection that didn't remind him of it daily. He could give the young crow hope.

Eiji and his grandmother both looked at him with the same perturbed expression.

"What do you mean?" Eiji asked. "How?"

"Healing magic. I'd only need about…fifteen minutes," Jun estimated.

The young man's brows drew even tighter. "You've done it before?"

"I have."

Eiji glanced at his uneasy grandmother. "Will it hurt?" he asked Jun.

"It may, but I'll attempt to offer some pain relief."

Eiji gave it a moment of thought before agreeing and asking his grandmother to leave. "I don't want you to see me in pain," he told her when she balked.

After sending her from the kitchens with the last of the morning cakes, he submitted himself to Jun's instructions and took a seat on a low stool, head tilted back and resting on the edge of the counter.

Jun stood over the young crow, whose face was taut with apprehension, and drew his magic into his fingers without trouble. A good sign. Seconds after the tendrils penetrated Eiji's cheek to begin restoring his flesh, the man made a tight grunt, face flushing.

He pushed a little pain relief into Eiji's cheek. "It's the setting powder," he explained, once Eiji appeared more comfortable, though the young man was already perspiring. "I'll need to draw it out as I go. Knock if you're able to continue."

Knock, knock, knock.

"Would you like to hold my hand?" Mikari asked, hovering close. Eiji didn't hesitate to grab her proffered fingers, and she began humming a soft, rolling melody that helped Jun focus as much as it helped distract Eiji.

"Do you have a cloth handy, lamb?" he asked a moment later. The young crow was sweating profusely, and the setting powder was beginning to darken and run like wet ash. Mikari dug into her sleeve with her free hand and produced a kerchief.

"Wipe when I say...now." He lifted his hand enough for her to wipe clean the partially healed skin. She let out a soft gasp of astonishment.

Minutes passed. Eiji sagged in relief every time Jun paused to let Mikari wipe away more of the setting powder, only to seize back up and hold his breath when Jun resumed.

"Breathe, lad. I'll dull it a bit more." He was keeping up a steady amount of pain relief, but he wasn't yet proficient and didn't want to overdo it, lest he send the young crow into a coma or even kill him.

"Done," he said at last, stepping back. He had certainly put his magic through its paces, but he had a comfortable amount of stamina left.

The young crow released Mikari's hand and slumped against the cabinet, eyes still shut. Mikari gently finished cleaning his cheek.

"It's over now," she crooned, dabbing at tears slipping from Eiji's eyes. "You did so well." She then gave Jun a warm, proud look that made him feel as tall as a mountain. "Both of you did well."

"Can I touch it?" Eiji asked hoarsely.

"You may," Jun said, flexing his still-tingling fingers. "Tell me if anything feels strange."

Eiji's hands trembled as he felt his mended cheek and swiped beneath his eyes. "It's been a year, but…I think it's healed." He sent Jun a look of incredulous awe. "Would I have been able to do what you just did? Heal people?"

"You still could, if the Divine One permits."

A sharp sob from the doorway preceded a crash as a tray full of empty bowls fell to the floor. Jun's hand darted to his hilt, but it was watery-eyed Kitsume at the threshold.

Eiji surged to his feet and went to embrace his grandmother. Relaxing his sword arm, Jun contentedly watched the two of them before he was distracted by a hand slipping into his grip.

"That was a good thing. A wonderful thing," Mikari murmured.

"It certainly feels that way," he agreed. "You were an excellent assistant." The compliment brought a smile to her lips, and he turned to face her. "Now, when are you going to say it?"

At first, she was mildly taken aback. Then a playful light entered her eyes. "I believe I was the first to say it last time."

A grin tugged at the corners of his mouth. Indeed, she had chosen to whisper that she loved him in between one of the many goodbye kisses they'd always had at the end of one of their trysts in the maze, guaranteeing an even longer goodbye.

"But I did say it already," he contended. "You just don't understand Chouja."

She gave him a look of mock outrage, eyes smiling. "Well, that's hardly fair. I demand the full translation."

He gripped her hand tighter, lifting it to his chest, cheeks aching from holding back a wide grin. "I'm still waiting to hear it from you."

"Don't you want to save such declarations for a moment when we're alone?"

He dipped his head to lay a kiss on her palm. "I need something to sustain me until that moment comes. Something to inspire me."

"Last night wasn't enough?" she teased.

"There's no such thing as enough when it comes to desiring you." Coaxing her sleeve down, he feathered his lips over the pulse in her wrist. The sound of her soft, sharp gasp made his mouth curl with satisfaction. He firmed his voice. "Now, say it, lamb."

"I love you," she declared, breath catching. "So much that I believe my heart's been drawn to you since before we ever met. So much that nothing can overpower it, and it terrifies me. Even when you were lost to me, even as I mourned you, it strengthened me. I never want to be apart from you ever again."

Moved beyond words, Jun captured her mouth with his and breathed deep, as if he could inhale her love and suffuse his entire being with it.

The mass of magic in his core twirled and swelled, and Mikari arched with an abbreviated moan as it stroked her possessively. Damn him for not listening to his magic. It had known all along that she wasn't gone.

Reluctantly, he broke the seal of their lips, but a mere glimpse of her low-lidded, transported expression had him showering her freckled cheeks with kisses, and his voice emerged from deep in his chest. "I've only been half-alive the last twenty years. Half-awake. Half-sane. Lost in a blasted maze and thinking I'd someday find my way out when all this time the center was the way through, the way back to you. I love you," he whispered ardently. "You are the center of me, for my heart will only ever beat for you."

She spoke his name as if it were a plea, fingers curling against his back, and he answered her unspoken entreaty with another kiss, one that altered him down to his soul, that shifted his reality. He felt a tightening throughout his body, an awakening that stunned and entranced him. Their kiss was a revelation.

He didn't realize someone was clearing their throat to get his attention until a voice still wobbly with joy shouted, "*Ijaa*! Would you two stop it so I can thank you?"

Chapter Twenty-Two

Mikari could hardly believe how much Jun ate for breakfast, and half-expected his horse to toss him off for being too heavy. She pretended to eat while entertaining the family's children, and Jun managed to stuff himself despite an avalanche of questions from the adults. Every time she shifted upon her floor cushion, a deep and wonderful ache reminded her of his lovemaking.

Though he insisted that no one owed him anything for removing Eiji's brand, the family refused to call things equal until it was agreed that they'd pressure the temples into acknowledging the empress's rule using whatever means they had.

"The temples have their guards and soldiers," Yotarou said, "but we have substantial trade deals throughout Gozu. Money and hunger are powerful motivators."

Kitsume then packed up even more food for Jun to take with him, and the entire family came out of the house to see them off, including the children not yet able to toddle around. The sky was an icy blue, and a stiff breeze tossed about handfuls of fallen snow.

"There's more to you than what you've told us," Eiji said to Mikari, speaking low so the others wouldn't overhear. "My family's too grateful to say anything, not that I'm not grateful, too. But you don't look nearly as old as you claim you are."

"Not by choice," she replied.

"How? Magic?" he whispered, wide-eyed as he handed over Temu's reins.

She gave a sad smile and shrugged. "What else?"

From there, the road to Tetsutani rose and fell over the evergreen-choked foothills of a low mountain to their right. Pausing at the top of the highest crest, they were able to make out the snowy roofs of the mining town nestled in the next valley over, although it would take another couple of hours to reach it. Thankfully, nothing seemed to be on fire.

Once they found a suitable spot, they stopped briefly to allow Jun to once again cast the *mind cloak* spell that had protected them since midday yesterday, although he grudgingly refrained from applying it with his mouth this time. Instead, he gently stroked her cheek, gazing at her with such devotion that she barely resisted peeking at his surface desires. The scent of his love was already a devastating test of her discipline.

Mikari then decided it was time to don her fox mask. She had visited Tetsutani often enough over the last several years for the most prominent townsfolk to remember her, and they'd expect her to be in her thirties, at least.

The top of the final foothill was in sight when another traveler on horseback came over the rise, traveling at a perilous speed, their mount kicking up wide sprays of snow.

"Wait," Jun grunted, rising in his saddle. "That's Kie." Before Mikari could even react, he lifted his arm and called out a greeting in Common to his fellow crow.

"Commander!" Kie shouted back. "Oh, thank the Divine One." Then, once she was a little closer— "We've had trouble, and the capital said your speaking mirror was no longer working. Seita and I thought one of us should try to find you, but I couldn't leave in the middle of a snowstorm."

Jun yanked down his scarf, posture stiff and alert. "What trouble?"

"The delegates have all taken ill," she said in an anxious rush. "We suspected poison, but—Noriaki went into some sort of violent rage last night, and he attacked the apothecary who'd come to help. Bit the poor man on his hand and... Well, we were later informed that the apothecary's wife found him on the floor of their shop—incoherent with pain.

All sorts of powders were torn open, bottles spilled everywhere. We believe he was trying to cure himself."

"Sweet Garden," Jun blurted.

"We've been consulting with Houfu, but Seita and I—neither of us is at all familiar with healing magic. And we don't think our efforts are helping at all. Noriaki is doing *very* poorly."

"You said you suspected poison at first?"

Kie gave a hurried nod. "We'd just arrived at our suite, and someone from the kitchens brought a tea service. Moments after drinking, we all began to have stomach pain."

"Did you question the employee?"

"We cannot find him," she said with a desperate shake of her head. "I practically forced my way into the service areas to look for him. And that angered the innkeeper, of course, but he swears that I've met everyone he employs."

"You appear to have recovered," Jun noted. "Did you not drink much of the tea?"

"I had an entire cup," she said, incredulous, shoulders lifting. "So did Seita. But neither of us has fallen ill, not like the delegates have."

"But you felt symptoms?" he pressed.

"We all ended up vomiting, yes. And Seita and I remained quite nauseous for about an hour, but that eventually passed."

Jun was struck silent, his steely expression shifting toward dread, as though he were grappling with a terrible suspicion.

"Let's get moving. We'll speak more on the way," he bade, urging his mount past Kie. "Tell me, where is your speaking mirror? Which of you has it?"

"I left it with Seita," she said, turning her horse to follow him. Mikari brought up the rear. "What happened with yours?"

"Suffice it to say we've had trouble of our own," he said, his tone brooking no further questions. "For now, tell me everything that happened since your arrival."

Kie did so, recounting the last twenty-four hours as the three of them hastened toward the prosperous mining town. According to her, the delegation reached Tetsutani mid-afternoon yesterday and sought lodgings at the Silver Hammer, the town's largest inn, where Mikari always stayed during her visits.

Noriaki was parched when they arrived at their two-room suite, and downed two cups of tea before anyone began feeling unwell, starting with an icy tingling on the tongue and throat and a general ill feeling. Kie's magic then forced her to vomit. So did Seita's.

Quickly realizing the delegates needed to do the same, the two of them got the brownies to empty their stomachs, shoving fingers down throats. They examined the teapot, but they didn't see or smell anything unusual, nor had the tea tasted off in any way.

Despite her residual nausea, Kie interrogated the inn's dozen or so employees and learned that the kitchen had prepped several refreshment trays over the last half-hour. They'd not received any complaints of tainted or missing tea.

Any further attempt to locate the employee whom they suspected of poisoning them then had to be dropped in favor of helping the delegates, whose symptoms worsened just as Kie and Seita's nausea faded. The three brownies complained of blurred vision and then a splitting headache, eventually becoming so disoriented they could barely speak.

A concerned black-haired maid brought them headache powder as well as a medicinal tonic for relieving nausea, neither of which worked, and Kie and Seita both attempted to use magic that would at least ease the delegates' symptoms, but they saw no change.

They ended up consulting with several people in Houfu who attempted to teach them more complicated healing magic through the speaking mirror.

But the delegates continued to suffer, especially Noriaki, whose symptoms escalated sometime after dinner, with Iwa and Natsu following another hour or so later.

At that point, the innkeeper summoned the apothecary, who quickly ruled out the most common poisons that could cause similar symptoms. He had been coaxing a sweating and moaning Noriaki into swallowing a powerful pain medicine when Noriaki turned violent, biting the apothecary's hand and drawing blood.

Kie spoke haltingly as she described the one or two interminable moments it had taken for her and Seita to subdue their translator so that Seita could apply sleep magic, currently the only thing keeping the delegates in any state of comfort.

They'd received no further help from the injured and fiercely scowling apothecary, who had snarled that they were on their own before abruptly departing. When news of the apothecary's ill health reached them a few hours later, they realized they were dealing with something other than mundane poison. Something far worse.

The innkeeper's manner toward them quickly went from strained politeness to open distrust and callousness. He relocated the other guests staying in their part of the inn, which Kie did agree was for the best, but he also warned the delegation that he wouldn't tolerate further trouble, which Kie had assumed meant either kicking them out into a raging snowstorm or turning them over to the town guard.

After that, the only staff member to interact with them had been the black-haired maid, who had brought them fresh linens, icy snowmelt for cooling the delegates' fevers, and food and drink for whomever could eat.

"I imagine her help was involuntary," Jun commented.

"Nene's been very kind," Kie said. "Nervous but kind."

The delegates' health had slowly deteriorated overnight as the unknown disease had drained them of strength.

Then, shortly before dawn, Noriaki's symptoms had turned truly horrific—racking pains, violent spasms, and serrated breaths. Before Seita had put him back to sleep, his only coherent words had been *"kill me."*

Houfu could only reassure them that Jun and Mikari were on their way to Tetsutani, but it was undercut by the news that his speaking mirror had lost its magic and attempts to scry his status had failed.

Kie and Seita had known without question that the delegates had only hours left, so they decided that Kie should ride out the moment dawn broke and attempt to hasten Jun's arrival, for he and his healing magic were almost certainly the delegates' last hope.

Which brought them to now. The three of them ran their mounts toward the next zigzagging rise, beyond which lay the town, and Jun continued asking questions, starting with a full summary of the delegates' symptoms.

Though Mikari had been listening in anxious silence since the moment Kie had intercepted them, she found herself growing distracted as Kie repeated the progression of the delegates' illness, for their symptoms sounded awfully similar to a rare bit of folklore she'd memorized.

One of the suppressed chapters of *Aya the Vigilant* told the story of

Aya's encounter with a beast so dangerous that only extreme measures could guarantee its eradication.

Nowhere in the stricken section were the true origins of "blightspawn" made clear—only a single line that referred to them as being "outside the intended magical order."

However, once established, the blightspawn somehow multiplied through its bite, which at first caused nausea as well as temporary, partial numbness at the site of the wound, resulting in a loss of sensation similar to being exposed to freezing temperatures.

The victim was then disabled with a migraine so acute that they could hardly open their eyes in a well-lit room or "voice the simplest thoughts."

As the blightspawn's minuscule young spread inside their host, eventually growing large enough to feel them crawling about one's insides, the victim experienced "advancing paralysis" from the site of the initial bite, followed by intense agony as they were eaten from the inside.

And then, once the host died... Mikari shuddered, and not for the first time since she'd learned the gruesome details.

The stricken chapter was a highly unflattering account of an incident at a Gozuan temple where blightspawn had killed most of the non-ordained staff in less than thirty-six hours. Aya and her adventuring companions ended up discovering that the cowardly priests had contributed to the staff's deaths by locking them up together in one of the temple buildings to die, whether they'd been bitten or not.

Aya's party managed to save the few surviving staff, though little detail was given regarding their method for helping the ones who'd already been infected. There was only a reference to "fervent prayer," which Mikari suspected had been an early attempt at revision before those in power decided to prohibit the chapter entirely.

However, according to the stricken section, Aya herself was bitten, initially making her ill enough to vomit, but the blightspawn's "venom" ultimately failed to take hold in her. Had her magical gift helped her resist the disease, in the same way Kie and Seita's magic had?

Mikari, Jun, and Kie rode doggedly the rest of the way to Tetsutani, but it was midday by the time they arrived. They were forced to pick their way through several narrow streets choked with uncleared snow and crowded with street vendors, as well as the usual foot and cart traffic.

Of the three of them, Mikari received most of the curious looks, but Jun and his massive stallion also had a few shoppers and vendors turning their heads.

All sorts of shop and trade banners were out. There was a lamp-oil merchant, a woodmonger and stationer, a secondhand clothes dealer, a myriad of metalworkers...but Mikari did not see an apothecary's typically green banner. She spotted what she believed was the correct location, but the unadorned entrance was shut tight.

The massive Silver Hammer Inn stood several stories higher than many of the town's buildings, its outer walls made of plaster panels atop dark timber, its roof done with tiles rather than thatch, although it was hardly visible beneath a thick layer of snow, which also frosted much of the inn's decorative, paneled storm doors.

Moving with haste, they tied their mounts to the posts in front, gathered their belongings, and went inside.

The inn's spacious reception area was familiar to Mikari—all-wood flooring, coffered ceilings, and interior paneling done in forest green with black and white framing. Nothing about it had changed in the few months since she'd last visited.

She spotted the innkeeper, Master Hayashi, through the open doors of the large communal dining space to the right where he was speaking to one of about a dozen guests just starting a meal.

His back was to the entrance, so he didn't notice their arrival, which no one cared to rectify as they quickly shucked their boots and carelessly stowed them in the grid of cabinets set next to the sunken, stone vestibule.

Kie then led the way toward the delegation's suite on the third floor, going first up the central, switchback stairs. Having slipped past the innkeeper, Mikari removed her mask and attached it to her waist.

Though the atmosphere inside the inn seemed calm, her stomach was knotted with fear, not only on behalf of the poor delegates, whom she worried might be beyond even magical help, but also because the murderous employee had not been found.

Kie and Jun were rounding the second-floor landing ahead of her when they heard a man's shout from the floor above. There was an odd, reverberating thump, followed by a crash that sounded like a body had been thrown against a wall.

"Seita," Kie rasped, dropping her saddlebags before launching herself up the stairs. Jun and Mikari followed, both leaving their belongings behind.

Mikari tried to keep Kie in sight—the woman already had her sword out—but Kie seemed to move with augmented speed, and she quickly disappeared down a third-floor hallway.

Jun drew his sword while muttering under his breath. His pace abruptly quickened, and Mikari was forced to tap into her inhuman abilities to keep up.

"Take this," he ordered in a focused but frenzied tone she'd never heard from him before. He held out the magical dagger, hilt first. The second she held out her hand, he slapped it into her palm.

Kie's battle shouts and the unmistakable clang of swords meeting echoed from the only open door. Another strange-sounding thump shook the air, followed by a heavy crash. Somewhere below them, others were shouting with bewildered panic, the uproar quickly spreading.

"Follow wisely," Jun growled before ducking into the room.

Heeding his advice, she stopped short of the door and peeked past its edge, tight all over with the need to curl into herself.

It was chaos inside the two-room suite. A close-quarters swordfight atop a sickroom.

The translator, Noriaki, and one of the female delegates both seemed to be unconscious, or perhaps too ill to move. The other female delegate, however, had wormed her way to her partner and lay across her protectively, even though her arms were tied behind her. The delegates were all bound like hostages.

Jun and Seita were meanwhile battling a brown-haired man across the open partition between the two rooms, their fight occurring dangerously close to the delegates—the walls and ceiling, too. Not an ideal place for a clash with long swords. Blood ran down Seita's face from a nasty gash above his brow.

Behind the three combatants on the far side of the suite, Kie winced as she struggled to her feet, the wall next to her cracked.

The assailant was dressed for travel and a quick escape. He wielded a well-forged sword in one hand and a…a ball of churning black smoke in his other. A baffling sight.

Jun and Seita swung their weapons in a coordinated attack, but the assailant blocked them with what appeared to be little effort, parrying one while dodging the other. He then focused his attention on Jun, who instantly sank into a defensive stance, a shimmering, bluish shape appearing before him like a shield.

The ball of smoke shot from the assailant's hand with the same eardrum-tapping thump from a few seconds ago and struck Jun's translucent barrier as harmlessly as a snowball hitting the side of a house, before dissipating.

The assailant's sword quickly followed in a vicious arc that put Mikari's heart in her throat. Jun slapped it aside with brutal strength, knocking the weapon out of his opponent's hand and sending it flying into the hallway.

Without missing a beat, the assailant dodged a lunging strike from Seita, twisting his body with a soft grunt and spinning out of anyone's immediate reach. Noriaki's eerily still form was only a step behind him.

Confoundingly, he had another sword in his hand, one that was more opaque shadow than metal. Could one conjure a weapon using magic? How was a brownie wielding such power?

Jun and Seita advanced in another coordinated attack. Seita's head wound bled profusely, dripping down his face, and he was forced to wipe the blood out of his eyes. Kie began moving, stiff but quick, toward the other of the suite's two hallway doors, likely to come back around from the first one, where Mikari stood.

"*Kushi no ryokuba!*" The assailant made a sharp motion, his arm trailing thick strands of black smoke.

Out of nowhere, a spear of shadow appeared and stabbed downward at an angle, skewering Kie right through her middle. She made a horrible sound, like the scream of a deer. The sight was horrendous, and Mikari's legs threatened to buckle beneath her.

Seita lunged forward, teeth bared in a snarl, and put himself between the assailant and the two female delegates. Jun entered the fray at the same time, coming at the brownie's other side with a powerful strike just as Seita swung his sword in a swift, controlled slash.

But the assailant blocked Jun's strike as though his sword arm were made of stone while dodging Seita's attack with the agility of a cat.

With one expert move, he pushed aside Jun's sword and spun while arcing his shadow blade, slicing it across Seita's chest—

"*Kandou!*" the attacker invoked.

Seita disappeared in a blink. In his place, a swoop of black vapor. Before Mikari could even gasp, he reappeared in the other room, screaming in pain and collapsing against the already cracked wall. And his newest wound, it...was smoking.

Kie cautiously attempted to move her limbs, but she remained impaled. She'd held onto her sword, somehow. Mikari didn't see any blood or even the suggestion of a physical wound, but the woman was in agony, and whatever magic held her seemed to have defeated her temporarily.

Jun alone now stood against the assailant, and they began trading blows. Neither landed a hit, both of them contending with some sort of defensive magical repulsion. A soft blue light surrounded Jun, whereas his opponent's aura appeared black.

They shuffled and lunged about the room, barely avoiding the helpless delegates. Mikari anxiously looked to Seita again, hoping he'd rejoin the fight, but he was struggling to remain on his feet, half-standing, his face taut with pain.

She wanted to help, but how? She had little experience wielding a weapon and didn't think jumping on the assailant's back would be all that smart.

Should she try her new ability, the one that had knocked Jun down like a bear's charge? If she did that, she might accidentally hit Jun or the delegates, and it would drain a considerable amount of her energy.

What should I do?

A whisper answered. *Allow me.*

Mikari started at the voice in her head. It wasn't the inquisitor. A woman?

She glanced down at the magical dagger in her hand—a living object, Jun had said. It was a comfortable weight. And warm. She could feel its heat even through her gloves.

What do you mean? she asked.

I can take over.

No was her instant response, especially after the events of yesterday morning.

Then use me. Stop standing here.

I don't know how—
You do. Kie first.

The silent discussion took only a second or two, after which Mikari darted to the second door leading into the suite. The clang and scrape of clashing swords rang out. She whipped open the door and went inside.

Kie raised her sword as though to defend herself, face flushed and perspiring. Once she recognized Mikari, she lowered her blade. "Get...help."

Slash at the spear.

Ignoring Kie's command, Mikari swung hard, expecting resistance, but the dagger cut through the spear as if it were as insubstantial as a shadow. The spear then vanished with a wave of heat and a smell like boiling metal. Kie fell to her knees with a yelp, gulping air.

Now we help Jun, came the voice, a little stronger now.

Mikari turned her full attention to the main fight just as Jun whipped his sword upward, slicing through the assailant's clothing as well as the strap of his satchel. The bag began to plummet, forcing the brownie to reach back and grab it with his free arm. Meanwhile, Kie staggered upright, sword in hand.

Pressing his advantage, Jun delivered a powerful follow-up swing. The assailant dodged with a twist, the gash in his clothes parting to reveal freshly drawn blood. He narrowly blocked a third, blurringly fast strike, the satchel clutched against his chest. Were its contents that important?

Peering closely at the visibly frustrated assailant, Mikari was stunned to realize that he looked familiar, in the same sense that all of the inquisitor's aides had looked to be blood-related. Something about the shape of his nose, the proportions of his cheeks and jaw...

Maze take her, he was a lust eater as well. None but eaters smelled as he did, like fire. The acrid odor of smoke and insatiable hunger. Atop that was the sweetness of his last feeding.

The assailant also saw her, his expression widening with surprise, perhaps even recognition, before hardening into cold resolve.

A terrible realization lurked at the edge of her thoughts, but she hadn't the time to confront it.

Half-thinking she'd distract the assailant to give the others an opening, she moved closer in an awkward lurch, dagger raised.

Unlike her, Kie didn't hesitate to leap, cleanly inserting herself into the fray and swiping at the assailant in the same instant as Jun.

But the brownie evaded them both with a backward leap, clearing Noriaki's supine form to land on the other side.

However, someone must have hit him, or rather his satchel, because its contents began spilling out of a tear near the bottom. Vials, small sacks, a rolled-up cloth.

Something hard, black, and glossy became caught in the tear—a prayer book—and it slipped out as the assailant panicked. Grabbing for it, he caught the thick tome against his leg with the flat of his fingers, his shadow blade having vanished into a puff of black smoke.

Mikari's attention became split between the assailant and Kie, who staggered with a sharp gasp, then sank to her knees, her free arm bent in front of her at a painful angle, as though the muscle had cramped.

"C-can't...cast anything," she gritted out.

The spear disrupted her magic, the dagger curtly explained.

Cursing silently, Mikari edged closer to the assailant. Then Jun lunged forward, his free arm extended. Her breath ceased the instant he grabbed the prayer book, the same instant the assailant jabbed him with the heel of his palm.

"*Kandou!*"

Jun disappeared, turned into a swirl of black smoke.

Horror sunk its claws into her chest. She was halfway through a soundless cry when there was a *thud* directly behind her, then a loud, sucking breath.

Her first instinct demanded that she rush to Jun's side, but she managed to resist, causing herself physical pain akin to swallowing something sharp, which then became lodged halfway down.

Is he all right? she silently beseeched, widening her stance protectively, even though she knew the assailant could go right through her if he wished.

Yes, the dagger said. *Focus on the threat.*

The assailant was looking at her, eyes wide with battle fury. He didn't notice the prayer book's front cover had come loose and was in freefall, its weight dragging pleated paper behind it like an unfurling streamer.

The book was filled with strange writing and even stranger drawings, ones that looked a lot like the magical array on her stomach.

Grab it, the dagger urged. *Now.*

Mikari rushed forward. She'd stab the assailant if she could, but she needed to get that book. In the same instant, Kie swiftly dragged Noriaki out of the assailant's reach.

The brownie made a familiar, sharp motion with his arm. "*Kushi no ryokuba!*"

Block! the voice sharply commanded.

Mikari raised the dagger without thinking as an unseen force pushed at her, jolting her weapon arm.

The assailant had a split-second to look surprised before a spike of shadow impaled him where he stood. He slumped forward with a choked gasp, face turning red, the satchel slipping out of his slack grip.

She lunged for the prayer book and grabbed the loose end with her empty left hand. She didn't dare get close enough for the assailant to touch her.

Footsteps pounded somewhere beyond the room. They were growing louder.

"*Dazu*," the assailant seethed, barely holding onto the other end of the book. He made a sloppy attempt to gather up the spilled banner of pages, his movements limited.

Wary of ripping the book in her urgency to claim it, she chanced a quick slash at his closest hand.

Unexpectedly, the blade carved through the side of his wrist as easily as a spoon through pudding, opening a deep laceration. A river of blood spilled out, splashing onto the pages and the floor. The assailant screamed, and yet he did not relinquish his end of the book, though he clutched it awkwardly.

Mikari barely held onto her prize and stared in horror at the enormous, gushing wound she'd caused.

I've broken his glamour, the dagger said.

She looked up to find his appearance had changed, or rather... emerged. His hair was as black as a crow's wing. The indeterminate shade of his eyes was now a rich amber. He had been handsome before, albeit strangely indescribable, but she could now say he had a strong chin, naturally devious eyebrows, and widely spaced dimples brought out by his grimace.

New voices cried out in unison as the pounding footsteps came to a halt outside the suite.

"Master Komatsu?" a woman breathlessly exclaimed.

"D-divine One have mercy!" came an older man's voice.

Master Hayashi and a crow woman stood in the open doorway, both of them wearing stunned expressions, the woman's clothes marking her as an employee.

"Help me," the assailant rasped, lifting his hand to the two newcomers. His name was Komatsu?

"Nene, stay back," Seita barked.

"It's not what you think," Komatsu pleaded, convincingly earnest. "Please, help me." Nene started forward, her worry-filled eyes only for him.

"No!" Seita shouted.

Komatsu yanked hard on the prayer book, ripping the banner of pages somewhere in the middle. He grasped at something beneath his shirt just as Nene wrapped her arms around his hunched shoulders.

Mikari heard him crush something, the sound like snapping glass.

And then he and the maid were gone, nothing left of them but a dissipating cloud of black smoke.

Chapter Twenty-Three

Nene floated in a sea of darkness. She tried to gasp, clutching tight to Komatsu, her only anchor, but there was no air. Nothing to breathe at all. And nothing beneath her feet.

Her lungs burned. Her chest strained to draw something in, anything. She swore she heard it wetly creaking.

A sudden burst of light and air shocked her—*what happened? Am I safe?*

She wobbled on her feet, stomach flipping as though she'd been falling backward, only to have the ground jump up to catch her. Breathing hurt almost as much as being unable to do so, the high, sucking sound as she filled her lungs nearly drowning out Komatsu's more controlled gasp.

She'd hardly oriented herself when Komatsu straightened to his full height, forcing her to let go of his shoulders. She clutched his waist instead, panting fitfully as she fearfully observed her surroundings.

They were in some sort of underground chamber, a rather large one. The air was noticeably cooler than before and smelled strongly like a smith's forge. Light from yellowed lanterns revealed dark pitted walls and a stone ceiling covered in pendent formations similar to icicles.

Numerous sets of shelves and tables held a dizzying variety of objects, many of them dusty with disuse. A basin made of what looked like clear quartz briefly caught her attention, the cloudy pool of liquid within subtly gleaming.

Heavy cloth hangings largely concealed other parts of the chamber, including any exits, their upper third dyed a flat red that darkened to pure black at the base.

One set of curtains, loosely drawn back, helped surround a sleeping space, the bed within sitting high off the ground. She was unnerved to spy a pale hand protruding from several layers of furs.

At least, she thought it was a hand. It was awfully thin, the back of it bruised. Was someone asleep in there?

"What happened?" she whispered shakily. "Where are we?"

"Far from where we were," Komatsu replied, sounding tired.

"H-how did we get here?"

"With magic."

"Magic?" she exclaimed. "How can that...? I-I don't understand."

Only seconds ago, she had been standing at the threshold of the delegation's suite, shocked to find Komatsu...impaled on something. A spike of shadow, it had seemed.

She'd been just as shocked at his altered appearance, his hair now black, his face both familiar and new, like seeing a childhood friend after years spent apart, the softness of youth having given way to the maturity of adulthood.

Even though she had run to the suite out of fierce worry for another, she hadn't been able to resist Komatsu's pleas for help, her innate response to seeing someone in pain taking over. While crossing the room to care for him, she had barely heard someone imploring her to stay away.

The southern male crow, she realized. She still hadn't learned his name, not in all the commotion after the delegation had swiftly and mysteriously fallen ill. He had avoided leaving his sick companions, so she had mostly spoken with Kie.

When she and the innkeeper had heard shouting and crashing sounds, she had worried that one of the delegates had become violent again, but...hadn't she seen a sword on the floor of the hall?

"Why would you bring me to this place?" she asked Komatsu. "Without even warning me?"

He turned in her embrace, dropping what looked like a torn book onto the ground, blood dripping freely from a horrific gash down the side of his wrist and hand. "Help me, and I'll explain."

"Divine One's grace!" Stunned that she'd forgotten the gushing wound, she pulled a clean kerchief from inside her dress and hastily applied it to his injury. "We—we need more bandages, clean water, a needle and thread…"

"Just wrap it up tight for now," he told her, removing his inner cloth belt with his free hand. The movement drew her attention to a gaping tear in his clothes, where there was even more blood. Were these sword wounds?

Mind spinning with confusion, she took the belt from him and efficiently bound his injury, hardly aware of what she was doing and relying entirely on experience from helping her father with his patients before the temple took her from him.

"Nene, stay back. No!"

The southern crow had sounded as though he were in pain, his voice gravelly and pinched. Had he been hurt as well? Maze take her, she'd been too distracted by Komatsu's impalement to notice much else in the room.

She wanted to go back and make sure everyone was all right, but how far away had Komatsu taken them?

Why had he been in the delegation's suite? She tried to recall her last conversation with him but found that she couldn't. Had it been early this morning? The day before?

"Well done, doctor," Komatsu said as she tied off the ends of his improvised bandaging, a note of amusement in his voice. "For someone as used to betrayal as you are, you really are much too tenderhearted." He took gentle hold of her chin and tilted her head up.

His smile was contemptuous, as though he considered her adorably pitiful. In her distress, she tried to blame his sinister countenance on the pain of his wounds, or perhaps his steep eyebrows.

But the foreboding in her heart was too great to wish away, the truth too dire to deny.

She hadn't listened to the right person. Instead, she'd gone to a man who had been hiding not only his appearance but also his motives. He had dragged her into this pit, where no one would know to look for her. He had gone to the delegation's suite to harm them, which meant…

"You were the one who tampered with their tea," she softly accused, backing away. "Why?"

His expression turned smug. "You should be glad you're not there anymore because the worst is yet to come."

"I don't care. Take me back."

"Although, in fairness, your new situation is not much better," he continued as though she hadn't spoken, gesturing about the chamber in the manner of one giving a tour. "This is the last room you'll ever see. But I can at least promise that your time here won't last nearly as long as it normally would."

She turned and ran well before he'd finished speaking, desperate to escape, the stone floor cold beneath her stockinged feet. She flung aside one of the curtains, its heavy length dragging across the floor. There was nothing but a stone wall behind it.

"You won't even be aware most of the time," Komatsu called with spine-chilling nonchalance.

Panting noisily past the sob stuck in her throat, she hurried to another set of curtains and threw them open, the heavy cloth cold to the touch.

Instinct made her freeze at the sight of another strange object, what appeared to be a freestanding mirror the size of a door, only it didn't reflect her. Instead, it gave her the sense of looking out a window at a moonless night sky, specks of white twinkling distantly like stars.

She might have assumed the heavy oval frame was empty but for numerous, inconspicuous cracks all along the edge, from which a small shard was missing near the bottom, revealing the gray metal backing beneath.

"Master Bane's speaking mirror," Komatsu patiently explained. "One of a triad, albeit formerly. He uses it to commune with his patron."

None of his words made sense to her, their echo indicating he hadn't moved. That he wasn't chasing her did nothing to calm her racing heart. He was confident that she couldn't escape.

A chill not born of fright wafted over her, condensing her loud, rapid breaths into billowing puffs of white. Frost crept across the black surface of the mirror, while wisps of freezing air slipped down the glass.

She stumbled back, tight with fear. Her teeth began to ache, and she realized the low buzzing in her ears was coming from the mirror, which was vibrating hard enough to blur the starry field and disturb the whorls of cold air.

"Master Bane believes the darkness is magic itself. Raw, unlimited," Komatsu rasped. "The primordial collective is born of it, made of it. And unlike the Divine One, my master's patron does not hide the truth."

Panting in sobs, heart pounding, she did her best to put distance between her and the mirror while avoiding Komatsu. But it was impossible to look away from the shifting image in the glass, stars now flowing in all directions, following unseen currents.

Something was moving on the other side.

She yelped as a hand on her arm wrenched her around, bruising her with its grip. A male crow she didn't recognize stared down at her with ruthless, blue eyes, his long face capped with a square chin.

Though it was futile, she fought against his hold on her, jerking her arm while pulling at his wrist. He retained her easily, hardly budging.

"I could not finish off the delegation, Master Bane," Komatsu said with regret. "And I failed to bring you the bard. But I did secure a new blood meal for you."

Her eyes widened. Blood meal?

The one holding her, Bane, frowned at his servant with a sidelong look. "You waited too long."

Komatsu didn't reply. She tried kicking at Bane's legs, but he smoothly sidestepped her.

"Let me go!"

She cried out, scalp burning where he'd pulled her hair, dragging her head to one side. Clawing at his fist, she watched with dawning horror as the teeth behind his snarling upper lip extended into four fangs. She tried twisting out of position, but he lifted her to her toes, her scalp and arm throbbing.

His monstrous teeth punctured the side of her neck, and her mind closed in on itself, pushing out everything she was seeing and feeling, even her own choked screams.

Instead, she found herself back at the inn, standing before a man whose name she would never learn, but whose earnest face she would never forget.

How long would he have waited before betraying her, too?

AT THE MAZE'S CENTER

Jun was still gripping his sword as he knelt to examine Seita's injuries, his heart pounding and his flesh humming with the echoes of body-transfiguring magic.

Behind him, Mikari was speaking with the innkeeper, a neatly dressed man who stood half a head shorter than her. Several of his staff had arrived a moment ago with various makeshift weapons that they'd since lowered, the commotion having come to an end.

Master Hayashi spoke Gozuan far better than he did Common, so Mikari was doing her best to calm everyone down.

Kie stood as a buffer between Jun and the others, weapon held discreetly at her side. It seemed likely her magic was arrested or damaged in some manner, and he'd offered to examine it after tending to Seita, but she'd insisted that he help everyone else first.

Seita sat in a half-slump against the cracked rear wall of the suite, his expression one of suppressed pain and inner turmoil.

The second that this "Komatsu" had disappeared with the maid, Seita had lunged forward as though to take her back, then dropped to his knees with a wordless howl, eyes trained on the spot from which Nene had vanished.

"What just happened?" had been the first sensible thing out of anyone's mouth, spoken by Kie. No one had responded.

Indeed, Jun knew little about half the magic Komatsu had employed against them, particularly his ability to...displace, Jun supposed he'd call it.

Thus, he didn't know where Komatsu may have gone with the young maid, whether he could return at any time, or even whether his escape was thanks to the same ability as the one that had blinked Jun five paces backward.

What he did know was that he wouldn't let it work on him a second time. Though his forced trip had been nearly instant and left him without injury, he'd had the distinct and unsettling impression of being somewhere dark and airless, and it had left him disoriented for a few precious seconds.

"I need to look for her," Seita said to Jun in a guttural rasp, shifting as though he meant to try standing again. "She could be nearby."

Jun stayed him with a firm grip on his shoulder. "None of us know that. And whether she is or isn't, you need healing now."

Even without any intervention, Seita would fully recover on his own, but it would take at least a couple of days and Jun needed him up and able to fight far sooner than that.

Using his empty right hand, he reached out with his magic.

The gash across Seita's forehead could be sealed quickly and easily, but the laceration across his chest was deep, the tissue partially dissolved as though the blade that had cut it had been coated with sandsnake venom.

Any deeper, and the damage the toxin would've done to his major blood vessels would have killed even an experienced crow in a matter of hours unless he received either the antivenin or magical healing, both exceedingly rare options in Gozu. Such a slow death would've been excruciating. As it was, Jun sensed dozens of small hemorrhages beneath the necrotic wound.

"I had nothing left to fight him with," Seita said with a thick voice, shaking his head slightly. "Spent all I had keeping the delegates asleep. Noriaki, he…passed away an hour ago."

Jun wasn't surprised at the news. If the delegate's eerie stillness hadn't given it away, then his bloodless complexion would have. But discovering he'd been a mere hour too late made Jun shut his eyes and give a tight sigh.

Could he have arrived that much earlier? Left the orchard the moment the snowstorm had begun to dissipate in the brace before dawn? If he had, Mikari might not have spoken with Eiji, and they might not have learned the likeliest place to find the inquisitor.

No known magic could reverse death more than a few minutes after it had occurred, nor would Jun ever meddle that far into a soul's journey, even if he could restore life. The only person currently known to have brought anyone back from death was the empress.

"Divine One keep him," Jun murmured.

"Nene had gone to make arrangements for him. I…I thought maybe his daughter would want his ashes." Seita shook his head again, worry sharpening his already crisp features. "Why did she go to him?"

Presumably, he referred to Nene. However, considering the intensity of Seita's reaction to the maid's disappearance, Jun decided not to answer. Seita was more than clever enough to come up with the two most obvious guesses.

Either Nene had been working against them, or she was a victim. Neither possibility was palatable.

"I don't know," Jun murmured. "We'll help her if we can, but the delegates have to come first."

Seita gave a resigned nod.

Though Jun was certain he could mend Seita's wounds, he had to spend his remaining magical stamina wisely, so he decided on an avenue of treatment he typically avoided, one that allowed him to lend his supernatural healing to another.

For Seita, a dozen hours of magically enhanced recovery would be reduced to a mere moment. For Jun, he would have to hope that he continued to avoid injury until his resiliency returned.

He placed his palm on Seita's middle and spoke the command for *sympathetic healing* in his mind.

"Yes, I know that I look quite young," Mikari said to the upset innkeeper, "but I am the same Mikari who's roomed here and entertained your guests a dozen times in the past. You know me. And I vow that the man whom you just saw vanish into thin air was the one instigating trouble, for you and the delegation. They're here as diplomats, not soldiers or spies."

"None of this ruckus and bloodshed occurred until these 'diplomats' arrived with two unbranded crows," Hayashi harrumphed. "I took a risk letting out a pair of rooms to them, and they ended up bringing evil into my establishment. Endangered my guests and my business."

The innkeeper apparently didn't think his missing employee was worth mentioning. And by now, half of his staff present had turned their attention to shooing away other curious guests.

"Do you really think I've forgotten that you once forced your kitchen to serve spoiled fish, which sickened nearly thirty people?" she coolly reminded the innkeeper. "Or that you accept a cut of the proceeds whenever the local gang runs its fixed dice games in your back rooms on the second floor, where a guest was stabbed last year?"

Having cited the innkeeper's hypocrisy, Mikari moved on to flattering his business savvy with the suggestion that he'll have realized, of course, how much his business would suffer were it widely rumored that not only had he rented out a room to an assassin, likely also a kidnapper, but that his inn was also the source of an outbreak of disease.

Many of his current guests would flee, refunds would be demanded, and few would dare to room at the Hammer until the news died down.

Jun suppressed a grin as the innkeeper blundered his way through a response. Maze take him, he loved that woman.

"Close one," Seita tiredly remarked, staring at the gaping tear in his clothing. The cut on his brow had healed, and the wound on his chest had been reduced to a raw red mark, which would fade to nearly nothing by the next morning.

Seita put his head back with a sigh. "Fuck, was I glad to see you and Kie."

"I'm glad we weren't too late," Jun said. "For you, at least."

Seita gave a tight nod. "I hope you can help the others."

"So do I."

Healing injuries was one thing. Treating disease was another. He had become better at diagnosis, but the method of magically curing something as common as sugar disease still eluded his entire house.

Worse, the fact that Kie and Seita had experienced symptoms, despite crows being largely immune to communicable illness, could only mean the affliction was magical in nature, making it even more difficult to diagnose let alone treat.

Magical illness was often deadly to anyone without a metaphysical organ to help them resist it, which meant that if Jun couldn't help the surviving delegates and possibly also the apothecary, then all of them would likely die.

Mikari managed to convince the innkeeper to keep quiet about the most recent incident, and even fabricated for him an excuse to give to nosy guests, that an overly strong dose of medicine had made a delegate delirious to the point of violence resulting in a quickly quelled scuffle. Rumor had already spread that the apothecary had sustained an injury while attempting treatment last night, which helped sell the story.

She also requested a new room for the delegation, for their current suite needed to be where Noriaki's body remained until it could be discreetly carried out and cremated, not to mention the large blood stain that would require several new floor panels.

Seita changed into clean clothes, then their group spoke briefly, all of them agreeing that Jun should assess the female delegates before anyone even considered a longer conversation. Kie and Seita asked to remain in the room, unobtrusively, but with two lives counting on him, Jun couldn't afford even the smallest distraction.

So instead, Kie went with the two lingering employees to see to their mounts and abandoned belongings, and Seita was to brief someone in Houfu about the attack and the items Komatsu had left behind.

"I can join Seita and give our account," Mikari offered as she and Jun removed their overcoats.

"No, I'll need your assistance," Jun said, to which she gave a firm nod.

"I'll keep it down," Seita said before closing the partition between the two rooms.

Jun started with Iwa, who hardly looked like the same woman with whom they'd been traveling. She was glistening with sweat, body twitching and juddering in pain. Her crackling breaths came in slow, shallow gasps. He made note of her pallor, which only emphasized the dilated veins in her cheeks and forehead.

Then he examined her bound limbs as best as he could without untying her, a precaution Seita had been forced to take with all of them after Noriaki's outburst last night. Her arms and legs were splotchy and puffy.

He parted her robe...then silently cursed.

Her midsection was distended, the dappled skin a decidedly unhealthy spectrum of colors, from dark pink to red to almost brown. It was somehow worse than what Seita had described, and the young crow was decidedly blunt. Jun didn't need magic to know that she had perhaps half an hour to live.

"Divine One's grace," Mikari said softly next to him.

"Back up, lamb." He squeezed her knee. "I don't want you in arm's reach."

Once she'd shifted back, he conjured a field of magic between his palms. Widening his hands, he stretched the field into a larger size, then sank it into Iwa's torso.

Sweet Garden.

There was extensive tissue damage, mostly to muscle and nerves, though her lungs, liver, and kidneys were beginning to break down as well. She was also having a severe chemical response as though she'd been repeatedly stung, and he detected several foreign masses of what seemed to be tissue...but not Iwa's.

Disturbed, he briefly concentrated on her stomach, from which he sensed a sort of skittering resonance that echoed throughout the rest of her. Definitely a magical disease, although he hadn't doubted it.

Like mundane medical treatment, magical healing was a combination of experience, skill, and intuition, and there was no catch-all magical cure. One had to make a plan.

With the delegates, he would need to eradicate the foreign masses, restore her damaged flesh, neutralize the venom breaking down her tissue, and counteract the diseased resonance.

It was a lot of moving parts.

But a filament of inspiration began worming through his mind like slow-moving lightning, granting him clarity and filling him with awe.

Recognizing the sensation as a blessing from the Divine One, he surrendered to it with quiet rapture, the welcome revelation arriving on a wave of hope and love that brought tears to his eyes.

Still, purging Iwa's affliction would take enormous concentration. Thankfully, Jun knew where to find it, though he had to swallow back tears to free up his voice.

"Will you hum for me?" he asked of Mikari. "Something soothing."

"Of course."

She needed only a few seconds to ponder his request. Then her voice emerged, soft and smooth, producing a lullaby-like melody. He allowed a moment for her calming tones to wash over him, eyes closed, before reviewing his plan in his mind.

Eradicate, restore, neutralize, counteract.

Then he got to work, first applying some pain relief and then widening and strengthening the magical field suspended between his palms.

Shujutsu, he silently invoked, drawing the charged magical field through Iwa's flesh like a fishing net to isolate the foreign masses.

He chose a growth at random and focused on it with destructive intent, until it had completely disintegrated, noting that it seemed to have a...structure to it.

Minutes passed as he destroyed them all, his effort aided by Mikari's soft humming. He repaired Iwa's tissue, requiring another spell, and scrubbed the toxin from her blood and organs—a third spell. Her erratic heartbeats began to normalize, her breaths becoming quieter.

Counteracting the resonance required the most concentration. The most effort. Doing so was like trying to reach out and quiet the vibration of a lute string without the benefit of sight, and from the edge of the room.

Byouki no jokyo.

In his mind, he created a spiky surface and turned it inward to form a cube. Then another cube outside of it. Then another. He slowly compressed them upon the source of the resonance, his magic churning hot and fast inside him, making him sweat and his heart race.

He knew that he'd succeeded when the cubes abruptly squeezed down to nothing, all resistance gone.

Panting and shaking, he toppled back into Mikari's ready embrace, the blue glow of his magic fading.

"Maze take me, you did it," she whispered effusively. "At least I think you did. Look."

Iwa's hair was still tangled and matted, her clothes disheveled, but her complexion was back to normal, the distension gone. She looked tired but otherwise healthy.

"Thank the Divine One," he breathed.

Mikari gave an airy chuckle. "Thank *you*. You did this."

"With the gift he gave me, and the words to channel it."

She pressed her cheek to his. "And with the strength of will that is yours alone."

Her sincere praise made his chest swell with pride. "I should have enough stamina to treat Natsu."

"And the apothecary?" she asked in a careful tone.

"Yes, him too, though it'll probably take all my remaining stamina. We'll be even more vulnerable for a while."

"How long does it take to regain your strength?"

"A crow's magic recovers at a set time every day based on when it first manifested. For me, it's in the second half of the brace of rose." Which was thirteen hours away.

He felt as much as heard her swallow. "In that case," she said lightly, "I suppose we'd better hope for a quiet evening."

"We can hope. Certainly eases me to know that Komatsu's magic is surely suffering the way Kie's is. Was that the dagger's doing?"

"Indeed, she helped me. Even spoke to me," Mikari said with soft awe. *She?* "Told me she'd broken his glamour?"

"Hmph, I saw that. But before it faded, I could have sworn that—"

"That he looked like one of the inquisitor's aides?"

"Then you saw it as well."

"Not only that… Jun, he's a lust eater."

Surprised, he turned to face her. "How…?"

"I could smell it on him," she explained.

"Could he be the one whom you've been tracking in your journal? Impressive work, by the way," he quickly added, before seizing the opportunity to blurt out even more. "That first night, you were willing to share it with me, with the Dark Court, and like a complete arse, I refused to listen. I apologize."

A shy smile pulled at her lips. "I'm certain it's him. A previous victim spoke of someone named 'Komatsu' to her neighbor, and the glamour would explain why his description is always so vague."

"But the powerful magic he wielded, the energy it must've required, how could a lust eater…?"

"I believe that, unlike me, he doesn't let his victims live."

Sweet Garden. That poor maid.

Mikari seemed to have the same thought. "He has to be the one whom the inquisitor meant for me to meet. If I'd come straight to Tetsutani, that maid might not have…"

"Don't go claiming guilt that's not yours," he said, his hand finding its way to its favorite spot behind her ear. "And don't ever suggest that your life has less value than another's, especially not to me. No other life means more to me than yours."

She gave him a gentle nod, her freckled cheeks turning rosy.

Recovered enough to use his magic again, Jun took a brief moment to help untie Iwa and straighten her clothing, but further care would have to wait until he'd seen to Natsu or until Kie returned.

Just then, Kie walked into the suite as if summoned, took one look at Iwa and stopped short, eyes round with astonishment. "D-Divine One's tears," she stammered.

Seita chose that same moment to approach them and ask whether was now a convenient time for something, but he lost track of his sentence the instant he saw Iwa, the muscles in his face and neck standing in stark relief.

After a hard swallow, he abruptly returned to the other side of the suite. "I'll tell them you're still busy."

Jun was more efficient at healing Natsu, having learned from curing Iwa, and felt less spent afterward. Their lead delegate would live.

Then he and Kie moved the delegates and everyone's things to their new room across the hall, while Mikari slipped away to deliver the letter from the old brownie woman in Okususo. Noriaki's covered body would remain in the original suite until the innkeeper and his staff returned to transport it.

When Mikari returned less than a quarter-hour later, they all convened for a quick meeting with the usual trio in Houfu, but Elder Mai was summoned once Jun mentioned the magical dagger.

He and Mikari gave their account of all that had happened since they'd last updated the capital, though Jun largely omitted their activities in the orchard's guesthouse. No one needed to know how thoroughly they'd enjoyed one another.

"You were given essence of moose velvet?" Rosuke asked, eyebrows raised. "How did you manage the...secondary effect?"

Jun remained stoic in his reply. "Slept through it, I suppose."

Vallen softly smiled, while Rosuke gave a knowing nod. "Of course."

They then discussed the magical dagger—Vallen acknowledged that Living Objects were known to grow in power, their voices becoming stronger the more they were utilized. He warned that a handful of such artifacts could become powerful enough to take over a wielder's mind, especially when used to do harm.

"Take care with it, Madam Bard," he stressed to Mikari.

Elder Mai encouraged Mikari to try speaking with it again, but the dagger had gone silent.

The conversation returned to Komatsu and the affliction, with the empress informing them that whatever spell or potion he'd used to infect the delegation was not described in the portion of the prayer book they'd retained, though it did detail much of the combat magic he'd deployed against them. It would be translated as soon as possible.

Unfortunately, there was nothing in the book about Mikari's curse, which made her deflate a bit. Jun squeezed her hand.

"However, we may have discovered an exception in the language of the curse binding your magic," the empress revealed, lowering her gaze to a piece of paper in her hand. "It allows anyone who can invoke the array to harvest the magic it suppresses, including you, I believe. With the right invocation, you should be able to reclaim your magic all on your own."

"Won't she need the exact invocation and the magic to power it?" Jun asked, trying not to get excited just yet.

"You should certainly be well fed before reciting it," the empress said to Mikari. "And as for the specific words, I've crafted something that I'm confident will work." She held up another sheet of paper. "It may not exactly match whatever the inquisitor drafted, but Mahou is not so rigid as to require only one solution to achieve a desired effect."

"This invocation," Mikari began, her voice nervous, "if it doesn't work, then what's the chance something bad will happen instead?"

The empress kept her expression carefully neutral. "I cannot say there's absolutely no risk. And you should be careful how you practice the invocation. Don't speak it out loud until you're ready. In fact, no one in your group should speak it out loud."

"Why?" she asked as though afraid of the answer.

"Invoking a magical array sometimes only requires proximity rather than touch, and if someone there read these words while standing too close to you, they might end up harvesting you by accident."

"Mikari should be the one to write it down, then," Jun suggested. To Mikari, he said, "And keep it somewhere safe until you're prepared."

"What if I don't wish to take the risk?" she tentatively asked.

The empress spoke with sympathy. "I don't think you can afford not to."

"As for the lust-eater curse," Rosuke said, "while Vallen and I cannot prove it, we suspect that once your magic is no longer bound, it will purge the remaining curse."

"Really?" Mikari exclaimed. Jun nearly echoed her.

"According to the ritual that was used on us, sundering a crow's magic appeared to be a prerequisite to cursing them, which makes us believe that ours would've otherwise protected us."

"I see," she said, anxious once more. "I hope you're right."

"So do I," Rosuke said with sincerity.

Mikari asked to copy the invocation later that evening so that she could accompany Jun to the apothecary, who likely had only a handful of hours left. Jun was indeed anxious to see to the man, but...

"The sooner you copy the invocation, the sooner you can start practicing it," he told her. "I'll manage the apothecary on my own."

Considering that they'd already lost one of their two speaking mirrors, Jun didn't want to take the chance that they might lose the other before obtaining the spell that could cure her.

"Are you sure?" she asked.

Jun nodded just as Kie, who'd been standing sentry at the door, interrupted them. "The innkeeper's coming."

"Is he here for Noriaki?" Seita asked, pushing up to his feet. Jun did likewise.

"He's got two big men behind him with a stretcher, but they're carrying improvised clubs," she said with a disapproving frown. "Do they expect a dead man to attack them?"

"Can you blame them?" Seita muttered.

Recalling the strange growths that had been moments from killing Natsu and Iwa, Jun joined Kie and Seita out in the hall.

"I'm going to examine the body before they move it," he warned them, taking care to close the door behind him so that Mikari could copy the invocation in private.

Kie frowned. "Do we dare ask why?"

"You're not gonna cut him open, are you?" Seita asked, voice low to avoid being overheard.

"Wasn't planning on it," Jun said drily, "but be ready for anything." Seita cursed under his breath.

Jun gave the innkeeper a short update, saying only that the rest of the delegates would recover and that he intended to check on the apothecary within the next quarter-hour. Hayashi imparted that he'd arranged a discreet route out of the building to a waiting wagon, which would take their deceased translator to a cremation pyre.

He had the same antsy reaction as Kie and Seita when Jun said that he'd be examining the body. "What good would that do now?"

"Just a precaution," Jun said.

"Precaution for what?"

"I want to make sure the body isn't contagious."

The innkeeper contained his shock admirably. "Hadn't thought of that," he said grudgingly. "All right, then. Let's get this over with."

Jun gave a curt nod, opened the door to the suite, and was instantly bombarded by a terrible stench.

"Divine One's arse," he swore, cupping his hand over his mouth and nose. His sentiment echoed behind him as the others likewise covered their faces.

He entered the room, stomach twisting with disgust and dread as he eyed the corpse laying in the center. Noriaki's overcoat had been draped over his head and torso, concealing him from view. Jun suspected that something horrific was happening beneath.

It was far too soon for decomposition to have produced such a pungent odor, and yet the bedding beneath Noriaki's body was already discolored, something that shouldn't happen in their current environment for at least a couple of days.

"Damn it, this smell will carry through the entire inn once we move him," Hayashi groused from the door, voice muffled behind his hand.

"Another hour, and it'll spread regardless," Jun replied. "Get that stretcher ready. I'll be as quick as I can."

Breathing through his mouth as little as possible, he went to Noriaki's other side and knelt. The two employees tasked with removing his corpse quickly laid the stretcher out next to him, on the side nearest to the door, then backed up.

Everyone was staring with morbid dread, all awaiting the moment Jun lifted the overcoat.

"I expect it's bad," he warned them. There were a few hasty nods. One of the stretcher-bearers wisely looked away.

With the thought that he'd thoroughly wash his hands once he was done, he grasped the woolen layer and carefully lifted it. His whispered curse was one of many horrified utterances.

Noriaki's face was grotesquely swollen, his tongue protruding, his skin a ghastly color—more green than red, yet strangely pale and waxen. Brownish-red fluid had seeped from his nose and mouth.

Their translator had been a portly man, but the distension in his abdomen was conspicuous. He parted Noriaki's robe, secretly grateful that the body was still bound in rope. Here, the skin was darker and marbled, close to blistering.

If Jun had come across a body like the one before him without knowing the time of death, he'd assume the person had perished at least a day ago of blood infection and the attendant fever, if not three or four days ago of a different cause. And he'd assume the distension was the result of the gases created during putrefaction.

But knowing exactly when and approximately how Noriaki had died made him suspect otherwise.

Hoping he'd turn out to be wrong, he prepared a magical field between his palms, so intent on his task that he didn't hear the door across the hall slide open.

The extrasensory field would tell him more about the state of Noriaki's insides than his fingers might, but Jun pretended to palpate the distension to avoid unwanted notice, using extra care to hide the soft blue glow of his magic.

He immediately felt movement beneath his hands, sensing it in greater detail through his magic.

Whatever the growths were, they were still alive. And based on the devastation to Noriaki's tissues, they had been eating him, leaving his organs for last, their corruption in his flesh rapidly advancing his decay.

Jun fought to suppress his horror so that he could count their exact number. He estimated about two dozen. And their general shape... Maze take him, they seemed to be—

Snatching his hands back, he watched alarmedly as the dead man's bloated stomach shivered and boiled, the creatures within teeming like a disturbed bee hive.

"Jun, get away from there!" Mikari exclaimed. He looked up just as she yanked the wide-eyed innkeeper from the room. "Stay out here."

"Divine One have mercy," Seita rasped. Jun jumped to his feet and backed up.

To their credit, the two staff members were braced for a fight. One wielded a broken table leg, the other a small shovel for cleaning out firepits.

"H-how is he moving?" Kie asked, pressed tight to the wall, hands clamped onto her sheathed sword.

"Blightspawn," Mikari answered as she shut the door of the suite, dagger already drawn. She repeated herself in Gozuan when necessary. "We can't let even one leave this room alive. Their bite spreads the sickness."

Jun wanted to ask how in the Maze she could know what they were dealing with, but he never got his question out.

Noriaki's distended belly suddenly split, releasing the foulest smell Jun could ever imagine, one that had him gagging.

Pale, fist-sized creatures began pouring out, scrabbling fast and covered in clots of blood and tissue, spreading in all directions. The sight was truly nightmarish.

Spiders. Make take him, it was a clutch of spiders.

Realizing the consequences if he used his magic now, Jun hastily drew his sword, too choked with adrenaline to add to the collective cry as everyone defended themselves with thwacks and shouts.

He stabbed the nearest blightspawn skittering toward him, the tip of his blade penetrating all the way to the woven-mat flooring. Jerking his sword free, he was repulsed to discover that the creature stuck on the end wasn't dead.

Divine One preserve us.

In the same instant, Table-Leg swung his improvised weapon, smashing another of the vermin in a sickening splat of blood and yellowish insides. Taking a cue from him, Jun swung his sword in a downward chop, then twisted and dragged it free of a fresh gash in the flooring to remove the dead creature.

Reflexively chopping at another one scuttling toward him, he tried to keep half an eye on Mikari, but there were too many to split his attention.

They were fast, acting on more than just instinct. He had missed the one aiming to attack him but jumped back before it got too close. Something wet and fleshy burst beneath the heel of his sock as he sliced the attacking blightspawn in half.

"You! Back of your leg," Kie shouted.

"Fuck!" came Shovel's reply in Gozuan.

Chop. Stomp. Slash. Smack.

He missed as much as he hit, some of them glancing blows that sliced off a limb or two. None of the vermin were on him long enough to bite, but Maze take it, how many were there?

A high-pitched gasp from Mikari's direction made his heart turn to ash. A second later, he glimpsed the red blur of her leg kicking a blightspawn across the room toward a broken pile of furniture that had once been a tea table.

The damned thing flared its pale legs mid-air, righting itself, and landed on its feet.

Slice. Stomp. Chop. Fuck, he kept missing. *Chopchopchop.*

"Ahh!" a low voice shouted.

"Shit! Shit, I'm sorry," Shovel cried out.

More chopping and stomping. Jun whacked his blade at anything small and pale that moved. Then at anything small and pale, whether it moved or not, until no threats remained.

Breathing hard, forehead tingling with sweat, he looked about for more to kill. Seeing nothing immediate, his gaze flew to Mikari.

She was also worriedly looking him over, her color high, eyes a little wild.

Shovel was engaged in pulverizing a dead blightspawn, but most of the others had stopped attacking the floor and walls, and were now twitching with fearful anticipation, eyes darting everywhere. Seita was frantically batting at himself.

"There's none, there's none," Kie assured him.

"Is anyone bitten?" Jun asked the room at large. More than one person did a quick skim of their body.

"I don't think so," Kie answered. Seita and Shovel both shook their heads.

"No, though I may have a cracked rib," Table-Leg grunted.

Shovel looked over with a wince, the blightspawn before him now reduced to paste. "I'm sorry."

Mikari wore a strange expression, a bit choked, as though she were about to cry. He froze in terrible suspicion, a deep cold entering his veins, every inch of him petrified.

She shook her head. He blew out a breath, immensely relieved.

Not bitten, then. But certainly not all right. Neither was he.

Lowering his blade, he crossed the room to draw her against him. She held him tight, nose tucked into the vee of his collar as though seeking his scent. The realization sent a tendril of tenderness through him.

"What in Oblivion were those things?" Seita asked.

"They were…n-nesting inside him," Kie said.

"Correct," Jun acknowledged. "They're responsible for killing Noriaki, and what almost killed the others."

"Blightspawn," Mikari said, casting him a guilty look as she pulled from his embrace. "I couldn't be sure at first, and it seemed impossible. But the smell that hit me when I came out of the other room…"

"Is it ov...er?" The innkeeper had opened the door, and now silently gaped at the carnage. Or perhaps just the damage to the room, regardless of the dead creatures.

Ignoring him, Jun returned his attention to Mikari. "Tell us what you know."

Chapter Twenty-Four

Alone at last in the unoccupied half of the delegation's new suite, Mikari sank somewhat gracelessly to the floor, having shut the partition and doused the lantern on this side.

Never had she relied so heavily on pure performance, covering up every twinge and forcing every smile.

The bite on the back of her right ankle didn't hurt. Everything below mid-calf was thankfully numb, so moving about was merely awkward. But the initial nausea had made speaking normally an extraordinary effort that had left her exhausted.

She had somehow managed it, though. Jun had given her a concerned look, but she'd passed off an irrepressible gag as being the fault of the pervasive fetor.

In answer to Jun's appeal, she'd given a brief summary of the suppressed chapter of *Aya the Vigilant* where the holy warrior encountered blightspawn, explaining that the stench of rancid meat preceded the final, postmortem stage of the affliction, which had alerted Mikari to what was coming.

Then she had warned Master Hayashi that the contents of the room at the time of spawning would need to be burned, including every single panel of flooring. This in addition to the cremation of Noriaki's corpse, which had been since been wrapped up and carried away.

Laundering everyone's clothing would also be prudent, which was why Mikari now wore one of the inn's complimentary robes. Fortunately, she'd found a larger-sized one that was long enough to conceal her right foot.

The innkeeper had balked at her urgings until she'd informed him that the only other way to ensure the blightspawn had been eradicated would be to torch his entire inn.

"That's what Aya and her companions did after one of the surviving staff became infected again while cleaning the building where they'd been isolated," she'd said. Hayashi had relented after that.

The five-minute conversation had been exhausting, but once she'd explained what she knew, Jun had taken himself off to help the apothecary, and his fellow crows had not questioned it when she'd asked for time alone to "practice" the invocation.

The spoken spell she'd copied had turned out to be rather short. One sentence to prime the magical array, and a command word to execute it. She'd been surprised to learn that the language of magic was pronounced rather like Gozuan. Was the latter derived from the former?

"There are crows, like Jun, who can cast some magics silently," the empress had said. "But this invocation is too advanced for that. You needn't worry about practicing it in your head."

"How will I know if I've fed enough?" Mikari had asked.

"Jun's love for you is potent. I have a feeling that one full dose will suffice."

However, the energy currently sustaining her was draining fast. She'd spent a large chunk of it hiding her symptoms, and the scant remainder was slowly leaving her, a weak healing response to the infestation. Too weak to fight it off. And yet she couldn't stop the slow loss.

If the blightspawn didn't kill her first, the starvation would.

Her current hope, which she still desperately held, was that she'd last until Jun's magic recovered.

Those things are growing inside me.

Red-faced and sweating, head pounding as relentlessly as a waterfall, Mikari parted the bottom of her robe, leg bent to the side so that she could see the back of her ankle.

A breath shuddered out of her. It could look worse, she supposed. Four small, red punctures surrounded by dark, puffy flesh.

It rather looked like a snakebite, which was why she decided to take the likely ineffective measure of tightly tying a thin length of linen around her leg, just below her knee, to slow the flow of venom-laced blood.

Once that was done, she leaned back to rest against the wall, hoping she wouldn't be disturbed until Jun came back, and that he'd understand why she'd hidden the bite from him.

Time seemed to slow as a migraine settled in deep, encompassing her brain and squeezing it like a vise, more pressure than pain.

But oh, was there pain. She would've given into tears, but doing so was guaranteed to take her from terrible discomfort to true agony.

Blood pulsed through her head with an audible woosh. Her robe became damp beneath her arms and between her breasts. And yet the room was painfully cold.

Chills had set in by the time she heard Jun's deep, distinctive voice through the closed partition. Thirty minutes may have passed since he'd left, or perhaps it'd been two hours, she couldn't tell.

She peered down at her ankle. It remained swollen, the skin becoming even darker, and the numbness had advanced upward.

"Indeed, it's done," Jun said, and Seita informed him that both delegates had woken briefly and taken a few sips of water. Something like relief filled her chest, but it hurt. "Where's Mikari?"

Seita mumbled a reply. Footsteps approached the partition.

It opened, flooding the darkened space with light from the lantern burning on the other side. She shut her eyes as a spike of pain pierced her forehead.

"Mikari?" Jun gasped. He was at her side in an instant, cupping her cheek and checking her pulse, his scent like astringent, sweet resin. Love mixed with fear. "What happened?"

Quickly discovering the problem for himself, he gently touched the pressure bandage around her exposed leg. Seita and Kie both stood silently in the open partition, their bodies blocking the bright light that hurt Mikari's eyes.

"Did we not get them all?" Jun asked in a horrified rasp. He hadn't yet figured it out.

"We did," she assured him, throat feeling pinched. She spoke in Common for the others' sake, but translating her thoughts was unexpectedly difficult. "I wasn't...when I said I wasn't bitten, I lied."

He grasped her shoulders. "Sweet Garden, *why*?"

She gave him a sad smile. "I knew you'd try to help me first, but I still have time. The…"—she struggled to remember the word for *koabakasha*—"the apothecary didn't."

"I might've been able to help you both!" he seethed, no doubt wanting to shake her but refraining. "If you'd told me right away, it might not have taken much stamina to cure you, but now that it's set in…"

"You might have," she agreed, closing her eyes in a long blink. "Or you might not have, and you wouldn't know until you'd reached the apothecary."

Granted, he might've slowed the disease in the apothecary with what little stamina he had left, and thus might've earned enough time to try again after his magic recovered, but doing so would've only extended the apothecary's suffering.

Or the affliction might've outpaced Jun's healing and ended up killing his unfortunate patient. Either way, she couldn't stand the thought of someone suffering even longer, possibly dying, just to spare her a few hours of misery.

"Anyway, doesn't matter now."

"It *does* matter," he erupted, squeezing her shoulders, eyes glittering with hurt. "We don't know how this disease affects your kind. It might kill you faster."

Considering the fact that her remaining energy had begun leaking at a greater rate, she suspected he was right.

She took a painful swallow, fear lodging itself in her heart like an ax to the chest. Fear, but not regret. Not for her own sake, at least. Maze take her, how her head hurt.

"And if I had to choose between your life or anyone else's, I'd pick yours," he vowed. "*Every time.*"

"Which is why I lied," she whispered, the joy his words gave her only making her feel worse.

"Shh, don't cry, lamb," he cooed, wiping his thumb across her wet cheek. "We'll find another way. There must be something in that prayer book. Because without your… Wait."

"What is it?" she asked, both hopeful and anxious.

"You could use the invocation. Then your magic could fight it off."

"I-I would need to feed first, and—"

"Then we shall do so."

"But you'd be giving me your physical strength, which you need."

"I don't need it more than your life."

She wanted to argue with him on that point but moved on to another. "I'm...not exactly in the mood right now."

"I have a sip of power left. It's enough to mask your symptoms for a short time."

"I haven't had any time to practice the spell."

"Pronouncing Mahou is just like Gozuan. And don't underestimate your talent with words. You'll do fine."

Tears tumbled down her cheek, despite Jun's plea. Having run out of all other concerns, she nodded. "All right, then."

He needed only a few seconds to gather the last of his stamina, which manifested as a puff of mist in his palm that he released above her head. A cool, lovely wash of relief flowed through her, dispersing the pounding pressure on her brain and quieting her nausea.

She took a full breath for the first time since she'd been bitten, and then let out a blissful sigh, releasing an enormous amount of tension.

Before she could even think about standing, Jun draped her arms across his shoulders, slid his hands beneath her, and lifted her from the floor.

A thrill shot through her at his masculine display, compounded tenfold by his naked devotion. He couldn't be using magic to augment his strength, so the ease with which he held her was all the more impressive and exhilarating.

"Anything we can do?" Seita quietly asked, making way for them. Kie silently reached out to adjust Mikari's robe and hide her injury.

Jun shook his head. "I secured another room before coming up. But I'll let you know if anything else needs to happen tonight. In the meantime, update Houfu, then get some rest. If all goes well, we'll see you just before breakfast, and we'll make a plan then."

"Your belongings?" Kie asked, opening the door for them.

"I'll have a staff member fetch them later." Jun spoke calmly and without strain, but his heart was thumping like a drum where they were pressed together. "For now, all we need is the invocation...and privacy."

"I-I have the spell in my pocket," Mikari confirmed, face flushing inexplicably at the word *privacy*. And here she'd thought she was beyond feeling bashful.

Jun bid the others good evening and carried her away, bearing her weight with continued ease. She couldn't bring herself to look back.

Needing to push past her shyness, she brought her lips to his ear. "You must be quite eager if your first thought when you returned was to get us a private room."

And then, because it was right there, she wrapped her lips around his earlobe and teased it with her teeth, until it popped from her mouth.

He made that deep, scratchy sigh she liked, holding her even tighter to his chest. Late-afternoon's brace of rhubarb couldn't even compete with the heady, complex aroma he produced in reaction to her playful taunting.

"I've many reasons to be eager," he uttered roughly, passing the stairs on their way to the longer side of the third floor. "As you crudding well know."

Indeed, she did. Even now, he was picturing himself pinned beneath her and bowing upward at the peak of pleasure, imagining her with her head thrown back in rapture. She planned to give him exactly what he craved.

"How far are we going?" she asked as they walked past the more affordable accommodations near the front.

"I asked them to set out the bedding in one of the better rooms. One without any neighbors," he admitted, his insinuation sending yet another unexpected surge of bashfulness straight to her burning cheeks. "They'll send up a dinner tray at the start of wisteria."

A realization hit her. "You'd already planned to feed me this evening," she whispered, "even before you learned I was ill. You wanted me to use the invocation tonight."

"I wanted you to have the option." He looked at her—no, *glowered* at her—so full of desire that it had pushed him into a possessive state. "And then I just wanted you."

One of the inn's employees emerged from a door at the end of the hall. Spotting Jun, they bowed just deep enough to show proper respect to a guest.

If they were at all curious as to why Jun was carrying a young woman, they didn't show it. But surely, they already knew, having just prepared the bedding several hours before most people went to sleep.

Maze take her, could her cheeks turn any hotter? She swore they'd soon be steaming.

"Everything's ready, Master Jun. Please enjoy your evening."

Hot, electric currents that had nothing to do with magic were racing up and down her body. Jun nodded his thanks, then conveyed her into their accommodations.

She reached out to shut the door behind them. Then he bore her past a folding screen placed just inside the room, which offered extra privacy and blocked any drafts from the hallway. She barely noticed that it was intricately painted with frosted flowers, her attention drawn to the rest of their luxurious suite decorated in rich greens and browns, the solid-wood walls papered with patterns of evergreens and snow-capped mountains.

A thick mattress covered in fluffy, white bedding had been laid out in the main area, which was larger than the delegation's entire suite. Small standing lanterns glowed at all four corners of the bed, just out of arm's reach. The room's other amenities included a small writing desk, a separate dining space for two, and a private water closet.

If Mikari could have allowed herself to imagine the perfect setting to feed from Jun without restraint, this would be it.

"I must admit," he said, speaking from deep in his chest, "I wasn't thinking of your cure when I asked for this room. Nor am I at this moment."

He carefully set her down in the center of the bed, his gaze so intensely carnal she could practically feel a lick of heat wherever it touched her.

"I know," she said, well and fully aware of what he was thinking. Currently, it involved freeing her breasts and feasting upon them.

"Mm, I suppose you do." He knelt before her, his outer belt already undone, and set his sword aside—out of the way, but still within reach. "I should exploit that wicked ability while I can."

She gasped, completely caught off-guard, scandalized by the vivid mental image he sent her of a frequently recalled memory of sinking his oiled fingers into her arse.

Pawing at her belt, she yanked on the first loose end she found, but the belt remained firmly tied. Maze take it, had she just created a knot?

Jun quickly removed his clothing, each item thrown somewhere in the vicinity of the writing desk.

The last time he'd undressed like this, with hasty greed, had been the night they'd first made love as mature crows. Now, as then, she was lit up with desire, heart pumping, heat prickling her skin.

Meanwhile, she'd managed to create a knot as tight as a stone. "Divine One have mercy," she shakily swore, picking futilely at it.

Jun drew her up to her knees, then tugged at the robe until it was loose enough to draw it over her head, her shoulders barely squeezing through the circle of the belt. She emerged embarrassed but relieved, hair mussed, and the cursed robe disappeared somewhere far behind him.

She reached for him. "Kiss me."

"I'll do more than that," he growled, hooking his steely arm around her waist.

Their bodies met from chest to thigh, lips crashing together. Glimpsing his intent, she remained pliant as he shifted backward, sitting her on his lap and dragging her thighs around him, the hard length of his cock cradled rightfully against her lower abdomen, where she also faintly sensed a response from his magic like an exhausted lover's fumbling touch.

Having wanted this moment for so long, and knowing she might not survive the night, she seized his lustrous hair in her fists and held on tight as she drank deeply of his desire—at first salty-sweet, then a dark and tangy citrus, with a warmth that lingered...and a note of honey evincing the submissive pleasure Jun received from her grip on his scalp.

His divine flavor blasted away any rationality she had left, turning her dizzy and uncoordinated. She could do nothing but surrender when he broke off their kiss to skate his lips beneath her jaw and down her neck, all while making those low, rough sounds that drove her wild.

His beard brushed a sensitive spot above her collarbone, raising the fine hairs on her nape and drawing out a soundless, shuddering sigh. Then he continued lower, tilting her backward and supporting her as his mouth captured the beaded peak of her breast.

"Oh, Jun," she moaned, head tipping back. With her nipple gently pinched between his teeth, he hollowed his cheeks and flicked his tongue.

She drew in a quick breath and held it, pleasure needling through her like a thin rope sharply tugging between her thighs.

He began teasing her other breast with his free hand, palming its weight while pinching and tugging at the stiff crest trapped between his fingers, making her eyelids flutter.

Mindless with want, she put her hands back and worked her hips against him, needing him inside her and yet seeking to delay the moment of joining. His shaft trapped between them seemed impossibly thick and hard, and she became obsessed with the sensation of its length sliding against her slippery cove.

Jun's attentions quickly devolved, becoming more primal. His hot mouth roamed her flesh with aimless greed, like a thief in a room full of treasures. He sucked the skin over her collarbone, dipped his tongue into the hollow of her throat, scraped his teeth against her neck, and jerked her upright to gain access to her mouth, which he then plundered.

The air around her was so thick and heavy with lust, she could practically feel it sticking to her skin, could breathe it in and feel it in her lungs like the hot, humid air of a sauna.

She'd never felt so snug in her body and yet so unbalanced and overwhelmed, clutching his shoulders and responding to his kiss on instinct alone. She didn't realize he had lifted her until she was sinking again, his cock impaling her with one slick push.

They moaned as one, the seal of their lips breaking, every part of her gripping him tight. Maze take her, the taste of him was potent now, practically gluttonous, and already these first sips of his love had her reeling with euphoria.

She clung to him desperately, trembling as she surrendered her last scrap of sanity, both to her hunger for him and to how he made her feel.

He began to rock beneath her, hand planted behind him for leverage. Over and over, the head of his cock pressed hard on a spot deep inside, stalling her breath with waves of heavy, rolling sensation. She arched her back to increase the angle and was rewarded with a flood of heat.

"Look at me, lamb." His voice was hard, guttural. "I want to see it take you."

He rocked upward just as she opened her eyes, and they refused to focus at first.

"No pulling out this time," he said, not demanding but announcing, hips tilting sharply beneath her. "You'll take all of me, *own* all of me."

Keeping her eyes open was difficult, but the look on his face was worth it. He watched her with fanatical fervor, brow deeply furrowed, gaze reverent, mouth held open by silent groans. She undoubtedly looked much the same.

A dozen thoughts crashed together in her head. Curses, declarations, pleas, confessions. Too many to sort, too many to keep in. They came pouring out as full-throated moans, rising in pitch as the pressure built, until she was quaking.

She thrust against his bucking hips, shattering the tension. Breathstealing bliss swept through her, and try as she might, she couldn't stop her eyelids from sliding shut as every bit of her that was wrapped around him started to melt.

One hot pulse later, pleasure's stranglehold on her loosened, and she began moaning anew. Jun made a rough sound that was half-growl, half-purr. He slowed to let her ride out her orgasm.

The heat of ecstasy left her soft and languid in a way that a long soak in a hot spring never could. Tears clung to her lashes as she kissed him, overwhelmed with feeling, hands framing his bearded jaw.

He responded by leaning forward to encase her in his arms.

At last, she managed to speak. "I love you."

Jun echoed her words, holding her tight to his chest, where his heart pounded like a drum. His strength gave her the moment she needed to recover...while wanton inspiration took root in her mind.

"Lie back," she softly instructed, pressing him flat. Then she rose on her knees until his staff slipped out.

"No—fuck," he gritted, reaching for her. "Inside you, lamb. Please."

"Soon." She pushed his hands back down to her thighs, which he gripped obediently. "Let me look at you."

He was gorgeous spread out beneath her, his wavy gray-streaked hair mussed from her hands, his pecs and thickly muscled midsection gleaming with a sheen of sweat. The scars he'd acquired—some white with age, others still tinged red—only added to his appeal.

While subtly preparing herself for a visit using her own lubrication, she ran her other hand admiringly across his torso, stroking as though discovering him for the first time—the ridges of muscle, the texture of his skin and hair, and the twinges her touch evoked.

By the time she was ready for him and had shifted a little higher, his grip on her thighs had gone from gentle to unyielding, every visible inch of him clenched.

Flushed with anticipation, she reached back to take hold of his stalk, still wet from her orgasm, and eased its thick crown into her rear.

Sweet Garden. He was a knife's edge away from exploding inside her. Had been since the second her eyes had glazed and her silky flesh had begun to throb around him.

Rather than thrust to completion, he had managed to slow down in what had to be a ridiculous attempt to increase the pleasure, having also increased his pain.

And now the pressure of her hand upon his chest as she sank his cock into her arse was about to overwhelm his last dregs of control.

He had already shut his eyes to the sight of her lush form braced over him, but the image of her wavy hair tossed to one side and her berry-tipped breasts begging for his mouth persisted, and refusing to look only heightened his other senses.

She held him down with more than just her weight, thighs firm with effort, softly grunting as she drove him inside her over and over. If he dared to listen carefully, he'd no doubt hear the soft squelch of his cock hitting deep.

Not that he couldn't feel it, too. Not that he wasn't literally aching to hold himself there and let go. To claim this part of her.

But if his pleasure fed her, then he'd give her as much as he could.

At least, that had been his plan before going from the knife's edge to its tip.

"I can taste how close you are," she moaned. "F-finish claiming me, Jun. I want it all."

He snatched her waist with a choked sob, shock at her words sharpening his desire, jaw clenching tight. He forced his eyes open.

She was pleasure made manifest, poised above him and limned in golden light. A goddess demanding an offering. He was more than eager to throw himself upon her altar.

Holding her in place, he slammed repeatedly into her, feet and shoulders braced, scalding heat surging up his shaft. Mikari was panting in moans, an alluringly desperate look on her face. At the last possible second, he pulled her down on his cock while lifting his arse.

A harsh growl tore from his chest. Pleasure declared itself like a taut rope snapping, the lost tension shooting outward in darts of heat. Mikari mewled with approval as she rocked her hips, milking him of every drop. Although his magic softly vibrated in sympathy, it had nothing to offer her. Instead, white mist rose from his skin, stinging the same way icy air sapped one's heat, and flowed into her.

Her deepest muscles pulsing, she absorbed his sexual energy the same way one slips into a hot spring—with gasps and hisses followed by grateful, sensual moans as she melted, softly shivering.

He collapsed in the same instant she did, both of them sweaty and spent. The plush bedding seemed to swallow him, or perhaps it was the fatigue of feeding her that had made his body feel as heavy as iron. He managed to put his arms around her, grateful for the warmth she imparted, for the rest of him was cold.

But in the exhausted afterglow, primitive delight burrowed deep in his chest—unreasoning pride for having satisfied her and her needs.

She softly giggled, then turned her face into his chest as though to smother it.

"You all right?" he asked, his voice rough.

"Oh yes, it's…I imagine it's like being drunk." She giggled again. "I'm drunk on love."

She lifted her head, her smile so euphoric it stamped its image directly into his memory—thankfully before worry replaced it an instant later as she popped up to her forearms, gasping with dismay. "Are *you* all right? I'm amazed you're still conscious after how much energy you gave me."

A corner of his mouth quirked smugly. "Was it enough?"

"I hope so. Give me a moment?"

"I'm not going anywhere," he said wryly, body aching as though feverish.

"You'll get a second wind soon. 'Til then, I'll take care of you." She dropped a kiss onto his lips and pulled away, taking the time to cover him with a blanket before gingerly but steadily padding away, the bite on her ankle still dark and swollen. Once she'd located her knotted robe, she snatched it up and disappeared into the water closet.

When she emerged a short while later, she wore a different robe made of dark-green silk that fit her far better, and she brought him a damp cloth that he used to clean himself up.

That he managed to drag himself upright to drink the cup of water she then offered was the first sign of his energy returning, albeit less than before.

"The relief I gave you earlier is wearing off, isn't it?" he remarked, having noticed her tight forehead and flushed cheeks. She nodded tiredly. "It's time, then."

"I can't believe this is happening," she said, producing a fold of paper from the pocket of her robe.

"I'll be here." He reached for her empty hand. "I love you."

Expression softening, she leaned toward him for a sweet, lingering kiss. "And I love you."

"This will work." He squeezed her hand before letting go.

Taking a deep breath, she untied and parted her robe to reveal the magical array on her stomach. Holding the written invocation in one hand, she placed her other on her midriff. Then she briefly closed her eyes as though in prayer.

He held his breath.

"*Gensen toshitemo, sadousha toshitemo...*" She spoke slowly and with great care, her gaze fixed upon the paper, her color high.

He didn't understand most of the Mahou she was speaking, only recognizing the word "invoker," but his magic stirred with awareness.

"*Mahou-kikan to...reikon wo—*" She stiffened as if surprised by an unfamiliar sensation, then continued with greater resolve. "*Motsu-kenri wo shuchou suru.*"

Power flared, emanating a low buzzing that he felt on his skin, surrounding her in a wavy aura like heat rising from a flame.

The array was primed. Jun's heart was in his throat, his magic alert.

Looking up from the page, she met his stare with wild determination. "*Sadou.*"

A jolt went through her that sent the slip of paper flying. Her eyes rolled up and her head fell back, the air around her crackling. The marks on her body glowed with an iridescent light, one bright enough to throw shadows.

Jun managed to seize her before she crumpled, and then cradled her in his lap.

She arched away from him with a cry, nearly escaping his hold. Her open robe slipped from her shoulder, and she grasped his upper arm in a claw-like grip that sent her fingernails into his flesh.

Grunting in pain, he watched as a deep flush bloomed on her freckled cheeks. Her familiar, feminine musk tinged the air, sending molten heat straight to his cock.

And when she cried out again, it was decidedly carnal.

The glow became even brighter. She clutched herself closer to him, turning her face into his chest. The flush on her cheeks spread to her breasts, turning her nipples dark and tight.

She stiffened in his arms then relaxed by degrees, overwhelmed with sensation. The glow intensified, and he was forced to close his eyes against the brilliant light.

Then he felt it. A glancing, accidental touch. He held her tighter, lifting her, his magic shifting with unexpected vigor.

The cherished touch returned, seeking. He reached out with his magic...and was met with a metaphysical embrace. They both let out sobs, clinging to each other in more ways than one.

In that moment, Jun was more afraid than he'd ever been. The next few seconds could destroy everything. Their happiness, their future...

He sensed a rising pulse, like lightning about to strike, filling the air with a tangible field of electric pinpricks. The hair on his head and arms stood up.

She began shaking, body arching in jerks. The hot puffs of air against his chest ceased as she held her breath, or perhaps couldn't relax enough to breathe.

A frantic, half-formed prayer passed through his head just as the pulse peaked, rocking him backward and nearly throwing him off, but he held onto her tight, even as pinpricks of magic washed over him in a swarm, only to dissipate like steam.

The preternatural glow vanished, and Mikari sagged in his arms. Panicked, he pulled back to look at her.

Her eyes were shut, lips parted, but she was alive. He could see her breathing easily enough. Her face, though flushed, remained that of a woman on the cusp of her majority, skin smooth and supple. Tears clung to her lashes and wetted her cheeks.

The curse upon her midsection was gone, as if it had never existed, revealing creamy, pliant skin. Her right, lower leg still showed signs of a recent injury, but the swelling was gone and the discoloration had mostly faded.

His magic anxiously sought hers, and he let out a sigh of relief when he found it, still intact and thrumming with power.

Maze take him, she was cured—no longer marked for harvest, her magic no longer suppressed, the affliction defeated. Had she been purged of her lust-eating curse?

"Mikari, my lamb," he crooned, cupping her jaw. "Speak to me, please."

She grunted with displeasure, the space between her eyebrows furrowing. He did his best to adjust his hold on her, thinking she was uncomfortable. Her eyelids drifted open.

"Jun," she pleaded softly.

He released a sigh of relief. "There you are."

She made another sound of discomfort and grasped his arm again, more gently this time. "Help me, Jun. Please."

Worry seized his heart. "Are you not free of the second curse?"

"I'm almost— I suspect that...pleasure must open the way." She skimmed her hand up his arm and pulled him closer. "I only need one last push. Please," she begged, shifting her legs open.

At last, he realized what his loins already knew. "Don't worry, lamb. I'll make it better." He turned her to lay her upon her back then followed her down, yanking the blanket between them out of the way.

"Please, please," she softly chanted, parting her thighs for him. He pushed into her...

"*Fuck*," he choked, back tensing.

Maze take him, he was two pitiful thrusts from spending himself. Merely holding still was taking every drop of concentration he could muster.

Thus, his magic enjoyed free rein, stroking and pulsing against her, the sensation so crudding fantastic that he was in danger of coming without even moving.

He would have to use his mouth to give her the release she needed, but before he could withdraw from her, she hitched her legs around his waist and began thrusting upward, burying sweet little moans into his chest.

Climax clawed its way up his shaft, and he swore again, even more viciously. Desperate and unthinking, he tried lifting his hips, but of course, she held onto him with her limbs.

Then, mercifully, she made a high, breathy moan of release. Her heat gripped his rigid flesh, soaking it with hot cream. Her magic fluttered, changing states in an almost indescribable way, as though it were reaching a new equilibrium.

He buried his face in her hair and came, shaking, gasping, the pleasure so intense he felt it from head to toe, every single nerve sizzling.

Their magics merged, fitting together at a level his mind couldn't comprehend, one his body could only withstand for a second or two.

They were not two bodies, two minds, but one. If ever a mortal could feel ultimate joy, this was it.

Sensation exploded between them, drawing out cries. He came again, or perhaps had never stopped. The room seemed to brighten for an instant, but he wasn't able to open his eyes in time to know for certain.

Unconsciousness beckoned him, dizzy and dark. So, with his last grain of strength, he shifted onto his side and succumbed to exhaustion.

Chapter Twenty-Five

When Mikari returned at last to the mortal realm from wherever her second climax had sent her, she opened her eyes to discover Jun lying alongside and watching her, his chin braced on his hand. His small smile seemed bittersweet.

Breathing in, she stretched experimentally, seeking to understand why she felt different. Different but very good.

She did have her magic back, but the memory of its metaphysical weight had never faded, so its presence within her wasn't entirely novel —closer to an emotion than a physical sensation. And yet, it evoked physical responses the same way dread filled her stomach with stones or the way arousal suffused her most sensitive flesh with warm honey.

Currently, her magic reminded her of a cat curled up on one's middle. But its restful mood still didn't entirely explain why she felt so at ease.

Her hunger for lust…it was gone. In fact, she was well and truly sated. Supple with afterglow. The realization was overwhelming.

Oh, she still felt desire. She couldn't look at Jun and not imagine how they might next pleasure each other. And the sweet pangs of love were all the more affecting, urging her to hold him and kiss him.

But the clawing itch to feed, to seek the delirious high of her cursed addiction, was blissfully absent. In its place she felt a strange sort of grief, tempered by the joy of her new freedom. She had derived a great deal of pleasure from both seeing and scenting his love and desire for her, but those senses were notably absent now. To think she would ever miss them...

"I can hardly believe it," she whispered, eyes stinging.

Jun must have noticed a change in her expression. He leaned over her, concern pinching his eyebrows, and gently kissed her.

"I can only imagine how you must feel," he murmured, hovering close. "If you wish to talk about it, I'll gladly listen."

"I assume I don't look any older." He shook his head. "I rather hoped I would. I feel left behind in a way. And also, as though something was stolen from me. From us."

"Time," he said simply. She nodded. "I feel similarly. It would be selfish of me to hold onto you. I've not been chained to a curse in the time we were apart. You should enjoy your freedom, pursue your dreams."

Ah, so that was the reason for his pained smile—pain she shared. Even if they survived confronting the inquisitor, Jun was still decades ahead of her and ready to put down roots, whereas she dreamed of spreading Gozu's bardic tradition. And she couldn't help thinking of how strong the likelihood was that he would join the Divine One in his Garden many years before she did.

If only there were a way to close the gap. Perhaps by magic? Despite everything she had seen it do, the possibility was surely slim. Or even blasphemous. Not that it would help all that much. No, she needed to think of another way to align their futures.

"Let's not worry about that tonight," she whispered, sliding her arms around his shoulders. He gave a small nod as he lowered his head, and they came together in another kiss, slow but fervent.

Then a sharp grumble pierced their bubble of intimacy. It had come from her.

More specifically, her stomach.

They drew apart, both smiling. Mikari laughed with embarrassment. "I do believe I haven't eaten actual food in a long while. That's next, right?" she whispered gleefully, earning from him an amused smile.

"Wisteria just began. Our dinner should arrive soon."

Indeed, the current brace's floral musk was rather strong. She suspected Hayashi was burning extra incense, for reasons she didn't care to contemplate at the moment.

"Hm, then I suppose I should attempt to appear as though I didn't just pass out from pleasure."

His lips spread into a wicked grin. "You could be freshly washed and in full bardic attire and they'd still know, lamb. Neither of us was very restrained in voicing our enjoyment."

Much to her unexpected chagrin.

"Better hurry." He kissed the tip of her nose then left the bed, lurching to his feet as though a boulder rested on his shoulders. The effort instantly winded him, and his legs visibly trembled.

Up in a flash, she tried to help him in his search for a sleeping robe, but the soft look he gave her as he shooed her toward the room's private water closet persuaded her to relent.

When she emerged a few moments later, clean and dressed, the room looked far more presentable. No tousled bedding and no pile of hastily discarded clothing. Surprisingly, Jun had found a robe that fit his chest and shoulders, although it was still too short.

They awaited dinner in the dining nook, where they quickly became engaged in seeing how well she could manipulate her newly woken magic.

Quite well, as it turned out. Though her knowledge of magic was currently that of a novice, she'd become fairly adept at channeling her power as a lust eater, and it came even easier to her as a mature crow. She conjured a flame on her thumb without difficulty and learned that its blue tinge indicated which season's magic she had an affinity to.

Judging by his puffed-up chest, Jun was unaccountably pleased that she was a winter crow like him. "I was certain you would be a spring crow. They're quite adept at bias magic, which is what your coercions are."

Her proficiency with bias magic therefore stemmed from the fact that she'd been born within a week of the spring equinox, according to Jun.

Fascinated, she listened raptly as he briefly explained each season's strongest talents, excitement evident in his voice.

He offered, with charming alacrity, to teach her everything he knew, and was in the middle of describing how to conjure a magical projectile when a light knock sounded on the door.

Moments later, two trays of food had been unpacked onto the table between them, including a small plate piled high with sweet rice dumplings. Far more than the usual two or four that other guests received.

"I couldn't find any strawberry dumplings in our cold storage," the employee said by way of apology, "but we had plenty of plum ones."

"Thank you," Jun said to him.

"You remembered," Mikari remarked with soft surprise, referring to the wish she'd written in her journal to stuff herself with the chewy dessert now within reach.

She was tempted to snatch one up and shove the entire thing into her mouth, regardless of the employee preparing a pot of tea for them. She gave into a grin instead, feeling so silly over a few dumplings that she bit her lip in embarrassment. And yet, Jun gazed warmly at her, unabashed by her delight.

The second the employee left, taking with him a message for the delegation and a few other instructions, Mikari plucked a dumpling from the plate and sank her teeth into it, shutting her eyes with a small *mmm* as a fine layer of sugar powder dusted her lips. Sweet Garden, she'd missed real food.

Sighing with satisfaction, she popped the second half of the dumpling into her mouth, then chewed with a close-lipped smile. When she opened her eyes to grab a second one, she found Jun watching her, smiling with pleasure.

In response, she leaned across the table and planted a sugary kiss on his lips.

They took their time eating and finished off every crumb. Mikari had never moaned so much during a meal. Jun then stacked the empty dishes onto the tray the employee had left, and set it outside their room.

Sluggish after her big meal, Mikari tucked herself into bed, where Jun joined her after dousing the lanterns. She lay against his side, tucked under his arm, her cheek on his chest. Despite the welcome drowsiness that would soon send her to sleep if she let it, lying down to slumber had not been in her routine for so long that doing so felt strange.

And of course, her worries chose that moment to occupy her mind. The inquisitor and his servants were still out there, as was Nene, for whom Mikari feared the worst.

In the morning, they'd likely set out for Ajiro Temple, and they'd have to assume the inquisitor might send someone after them, which meant taking the lesser-known side roads to get there. But doing so might slow them down...

"Try not to think of tomorrow," Jun softly rumbled. "It'll come soon enough."

She gave a soundless chuckle. "How did you know?"

"Because my own mind was beginning to churn. And because I know you." He gathered her a little closer and kissed the top of her head.

"What should we think about instead?"

"Mm, I like the idea of waking up together."

"Waking up with anyone would be a first for me. I'm very grateful it'll be with you." And that he couldn't see her sad smile, for there was a strong chance they wouldn't have many more mornings together.

Jun hummed his agreement, his heartbeat steady beneath her ear, so she couldn't know for certain whether he was thinking the same thing.

PART FOUR
Ambrosial Devotion

Chapter Twenty-Six

For the first time in weeks, Jun had a peaceful night's rest. No maze. No frantic search. No carnivorous tree. The only interruption had been a brief moment when Mikari had been in the midst of her own unpleasant dream and needed comforting.

He doubted his nightmare was gone forever, but he was grateful for even one night's reprieve from it. Instead, a pair of soft lips upon his brow gently pulled him from sleep.

As he'd arranged, the delegation arrived at his and Mikari's suite shortly before dawn, the only private space big enough for the six of them to eat a meal and discuss their next steps without hitting elbows or being overheard. The two delegates greeted him with tearful hugs and thanked him for saving their lives.

"We don't remember much, thanks to Seita," Natsu said, her praise softening Seita's sullen expression. "But we know that he and Kie kept us safe until you could reach us. And we found out what happened after…after poor Noriaki passed. If not for the four of you…"

Indeed, Jun knew what would've happened not only to the delegates but also to the town of Tetsutani had even one of them done anything differently.

Though the two brownie women still looked a little thinner and paler than usual, they assured him they were more than healthy enough to set out as soon as their party had full stomachs and a plan.

Recalling his promise to Kie, Jun offered to examine the damage to her metaphysical organ, but she said there was no need. It had fully recovered at the same time of night it always did, which meant Komatsu's would soon recover as well if it hadn't already.

Half an hour later, they were nearly done with breakfast and discussing their options.

"It's not that I don't believe Master Eiji heard what he heard," Seita said, one hand cradling his bowl of wild-vegetable soup. "I only question whether we can truly infer that the inquisitor can be found at Ajiro Temple."

Though Seita was sitting casually behind his breakfast tray, one bent leg resting on the floor and the other folded against his front, the young crow wasn't at all relaxed. Lips tight, he shifted upon his cushion as though itching to abandon his barely touched food and race ahead on his horse.

"We know the inquisitor and his servants routinely travel to the minor temples in search of victims," Seita went on. "How confident are we that he's not currently at Genbi? After all, his servant Komatsu was here in Tetsutani and Genbi is the closest temple."

Jun sympathized with Seita's anxious urgency. Ajiro Temple would take several days to reach, but Genbi was only an eight-hour ride away —assuming they met with zero trouble, which was far from guaranteed. Going there first would delay them from arriving at Ajiro by another day.

Not that Seita was wrong to dispute their strategy. The information they had wasn't comfortably convincing. However...

"Thwarting the inquisitor's plan to make himself a god is our current mission, whether he's there to stop us or not," Jun reminded the younger crow, who had updated Houfu late last night and received new orders. "We're certain he's been preparing for decades, and that he's now gathering his victims."

Jun avoided the thought of what would've happened had Mikari escaped from him while her mind had been taken over, but he couldn't help reaching out to touch her, resting his hand on her leg.

"So, we must assume he intends to harvest them soon. And the conversation Eiji overheard last year indicates that the inquisitor has established himself at Ajiro Temple, so Ajiro is the likeliest place for his intended ritual. I suspect many of his victims are already imprisoned there, awaiting death."

"I agree," Kie said. "But what hope do we have of stopping him? I'd never suggest giving up, but he knows we're aware of his plans. He can perform his ritual at any point over the next few days, and there's nothing we can do to prevent it."

"Does that mean we'll be too late?" Iwa fretted.

"No," Mikari said reflectively, seemingly in the midst of a revelation. "He doesn't know we've discovered his lair, only that we're looking for him. He might even assume we're still in the middle of a blightspawn outbreak, which would at least hinder if not fully occupy us. If his servant came after you, then he must view the delegation as a threat. And if you're a threat, that means his plan's not yet ready."

She's right, Jun realized. *And crudding brilliant.*

The compulsion the inquisitor had placed on Mikari to force her to surrender herself to Komatsu would've been extremely taxing, even for a powerful crow using a special scrying pool.

So, the fact that human-born demons had been discovered well outside of Gozu meant that summoning all of them would require a lot of stamina and therefore several weeks. The amount of time that had passed since the Damned One's death.

And as Mikari had proven, some of the inquisitor's victims had a chance of resisting him, and the farther away they were, the better. They'd take even more effort to round up, which had to be why he'd sent Komatsu to collect Mikari physically.

But with the empress's attention turning toward Gozu just as winter was nearing, the inquisitor would not be able to beckon all of his victims before the passes closed and his plan was discovered.

The inquisitor needed Mikari, or rather the power he'd get from her. His ultimate goal demanded it. Now he'd need time to replace her.

"She's right, we do have some time," Jun said, full of hope. He then explained his reasoning. "As for replacing Mikari, he wouldn't be able to use the maid. She's been cleansed."

"Why take her, then?" Seita asked in a hard whisper.

Jun suspected that the maid, like the other women who had disappeared with Komatsu over the years, would serve some other purpose.

"I'd rather not guess," he deferred. "But my gut says we'll find her at Ajiro. The device Komatsu used to escape—if it's as costly to create as other magical objects, then its effect was determined well before he came to Tetsutani, and he'd have avoided using it unless no other option remained. Makes sense to me that it transports him to safety—to his master's lair."

At last, Seita nodded in agreement.

"To Ajiro, then," Kie said. "We'll have time on the way there to come up with an infiltration plan."

"I can help with that," Mikari offered. "My mentor retired a few years ago, and he lives in the city below the temple. He loves nothing more than knowing things, especially things he shouldn't. It's thanks to him that I was able to give any warning about the blightspawn, and I'm certain he can tell us more about Ajiro and its security."

"Lamb, I could kiss you," Jun said impulsively in Gozuan. In fact, he'd do just that the second he had the opportunity.

She gifted him with a smiling glance. "I think I can convince him to shelter the delegates, too. And I know a route to Eiroku that can get us there without a great deal of notice."

"Well, whatever the commander just said, I second it," Natsu happily announced.

Seita plunked down his bowl of soup, nearly spilling it. "Let's get to it, then."

They set out as soon as their mounts were ready, with the exception of Seita, who caught up with them just as the northeastern road began to ascend the next foothill, a new and unfamiliar bag tied to his saddle. It couldn't contain Noriaki's ashes. Those were riding with Natsu.

There was also something different about the lad's expression, a simmering desperation far more genuine than the boyish scowl he had become used to seeing.

He raised his eyebrows in silent question and slowed his horse to ride nearer. Seita met his gaze only briefly, as though self-conscious.

"I had someone pack a couple of Nene's personal things," he admitted in a voice stretched thin with worry. "They'll help me scry her location if we don't find her at Ajiro."

Not a bad idea, Jun silently acknowledged. "But not before then," he cautioned. Even with the protection of *mind cloak*, which Jun had granted to the entire party, scrying into enemy territory carried the risk of tipping off the inquisitor, should he or his servants detect the intrusion and gain control of the sensor.

And who knew what horrible things the younger crow might see if he successfully scried on the maid at any point over the next few days?

Seita nodded his agreement. "I told her we weren't there to make trouble for her," he then said, as though he couldn't help himself.

"You didn't," Jun asserted. "Komatsu managed that all on his own. Don't take what happened to her as a personal failing, lad. None of us managed to stop it."

"It became personal the moment I first saw her," Seita countered with quiet surety.

THE NEXT COUPLE of days passed without incident, the weather remaining overcast and calm, which allowed them to travel swiftly for longer.

With Mikari leading the way to Ajiro Temple, they were able to avoid larger settlements where they might encounter enemies and otherwise stuck to the main road that would get them to their destination the fastest.

Even though the idea of Mikari putting herself in danger alongside him at Ajiro turned his gut to ice, Jun knew better than to ask her to stay behind with the delegates once they reached the home of her retired mentor.

She, of anyone there, had the most right to confront the inquisitor. And the addition of a fourth magic user would improve their chances of stopping him, not to mention Mikari was brave in a fight and had proven that she was quite capable of channeling magic. All that remained was expanding her knowledge.

Thus, every spare moment of their journey went toward teaching her the combat spells she'd need and training her to use a sword, which they planned to procure for her in Eiroku. Unless her magical dagger had the ability to change its shape, it would serve her better as an ambush weapon or possibly an offhand weapon, while a sword would be her primary one.

Jun was prepared to be her sole instructor, but Kie and Seita didn't hesitate to join in, the four of them sparring in pairs or teams.

Mikari already knew how to enhance her strength and speed, which she used effectively during a training bout with him their first night on the road. Wielding a tree branch as a stand-in sword, she learned with impressive celerity how to keep her distance and her footing while maintaining awareness of her environment.

Jun had known that she'd be a dedicated student and evince a natural talent for magic, but he was pleasantly surprised by how much she appeared to enjoy sparring with a weapon, especially once their lessons began to take hold in her muscles the second night after they'd stopped to camp and rest.

Subtly glowing blue with magic, she deflected several of his strikes in smooth succession then danced out of range, putting a fallen tree trunk between them, her eyes alight with excitement. The obstacle allowed her an instant to conjure a magical projectile, which she didn't hesitate to launch at him. He barely got his *shield* up in time.

"That's it!" Kie cheered, watching them from the warmth of the campfire, where she and the rest were devouring a hot stew.

Jun raised his hand in a "hold" gesture to indicate they should disengage. "Well done," he told her, nodding with approval, trying his damnedest to suppress his innate reaction to the tempting look on her face. His loins were determined to interpret it as arousal.

Even if her breathless anticipation were sexual, he could do nothing about it, just as he'd been unable to do anything more than sneak a few kisses the previous night when they'd all stayed in the unused barn of a farmer who had given them shelter for a reasonable fee.

Jun had nevertheless derived a surprising amount of pleasure simply from holding her in his arms while they'd slept, and he was looking forward to doing so again tonight, curled up together by the transparent campfire Kie had summoned. It shed far less light than a normal one but plenty of heat, making it ideal for avoiding unwanted attention.

The unique ability was one of the perks of being a summer crow, whose strongest elemental power was fire. Not the easiest thing to deploy indoors.

However, thanks to the partial spell book they'd wrested from Komatsu, they could now infuse their weapons with elemental energy, the same way Komatsu had when attacking Seita with void energy, the highest of the five elements, which his book referred to as "aether."

How Komatsu had tapped into it was uncertain, for crows were constrained to the four physical elements—fire, water, wind, and earth

—with void energy comprising the immaterial—the metaphysical fabric of creation from which the Divine One had woven the world as they knew it.

Certain spells manipulated void energy, stretching and folding it, but the highest element could not normally be channeled into a physical attack, as far as most everyone knew, which was admittedly little.

And yet, according to the empress, there could be no mistaking the scent of aether, what Mikari had accurately described as "boiling metal."

Kle's elemental infusion was quite striking, a fiery aura surrounding her blade that left wide scorch marks on anything she swung at. Seita, as an autumn crow capable of channeling the wind, could now infuse his weapon with lightning, which danced along his blade, reaching out ahead of his strikes with snapping tendrils.

Jun's earth-based infusion was subtle, dusting the edge of his sword with a diamond-like glitter, but it allowed him to fell a mature tree in a single slice. Mundane armor would provide little protection, and even glancing blows to an opponent would result in deep wounds.

Currently, however, he was wielding a tree branch, the same as Mikari. With more time, he would train her in various techniques for disarming or wounding an opponent, but with only two days left until they reached Eiroku, showing her how to stand and keep an enemy's blade away from her body was as much as he could do.

"Your stance is solid," he said to her as he returned to his starting position. She did likewise. "That's the one thing I want you to keep in mind once we encounter hostility. That and keeping your wrists straight. You felt strain in your back wrist when you blocked that last strike, didn't you?"

"I was trying to redirect it, but the angle wasn't right."

"How's your stamina?" he asked, noting the small wince she made as she stretched her back. They'd been riding all day, sparring since setting up camp an hour after nightfall, and burning magic on physical enhancements for the last thirty minutes, which was approaching the metaphysical limits of most crows who were new to their powers.

Her small, flirty smile and breathy response nearly undid him. "I can keep going."

Maze take him, what he wouldn't give for even a few minutes of privacy. He'd show her how much further he could go as well.

She had always preferred to wear her hair loose, but he'd convinced her to braid and pin it for sparring. The soft, silky mass had been slowly escaping, and his hands itched to unravel it completely.

His need must have shown on his face, for she granted him a spot of mercy with a distracting comment. "I want to practice with a real sword."

He blinked away the lust fogging his eyes. "We will tomorrow night. For now, let's practice once more with our wooden version. Then we'll eat and get some rest." She nodded in response.

The clearing in which they'd chosen to camp was small, the result of a pine tree toppling over, leaving behind a splintered trunk. Its surviving neighbors blocked the wind and concealed them from the main road that lay just out of earshot.

There wasn't much room for a sprawling swordfight, which suited their purposes just fine. Jun doubted they'd find the inquisitor in the middle of an open field.

He readied his stance, flesh humming with magic and smoldering desire. Mikari did likewise, her weapon held vertically in front of her dominant shoulder.

Her goal was simple—fend off his attack, gain the distance needed to conjure a counterattack, and deploy it. If he could hammer that response into her before their mission, he'd feel marginally better about her safety.

He swung at her, leading with his weapon, his back foot following the forward motion as he stepped diagonally. He wasn't using his full strength but damned near it, confident she could defend a simple, downward strike.

She blocked him handily, her stance strong and stable. He changed his grip and tried to stab at her chest, but she shoved his weapon aside, stepping out of its intended path for good measure.

He came at her again, rotating his arm for an upward slash. Before he could connect, she clacked the end of his branch off its trajectory and scurried back, putting the splintered tree trunk between them.

She wasn't exactly smiling, but her expression wasn't one he'd ever seen in a skirmish. Rather, she only ever wore it when he glared at her with explosive sexual intent.

That eager look fanned his desire, weakening his concentration.

He therefore wasn't ready when she launched another bluish

projectile at him. He tried to dodge it, twisting his body to one side, but it hit him squarely on his bad shoulder with a sickening pop.

Pain exploded across his chest and down his back and arm. Wincing, he fell to one knee with a grunt, fingers tingling. Were he left-handed, he'd have lost his grip on his weapon.

"Jun," Mikari gasped. "I-I'm sorry!"

Mortification swamped him as she dropped her practice sword and rushed toward him, her blue aura fading. The soft conversation by the fire had gone silent, everyone no doubt staring with concern.

"Don't be sorry, lamb," he said, angrily tossing aside his branch to wrap his hand around his upper arm. "I'm the one who wasn't paying attention."

He lurched to his feet, too embarrassed to meet Mikari's worried gaze, and headed toward the campfire. No need to announce they were done for the night. Mikari comforted him with gentle strokes to his uninjured side, not responding to his terseness.

Normally, a hit like the one he'd taken would knock him back the same as a hard punch and leave him bruised. It shouldn't still hurt the way it did, as though the tendons were stretched to the point of tearing, nor should his arm feel stuck while rotated outward.

Which meant that his shoulder was dislocated…again. For the sixth time since that disastrous fall from a ladder at the age of nineteen. No doubt he'd find a hard bump right where the pain was worst—the head of his arm bone, jerked out of place.

"How can I help?" Mikari asked once they were seated with the others by the fire. "It's dislocated, right?"

He nodded, then described how to slide the joint back into place. He could resolve the displacement on his own, but having someone else do it was easier, and Mikari was guaranteed to be gentler than the mercenaries in his old group.

The process of re-seating his bone took only a minute, the others watching with sympathetic winces as Mikari carefully raised his arm. He let out a deep sigh of relief once the joint rolled back into its socket.

"I didn't think *flying fist* could do that," Kie murmured.

"The damage done to one's shoulder when it's first dislocated makes it easier for it to happen again," Jun explained. "This was the sixth time."

"Fuck me," Seita said under his breath.

"Use your healing magic," Mikari urged. "If you can cure the blightspawn affliction, then surely you can heal your shoulder." She leaned closer and lowered her voice, speaking to him alone, her brows knitted with determination. "You're not stronger for enduring it, my love. Not when you can do something about it."

She was right on both counts. He hadn't had the advanced knowledge before the Dark Court's reformation to repair the damage to his shoulder, but he did now. All he'd lacked was the will.

He also realized that his injury was yet another hurt he'd been holding onto since his escape from Nansen Temple. One he was ready to be rid of, at long last.

"That would be best," he agreed. The response she'd been hoping for, it seemed, her relief evident.

He examined his healthy shoulder first, eyes shut to concentrate on studying its structure with his magic. Though he was already knowledgeable of how the joint was put together, thanks to medical texts from the court library, every person's body had its peculiarities. The rest of the party remained silent, sensing his need for quiet.

When he examined his injured side, the differences were stark. There was far less cartilage surrounding the ball of his arm bone, and the stretched-out ligaments were torn in several places. He also detected fresh tears, some of them bleeding.

After muttering the correct invocation, he first took care of the broken blood vessels, then the shrunken cartilage, building it back up to match his healthy shoulder and numbing any twinges of pain as they occurred. Lastly, he repaired and tightened the cords of tissue that held everything together.

In all, it took less than ten minutes.

The physical relief was enormous, and yet not as overwhelming as the emotional relief. When he opened his eyes to several expectant faces, he was blinking back tears.

The mood turned far lighter from there, the others congratulating him as he tested his newly healed shoulder and discovered just how much range and strength he'd lost over the years.

Once everyone had eaten, Mikari entertained the group with a full recitation of the original version of *Aya the Vigilant*, stricken chapters and all, including a graphic but thankfully short section in which Aya and one of her adventuring companions made love.

Of course, Mikari teasingly asked him how to translate *idojo*, a

Gozuan euphemism for a woman's arousal, which she crudding well knew meant "honey."

He and Mikari then took the first watch. Out of consideration for their sleeping comrades, they kept any whispered conversation to a minimum, instead silently holding hands as they gazed at the fire in between glances at the surrounding trees.

"I'm eager to see you test out your shoulder when we spar tomorrow night," Mikari murmured at one point.

Barely holding back a grin while imagining another way to test out his repaired joint, he spoke directly into her ear. "Not as eager as I am for the next time we're alone."

She slid him a sideways glance, lips curled upward. "I have somewhere in mind."

Too tempted to resist, he snuck a kiss.

They camped again the next night, this time without any injuries. Mikari borrowed Kie's sword for her training, and he taught her a couple of ways to pull her dagger. The voice within even helped her grip it right.

On the fourth night, Mikari led them to a small inn built atop another hot spring, one that was happy to have the business of a large party of travelers and didn't care that four of them were uncleansed crows, for the family who ran it had black hair themselves.

With tonight being their last opportunity before they reached Ajiro and confronted the inquisitor, Jun and Mikari leaped at the chance for a private room where they could recreate Aya's night of passion. Which, incidentally, also took place before a major battle in her tale.

Hours later, Jun woke to the sound of Mikari using a spot of magic to light the lantern in the corner of the room. He sensed it was morning, but dawn hadn't yet arrived.

He turned his head just as she was replacing the lantern's shade. She then sat staring at it with a mixture of worry and wonder.

"Something wrong?" he asked.

She started at his voice, blinking with restored awareness, and glanced distractedly at him. *"Ie, kekkou desu."*

"What?" He sat up with surprise, for she hadn't responded in Gozuan.

Mikari gasped in realization, pressing her fingers against her lips and looking horrified—no doubt suspecting she was being manipulated again. But awe quickly replaced her fear.

"*Yume de wa nakatta,*" she whispered, before shaking her head. "I-I mean, I thought it was a dream."

"The Divine One spoke to you?" he asked, pushing the blanket away.

She gaped at him. "How did you know?"

"The empress speaks in Mahou for a time after she's communed with him," he explained, hastily pulling on a sleeping robe as he crossed the short distance to her. His answer seemed to stun her. "What did he say?"

She struggled to collect her thoughts and stammered through her reply. "I...didn't understand most of it. Was I supposed to?"

"If not now, then you will soon," he reassured her.

"He told me that our threads are beginning to tear—I think he meant all of us—and that I would need to 'open new eyes.'"

Jun nodded grimly. "We must have a tough fight ahead of us."

She bobbed her head to show she'd heard him, but her gaze was on the lantern. "He talked about the Veil, said it was losing strength. Then he spoke the final contemplation."

Goosebumps washed over Jun. "Everything made must someday be unmade."

Faith in the Divine One varied greatly across the land. In the far south and along parts of the coast, people believed that his realm was a free-floating island rather than a garden. Instead of a maze, souls in need of redemption found themselves on an icy, barren shore constantly buffeted by powerful waves, and one needed the strength of spirit to travel past them to their eternal rest.

Quite a few worshippers throughout the plains believed that the Damned One and the Divine One were opposing siblings whose progenitor would someday return to scorch the world. Accordingly, "by the dueling gods" was a commonplace phrase.

Jun had also heard the claim that the Damned One wasn't real. That his "demons" were fabrications meant to explain away the evil acts of ordinary people.

And more than once, Jun had come across pockets of cultists, or even just half-mad drunks, who believed the Divine One was not the only god, and they'd encouraged praying to some other deity who would act when the Divine One would not.

But all of these people, despite their conflicting beliefs, could recite the Divine One's major contemplations, including the last—*everything made must someday be unmade.*

The Divine One's priests interpreted it in various ways. *Life is finite, so do good with it. Don't focus on material possessions.*

In Jun's experience, the contemplation was most often spoken at funerals...or invoked whenever a temple asked for donations.

But for the Divine One to speak his final contemplation after telling Mikari that their "threads" were tearing and the veil of aether cocooning the world was failing...it put ice in his veins.

"We should inform the empress," he said solemnly, though he doubted their news would surprise her.

Indeed, Empress Shumei merely looked sad when they told her. Rather than answer him when Seita asked whether the Veil was truly failing and what that meant for the world, the empress advised them to focus on their mission.

"I know little more than you now do," she said.

Despite an inauspicious start to the day, the last leg of their journey went smoothly. To attract less attention, they arrived at their destination in smaller, separate groups—Jun and Mikari first. And rather than catch eyes in Eiroku with her bardic attire and white reindeer, Mikari wore normal traveling clothes and rode an inconspicuous horse borrowed from the inn, where her reindeer would remain until someone returned for it.

Though Eiroku sat on an important crossroads, the trade city was smaller than Jun had expected, not much larger than Tetsutani, but it was still home to easily a thousand residents.

Mount Nagura, the tallest peak in Gozu, loomed over Eiroku, its summit hidden behind thick clouds. A black archway two stories tall and ornamented with gold inlay marked the road leading up to Ajiro Temple.

Though the winter holidays were still weeks away, the city was already preparing for the first of them. The March of Souls honored one's ancestors, especially the recently deceased, with a beautiful display of paper lanterns in all different shapes and colors.

Silently riding past the square where several workers were erecting a temporary pavilion, Jun followed Mikari to the home of her retired mentor, who lived in the rear rooms of his shop where he sold refurbished musical instruments and taught music classes. His shop was one of many slotted into a larger building.

Seeing his banner was still out, they tied up their horses and let themselves in. Mikari called out a friendly greeting as Jun shut the door behind them.

The shop's interior was warm and uncluttered, inviting customers to relax as they gazed at a beautiful selection of instruments carefully arranged on well-dusted shelves and stands.

Beyond the shop space were two more rooms that led even farther back. The open one on the right was his teaching space. The other, once the door slid open, appeared to be his workshop.

Like the city of Eiroku, Master Atsuyori wasn't what Jun had expected. The man was lean and sour-faced rather than soft and kindly, with white close-cropped hair.

Though Mikari had told Jun that she'd trained and traveled with Atsuyori for nearly two years, and stayed in contact since, the old man greeted her with a frown and an up-and-down look. The only thing about him that seemed at all "bardic" was his deep, smooth voice.

"Still cursed, eh?" Atsuyori bluntly asked from the raised wooden flooring beyond the tidy entryway. "Where's your mask? And who's that mountain of a man with you?"

"I'm cured, actually," she said in a conspiratorial tone, as though sharing gossip with an old friend. She began to remove her snow-encrusted boots, so Jun followed her example. "But it's only been a few days."

"In that case, I'll probably be dead by the time you get your first gray hair." A reaction devoid of joy, surprise, or congratulations, but one might be able to interpret happiness in the way his eyes crinkled. "I'll want to hear the full tale."

"You'll hear it, I promise. The mountain beside me is a central character."

She introduced Jun using all of his titles—commander, demon hunter, former mercenary, and lover. Atsuyori's eyes slowly grew wider. She then explained their situation with concise clarity, taking no longer than the time required for a pot of tea to steep.

Atsuyori grumbled over her request to discreetly house the soon-to-arrive delegates but agreed when she pointed out that Natsu and Iwa would have plenty of verified reports from the southern lands to share with him.

"I told everyone that you'd be able to give us information about the temple," Mikari then said. "Rumors, the number and location of its guards, and especially a way inside."

Atsuyori set his teacup down with a wince, and Jun's heart sank. "I believe you'll regret making that promise. I know more than most, but not enough to help you. For years, the temple's been shrinking the number of days it allows worshippers to visit its grounds, and I made the mistake of pushing too hard while trying to get information from some guards having a drink at the tavern. The only person there who talks to me anymore is a young aide."

"Oh. Whatever you can tell us, then," Mikari said, dejected but sympathetic.

"That said..." He poured more tea into Mikari's empty cup. "Three times in the last couple of months, I've seen or heard of young-looking crows wandering around, acting strange. Well, the 'wandering around' is what was strange. They didn't seem to have a purpose, though I suppose they might've been looking for someone. Lost sight of the first one, but the other two were approached by a temple aide, based on their robes."

"Would you be able to describe the aides?" she asked, eyes slightly narrowed with suspicion. Jun silently applauded her question.

"Well, they..." Atsuyori frowned in mild consternation. "I know they had brown hair. Both were male...and good-looking, I suppose. I didn't notice much else. To be honest, I'm not sure if they were the same person or not."

"What happened once the aide approached these crows?" Jun asked.

"The aide appeared to greet them, then they walked away together. I couldn't follow them the first time I saw it, but I did the second. Went almost all the way up the gate-road. Had to hang back once they veered off into the trees on what I think was an animal path, and I lost sight of them. Kept following, but the path didn't lead anywhere, just to one of the temple's defensive walls. Couldn't see the crow or the aide."

"What about footprints?" Mikari asked.

Atsuyori shook his head. "Area's rocky, and there wasn't any snow on the ground at the time. I'd have looked around more, but I didn't want a sentry spotting me. Not that there was anywhere else to look."

"So, to your eye, they simply disappeared over the wall?"

"I wasn't that far behind. Would've seen them climbing up. The wall's at least two stories high."

Mikari glanced Jun's way, looking as befuddled as he felt.

Then she gasped, eyes flaring wide. "He told me I would need to open new eyes."

Jun instantly grasped her meaning, and his heart leaped. "A secret door, hidden by magic." He grabbed her hand on the table. "That's it. Our way in."

Thank the Divine One that Atsuyori wasn't kind or doddering. The spry, nosy old man had discovered how the inquisitor was smuggling cursed crows into his lair.

"What do you mean? Who told you?" the old bard asked, words sharp with interest.

Mikari grinned at her mentor. "I'll start at the beginning."

Atsuyori would not be dissuaded from hearing the entirety of her tale, and Jun trusted her to skip any prurient details, so he was the one to welcome the others as they arrived over the next hour, storing their belongings in their host's teaching space and securing stabling for the horses.

While he was out, he happened upon a black-haired swordsmith, branded of course, who sold him a finely made blade that he intended to give to Mikari. He was anxious to get it properly attached to her belt, but when he reentered the shop, she was fully immersed in a conversation with her mentor about a student or two of his who had shown interest in apprenticing with a bard, and looked rather excited, to Jun's unavoidable dismay. Rather than interrupt her, however, he apprised the others of their stabling arrangements.

Sunset came and went. An energized Atsuyori brought in his shop banner, and numerous lanterns illuminated the streets.

Once introductions had been exchanged over a quick meal, Atsuyori provided them with a map of the temple grounds. However, it was several years old and no longer completely accurate—the temple changed the pattern of its maze every year to keep its most dedicated visitors from memorizing the way through.

As with all Gozuan temples, Ajiro's maze was the first structure a visitor was meant to encounter, unless they made a significant donation, of course. And it was enormous, much larger than the maze at Nansen.

Atsuyori had already marked the location of the trail that would take them to the hidden entrance, and instead drew their attention to the center of the maze and an icon labeled "pavilion." The symbol was of a square inscribed inside a messy circle, and did not appear in the map's legend. He frowned as he told them he'd never met anyone who had found the way to it.

"I've tried to reach it myself, unsuccessfully," he said.

The retired bard then moved on to pumping the bemused delegates for news from the empress's court while the rest of them conferred in the classroom.

"It would take me hours to get through this," Seita muttered, glaring at the map spread out on the floor between the four of them.

"There's a way to find the exit without remembering which turn you took," Mikari told him, "but it would take a terribly long time for a maze as large as this."

"And what's that?" he asked, glancing up at her.

"Simply choose one side, right or left, and follow that wall until it leads you out. However, it doesn't work if you try to follow a wall that doesn't connect to the outer boundary, and there are a few such 'islands' in this maze."

Seita glared even harder at the map. "Fuck me."

"Any objections to leaving at the tip of camphor?" Jun asked. There were none. "Let's review, then."

The plan was simple, if only because it was unavoidably incomplete. They knew where to infiltrate and what their objective was, but they had little idea how the first would lead to the second.

The hour grew late as they discussed a variety of contingencies, and the streets outside quieted. Inside, Seita grew more and more agitated, unable to sit still for long.

They received a final message from the empress wishing them luck and informing them that someone would be monitoring their mirror throughout the night.

Everyone dressed for a cold hike and a fight. Mikari wore her new sword, which she'd had no trouble drawing from its sheath. Jun prayed she wouldn't have to.

He then drew a magical array in chalk upon the wooden floor of

Atsuyori's shop, which would grant a few hours of immunity to the specific spells Komatsu had used against them in Tetsutani.

The magical protection wouldn't apply to anything else the inquisitor and his servants had up their sleeves, but it would be far better than nothing.

Atsuyori and the two delegates were still awake when the time came for the four crows to leave, and they all joined together for a short prayer. Should Jun and his fellow magic users not return by midday tomorrow, the delegates were to remain with their host until the empress sent them word.

They then slipped out of Atsuyori's shop, leaving all but their weapons and a few supplies behind.

Before night had descended, the sky had been heavy with clouds promising more snow, but none yet fell. Any townsfolk who were still awake would hear only the gusting wind as their group glided along the darkest path through the intermittently lit streets and alleys to the gate-road.

From there, the path up the mountain was pitch-black, but they couldn't afford to light their way with mundane methods, which would give away their approach. Instead, they used the same echolocation spell that had seen Jun and another group of crows through the sewers beneath the demon city in Oblivion.

The darksight spell was just as efficient at showing them a faint outline of their surroundings as it had in the sewers, thanks to the silent pulses their magics sent out.

They hiked up the gate-road in single file, with Kie leading the way. She had the most experience hunting and tracking animals and would search for the side path Atsuyori had spoken of.

Even though Mikari was only a few steps behind him, and even though Seita was watching her back, Jun couldn't help glancing over his shoulder practically every other minute to verify that she was there.

The farther they went from the dwindling lights of Eiroku, the more he felt that his nightmares of a dark, icy maze had prepared him for tonight. That somehow, he would be separated from her. Or worse, that he'd lose her forever.

But not if he could crudding help it.

Chapter Twenty-Seven

Mikari would have marveled at the softly pulsing, colorless outline of her surroundings were she not also frightfully aware that she was one of only four people trekking up a snowy mountain on a starless night, headed toward mortal danger.

However, the prospect of staying behind was unbearable, not to mention pointless. She was going to fight for her future, not hide in a corner and let fate decide, especially not while the man she loved did the opposite. Not again.

Atsuyori had said that the path he'd discovered was only shouting distance from the front gate, so their group moved with greater caution the closer they drew to the glow of the temple's many bronze lanterns, staying low and taking advantage of whatever terrain they could to conceal their approach.

To Mikari, the crunch of her footsteps through the icy snow sounded thunderous. In reality, it was no louder than a cough, which the wind and the rustling evergreens would muffle, at least as far as the tree line standing a stone's hard throw from the ramparts.

Like all Gozuan temples, Ajiro was surrounded by a stone wall that was sloped to take advantage of the steep terrain, its main purpose being the repelling of invaders, specifically demons. And now, them.

Atop the defensive wall were the temple's barrier charms, barely discernible across the distance despite the numerous lanterns along the top. Mikari's darksight offered some detail of the long cable strung with hundreds of prayer plaques swinging in the stiff wind.

Not one of their party believed that the barrier truly throttled magic, not only because Ajiro Temple did not take in wards, but also because it would interfere with the inquisitor's ritual. They'd find out soon whether they were right.

The towering hedge maze lay just past the ramparts and occupied the front of the temple grounds, beyond which the usual set of buildings stood, rising from higher and higher elevations. Some were for visitors and non-ordained temple staff, and some were only for authorized clergy. Reaching them involved navigating more walls, steps, and courtyards arranged in complex patterns meant to slow an enemy force.

The only movement came from a lone, torch-bearing figure walking along the ramparts in the opposite direction from the one they intended to take, but another guard stood sentry above the temple's closed front gates, which sat at the top of a final, steep incline and a set of stone steps.

Up ahead, Kie paused to examine the terrain to their right, prompting everyone else to pause as well. Looking back at them, she gave a nod and pointed at what had to be the narrow trail Atsuyori had spoken of.

The path took them a fair distance from the gate-road, to a section of the defensive wall that looked as unscalable as any other. Nothing about it or the denuded ground in front of it indicated an entrance.

Clustered together at the edge of the trees, they pushed back their hoods and set their gazes upon the ramparts to watch for patrolling guards. Mikari saw one deposit his torch into a bracket and disappear into one of three watchtowers spaced along the wall. There was no other in sight.

Since this morning, she had feared that whatever inspiration she'd expected to receive wouldn't come. That she'd failed to understand the Divine One's pronouncement…or wouldn't have earned his blessing.

But when Jun placed his hand upon her shoulder to ask if she was ready, insight claimed her like a long-lost memory, guiding her toward revelation. The experience left her awestruck, her heart racing.

At her silence, Jun softly called her name. She didn't need her darksight to know he was anxious on her behalf, and whispered *I'm ready* with as much calm as she could muster.

"Be careful, lamb."

"I will."

The others gave her encouraging nods. After one last glance at the wall walk, she let go of her darksight magic, allowing the night to cloak her surroundings once more. Then she removed her gloves and pressed her palms together.

Drawing power into her hands took a moment of concentration, then she formed a window with her fingers. *"Shinjitsu."*

The window of her fingers subtly glowed, no brighter than a swiftly cooling ember, and her heart leaped. Would casting magic ever fail to thrill her, she wondered as she raised her hands to peer through them.

Almost directly ahead of them, at the base of the defensive wall, there was a strange shimmer that looked like starlight reflecting on a rippling pond.

She raised her head to see without the aid of penetrative magic and could see nothing but perfectly still stone blocks.

"I see it," she whispered excitedly. "Wait here a moment."

There was silence behind her as she moved quickly but quietly across the open space between the forest of evergreens and the sloped base of the wall, still getting used to the weight of her sword on her left hip.

Her pulse fluttered as she neared the irregularity, which projected an unbroken slant of tightly mortared stone. Behind the illusion, there was a vertical break in the wall's canted surface that contained a normal, wood door.

Though the wind had erased any evidence of other footprints, swipes of snow were missing from one side of the door where someone had pushed it open.

She stepped cautiously into the secret cutout, and yet the illusion of a sloped wall remained, the only change being the bizarre sight of her lower half sunk into the stone.

Her hands were beginning to ache from the cold and the sharp pressure the *reality* spell put on them, so she collapsed her framed fingers and continued forward, breath held as the rest of her passed through the illusion and beyond the others' sight.

With the hope that it wasn't locked, she pushed at the door gently, then with more effort when it didn't budge.

At first, the door opened slowly, *loudly*, its bottom edge scraping the frozen ground. She shoved harder, wincing with anxiety. A tense second later, the door opened the rest of the way, and she stumbled forward into total darkness.

Catching herself, she held still and listened, but heard only the wind behind her. She took another careful step, reaching to the right and finding a rock wall. Something hanging on the wall clunked into her hand, stopping her and sending her heart into her throat. She hastily stilled the lantern she'd accidentally bumped.

Going by touch rather than spending stamina on her darksight, she opened the lantern and found the unlit wick inside.

She knew she should turn back. Her only role at the moment was simply to lead them through the illusion, and Jun was undoubtedly anxious. But she took a few more tentative steps, one hand on the wall and the other suspended in front of her.

Heat and pain began radiating from where the dagger sat on her right hip. A warning, she sensed. Magic filtered into her palm, practically without thought.

She jerked back the second she felt it—a sort of field or...skin that clung to her fingertips. After a brief hesitation, she put forth her hand again and explored the strange magical effect. It seemed fragile, like surface of a puddle starting to freeze. Probably not a good thing.

Would the dagger be useful? She had no idea. But perhaps one of the others did.

She turned just as the soft crunch of several pairs of feet reached her ears and made it only a couple of steps before she was engulfed in an embrace against a tall, wide body.

Jun blew out a breath as if he'd been holding it ever since she'd left his sight. His heart by her ear pounded.

"Oh! I'm sorry," she whispered, hugging him. "I wanted a sense of what was on the other side of the door."

He held her a little longer, making no comment, then released her, though his hand stayed on her arm. She rubbed the back of it as she told them about the magical field and what it had felt like.

Jun sighed. "A *sentry* spell. Anything bigger than a rat will trip it, and whoever cast the ward will know instantly that someone is where they're not supposed to be. We're lucky you didn't set it off."

His last remark made her heart trip. "Do you know how to get past it?"

"Only for myself, and I'm terrible at it," he said, voice hard with frustration. "The minor advantage I have with autumn spells doesn't extend to wind magic. Not to mention, transfiguring into gaseous form takes a lot of power if you don't have the affinity."

"And now is certainly not the time to teach it to them," Seita concurred.

Mikari's mind tripped over the realization that Jun could turn himself into a cloud, despite what she'd already come to know about magic. It tripped again when Seita all but admitted that he could do it, too. He even had an affinity for it.

Thankfully, she was able to refocus. "We know the dagger can disrupt magic. Could that work?"

"It might," Jun hedged. "Or it might set off the alarm. But unless we want to find another way in, we'll have to risk it."

"At least we know that magic works within the temple," Seita observed. "We're definitely inside the barrier charms."

Kie lit the lantern, revealing a corridor supported by wooden beams. It went in a considerable distance before turning. The walls and ceiling barely allowed Jun any clearance as he walked forward with his hand out.

Once he'd confirmed the location of the ward, he took two steps back and turned to face them. "This is it, then. The point of no return."

"I'm ready," Mikari affirmed, drawing the dagger from its sheath. It was warmer than usual.

Finally, it said.

"As am I," came Seita's voice from behind her. Kie echoed his words from her position at the tunnel's entrance.

"Whenever you're ready," Jun said to Mikari, squeezing to one side of the tunnel. He briefly gripped her shoulder as she passed.

She sent a thought to the dagger. *Can you disrupt—*
I can, but my abilities aren't endless. I may not be able to help later.
I understand, Mikari thought.
Very well. It then gave her brief instructions.

"Here goes." She touched the blade tip to the magical field, sensing pressure where the two met. A translucent wave instantly rippled down the corridor, its subtle light filling the tunnel's dimensions as it rolled away before disappearing around the corner.

She reached out to see if the ward remained, but there was nothing but cold air.

Sheathing the dagger, she nodded at Jun.

He drew his sword. "Let's go."

They proceeded single file, weapons drawn, with Jun leading the way. The lantern they left behind, out of concern that its glow would expose their presence prematurely.

Was that…moaning up ahead? He stopped at the bend in the tunnel and leaned for a quick look, stomach tight and magic alert.

However, the tunnel abruptly ended at a tall stack of crates that blocked sight of whatever lay beyond. Dim, yellow light limned any gaps.

He crept close enough to peer through them and spied what appeared to be a storage room. Weak light from a door left ajar revealed piles of crates and barrels lining the walls and covering most of the floor. The boxes blocking the tunnel were set back just far enough for a person to sneak around them.

Jun motioned for the others to follow, then slipped into the musty storage room, making his way toward the door. A brief search of the containers he passed found them all empty, but some still smelled of fermentation, indicating they had once held offerings of rice wine and various staple foods.

Were they currently in the temple's undercroft? One with a long-forgotten and now-hidden escape route from invading demons?

Jun crouched by the door and peeked through the gap, the moaning he'd been hearing growing more distinct, turning into a woman's low, tired cries for help—eerily similar to the lure of the soul tree. Though goosebumps washed over him, he nevertheless resisted the instinct to look at Mikari and confirm she was safe.

AT THE MAZE'S CENTER

A single, dingy lantern lit the plainly constructed stone corridor ahead, which eventually turned left. The dull light source was set between an open archway to their immediate left and a closed iron gate, beyond which lay a series of openwork wood doors spaced close together—prison cells.

Meeting the others' grim gazes, Jun nodded to signal that all was clear. Then he pushed open the door and moved quickly down the corridor, which was thankfully wider than the previous tunnel, if not taller.

The open archway led into what looked like a ritual space, bare of all but the most basic supplies for working magic. The unpleasant odor of aether lingering in the air suggested that the room had been used recently.

Seita went past him to the iron gate and gently tested it. Locked. Without hesitation, the lad turned the latch with a swipe of magic, and it swung open with a low rasp.

Jun followed him through and went to the closest cell on the left while Seita went right. Through the square spaces of the door, Jun spied a lax human form upon a thin mat—a woman, her face turned away.

She seemed to be asleep, but she certainly wasn't resting. Her breaths were labored, limbs twitching. The light was too weak for him to be certain of her hair color, but it appeared to be brown.

He turned away to check in with the others. Kie had gone ahead to look into the next cell, where she stood stiff with shock. Seita meanwhile had his back up, gaze locked on whoever occupied the cell before him.

The lad abruptly turned and rushed past Jun to the door behind him, searching for someone in particular, Jun realized. By the time he strode across the hall to look at what had spooked him, Seita had already moved on to the next door. Kie had backed away.

"Maze take me," Jun couldn't help muttering.

A black-haired woman had crammed herself into the corner, legs pulled in, head back, arms slack at her sides. Her waterfall brand still glowed, even though her eyes were open but unseeing, her mouth frozen wide open in a silent scream.

If he had to guess, he would say she had died of fright.

Mikari appeared next to him, also looking in, her expression one of quiet shock. Sweet Garden, why hadn't he begged her to remain with the delegates?

Their eyes met. Something fierce hardened her gaze. "Jouse Temple," she whispered, referring to the woman's brand.

Digging deep for similar resolve, he began checking the other cells, Mikari not far behind. In the next was a brownie man, also dead, his lower half unclothed. Opposite that one was another brownie man, seemingly alive but unconscious.

Jun didn't want to believe it, but only one thing explained why people with no magic were imprisoned here. They were food. And only then did he realize the pleas they'd been hearing had gone silent.

Seita was closely peering into the last cell at the end of the hall, opposite the turn, when they all heard a low commotion of voices from around the bend, sharp and demanding.

The lad swiftly retreated to the inside corner of the hall, concealing himself just as the clank of a lock sounded. Jun and the rest hastened to join him.

A door opened somewhere past the bend, flooding the hall with the unmistakable flicker of torchlight.

"How much longer are you keeping us here?" a woman shouted from somewhere distant.

Jun silently called upon his magic to enhance his strength and speed, sensing an imminent need. He tapped Seita's arm, then switched places with the lad.

Sword at the ready by his shoulder, he sidled up to the corner for a glimpse.

A familiar crow had entered the corridor from a larger room beyond, a torch in his left hand. However, instead of common traveling clothes, Komatsu wore a loosely belted robe of dark red shaded into black, the hem speckled like a starry sky, beneath which he appeared to be wearing pants and thick boots still wet from trekking through snow.

Jun was prepared to slice the man in half the second he was in range, but Komatsu stopped at one of a handful of cells around the corner, a cruel smirk on his face.

"I knew you'd give in eventually," the villain said in Gozuan.

Another male voice made a vicious reply. "Damn you to Oblivion. I almost killed her."

"It's a pleasant enough end, isn't it? Far better than the alternatives."

"You soulless bastard."

"Not true, on either count, though I have burned through quite a few souls. *Kyousei.*" In the same instant that he invoked the Mahou word for *compel*, Komatsu gestured as though plucking a large fruit from a tree. "Return to your original cell, and don't cause any trouble."

Another gesture unlocked the door with a soft clunk. It swung out, and a lean, tall man emerged. He was black-haired, gait stiff as though he were fighting the compulsion. Jun could tell little else. The lust eater preceded Komatsu toward the large room at the end, which had since quieted.

Were more of the inquisitor's servants ahead? Or was Komatsu alone?

Jun slunk down the hall, closing the gap between himself and his prey, certain the others were following in like silence.

In the room beyond, there appeared to be a long wall similar in construction to the prison-cell doors, but the thick, perpendicular beams were not made of any ordinary wood or metal. The onyx-like material did not reflect the torchlight and instead emitted its own radiance, which shined like distant stars.

Voices began shouting again. "Why are we here?" one yelled. "Why keep us alive?"

Another few steps would bring Jun to his target. He had to duck through the door, then emerged into a cavernous space, with cage walls on either side that extended from floor to high ceiling, dozens of individuals behind them. A few darkly lit, glowering faces stared at their captor walking by.

"Answer me, damn it!" A man slammed against the cage wall to the right and reached for Komatsu through the fist-sized spaces. He then made a disturbing croak of pain, having touched the wall, and the smell of boiling metal singed Jun's nose.

Komatsu had turned at the outburst and saw Jun behind him. His eyes widened.

Jun leaped forward with a life-ending strike, teeth bared. And hit nothing but air.

335

Mikari was last through the door into a large holding area with cages that radiated aether. In the central aisle, Jun and Seita were engaged in a complicated fray with none other than Komatsu, Kie at the ready behind them, a cacophony of shouts, grunts, clangs, and thumps echoing inside the stone chamber.

An unfamiliar and disheveled crow with a boxy face watched the violence from the other side, the intense discomfort on his face indicating that he wished to do otherwise.

Mikari maneuvered closer to the two-on-one sword fight, heart beating painfully, magic vibrating like a plucked string. Jun was on the offensive, but knowing that did nothing to quell her skittering anxiety.

She wished she could help, but there was hardly room for Jun and Seita to face off against Komatsu side by side, let alone room for her or Kie to flank.

Kie didn't let that stop her. A wave of heat rolled off the female crow as she hissed a word of Mahou and ignited Komatsu's sleeve, distracting him long enough for Seita to slice open the scoundrel's side, lightning arcing from his blade. The prisoners whooped with violent joy at their captor's scream of pain.

Komatsu quickly ripped off his burning sleeve, then blocked what would've been a decapitating strike, but his defeat seemed imminent as Jun and Seita pushed him back toward another door while opening up wound after profusely bleeding wound.

His aether projectiles were all fizzling thanks to the limited immunity Jun had bestowed, so the scoundrel tried displacing him and failed at that, too, the attempt nearly ending in his evisceration.

How Seita knew to duck rather than look over his shoulder when Kie called his name, Mikari didn't know, but he sank to his haunches just as Kie launched a fiery sphere at Komatsu.

The orb slammed against his chest in a jaw-dropping explosion wide enough to lick the cage walls, knocking him flat at the feet of the nameless eater and scattering the nearest prisoners. That the ball of fire hadn't killed him outright spoke to the strength of whatever protective magic he'd summoned, though his clothes were now blackened and torn.

At a point where some might freeze in shock, Jun and Seita quickly advanced on Komatsu, swords raised, a dozen voices cheering them on. Kie followed, her blade glowing hot as if pulled straight from a forge.

Komatsu's eyes were round with alarm. He grabbed the ankle of the eater standing numbly behind his head and displaced him with only a word.

The eater didn't go far, only to the ceiling directly above Jun and Seita. He flailed as he fell, and landed mostly on Jun. The two of them crashed painfully onto the floor...right where Komatsu no longer was.

Shouts of surprise echoed sharply. The dagger on Mikari's hip warned her with a flare of pain. She whirled around.

"No!" Jun shouted.

A blur of movement at the top-left of her vision. Instinct tempered by her recent training drove her to stop the incoming blade with her own, the sharp peal of metal on metal ringing out.

The force behind the hit would have overwhelmed her had she not tapped into greater strength a moment ago. Even so, she felt a wobble in her dominant wrist that jolted her already-racing heart.

Komatsu adjusted his angle, seeking the closest opening. She shoved the hostile blade away and stepped back, but not to retreat, an outrageously bold response taking root in her, surrounded as she was by others like her, with whom she might now be caged if not for Jun and the rest.

Careful of her balance, she kicked at Komatsu's wounded side and managed a glancing blow. The pain made him stagger back, his handsome visage turning horrific with rage.

The move gave her the second she needed to draw power into her hands and slap them together, cupped palm against fist. "*Hakushu!*"

Coruscating energy leaped out, hitting him hard enough to rip his sword from his hand and fling him halfway to the door. He slammed onto his back just as Kie raced past, Seita right behind her. A few cheers erupted.

Mikari jumped when a steely arm wrapped around her, before realizing whose wide, muscular frame was behind her, his bearded jaw roughly nuzzling the side of her head. She leaned back gratefully.

"I think I just aged another twenty years," Jun said in a ragged voice.

"Where is she?" Seita demanded, the tip of his sword tucked beneath Komatsu's chin. A wet croak was his only answer. Seita snarled with frustration. "Kie, watch him."

"Go," she responded, extending her sword toward Komatsu's stiffly writhing form. Seita hastened back the way they'd come, to search the other prison cells, Mikari surmised.

"Are you all right?" Jun asked even as he turned her around to examine her, looking concerned but also furious.

"That wasn't my first melee," she reminded him, thankful her voice was steady. "And I had a rather good instructor."

He glowered in response, likely preparing to chastise her for hitting back when he'd taught her to retreat.

"Why do you wait? Kill him!" one of the prisoners hissed.

"Let us out!" another begged.

"We don't even know who they are. They might kill us, too."

"Or leave us here to die."

"I don't want to die here!"

More and more voices began pleading with them, the din growing louder. The eater whom Komatsu had been escorting said nothing, though he postured in a way that reminded her of a dangerous animal caught in a snare—aggressive, fearful, and desperate.

He appeared to be waiting for his cell door to open, which meant he was still under a magical compulsion and could do little else.

Mikari hated knowing how powerless he was feeling—thanks to personal experience—when she knew she could do something about it. And yet she didn't trust that he'd hear them out otherwise.

"Enough," Jun snarled, turning about. The prisoners fell into an uneasy silence. "We know what you are and how you survive. Her Imperial Grace, Empress Shumei, sent us here to track down your kind."

"I knew it," a female eater fearfully whispered. "They're going to kill us."

"We're here to cure you," Jun averred. "Not to kill."

Shock rippled through the holding area. "There's a cure?" one of them asked.

"There is," Jun confirmed. "But applying it to everyone would require far more time than we have, nor would you be any safer running away—not when the inquisitor would only force you back here should we fail to defeat him."

Mikari also suspected that only some of them could muster enough energy for the invocation.

"Your only hope is to help us kill the bastard. After that, I promise we can cure you."

"How is that our only hope?" someone fumed. "What's to stop him from tak—"

"*We* are what's to stop him, the forty of us," another said. "You can count me in."

"And me," said a third, then several more.

"But…s-some of us have killed. You would still cure us?"

"Yes," Jun said, "but don't expect to go on your merry way afterward."

Any further discussion came to a halt the second Seita stormed back in, his angry strides eating up the floor, the air crackling around him.

The exact source of his wrath was indiscernible. Even finding Nene alive and unharmed didn't strike Mikari as an outcome that would calm him. But his target for retaliation was abundantly clear. He homed in on Komatsu with an expression so stark she couldn't bring herself to ask whether he'd found the maid. She suspected the others were likewise reluctant.

Kie sensibly backed away from Komatsu, whose limbs were contorted with the agony of slowly dying. His face was ashen, and blood had pooled around him. No one dared to speak.

Seita stood over him, tight with anger, sword raised for a killing blow as crooks of lightning skittered up the blade. "Where. Is. She."

Komatsu gave him a wan but bloody smile, a strange gurgle emerging from his throat. Wet and gasping. It grew louder, and he began to shake.

He was laughing.

Seita brought his sword down in a vicious chop, metal striking stone, blood spattering. Mikari instinctively moved closer to Jun, gasping at the sight of Komatsu's head separating from his body.

Seita slowly straightened, his fury giving way to detachment as his gaze turned inward, giving Mikari the sense that his mind was either crowded with thoughts…or completely silent.

Certain he was close to unraveling, she glanced worriedly at Kie and Jun and saw the same concern in their eyes. She wished one of them would say something. But what was there to say?

"It's not over, lad," Jun declared, gentle but firm.

Seita blinked, awareness sliding back into place behind his eyes. He turned toward them and nodded, avoiding eye contact.

"There are a few things you should know," a male voice bravely volunteered after that show of violence. The eater separated from the rest was no longer mentally captive, his relief evident enough.

"First, no one is breaking out unless you know how to deal with whatever foul magic is on these cages." He gestured at the bars pulsing with aether. The other eaters were careful not to touch it, she'd noticed.

"We may have a way," she said, briefly meeting Jun's gaze. He glanced at the dagger at her waist and subtly nodded. "What else?"

"There's two more of him." The eater gestured toward Komatsu's corpse. "And their master isn't only the inquisitor. He's also Gozu's Keeper."

Chapter Twenty-Eight

The revelation hit Jun like a dousing of freezing water, shocking him into silence.

"H-how did you learn this?" Mikari asked, aghast.

"He visits every few days," the lust eater replied. "Calls us his 'covey,' because we're all crows, right? One of us demanded to know how he'd kept his operation a secret from the Keeper, and he said the Keeper already knew. Then he…changed into the Keeper before our eyes. Just like the one you see in the temple murals, white hair and all. Only his eyes weren't quite right, like you could still see his soul through them. Or what's left of it."

While the lust eater spoke, Jun's mind spun furiously, jumping from one realization to the next. He noticed Mikari looking at him with a stricken expression, one that told him she was also circling the same conclusion.

If the inquisitor could look like anyone, there'd be no telling how long he'd been occupying the highest religious office in Gozu. Perhaps only recently. Perhaps far longer. He could even be responsible for establishing the practice of cleansing in the first place.

But now was not the time to ponder the implications, and Jun forced them aside to address the prisoners, speaking to them with deadly calm.

"Regardless of whom he pretends to be, the inquisitor must be stopped. Anyone who runs instead of fighting should expect to see one of us again before winter's end, and anyone who attacks us should expect to lose their head here and now."

There were a few resentful grumbles and frowns, but no further objections. He looked to Mikari for the next step.

"Stand back," she warned as she approached one side of the holding area, drawing the dagger once more. Jun reluctantly obeyed, but he was ready to leap in at the first sign of trouble.

She stared at nothing for a few seconds, head tilted as though she were listening. Then she used the dagger to draw the outline of where a physical door already stood, cutting a hole in the magic through which to escape.

The pungency of hot metal filled the air as the aether contracted like melting ice, quickly fading. The white glitter within flipped through a rainbow of colors, including some seemingly impossible shades.

The door had no physical lock, and it almost instantly slammed open. Mikari hastily retreated as eaters poured out, some cursing or gasping with relief, a few thanking them, all understandably eager to leave their prison.

Jun held Mikari's shoulder in a comforting grip, braced for every single eater to stampede past Kie and Seita toward the exit. But to his surprise, only two ran. Then three more from the other side, once Mikari created an opening.

He did his best to memorize the faces of those scurrying away and did not care whether they found the tunnel leading out.

Unsurprisingly, the eaters who remained had been stripped of their possessions, including any weapons. But even barehanded, most would be able to move and fight with inhuman speed and strength. Jun hoped that would be enough to tip the scales.

"What's your name?" he asked of the lust eater once Kie and Seita rejoined them in the center of the holding area, leaving Komatsu's body where it lay.

"Kyubei."

"Any idea where to go from here?"

"That way, for certain," Kyubei said, pointing at the door ahead. There was light on the other side. "But none of us have been through there."

"Follow my lead, then," he announced, heading toward the door. "And stick together."

The door was unlocked, the smoothness of its fixed, wooden handle indicating that many hands had touched it over the years.

Jun went first into a chamber the same length as the holding area, but it appeared to be naturally formed rather than dug, its ceiling high and craggy. Two large holes in the floor had been patched over with wooden slats.

Besides another dingy lantern and a few open crates to the side, the cavern was largely empty and cold. A set of wood steps at the other end went up a narrow chute, likely to the outside.

"Check those crates," he said from the middle of the chamber. Kyubei and a few other eaters hurried to do so.

"It's our things," Kyubei confirmed, pulling out packs, coats, and thankfully several swords.

"Take only what you need for a fight," Jun advised. "Come back for the rest."

Only there wouldn't be enough time. A heavy clank sounded, followed by pounding footsteps as torchlight filled the stairway. Drawing once more on his magic, Jun looked to make sure Mikari had her sword up.

Two black-haired men burst into the chamber. One had a deep scar across his mouth. The other carried a torch and bore a rather close resemblance to Jun's old mercenary boss, Masanori—an objectively handsome man, but one with a smirk so cruel it made him ugly.

They seemed rather surprised to find their master's entire covey had escaped. Surprised and livid.

"*Fuminami*," Jun declared, bringing his leg forward and stomping hard. The impact ripped across the cavern floor, breaking the surface in a swift straight line like a tree root tearing from the ground, the sound of cracking stone echoing loudly.

Scar leaped back, onto the wood steps, just before Not-Masanori—Notanori—had his feet swept out from under him. Falling prone knocked the torch out of his hand, which spun and rolled away.

Jun rushed forward with a battle cry, the others closely following.

Notanori surged to his feet as if supernaturally aided, and snapped at Scar in an unfamiliar tongue. He then swung his arm out and grabbed at the air, aether cupped in his grip. "*Ue wa sh—*"

"*Chissoku*," Seita snarled, cutting him off with the Mahou word for *suffocation*.

Notanori clutched at his throat, aether seeping from his casting hand. Wide-eyed with alarm, he flung himself onto the stairs, barely dodging the fireball that instead smashed into the wall behind him. Scar meanwhile was fleeing up the tunnel.

Jun prepared to leap, sword glittering.

"*Ue was shita*," Notanori croaked, twisting his fist in the air, face red.

Jun fell upward just as he thrust his blade, nicking his target instead of skewering him. Shouts of alarm rang out. He barely avoided hitting the puckered ceiling head-on, twisting just in time to roll off his shoulder when he landed, the air knocked out of him.

He wasn't the only one for whom up was now down, judging by the dozens of thumps and yelps, and a loud crash as the crates shattered against the ceiling.

"Fuck me," Seita spat. "I couldn't hold the choke."

Jun lurched to his feet, temporarily disoriented until he was able to lay eyes on Mikari, who was already standing. She gave him a nod, her braided hair now mussed.

He looked up at the mouth of the exit tunnel sitting high on the wall, just in time to see a pair of boots scrabbling out of sight. The wood steps leading out now appeared to hang from the top of the tunnel.

"Be ready to drop again," he bellowed over the din of confused cries, certain that such a powerful effect couldn't last long. Indeed, only a couple seconds later, he felt his body growing lighter and reflexively crouched down. "Here it comes!"

Gravity reversed once more. He pushed off the roof with his hands, flipping himself feet first, and stuck to the ground with hardly a stumble, though he was certain his knees would ache terribly later.

He glanced briefly at his fellow crows to make sure they'd recovered, then pounded up the stairs in pursuit of the two servants. The rest of his party quickly followed, all three of them shouting encouragement to the eaters.

"After them!"

"Don't let them get away!"

The tunnel was dark, but the cold air rushing in told him it led outside. With his magical darksight, he spotted Notanori climbing out of a small opening not far ahead, and launched himself the last few steps in one grunted, magically charged push.

Fully expecting to be attacked the instant he squeezed through the exit, he had only a second to absorb his surroundings. But that was more than enough to make his stomach sink with dread.

Sweet Garden, he was in the maze, encompassed on all sides by towering hedgerows, having emerged from a tunnel concealed beneath one of its contemplative features—a menacing sculpture of a person thrusting an absent sword, their arm extended, and finding themselves stabbed by their own blade. Scar, the other servant, was nowhere in sight.

Jun, skirting the ragged edge of panic, put his all into blocking Notanori's swift and brutal overhead strike. Muscle memory took over as he twisted his grip, aiming the point of his sword at Notanori's neck.

Rather than get impaled, his opponent leaped back with supernatural strength, almost to the nearest hedgerow, and landed a step away from one of two exits. Jun advanced while his allies poured from the tunnel behind him, ice crunching beneath their boots.

Though his darksight allowed him to see, he couldn't tell which way Scar had gone. The snow on the ground was several days old, and there were tracks leading everywhere.

Mikari, appearing next to him, didn't hesitate to launch a *flying fist* at Notanori just as the servant invoked his magic. Notanori swept his arms in the way one donned a cloak, and dodged her well-aimed attack in the same motion, waist bent at an unnatural angle.

"The other one?" Seita quickly asked. "Did you see which way?"

"No." Jun stomped again, the ground ahead of him breaking in a jagged line that shot up shards of snow and earth. "Split up. You and Kie."

Notanori deftly evaded the attempt to trip him, then hurled a shadowy orb the same instant Mikari threw another projectile. The dagger, Jun realized.

He resisted shielding himself from the servant's attack, knowing his limited immunity would protect him. As expected, the ball of aether hit Jun's chest without any force and vanished, and Notanori cried out as though hit.

But the notion that something was wrong immediately took hold.

How could this place look and feel exactly like the maze of his nightmares when he'd never been here?

He tried to focus on Notanori, who ran into the nearby gap, stiff and hunched. But the chain of his thoughts broke before it could form, filling his head with bits of nonsense parading as knowledge, and pushing him further toward panic.

The red moon, warping, twisting. Creeping, boiling color, digging at the edges, bursting through the cracks. The Veil holds it back.

I wish I didn't know.

Jun blinked as terse whispers briefly grounded him. It was Seita and Kie, the former leading half of the eaters toward the maze's other path.

"We'll try to find the center," Kie said in a rush from over her shoulder, hastening to follow them. Seita was already gone.

Mikari stood in front of him, tense and alert, moving with obvious impatience toward the gap where Notanori had disappeared.

"Come on," she urged in a loud whisper.

Jun gave a hasty nod and hurried forward, unable to speak past his hammering heartbeat. He entered the maze with Mikari at his side and more than a dozen vengeful eaters at his back.

What purpose brought me here? Do I remember? If I can't...

"I can barely see," Kyubei hissed a few steps behind him. Indeed, the light of the temple's lanterns could not penetrate past the tops of the hedgerows.

"Keep hands on each other," Mikari advised. "I can guide."

At the first junction, they ignored a turn that immediately dead-ended, and continued straight, following the path as it twisted through the maze.

Is this a dream, or did I die? Is this a test, and I forgot?

"I see something, straight ahead," Mikari softly announced. She pointed at a junction with two right-hand turns, one after the other. Jun saw nothing of note, though his darksight seemed to be working.

How many times have I failed this test? A thousand?

Then he spotted something atop the trampled snow at the second turn—a long, dark stain from a sudden gush of blood, suggesting a blade had been pulled from a wound. The scent of aether hung in the air.

How many times have I watched her die?

"Through here," she whispered.

AT THE MAZE'S CENTER

Though he heard her words, they failed to penetrate. He glanced down the second turn, spied another bloodstain, and sprinted to follow it, his magic bucking inside him like an animal in a net.

Did I die in Oblivion? Am I now food for the weeping willow? Or did the riven, red moon pull me into a million pieces?

He poked his head down several dead-ends, following the corridor as it turned and looped around, searching for a sign of where Notanori had gone, before reaching a heavily trampled intersection. He chose a direction at random and ran until he hit another dead-end.

When he returned to the intersection, he discovered he could no longer recall which way he'd come from. Only then did he realize what had happened, his mind clearing.

Notanori must have channeled something into that *flying fist* of aether, and it had warped his sense of reality. The temporary paranoia was fading, but the damage was done.

He was alone. And lost.

To KEEP HER HANDS FREE, Mikari had applied the *reality* spell directly to her eyes the moment the inquisitor's goon had run, and they were already beginning to smart, the same way they would if she refused to blink while facing a stiff breeze.

She had no choice but to endure the discomfort, though, for the maze was riddled with illusions, many of them hiding paths that were still pristine—no tracks in sight. However, straight ahead at the first intersection, she spotted a fake hedge that concealed a well-trodden corridor. Just before it was a puddle of blood. The servant's, no doubt.

Throwing the dagger at him had been impulse after missing him with her *flying fist*. She would have undoubtedly missed again, were it not a powerful living object, but the dagger had adjusted her aim and ensured she would hit.

It had already returned to its sheath, where it had pulsed to announce itself. The servant must have stopped to rip it out and toss it away.

With the assumption that Jun had his eye on her, Mikari led the way through the illusion, briefly taking the forearm of an eater named Kyubei who was directly behind her.

From there, the trail of blood was easy to follow, leading her the right way whenever she had a choice to make. Then, at last, she spotted the servant at the other end of a rather long straightaway, his hand pressed to his side, pace tired and uneven.

"There!" she whispered, pointing while glancing at Jun.

Only Jun wasn't next to her. Nor behind her, she discovered, wheeling around with a gasp.

"Jun?" she softly called, painfully aware that she couldn't go back without giving up the chase. "Did anyone see him split off?" Her question was passed down the line, but no one seemed to know the answer.

"Divine One's arse," she swore, throat tight with worry, mind racing for a solution as she turned and sped up. Should she continue pursuing the servant, or find Jun and then follow the blood trail?

"Spread out," she ordered. "Stretch yourselves back as far as you can remember. Try to find him."

Her command made its way down the chain, eventually fading. Only Kyubei continued on with her. At the end of the straightaway, she cautiously rounded a U-shaped turn, then leaned for a look into an opening on the left side, where the path ended.

"Maze take me," she breathed. Probably a poor choice of words.

It wasn't immediately clear whether the aging pavilion had been built around the hibernating *runtida* tree—the largest she'd ever seen—or if the tree had grown out of it. The tree's massive roots appeared to lift the base of the enclosed pavilion, and its trunk grew flush against a hole in the weathered but undamaged roof that was standing strong against a flurry of wind-whipped branches.

Both tree and pavilion took up less than half of the maze's otherwise empty center, and a single lamp next to the entrance shed just enough illumination for her to dismiss her darksight.

Everything shimmered with illusion magic, of what she couldn't say. But either way, she had to maintain the *reality* spell, eyes now throbbing with pain. She swore she could feel the surrounding muscle strands stretching and flexing with her every glance.

The wounded servant trudged doggedly toward the pavilion, using his sword like a cane for support, his left side shiny with blood all the way down to the hem of his robe.

She was certain she wouldn't best him in a swordfight, so she drew hard on her magic as she rushed forward, Kyubei keeping pace beside her.

The servant turned at the sound of their footsteps, a massive ball of aether swirling in his palm. It came at her so fast that she reacted out of instinct, aiming her attack at it instead of her opponent.

"*Hakushu!*"

The dark orb burst like a sack of black powder, spraying both her and Kyubei with dry, pungent aether that evaporated like steam.

She felt no pain other than the stinging in her eyes—even blinking hurt—but something was nevertheless very wrong, the suspicion only confirmed as she glanced frantically about at her altered surroundings, heart squeezing with dread.

There was no snow anymore, only barren, hard-packed earth. The tree and pavilion remained, but a round red moon directly overhead lent everything in sight an ominous hue, particularly the fleshy, pale fruits hanging from the tree.

"Am I dead?" Kyubei asked with a tremor of fear.

Instinct told her to disbelieve her eyes, but she couldn't articulate why, even though she could feel snow compacting beneath her feet, even though the tree didn't move despite sheering winds, and even though the pain in her eyes was fading.

In her mind, none of these facts connected, leading to the illogical yet glaringly obvious conclusion that she had succumbed at last to her magic's corruption.

Maze take me, why did I let it in?

The dagger at her waist pulsed sharply enough to make her hiss, but she lacked the awareness to heed its warning, instead seized with wide-eyed horror as several black tentacles burst from the servant's wound, stanching it.

"*Kyousei,*" he declared, plucking something invisible from the air, less pained than before. Kyubei gurgled strangely, then hunched as though in anguish.

She tried to understand what was happening, but her thoughts refused to crystallize.

Did I ever have control?

Weak, weak. I'm too weak.

The servant was smirking when he jabbed his finger at Kyubei. "Take her sword, and gut her with it."

Panic left her frozen. She couldn't even speak let alone resist as Kyubei snatched her weapon and assumed a practiced fighting stance.

No! I'm stronger than this, she silently screamed, her power surging in response to her will, aiding her. *I won't give in to fear again.*

The temporary madness gripping her vanished in a few quick blinks, leaving only blessed clarity. She pulled her dagger in an instant thanks to Jun's training, and grabbed Kyubei's dominant wrist with enhanced strength, preventing him from attacking her just long enough to help him.

Nick him, the dagger said, already aware of what she intended.

The blade's sharp tip sank easily into the outside of his arm, delivering what felt like a subtle jolt to her but which caused a full-body spasm in Kyubei.

I have nothing left, the dagger warned her.

A column of fire erupted somewhere else in the maze, drawing Mikari's attention. A hair-raising howl of agony followed. If she had to guess, she'd say Kie had just killed the other servant, the one with a scar.

The one Mikari had wounded also cried out, swiping at himself as if being attacked—no, as if he were on fire. He shook himself back to full awareness right as Kyubei, still wielding her sword, ran to engage him with blinding speed and a bloodthirsty roar.

Kyubei gave the servant no time to cast any magic, swinging and stabbing with impressive expertise. Unfortunately, the fight seemed rather evenly matched.

What do I do? Her dagger had no more help to give and didn't even respond to her silent plea. She had enough magic left for one last burst, so perhaps…

She spun around before knowing why, only sensing the danger, every hair on her body standing in response to a malicious, all-too-familiar glare.

A cloud of aether faded into existence before her and swiftly coalesced, becoming the shape of an arrestingly handsome crow of indeterminate age, but whose ruthless calm revealed him to be far older than what was natural.

The inquisitor.

She staggered back as something cold and sharp grabbed at her magically shielded mind, the sensation so terrifying and painful that fighting it off took nearly all of her concentration.

He was trying to take control of her. Again. Instinct told her that if he succeeded, she'd never get it back.

I'm going to make you kill him, a hard voice pushed into her mind. *Then I'm going to rip out your magic and eat your soul.*

Time slowed as she reached out with the last of her stamina, pushing farther and farther, well past the maze's center, until she found what she sought.

"Jun!" she called out, with both her voice and her heart. "Jun, help me!"

Chapter Twenty-Nine

Not even his darksight could tell Jun which of the dozen set of footprints belonged to him. The only thing he knew for certain was the direction he'd just explored, and he quickly marked it by slashing an X on the ground with his sword.

Figuring he'd have chosen to go right when first arriving at the confounding intersection, he took a left from the X and hoped it was the way back.

It wasn't. He came upon something he hadn't yet encountered, a wind-torn section of hedge lying across the path, and turned back with a sharp curse, his terror mounting.

Back at the intersection, he carved another X into the ground, then briefly considered which of the unmarked paths to take next. Picking the one directly across from the first X, he ran down it at full tilt.

His mind likewise sped through every reason he could think of why this time in the maze would end differently than in his nightmares—why it *had* to. But his wildly beating heart remained desperate for the reassurance of having Mikari safe in his arms, and his magic bucked violently inside him as a result.

Something bright lit up the maze from somewhere behind him, roaring like fire and startling him enough to break his stride. He whipped around in time to see a pillar of fire dissipate, leaving behind a yellow glow several hedgerows away. A man's harsh shriek told him someone was in a great deal of pain.

AT THE MAZE'S CENTER

Please let that have been Kie's doing, he pleaded, continuing on.

Thankfully, the path he'd chosen felt familiar. He was certain he'd find a short stretch and another left past the turn up ahead, and was relieved to be proven correct.

He ran faster than he should, frantic, slipping and nearly falling twice. Then at last, he spotted the dark patch of blood that had led him astray and hurtled toward it, only to careen to a halt when a familiar metaphysical touch hooked onto his magic.

"Jun!" Mikari called, sounding much too far away. Her cry then echoed loudly inside his head, fear and effort straining her voice. "Jun, help me!"

He let out a sob, feeling equal amounts of relief and terror, heart drumming painfully.

"I'm coming, lamb," he whispered out loud while yelling it inside his head. *I'm coming!*

He could still feel her connected to him, their hearts and magics interwoven like the strands of an invisible rope that pulled him toward her, turning him to face the hedge to his right.

To the Maze with it, he thought, summoning a flood of magic that cloaked him in a bright blue glow. He focused it downward, grimacing with effort, until he'd contained it in his right leg, flesh tight and tingling, bones aching.

"*Fuminami!*" He drew his foot forward and stomped, the ground cracking loudly enough to echo as it ripped a line through the maze, tearing the hedgerows apart to reveal a direct path to the center.

The subsequent wave of fatigue left him weak-kneed and gasping for breath, but he nevertheless charged forward, stumbling at first, eyes focused on Mikari's familiar form. She appeared unharmed but she certainly wasn't safe, barely two steps away from yet another crow in cultish robes, neither of them moving to strike, both engaged in a mental battle.

Sweet Garden, was that the inquisitor?

The closer he came, the more his strength returned, and the better he could see Mikari's desperate expression, her attention focused on her opponent.

"I...can't hold him," she gritted out once Jun was close enough to hear.

Hold him? Jun didn't understand, but the second he was in range, he leaped forward and swung, slashing deep into his enemy's back.

Mikari sagged, then fell to the ground, sitting up but spent. The inquisitor staggered forward, shoulders back and roaring in pain.

Jun would have followed up with swing after swing until the villain was dead, but the sudden change in his surroundings was too surreal to be dismissed.

That he stood within an illusion was obvious enough. Oblivion had been destroyed, and he could feel the icy wind. But the sight of an enormous weeping willow over an ominous, one-story pavilion was heart-stopping.

In that empty heartbeat, he spotted Kyubei battling Notanori. Both appeared tired and injured, and horrid black tentacles had sprouted from the latter in several places.

The wound dealt to the inquisitor did little to slow him, the long gash quickly filled in with a row of the same horrid tentacles, which smelled unmistakably of aether. Some sort of healing response?

The inquisitor spun to face Jun, his rage evident, and in the same motion caught the center of Jun's chest with the heel of his palm. "*Kandou!*"

The physical blow pushed Jun back a step, and for a split second, the air around him stilled and darkened. But his limited immunity prevented the inquisitor from displacing him.

Growling, Jun sprang at the inquisitor with the intent to sever his neck. The other crow leaped backward with supernatural grace, and a sword of aether appeared in his hands just in time to parry Jun's follow-up strike.

He brought all of his strength and experience to bear, entering into a battle trance, testing every possible weakness and finding little— nothing exploitable, at least. The inquisitor was unfortunately faster than he was, and could cast magic in only a blink of time, which allowed him to blur his image and make it harder to target him.

Harder, but not impossible. Not when Jun had all the motivation he'd ever need, too focused to feel much from a deep cut his opponent made on his arm.

He slipped in close and landed a satisfying stroke across the front of the inquisitor's leg, but missed with his finishing strike and leaped back, barely avoiding having his gut sliced open.

AT THE MAZE'S CENTER

Dozens of eaters then swarmed into the maze's center, Kie and Seita among them. Some had found their way using the path he'd created, and some appeared from two other entrances, including one he hadn't noticed on the other side of the pavilion.

A brief glimpse of the inquisitor's true face through the smeared image he projected evinced his deepening fury, as did his hiss of outrage when he saw Kyubei tug his sword out of Notanori's chest, the servant now lying motionless on the ground.

To Jun's dismay, the inquisitor then transformed into a thick cloud of aether and swiftly retreated like a sheet of wind-tossed snow toward the pavilion, deeper into his lair.

The eaters froze in shock and confusion. Kie and Seita were closer to the pavilion than Jun and followed their prey undaunted, moving swiftly but cautiously to the building's weathered front and peering inside over the lip of its porch.

Jun had nearly reached them when Kie gave a hard, frustrated sigh. "He's gone farther in," she announced. "Back underground."

Jun's immediate reaction was to gnash his teeth, a primal roar building in his heaving chest. But the heat of his rage quickly ebbed once Mikari appeared at his side. Then he could only marvel that she was unharmed, his shoulders slumping with relief.

"Oh, Jun," she lamented, looking at his arm with sympathy while unraveling a strip of bandaging she'd brought. "Maze take you for making me so scared and so proud at the same time. I think I might also be aroused."

In other circumstances, he would've laughed. Instead, he took her mouth in a hard kiss, hand clamped around her nape, too desperate for a taste of her to be tender. She softened nevertheless, feeding him a sweet little sob he knew he'd never forget.

Alas, one kiss was all the indulgence he could afford, and he pulled back.

"You saved me," she whispered. "Do you understand?"

Nodding, he held still while she quickly dressed the wound on his arm. "He didn't hurt you?"

"No, but he nearly took control of me, and...I don't know where it came from, but I got the idea to picture a mirror in my head, and suddenly, I was the one controlling him."

Jun looked at her stunned. And perhaps also a little aroused.

"I saw bits of his mind while I controlled it. Thoughts and memories. Most of it was jumbled. And terrifying." He winced as she tied off his bandage. "But I learned who he is, and what he's trying to do."

"I'm guessing it's not what we thought," he said with resentment. She shook her head. "Let's go meet the others, then. They should hear it, too."

She nodded in agreement, then jogged alongside him toward Kie and Seita, who awaited them by the pavilion steps.

The eaters themselves remained spread out but poised to follow. Kyubei offered Mikari's sword to her without a word, but she shook her head. "It'll be far deadlier in your hands." To everyone else, she was direct in bringing up her glimpse into the inquisitor's mind.

"Would knowing change how we go about killing him?" Seita asked, glancing impatiently at the pavilion.

She thought about it. "It might, based on who he is. Bane seeks to open a door to our world and invite something in."

"Bane?" Kie exclaimed. "*The* Bane?"

"Fuck me," Seita spat.

Jun absorbed the revelation in silence, chest tight with dread, though not from learning who their enemy was. He'd had his suspicions about the inquisitor before now and was far less surprised to have them confirmed than even he had expected.

However, the presumption that there was something besides the Divine One beyond the Veil gave him serious pause. That, and especially Bane's intention to open a door for it. Unbidden, his memory of the sky in Oblivion flashed before his eyes.

Creeping, boiling color, digging at the edges, bursting through the cracks.
The red, riven moon…

"He's convinced he'll get what he wants if his patron can enter," Mikari said. "All he needs to do is sacrifice a few dozen fully matured crows."

"Who is this patron?" Jun asked.

"I'm not sure," she admitted. "The only clue I have is…well, I can't really describe it."

"I think we've spent enough time talking," Seita insisted.

Jun nodded in acknowledgment. "My magic is all but spent, but allow me to lead."

Mikari scoffed. "Allow you to 'get hit first' is what you mean," she accused, correctly. "There's no need for such heroics, you're already too impressive. Jun, I'm serious," she said when she saw him grinning, chasing him up the pavilion's worn steps.

They entered together, closely followed by their allies. The inquisitor was smart, forcing them through a bottleneck and into a smaller space where he could make a better stand. The only path forward was through a large hollow at the base of the tree and into yet another tunnel.

Evidence of the ritual he planned to carry out was all around them. The walls and floor were covered in what appeared to be one large magical array that had been carved into the aging wood. Dozens of empty nodes surrounded the tree at the center, each containing an iron shackle at the end of a chain that was bolted to the floor.

He meant for them to die on their knees, in forced supplication, Jun realized, noting how short the chains were, the shackles too wide to be anything but collars. *One of these would've been hers.*

Bane's victims also realized what fate he intended for them, with the result that several glowering eaters ran past him toward the tunnel beneath the tree, only two of them armed with swords.

"Don't go in ahead of us!" Jun warned, to no avail. He ran after them. "Divine One's crudding arse!"

He had no greater fear of heights than anything else that was potentially fatal, but he hesitated at the mouth of the tunnel long enough to draw in a silent, anxious gasp, before rushing in. Or rather straight down.

Rough stone steps descended the nearly vertical tunnel in crumbling, gut-tightening switchbacks lit by the occasional bronze lamp, the air turning warmer than outside but still colder than what was comfortable.

As a large man near the edge of his supernatural limits, Jun was forced to go slower than the eaters recklessly plummeting the stairs, their lead quickly widening. They ignored his repeated calls for caution, running out of sight as the tunnel flattened out into a tall, wide corridor that was far older than the temple at the surface.

Here, the only light to see by came from a narrow gap between immense cloth hangings up ahead, at least until he spied the flicker of Seita's elemental infusion as the lad raced alongside him.

But even at a supernatural speed, neither of them could run fast enough to overtake the bloodthirsty eaters before they burst through the curtains into a large and well-lit chamber, where their battle shouts quickly turned to screams.

The two of them flung open the drapes as they barreled into the chamber, then skidded to a stop. Jun vaguely understood where they were, but he was too focused on the chaos before him to consider the magnitude of it.

Several eaters had been impaled upon spikes of aether, including one suspended in the air. They bayed in pain and horror, while the rest staggered about in frightened confusion.

Bane stood smirking before an open set of drapes in the back, his arm wrapped around the waist of an unfortunately familiar crow woman whose pallor was alarming.

Nene was barely standing, head drooping, eyes unfocused and only half-open. She wore nothing but a white, blood-spattered robe that was torn in several places where she'd sustained ragged wounds. And her neck…sweet Garden, it was shredded and bruised on both sides, as if she'd been mauled by an animal. A raw sound tore from Seita's throat.

Next to Bane was a large, ancient-looking magical mirror—the source of a disturbing resonance that affected Jun's heart rate as much as his ears, stars swirling behind its spelled glass.

A speaking mirror, he realized, the back of his neck prickling painfully. But where was its twin? With whom did he speak?

"It's over, Bane," he said, slowly advancing, backed by his allies and a growing number of eaters.

"Words I've heard before, more times than you have years. They've yet to be true." As he gave his retort, the source of Nene's numerous injuries became sickeningly evident, for there were long, thin fangs where his upper incisors should be.

"They…came true for…the Damned One," Jun struggled to reply, becoming more distracted the closer he came, his heart pounding as if he dangled over a cliff.

"Is the empress also here, then?" Bane taunted. "Because then I might be concerned."

Even parsing his words was becoming difficult. Jun retreated a step and shook his head as if clearing the debris from his mind.

It was that crudding mirror—the vibration it emanated. He swore he heard whispers. And distant screams. No doubt it was the reason the eaters had lost their senses.

"Wait, lad," he told Seita, who had gone ahead of him.

Bane shifted his gaze to the younger crow and grinned with cruel delight as he hissed into Nene's ear, "Look who's here." He then spoke to Seita. "Whenever I feed from her, she thinks of you."

The unlucky maid cringed fearfully as he nuzzled his way down her neck, crying out when his tongue swiped over her raw wound.

"You sick fucking—" Seita snarled, tensing to leap.

Jun grabbed the lad's arm as Bane began to laugh. "Any closer and you might lose your mind."

"Already there," the lad rasped.

"We need to do something about that mirror." Jun kept his voice low. "Kie?"

He heard her make a frustrated sound. "Nene's too close."

"Mikari?"

"The dagger and I are spent, so unless you need me to sing…"

Latching onto the brilliant suggestion, Jun jerked his head around. "That's it, lamb." She looked surprised. "Give us something else to hear."

Kie let out a cry as Bane grabbed one of the maddened eaters by the front of his clothes. With a sinister smile, the villain snarled as he tore open the poor man's throat with his teeth.

Blood spurted, some of it splashing onto Nene. Amidst a chorus of horrified cries, Bane licked his lips and then pushed the dying eater away, pulling something from his victim's body as it fell, something that glowed too bright to see whether it had a shape.

The eater's magic.

Bane regarded the stolen power with something like satisfaction, then threw it at the speaking mirror. Its light dimmed and slowed as it traveled through the air, sliding through every shade of every color before turning flat red and fading to nothing, becoming part of the blackness.

The metallic scent of aether filled the room as the temperature dropped. The vibration grew stronger, causing an ache in Jun's teeth.

Bane was trying to open the door right then and there.

"Stop him," Jun shouted. "Destroy the mirror!"

With no other choice, he plunged into the chaos, slipping between two impaled eaters and heading straight for Bane, who had grabbed another mindless victim.

Thankfully, Mikari's voice cut through the low, pulsing roar of the mirror. She'd chosen a song for the fireside, about weathering a storm, and it held back the whispers and the shrieks.

But the closer he came, the more the mirror drew his eye. The stars within weren't the only things in motion; the blackness also moved like a nest of snakes.

Something slammed into him and sent him stumbling to the side. He didn't know what hit him until he crashed into a set of shelves, then fell to the floor beneath someone, sword still in his grip.

Mikari cried out his name, then sang all the more forcefully, the familiar melody lifting him above the tide of madness, the lyrics promising survival. He pushed the slack weight off of him, grunting with pain, and sat up.

Seita was quickly circling Bane, searching for an opening, his expression deadly. Nene fought her captor with what little strength she had left, both hands latched onto his arm. Someone's magic shined in his grip.

Struck with realization, Jun looked down at the face of the eater who had been thrown aside like an empty jug, her throat ripped open, eyes blank with death.

Baring his teeth, he lurched to his feet just as the rest of the eaters swarmed, blocking his way to Bane. Seita attempted to strike the villain with his sword, but Bane dodged, dragging Nene and positioning her as a shield.

Though the maid held onto Bane's arm, he had no trouble sending the stolen magic into the mirror. It began to roar and squeal, filling the chamber with an enormous presence. One that Jun had felt before... when the red moon of Oblivion had begun to sunder to a voracious force from outside the Veil.

Sword held high, he made eye contact with Mikari, who sang as if their lives depended on it, then pushed his way into the sea of bodies. Kie struggled likewise, but she was closer.

"*Kushi no ryokuba!*" Bane summoned several more spikes of aether, striking the eaters near him and turning them into more obstacles. One had been standing next to Kie, and she jumped back.

The eaters' screams of pain scared the others into hesitating, but

AT THE MAZE'S CENTER

Seita charged forward. An instant before reaching Bane, the lad leaped, dissolving into mist, and swooped past Bane to resolidify behind him.

Bane held Nene against the left side of his chest, over his heart, and when the tip of Seita's sword burst from Bane's front, it narrowly missed her arm.

Bane flung the poor maid away as he whipped around, then seized Seita by the throat. Black tentacles still wriggled from the wound Jun had dealt him earlier, and they extracted Seita's sword as if it were no more damaging than a splinter. Jun shouted for the eaters to get out of his way.

Seita kicked futilely, his face dark red, as the helpful tentacles put the sword in Bane's other hand.

"You missed," Bane sneered, then drove Seita's sword right through the lad's heart.

Horror gripped Jun's entire body, turning his knees soft but snapping his spine straight. Yells and shrieks of alarm filled the air.

He heard Kie shout with anguish just before a tornado of fire exploded into existence and engulfed the mirror, heating the chamber like a bonfire. She came flying at Bane, her sword aflame, but she dropped it when Seita was thrown at her.

And when her magical fire dissipated, it took Jun's hope with it, for though the mirror's frame lay smoldering on the floor, the glass was undamaged and floated in mid-air. Aether now boiled beneath the surface, leaking past the edges, which were no longer distinct.

Despite Mikari's singing, the maddening vibration still had a strong effect on the remaining eaters, making them easier to grab and harvest, which Bane did to yet another victim, launching their magic at the mirror with precision.

Exhausted and out of magic, Jun wanted to tell Mikari to run but knew she wouldn't. And though he could face the growing certainty that he was about to die fighting, despair that Mikari would follow soon after hung about him like a mantle of iron.

But in that moment of desperation, Jun felt his magical stamina returning, as it always did during the brace of rose.

The timing stunned him, filling him with hope.

He tapped his physical enhancements, allowing him to move with haste as he elbowed past more eaters. Knowing he'd need it, he invoked his strongest protection magic, and his skin hardened to be as tough as steel armor.

He then ran at the mirror, sword glittering over his head, and poured his all into a vicious stroke that cleanly sliced through the glass. It buckled inward, fractures spreading across the surface before exploding in a spray of shards.

Jun took the brunt and was pushed back several steps. Thanks to his hardened skin, the explosion felt like nothing more than a blast of snow. The vibration ceased at last, the oppressive presence fading even more quickly than it had appeared.

Bane bellowed with furious disbelief. Jun turned in time to see the villain's confidence shatter, his blue eyes wide with fear, right before the eaters descended upon him and tackled him to the floor, where they used their supernatural strength to rip him apart with their bare hands.

Chapter Thirty

The sight—and sound—of the eaters' desperate rage was staggering, choking Mikari with booming, chest-sized heartbeats, their paralyzing weight plunging to the pit of her stomach the second the inquisitor's screams stopped.

Caught between a pent-up shriek and utter numbness, she was too overwhelmed to conceive why Jun hadn't suffered a single scratch, despite a thousand shards of glass littered about, bits of it caught in his hair and clothes as he stared, likewise appalled, at the brutality happening between them.

"Help! Somebody, help!" Kie cried out, freeing them from their horrified enthrallment.

Mikari dazedly turned her head, only to reel back with sorrow at seeing Kie hunched over Seita's body. *He was so desperate to save her.*

Wait, had his arm just moved? Maze take her, he was alive?

Mikari was so stunned she feared she would trip as she and Jun raced to their fallen ally.

Seita's face was ashen, his neck already bruised in the shape of Bane's hand, but he was still alive. Each slow, shallow breath he took appeared to require enormous effort. There was less blood than Mikari would've expected, but the placement of the wound was...not survivable. Not without powerful magic.

He was only a moment from death, so it was startling how fervently he stared at Nene as though determined to have her face be the last thing he ever saw.

Barely alive herself, the battered maid had crawled close enough to touch his outstretched hand, somehow finding the strength to squeeze his fingers.

"He must remain perfectly still," Jun said sternly, conjuring a gossamer sphere of magic as he knelt between Seita and Nene.

Heeding his command, Mikari quickly situated herself over Seita's legs while Kie got a firm grip on his arm and flank. Once they were in place, Jun lowered his magic's soft radiance into Seita's wound, careful not to bump the sword protruding from the younger man's chest.

Seemingly aware of what was happening, Seita rasped something she couldn't catch over the post-battle clamor of agonized moans, plaintive sobs, and Kyubei beseeching those still in a white-hot rage to go cool off.

Jun, however, was close enough to hear him. "*Aj'*, of course, I will," he chided. "*After* I see to you. Now stop talking."

"Should I sing?" Mikari proposed the instant she saw his anxious expression. He nodded vigorously in response.

She could think of nothing more soothing than what she'd sung previously when Jun had employed his healing magic—a wordless melody she'd found in a wealthy patron's library, tucked into a collection of traditional lullabies.

Though she had no proof other than her gut, she was convinced the song used to have lyrics, possibly in the same language once written on her, she realized.

Halfway to losing her voice after singing at the top of her lungs earlier, she had to adjust the melody's high notes, but the song's effect thankfully remained unaltered. Jun's air of panic began to evaporate, and as he exerted his magic, the agony constricting Seita's face subsequently vanished, transforming into drowsiness. Pain relief, she hoped.

Likewise bolstered, such that her heart slowed to normal for the first time since leaving Eiroku, Mikari was able to split her attention between singing, Jun's progress, and the rest of the chamber.

The chaos started dying down as Kyubei pacified the mob of eaters surrounding Bane's mangled corpse. She heard him suggest finding something to lay over the body and hide it from view.

"Get ready," Jun said, bringing his hand toward the sword's hilt.

Despite her calming melody, Mikari felt a pang of dread as she braced her position.

Swiftly but deftly, Jun drew the blade from Seita's chest. Seita bucked in reaction, the involuntary motion cutting off a harsh croak of discomfort as his sleepy eyes became wide with pain. Mikari and Kie barely managed to keep him from moving and further injuring himself.

"Easy now, easy," Jun said in a gentle rumble, hastily putting the sword aside with a clatter. The blade was stained with two different shades of blood—red and black.

Seita went limp, eyes rolling up as he passed out.

"*Aj*," Jun hissed with a frustrated grimace. "Let's hope I didn't just put him into a coma."

Another moment slipped by as Jun focused entirely on his task. The room grew quiet but for a few soft conversations taking place, and Mikari soon realized she had the attention of almost every eater, a gamut of emotions in their jaded eyes. She hoped her song gave them something else to listen to over the thoughts in their heads.

Jun let out a breath. "All right, let's roll him to his back." Doing so entailed unlinking Seita and Nene's hands as they repositioned him, with Kie's coat serving to cushion his head.

Mikari watched closely as Jun focused his magic once more on Seita's chest. She wished he were merely confirming that the nearly fatal wound was sufficiently mended, but his worried frown said otherwise.

He moved on with what looked like reluctance, shaking his head, and channeled his magic into Seita's darkly bruised neck. Within seconds, Seita's raspy breaths quieted and the contusion across the front of his throat began to shrink and fade.

Once it was gone, Jun sat back with a tired sigh and stretched his hands. "I've done all I can, at least for now. But I believe he'll live."

Sensing a brief lull, Mikari gave singing a rest, ruefully noting Jun's choice of words—*live*, not *recover*.

Kie sagged with relief. "Divine One have mercy."

"You all right, lamb?" Jun asked Mikari, reaching for his favorite spot behind her jaw.

She nuzzled her cheek into his palm and nodded. "You?" She now knew how he'd managed to withstand the explosion of glass, but it had still been a chaotic fight.

"Nothing that can't wait," he assured her.

Next, they tended to Nene. She said little, her misery as evident as her injuries, and instead communicated mostly in nods as Jun explained how he would help her, starting with her mauled throat.

Mikari was humming and gently wiping away residual blood with a spare cloth when Nene made an effort to speak.

"What—" The word caught in her dry throat, sending her into a coughing fit that Jun was quick to soothe.

"She's severely dehydrated," he remarked.

"Here," Kie said, unstoppering her water gourd.

Mikari gratefully accepted it, slid her arm beneath Nene's neck, and trickled water between her lips in intervals. "More?"

Nene shook her head and rasped, "What…is h-his name?"

"His name?" Mikari repeated, confused. Jun had already introduced himself. Unless she meant…

"I…never ended up…learning it."

Mikari couldn't contain her surprise. In light of Seita's behavior the past four days, she'd assumed far more familiarity existed between them. "His name is Seita."

"Seita," Nene whispered with relief. "Where am I?"

"Beneath the maze at Ajiro Temple."

"Aji…ro?" She was understandably confused and no doubt desperate for answers, but as Jun's magic eased her physical pain, she began to lose the battle against her utter exhaustion. "H-how many…days…?"

"Nearly five," Mikari gently replied, her heart aching for the poor maid. She couldn't imagine not knowing where she was or how long she'd been there, all while being tortured.

"I'm afraid…to close my eyes," Nene confessed, on the verge of tears, rolling her head from side to side. "Such…terrible dreams."

"I promise you'll rest easy," Jun said as he extended his hand toward her face. "You'll never see this room again."

"Hate…promises," Nene mumbled with a bitter frown. "They mean…nothing." But Jun touched her forehead, and she slipped into a magical sleep.

Hopefully a peaceful one.

Chapter Thirty-One

Days later, Mikari sank to the bed she had been secretly sharing with Jun, too tired to wait up for him even though they hadn't been in the same room together since dawn.

She didn't regret suggesting they install someone as the Keeper using the same glamour magic that had allowed Bane to occupy the role. But she wished Jun hadn't been the best candidate, being the only Gozuan-speaking male crow.

Her mentor, Atsuyori, would have been the ideal choice, for he knew more about Ajiro Temple's inner workings and staff than anyone else whom they could rely on to dismantle the tradition of cleansing young crows.

However, the magic that altered one's appearance only lasted a few minutes when applied to another person, and as a brownie, Atsuyori couldn't hope to cast such magic himself. Much to their distress, the spell involved the carefully preserved corpse of the priest who was last chosen as successor.

But her old mentor was indispensable otherwise, advising Jun on how to act and whom to pressure, based on his meticulous knowledge of Gozuan politics.

She had worried they were causing too much disruption in his life, but Atsuyori had allayed those concerns, saying that his retirement from bardic intrigue had begun to bore him, hence his obsession with learning Ajiro's secrets.

Though the Keeper's authority over Gozu's temples was absolute, convincing the entire region to throw out a centuries-old practice was a tricky proposition. But Jun, Atsuyori, and the delegates had hammered out a strategy that seemed to be working.

They based the Keeper's abrupt change of heart on a "revelatory vision" sent by the Divine One the same night that several guards and a few light sleepers witnessed strange phenomena in the temple's maze. For those still resistant, they put every possible bit of leverage to use— from personal contacts with the power to sway public opinion, to official diplomatic proposals from the empress and her Dark Court.

Mikari meanwhile had been following through on their promise to the eaters who had fought, some of whom were cured within hours of Bane's violent death. The rest had needed to feed before they could rid themselves of their curse, and arranging and supervising the feedings had taken a mental and physical toll on her.

At least Kie had been the one to ensure the people in the feeding cells, or their remains, returned safely home.

The last cursed crow had reclaimed their magic a couple of hours ago, and the person from Eiroku whose fear of fire had powered the invocation was now resting at home, their memory of the feeding altered to have been a nightmare.

As for the five eaters who had run rather than fight, Mikari had managed to collect a handful of leads to follow, based on her notes and whatever she could learn from the crows they'd cured.

But even though Kie and Seita could now glamour themselves to look like brownies, which would make travel easier until the populace had softened toward crows, neither of them spoke Gozuan.

Thankfully, Kyubei had overheard their predicament and volunteered to join them on their hunt. He and Kie had departed yesterday.

Seita, on the other hand, still needed some time to recover from his nearly fatal wound, despite Jun's healing magic. Jun had confided to Mikari that a strange resonance still hummed in Seita's repaired heart. He was confident Seita would be back to normal soon, but he hadn't sounded all that confident.

As for Nene, not even scars remained where Bane had repeatedly bitten her, but she had taken to covering nearly every inch of her skin, and Mikari had learned not to walk up behind her, the poor lass.

She had looked forward to seeing Seita and Nene spending time together after all of that, but they only seemed to avoid each other, despite the yearning looks. Seita had even asked Mikari to return Nene's personal things to her rather than do so himself, the bag suspiciously less full than when it had hung from his saddle.

Nene now spent much of her time in the temple's library, having received special permission from "the Keeper," while Seita spent much of his time in Bane's former sanctum, poring over every scrap of information it contained, as if looking for something.

Mikari knew his secret, of course. Had glimpsed it back in Koichino when he had been guarding her door that first night and his mind had wandered. She'd thought about offering him some advice so that he and Nene would stop dancing around each other, but he'd snapped at her earlier when she'd checked on him, refusing even to look at her.

Blearily, she glanced around the opulent bedchamber of Gozu's Keeper, where Jun daily donned and doffed his glamour of an elderly brownie who was shorter than she was.

Neither of them had wished to sleep in the same room Bane had occupied, let alone the same bed, but it had access to the glamour's gruesome spell component, and a hidden passage behind the sleeping platform allowed Mikari to sneak to her lover's bed every night.

A skilled artist had painted seasonal murals on every wall, and black lacquered furniture with floral detailing gleamed in the soft light of a pedestal lamp, one of eight. All but one of the painted straw curtains separating the bed from the chamber's exit had been lowered. Instead of a tranquil landscape, they displayed a rendering of Ajiro's maze.

The bed itself was a dream. Thick blankets engulfed a wide mattress lifted upon a black lacquer base surrounded by a canopy of silk curtains. She imagined few others slept so luxuriously.

If Mikari had any issue with the bedchamber, it was only that she and Jun had to swallow their nightly cries of passion, lest someone hear.

But that was something she needn't worry about for the next few nights, her monthlies having resumed. She was more disappointed than she'd expected, and anxiety had crept in once she remembered that her mother hadn't successfully borne a child until her forties.

The thought of the same thing happening to her and Jun was what had sent her to bed early, rather than the dull cramping in her abdomen or the exhaustion of her long day.

Frowning, she had no sooner shut her eyes than she found herself standing with Jun beneath the tree in Nansen's maze, shafts of moonlight shifting around them while wind bells rang overhead.

Jun wore a look of admonishment, a bloodied menstrual cloth hanging from his hand at his side. *Again?* he accused. Blinking back tears, she gave a shamefaced apology that only seemed to disgust him.

I should've known better, he said, walking away—for good, she realized.

She blocked his path, her heart breaking, and clung to his shoulders. His arms remained at his sides, even as she wept. He moved to leave her embrace, but she only held on harder, so he pulled firmly at her wrists.

"No!" she cried. The sound of her voice shook her loose of the scene's hold on her mind. Jun disappeared, and she was forced to catch herself rather than fall.

The night slid backward toward a sky in late afternoon. The tree and the hedges broke apart, as if made nothing but dry leaves, to blow away upon a warm wind. Flowers in all colors covered rolling grassy hills, and in the distance, she saw snow-capped mountains.

She had dreamed of this place before.

"He loves you regardless," a deep, gentle voice said. "Just as you love him, no matter his physical age compared to yours."

Her face turned hot with a mixture of shame and elation as she turned to see the Divine One walking toward her. He was rarely depicted in temple art, but always as a white-robed figure with light shining from the hood. He did indeed wear a traditional robe consisting of several layers of shimmering white, and the power teeming behind his softly smiling eyes was a deep well of aether, which his irises refracted into iridescence.

However, she'd come to realize that no mortal rendering could ever capture his beauty. Nor would any Gozuan temple dare portray him with such long, luscious black hair.

"I wish I didn't have such doubts," she said, frowning.

"They reveal your devotion. And they shall lessen over time. For now, take comfort in knowing that his devotion equals yours." At arm's length, the Divine One stood close enough for his aura to sweep away her anxieties. "Such devotion can even reach across time. Your time, specifically.

"With a bit of magic," he said, raising his hand, "it can bring you together."

She knew what to expect, but couldn't help the gasp she made when he touched her forehead. The contact was light, but the love that filled her made her sway with euphoria.

The arcane knowledge he then granted her made her weep with joy.

"Follow your heart," he whispered, laying her on the soft ground and settling her on her side. The sun-warmed grass was silky beneath her cheek.

He drew away, and her limbs grew heavy, her head drowsy. The ground dipped beneath her slightly, feeling like someone joining her in bed. Heat then surrounded her, as tangible as an embrace. And something soft brushed her cheek—a pair of lips and a beard.

"I'm here, my lamb," came a rumbling whisper. "You're all right. You're safe."

She woke at last, opening her watery eyes with some effort. Jun lay next to her, sharing her pillow and gazing at her with loving concern. Eyes growing hotter, she buried her face against his chest, where she listened to his heart.

Jun held her close and kissed her head. "Bad dream?"

"*Hajime dake,*" she said in Mahou. His arms tightened around her. "O-only at first. Then it was lovely."

"What did he say?" Jun asked, voice soft but chest pounding.

"To follow my heart." She lifted her face and looked into his eyes. "And my heart wants us to marry. How soon can we have a joining ceremony?"

He was stunned before a wide grin lifted his face. And when he spoke, he was almost bashful. "The ritual itself does not take long to learn. I could—"

"I already have it in my head. The Divine One showed me."

He blinked at her, stunned once more. "Oh. When...when we return, then."

Bane had been a tyrannical Keeper, maintaining power through corruption and murder, while extracting popular appeal from the reassuring lie that the ward system was "benevolent." He'd also been known to disappear on occasion, with little to no notice, for days or even weeks at a time—no doubt switching roles to travel as the inquisitor.

Jun and Mikari could therefore leave for a short while and make the three-day journey to visit Jun's sister without his absence rousing any suspicion, before returning to Ajiro ahead of a special summit with Gozu's Primaries to begin dismantling the ward system.

She was looking forward to their departure the day after tomorrow. "What about somewhere in Yuugai? I'm certain I could find us enough space."

The magic of a joining ceremony could be felt well beyond the confines of the two overlapping circles where they would bind themselves together, a phenomenon that would require more privacy than a door or two could offer.

Jun shook his head. "I'll take care of the space. But while we're there, you should obtain the appropriate attire."

They discussed a few more details while Jun's hands slowly roamed her body. When she expressed interest in painting her face for the ceremony according to the trend at court, he began tugging at her belt and she was forced to stop him.

"Not right now?" he asked lightly, raising an unassuming brow.

"For a few days. My…my monthlies," she awkwardly explained.

"Ah." There was no disappointment in his eyes, only understanding. Oh, this man. "I seem to recall that you experience some cramping the first day or two. May I?" he asked, splaying his hand over her abdomen.

She nodded, too full of love for him to speak. He examined her with gentle strokes of magic, murmuring all the while how fascinating he found the reproductive organs and of the differences a black-haired woman experienced once her gift manifested, such as a heightened awareness of her cycle.

He fell silent just as her uterus cramped again, making her wince. His expression was one of deep curiosity. Then he hummed as if to say "interesting."

"How's this, lamb?" he asked.

The pain receded, and she sighed in relief. "Oh. Much better."

"Good. I can teach that to you in the morning."

They settled in to sleep, pulling the covers higher. "I rather like having you do it."

The corners of his eyes crinkled. "Do you now? I suppose I could." Then he tucked her head beneath his chin.

"Want me to get the light?" she asked.

"Go ahead."

Lifting her hand from where it lay draped against his back, she used her magic to pinch out the flame of the only burning lamp. And this time when she fell asleep, she had a smile on her face.

Epilogue

Jun looked around the maze's center, stomach churning with a painful sort of giddiness. Before attending his first joining ceremony, he hadn't thought much about weddings. His wedding, specifically. Instead, scenes of married life had filled his more romantic daydreams. The erotic ones as well.

But after witnessing the empress and her consort link themselves metaphysically, he'd thought a lot about this moment. Even dreamt about it once or twice, waking afterward with a bittersweet taste in his mouth.

He hadn't pictured quite so much snow, nor had he imagined that most of the small crowd in attendance would consist of former demons rather than members of the Dark Court, as well as a pair of brownie delegates, a retired Gozuan bard, and his beloved older sister, Toyome.

He found he liked such details. They made the day more real, and he wanted to remember it vividly—the pavilion hung with blue banners, the shoveled path lined with lamps, and the stage next to him, which braziers at every corner kept warm and dry. He wanted to remember the large, gently falling snowflakes, the colorful array of umbrellas, and the occasional ting of a wind bell high in the *runtida* tree.

After the ceremony was over and the stage was disassembled, the plan was to dispel the illusion hiding them from view and begin returning Ajiro Temple to a state from before Bane had buried his secrets beneath it. The first of many steps Jun would need to take to remove himself from his temporary role as Keeper.

Now was far too soon to announce his resignation, but he had already found someone to designate as his successor. The priest was an Itinerant—traveling clergy who offered services of the faith to remote areas—and while he performed his role well, he had been forced into it as a result of his views. An outspoken opponent of the ward system, the priest was an outlier among his colleagues, and Jun had heard nothing but praise about him from former wards he'd questioned.

As for the former eaters, many felt adrift in their new freedom, and they'd remained near Ajiro to begin acquainting themselves with magic and the Dark Court, which was prepared to accept them once the passes opened in the spring.

In the meantime, they'd found catharsis in stripping and renovating the maze's pavilion. Instead of a one-room interior covered in chains and cryptic lines, they'd built a calm space for contemplating the reasons for the maze and the redemption it offered, while a well-hidden door allowed access to the base of the tree and the tunnel it stood over.

When revealing the location of their joining ceremony to Mikari, Jun had been prepared to explain why he'd chosen it and to offer an alternative if she didn't wish to marry in the same place where she'd almost been sacrificed.

But she'd immediately understood that he wanted their love to consecrate the space, to cleanse it. And she'd agreed wholeheartedly.

So now he stood, eagerly waiting for her to emerge from the pavilion in her joining gown. Though he hadn't yet seen it, he knew she'd chosen something to signify the color of her season.

For him, she'd obtained an expertly tailored set of clothes in midnight blue, the inner layer dyed cobalt, and a fur-lined black overcoat that fit better than anything he'd ever worn.

"What do I do with my umbrella?" his sister urgently whispered, clutching its handle. "When it's time for the *esorege*, should I put it down?"

He was considering their options when his older nephew offered a solution, albeit with a bit of exasperation. "I can hold it for you."

"That works," Jun said in agreement.

Toyome nodded in relief, then consulted the small slip of paper in her hand that outlined her role during the joining ceremony. Always a bit of a worrier, she was taking it as seriously as he'd expected.

"I'm glad you're here," he told her, which got him a happy grin.

A bell stick was given three hard shakes, sending his heart into a gallop. He stared raptly as the doors of the pavilion slid open to reveal his bride, and was startled to see her holding her fox mask before her face. Beneath her open white overcoat, she wore an icy-blue dress covered in snowflakes and dark blue swirls, and a white inner layer.

All were silent as she descended the steps of the pavilion, skirt hemmed to brush the top of her white leather boots. She did not carry an umbrella, and snowflakes quickly dotted her carefully arranged hair as she moved gracefully to the other side of the stage.

When the moment came to ascend the steps, Jun shut and handed his umbrella to his younger nephew, who bowed nervously low, as though humbly accepting a gift. Jun was so nervous himself he nearly barked with laughter.

He was afraid he'd trip going up the steps, but his body felt light as it climbed to the platform. There, he and Mikari took a moment to regard one another. He realized the swirls on her dress sparkled, and noticed a slight shake in the hand holding her mask. She then lowered it, slowly. His heart leaped.

She had painted her face to be similar to her mask, with red swirls at the outside of her cheekbones and more rising from between her eyebrows. A fine dusting of rice powder emphasized the shape of her face, softening the look of her freckles without erasing them, and she'd applied a small amount of pink to her cheeks and her eyes. The red upon her lips was dark and succulent, the edges sharp and begging to be smeared.

"My lamb," he wistfully sighed.

Her eyes smiled at him. "Your fox today. Your lamb forever after."

The next step of the ceremony required them to draw overlapping magical arrays upon the ritual platform, using sticks of willow charcoal, which Toyome heedfully handed to them from the ground.

Braced upon his haunches, he drew his array with great care, so focused on accuracy, and not clumsily knocking his arm into Mikari's, that he didn't notice the relative complexity of her circle.

Next, they stood in their separate halves, while Toyome passed an unglazed sipping bowl to each of them in turn, careful not to touch the rim. Rice wine was the court's tradition, but they had chosen to share a cup of freshly poured *esorege*.

Mikari drank first, tongue sneaking out to lick a dot of froth from the point of her upper lip. Maze crudding take him.

When his turn came, he placed his mouth upon the faint arch of red she'd left on the rim and took his sip, all while holding her gaze. The drink's spicy sweetness spread across his tongue, along with a lick of power that made his lips tingle.

As he returned the cup to his sister's waiting hands, he felt a metaphysical tug upon his mouth that led to Mikari, the same tension that always filled him right before they kissed. Tempted to step forward, he instead pushed his heels down.

"I vow before the Divine One, of my own free will, to become one with you," he declared to her in Mahou, summoning a swift surge of power.

His magic started to churn, becoming a storm whirling beneath his skin, one full of heat and thunder, roaring in his ears.

Mikari began to echo him, each syllable adding to the sweet tension urging them together, only her vow was a few words longer. She had promised to "give" something of hers, the word compounded with another that meant *divide*, and he had no idea what the Mahou word *jumyou* meant.

His confusion was no doubt obvious, and she beseeched him with her gaze to trust her. He nodded in response, the pull of their connection drawing him forward, into the area where their circles overlapped.

Able to touch her at last, he didn't hesitate to gather her against him, lifting her closer and banding her tightly to his chest. He'd thought holding her would give him a sense of relief, but she looked up at him with the most tempting expression, her eyes and lips soft with desire, and his hunger for her only grew, body tightening with the need to kiss her and consummate the ceremony.

But the invocation wasn't yet complete. Magic pooled on his tongue, ready to capture his words. Breathing in, he felt her do the same.

"*Eien ni*," they said as one, promising forever, before bringing their mouths together.

A Kiss of Power was just that—a consensual exchange of pure magic, often done with a kiss. With it, the tangible and intangible blurred in form, and yet were ever sharper, overwhelming one's senses.

Every hungry drag of their lips and tongues was like a stroke between his legs. Every shared breath tasted of devotion. Love echoed in their unified heartbeats, and joy fell from his eyes as tears.

She swayed in his arms as if growing weaker, and yet he couldn't recall the last time he'd felt so strong—no, so young. Looser of limb and firmer of flesh, free of the aches of advancing age.

Part of him realized then what she had done, although it still seemed impossible.

The flood of power ebbed, and their magics gently pulled apart, but not totally. They would never truly be separate ever again. Indeed, he still sensed her within himself, as if the tight mingling of their magics had resulted in transference.

After one last press of his lips, he lifted his head and opened his eyes, barely hearing the cheering and clapping of their audience.

At first, she looked no different to him, other than the smudged and faded lip stain ringing her mouth. Then he began to notice what about her had changed.

Her cheeks appeared more sculpted, having lost a bit of their youthful plump. Her other features also seemed more adult, or rather settled, in a way. Her eyes were a little deeper, her nose a little thinner. A couple of faint lines sat at the outside corners of her watery eyes, which gazed at him with adoration as she stroked the side of his beard.

What convinced him was the single, silvery strand of hair he spied on the right side of her head.

"It worked," she marveled, then softly laughed. "Of course, it did."

"What just happened, my lamb?" he rasped.

"I vowed to share my life with you. Ten years of it."

His heart pounded in shock. "What? You—?" He had nothing reflective to look at but could guess that most of his gray hair had disappeared, along with some of his wrinkles. In lieu of a mirror, he glanced at his hand, the texture of which appeared smoother.

"Why, Mikari?" he begged. "Why would you give up a decade of your life?"

"I'm not giving up anything," she contended. "I'm gaining ten more years with you."

He could only sputter in response.

"Besides, who in Houfu would attend a bardic college run by a girl of only twenty years? I'll get more students if I look older," she joked, her new smile lines deepening a little.

He laughed, a joyful grin splitting his face. Together, they turned to the amazed crowd of onlookers, one arm still wrapped around each other.

His sister was crying, of course, and both of his nephews blinked as though fighting the same. He saw Seita and Nene at the back of the crowd, standing far apart but looking at each other.

Even Atsuyori was wiping his eyes, frowning as though quite put out. "Yes, well—who's ready for some music and far too much wine?" The crowd responded with a small cheer.

They then left the stage and the maze behind, everyone heading down the mountain road to Atsuyori's home to celebrate.

And though the future would hold more challenges for them, Jun rejoiced to know that he and Mikari would navigate them together.

Afterword

Thank you for reading!
If you enjoyed Jun and Mikari's story, please help readers like you find this book by leaving a review. (It would also mean the world to me!)

Interested in some bonus content?
When you subscribe to my mailing list, you'll be able to set up a free account for accessing **Ruby's Parlor**, where you can view bonus content related to my books!

Join my mailing list here:
rubyduvall.com

Also By Ruby Duvall

(time-travel romance)
LOVE ACROSS TIME SERIES:
Stay with Me
Escape with Me

Eidolon *(BDSM romance)*
The Fisherman's Widow *(erotic horror)*

(fantasy romance)
THE DARK COURT SERIES, IN ORDER:
Caught in the Devil's Hand
Drawn into Oblivion
At the Maze's Center

Made in the USA
Middletown, DE
08 March 2024